WHO ARE YOU?

What did she really know about Morgan? What was it that made her trust him so completely? Why was it so easy to believe his tender looks and caring words?

Was it the way he made her heart race? Or perhaps it was the exquisite feelings he had resurrected within her body. Maybe she trusted him simply because she had needed someone to trust. But that was wrong. All wrong.

Suddenly appalled by the depth of what she was feeling, Lacey dropped Morgan's hands as though burned by their touch. She skittered away from him, rising to move across the room for some much needed space.

"What do you want from me, Morgan? Why are you involving yourself in a fight that has absolutely nothing to do with you?"

He smiled that charming, easy smile that Lacey wanted so much to believe was genuine. "All right, Lacey." He stood and tossed his hat onto the table. "Here's the truth for you." Crossing the scant distance between them, he gathered Lacey into his arms before she could protest. In one loud, thundering beat of her errant heart, Morgan's lips were on hers . . .

MORNING SKY

CONSTANCE BENNETT

DIAMOND BOOKS, NEW YORK

MORNING SKY

A Diamond Book / published by arrangement with
the author

PRINTING HISTORY
Diamond edition / March 1991

ISBN: 1-55773-471-2

Diamond Books are published by The Berkley Publishing
Group, 200 Madison Avenue, New York, New York 10016.
The name "DIAMOND" and its logo are trademarks
belonging to Charter Communications, Inc.

10 9 8 7 6 5 4 3 2 1

To the Hart family,
my dear aunts and uncles,
who have provided me with so much
love, support, and inspiration

Prologue

July 1886
Wyoming Territory

Angry, jagged streaks of lightning chased each other down the mountain into the valley, bathing the small ranch house, the empty stock pens, and the enormous oak tree in an eerie light that chilled the blood. The keening wind shrilled through the oak and made Riley Hanson's lifeless body, hanging from the remains of his son's rope swing, sway wildly in a macabre dance. All else was silent. As silent as death itself.

Speechless with horror, Lacey Spencer sat motionless in her carriage, hardly noticing when Zach, next to her on the seat, slipped the horse's reins from her numb hands. The wind plucked at her honey-brown hair, splaying tendrils across her face, but she was oblivious to it. Air would not come into her lungs.

Too late. She was too late. The rumor that the vigilance committee was riding on the Hanson ranch had reached Lacey too late for her to stop the slaughter, and now a decent, honest man was dead. She had pushed her horse to the limit, taking desperate chances on the nearly nonexistent road from town, but it had all been for nothing. Something inside her screamed in rage, but outwardly Lacey was frozen like a statue.

Another flash of lightning lit Riley's face, emphasizing the crazy angle of his neck, and Lacey tore her gaze away before the image became so deeply engraved on her memory that she might never be able to force it into the back of her mind.

The abrupt movement brought her back to a semblance of sanity, and she realized that the place was too quiet. Martha should have been in the yard, screaming in terror or weep-

1

ing pitifully—showing some reaction to her husband's hideous death. Dear God, Martha should *be* here. And Timothy.

Surely the vigilantes hadn't . . . No, no one could be that heartless. The blood of an innocent man was enough; they wouldn't murder a woman and a child, too.

Mobilized by sickening dread, Lacey grabbed Zach's arm to steady her as she leapt from the carriage. Lightning played across Riley's body again and Lacey froze.

"Cut him down, Zach," she begged, hysteria edging her voice. "For God's sake, cut him down now!" And then she was running across the yard, the wind whipping at her skirts.

The cabin door was ajar, and dim yellow light from a single lamp bled into the darkness. Lacey slowed, afraid to see what the room held, afraid not to see. Step by step: The room slid into view; red embers glowed in the stone hearth, and above it hung the head of the ten-point buck Riley had killed only weeks after bringing his wife and child to this Wyoming valley. Lacey tried not to remember how proud her city-bred friend had been that day.

Another step: She could see the table where three half-empty plates gave mute testimony to the moment of the vigilantes' arrival.

Step: Overturned chairs and scattered papers swirled on the floor like dancing ghosts, caught in the tempest.

Another step: Lacey was standing in the doorway, her hammering heart drowning out the rumble of thunder overhead. Sprawled just inside the room, a rifle inches from her lifeless fingers, Martha Hanson stared sightlessly at the rough-hewn beams of the ceiling. Gentle Martha, whose only crime had been blind devotion to her husband. Blood streaked her face from the wound where she had been clubbed with the butt of her own rifle.

Lacey wanted to retch, desperately wanted to flee, but she fought down both instincts and stepped gingerly around Martha's body.

"Timmy? Timothy!"

Her voice echoed in the stillness. Frantically Lacey pushed aside an overturned chair and darted into the tiny room where Martha and Riley had slept.

"Timothy!"

Desperate, she searched every corner, every cranny, then fled back into the main room and gathered her skirts to scramble up the ladder to the loft where the boy slept.

"Timothy?" she whispered, afraid that she was expending her last hope of finding the child. "Timmy, come out, please."

A shadow moved and Lacey, still perched on the ladder, peered into the thick darkness, waiting. "It's all right, Timmy. Come to Lacey. Come to me, please."

"Miz Lacey?" The tiny whine was so pitiful it brought tears to Lacey's eyes.

"That's right, Timmy. Come to me."

The shadow moved again, streaking toward her as fast as unsteady legs would allow. She gathered the child up, somehow comforted by the furious strength in his little arms. Timothy Hanson was alive. He was five years old and an orphan, but, dear God, he was alive!

"Men came for Pa . . . men with masks," he croaked tearfully between great wrenching sobs. "They broke the door—"

"Hush, Tim, hush," Lacey crooned, stroking his hair as his tears dampened her collar. "Come with me now."

Lifting him into her arms, she struggled to maneuver his slight weight down the ladder. One gentle hand kept his head buried in her shoulder as she rushed him into the night, past his mother's inert body and out onto the porch.

Thunder rumbled on the coattails of lightning that slashed the sky from night-black clouds down to the floor of the valley. Lacey gently rocked the sobbing child to and fro. Each stab of lightning intensified his cries, and as Lacey stroked his corn-silk hair she wondered how many years it would be before he would hear approaching thunder and not relive the terror of this night. Indeed, how many storms would she live through before she forgot?

To her right, Zach struggled with Riley's body and in the distance she made out the sound of horses approaching the house. No . . . one horse, she decided with relief.

"Zach?"

"Right here." As if by magic, the tall, blade-thin black man appeared beside her. Lightning danced off the barrel of the

Winchester repeater tucked in the crook of his arm.

Together they waited for the rider to near. Several tense minutes later the lone man guided his horse through the split-rail
gate that hung askew on broken hinges. Simultaneous surges
of relief and anger tore through Lacey as Ben Watson spotted
them on the porch and drew closer.

"Where's Riley?" she asked Zach softly.

"Beside the house, ma'am, covered with a blanket."

"Take Timmy to the carriage and wait for me," she instructed, fighting back tears when the boy clung to her neck
as she tried to pass him to Zach. "It's all right, Timmy. Go
with Zachary. No one will hurt you. You're safe now."

Her words seemed to comfort him, as did Zach's familiar
presence. He transferred his stranglehold from Lacey to the
aging black man, and Zach left the porch as quietly as he had
arrived.

"Well, congratulations, Sheriff!" Lacey called out, not
bothering to restrain the contempt she felt. "You're just in
the nick of time—as always!"

Ben Watson's craggy face was grim as he dismounted and
stepped toward her. "What happened here?"

"You know damned well what happened," she snapped
angrily. "C. W. and his pack of wolves struck another blow
for *justice*."

Watson's head shot up. In the six years he'd known Allyce
Spencer he'd rarely heard her speak in any but the most pleasant of tones. She was opinionated and sometimes a damned
nuisance, but she was a lady through and through. "Where's
Hanson?"

"Next to the house, over there. Zach cut him down and covered him."

"Cut him—"

"They hanged him, Ben," she spat, her voice as cold and
cruel as the act the vigilantes had committed. "They dragged
him out of the house and hanged him—from his own son's
rope swing! And then, for good measure, they bashed in his
wife's skull."

"What about the boy?" he asked tightly.

"He hid in the loft."

The sheriff's shoulders sagged with something Lacey thought might have been relief. "Then he's okay?"

Lacey's laugh was mirthless. "As okay as a child can be who's just watched the brutal murder of his parents. My God, Ben, when are you going to put a stop to this?"

Ben ducked his head guiltily, but he was spared having to come up with an answer when Zach approached silently and handed Lacey a ragged piece of paper.

"I found this under the oak. The wind must have torn it off Mr. Hanson's body." Zach's clipped, educated accent carefully concealed any emotion he might have been feeling. He turned away and stepped into the house. Lacey knew without looking that he was moving Martha's body.

Edging into the yellow light leaking through the doorway, Lacey strained to read the note, though there was little need. The men of the vigilance committee had a habit of repeating themselves, both in their actions and in the warnings that accompanied their wholesale slaughter.

" 'Beware, rustlers,' " she recited sarcastically. " ' The citizens of Willow Springs and all Wyoming will tolerate your thieving no more. Be gone or be prepared to die!' " With a contemptuous flourish she thrust the note at the sheriff, then muttered softly to herself, "You've gone too far this time, C. W."

Watson glanced from the note to Lacey. "You got any proof C. W. Rawlings had a hand in this? Did the boy see anything?"

"They wore masks."

"Then you can't prove nothin'."

"No, Ben, I can't prove it," she agreed softly, "but everyone knows Rawlings is behind the vigilance committee. He wants the little ranchers like Riley Hanson out of the valley because they cut into his rangeland."

"Thinkin' it and provin' it's two different things, Miz Spencer."

Lacey smiled and Watson felt a shudder ripple down his spine at the coldness in her eyes. "I don't have to prove it this time, Ben. C. W. just dug his own grave."

Watson frowned. "What's that supposed to mean?"

"Riley Hanson was no cattle rustler, nor was he just a dirt-poor rancher barely eking out a living. C. W. doesn't know it yet, but the man who was murdered tonight was the son of a U.S. senator. Riley's father is William Westgate Hanson, one of the most powerful men in the state of Pennsylvania. *And* he's a close personal friend of President Cleveland," she added with a wispy, joyless smile. "C. W. Rawlings may have the support of the Wyoming Stock Growers Association behind him, but even they won't be able to save him from Will Hanson."

The sheriff's surprise was obvious. "But why didn't the boy tell nobody?"

"Because he wanted to succeed on his own. That was all he ever wanted. He was determined to make his own way, without his father's name and fortune behind him. Unfortunately it cost him his life." She shrugged expressively. "So much for the value of pride."

Thunder rumbled as the first few drops of rain began to pelt the ground. "I'm taking Timmy back to town with me, Ben. First thing tomorrow, I'll wire Senator Hanson for instructions. He'll want the boy to live with him, I know. I'll keep Timmy until his grandfather comes for him."

Watson nodded. "I appreciate you takin' care of that, Miz Spencer. I'll see to the bodies and shut the house up tight until I can get someone out here in the mornin'."

"You do that, Ben." Lacey fixed him with her most penetrating gaze. "You tidy up the mess and send for the undertaker. And then you go back to your office and sit, because sitting is what you do best. There's a storm coming, Sheriff," she predicted coldly, anger honing the cutting edge of her voice. "And it's a tempest that's going to make this little thunderstorm seem like a lazy spring shower. But when it's over, Wyoming will be clean again, free of the stench of men like C. W. Rawlings. I don't know how it will happen, nor do I know when, but no matter what it takes, I'm going to see that Riley Hanson's death counts for something. Next time you see Rawlings, you tell him what I said."

She turned away furiously, marched toward the carriage, then whirled back. Continual streaks of lightning silhouetted her, and the wind plastered her skirt against her legs, making it billow out behind her. She was a magnificent virago, as dangerous as the fury of the tempest unleashed around her.

Over the howling wind, she warned, "Or better yet, advise him to read tomorrow's special edition of the *Gazette*! C. W. is about to learn firsthand about the power of the press!"

Chapter One

"I'm real sorry, Miz Spencer, but I just can't let you see them Wanted circulars!" Sheriff Watson shifted uncomfortably from one foot to the other, carefully avoiding the accusing stare of the slender woman facing him across his cluttered desk. To be truthful, he hadn't been able to look her in the eye since the night of Riley Hanson's murder nearly four months ago, and for good reason: She and C. W. Rawlings were locked in a battle that was going to be the death of one of them, and Watson didn't want to be anywhere near the middle of it.

Unfortunately it was a location he couldn't seem to avoid. It was his responsibility to tell her about C. W.'s latest dirty trick and to bear the brunt of her anger once more. Lucky for Ben, Allyce Spencer was a true lady who kept a tight rein on her temper. It was one of the things that made her so damned difficult to dislike.

"Let me understand this, Sheriff," Lacey said patiently, the glittering sparkle in her powder-blue eyes the only indication of her displeasure. "Last week I was allowed to look through the Wanted posters. And the week before that, too."

"Yep."

"In fact, I've had access to the Wanted posters every week for the past three years, just as my husband did before he died, isn't that right?"

"Yes'm."

"But this week I can't see them."

"That's right."

"Would you care to explain why?"

8

Watson shifted again, his eyes downcast. "It's the new town council rule."

"You mean it's the new C. W. Rawlings rule!" Lacey slapped the edge of the desk with her kid gloves, immediately drawing Watson's attention. His head snapped up and Lacey's demanding gaze captured him before he could escape. "All right, Ben, let's have a little honesty here. You may be nothing more than a mugwump, sitting carefully on the fence so you don't have to take one side or the other, but at least you've always been an honest mugwump. Rawlings is out to ruin me, and everyone in town knows it. If you don't have the guts to face Rawlings, at least have the good grace not to lie to me! Now"—she lowered her silken voice to a soft, commanding purr—"whose idea was this?"

Ben sighed heavily. Damn, but he did hate being in the middle like this. "The town council decided—"

"You mean C. W. Rawlings decided," Lacey insisted.

The sheriff looked at her meaningfully. "You know as well as I do, Miz Spencer, that C. W. *is* the town council. Whatever he says, they do."

"As do you," she pointed out sharply.

"It's my job, ma'am."

Lacey shrugged her shoulders dramatically. "I always thought a lawman's job was to protect the people."

Watson straightened and Lacey could almost see the hackles rising on his neck. "I keep order in Willow Springs, ma'am."

"Oh, really? And where are you every time Rawlings's men shoot out the windows of my office? And why haven't you found the vandals who stole the handle off my printing press last month? Or the ones who stole my entire stock of newsprint last week? And why is it that you happen to be conveniently occupied elsewhere whenever Rawlings's men harass me or Berta or Zach?"

"You don't have no proof who stole that fancy thingamabob of yours, or the paper, and you don't know who broke the windows, neither."

The sheriff's scraggly eyebrows went up in surprise as Lacey began laughing and turned slightly to sit against his desk. The laugh was a pretty sound, soft and throaty, but it also sounded incredibly weary. Watson's heart went out to the lovely young widow. C. W. had broken grown men, crushed their spirit and ground them into the dirt. Ben Watson was living proof of that. Yet this little slip of a woman seemed to bend like a willow, always snapping back, no matter how much pressure Rawlings put on her.

"Oh, Ben, that's funny, truly it is." She chuckled, regaining the sense of humor that had kept her going these past months. "I suppose you're going to tell me that ghost riders shoot out my windows every week and that the press bar and paper just got up and walked out all by themselves."

"No, ma'am, I ain't gonna tell you that, but what I am gonna say, you ain't gonna like to hear."

Lacey's delicate eyebrows arched in patient expectation, and Watson took heart. Maybe the widow Spencer was ready to listen to reason. Someone had to get through to her or she was going to get herself killed. "It's time you packed it in, Miz Spencer, and that's the long and short of it! Old C. W.'s got it in for you 'cause of all them stories you write about him and the rustlers—"

"*Ranchers*," Lacey interrupted sharply. "They're ranchers, Ben, and you know it. Their spreads aren't big, like Rawlings's, and they don't belong to the Wyoming Stock Growers Association, but they're ranchers just the same. The land's theirs, bought and paid for, and the only cattle they 'steal' are their own—the ones Rawlings's men have deliberately driven off and left straggling loose on open range."

"Well, that makes them rustlers, ma'am," Watson argued. "Accordin' to the new mustang law, any strays found on open range automatically belong to the WSGA. It's the *law*," he stressed, as though that made the ridiculous legislation palatable.

"It's an unjust law, and I plan to see that it's changed!"

"All by yourself? Jest like that?" Ben's gray hair, thinning on top, crackled as he ran both hands through it in frustration. "One little slip of a woman with no one to protect her but an old black printer's assistant and a German housekeeper who looks like she's ate too many prunes? The three of you are gonna fight the whole territory of Wyoming?"

"If we have to." Lacey smiled, unintimidated by the sheriff's assessment of her limited resources.

Watson stared at her in amazement. She was a purebred lady from the top of her loosely piled silken curls to the tips of the shiny black slippers that peeked out from beneath the skirt of her well-cut shirtwaist dress. A tailored jacket nipped in to define her tiny waist, but other than a simple cameo at her throat there was no adornment on her clothes. The outfit was simple by any standards, and yet one glance told a man that it was made of quality goods and that the soft, slender woman inside it was quality as well.

Her vivid blue eyes, twinkling with humor and intelligence, said a lot about her, too, but as far as Ben Watson was concerned, that was half her problem. It was pure trouble and nothin' but when a woman got educated and started thinkin' she had ideas. Why, a woman runnin' a newspaper! It was plumb crazy, that's what it was!

Of course the sheriff wasn't about to say that to the widow's face—no, sirree. Instead, he shook his head and muttered, "And I guess you think you're gonna win this fight?"

"I'm going to try."

"You're gonna get killed is what you're gonna get, Miz Spencer."

"Are you forgetting who my father is, Ben? I don't think he'd take too kindly to burying his only child."

Watson shook his head sadly. "Washington's a far piece from here, and that pappy of yours ain't gonna be much help when C. W. decides he's had enough. I don't care how many newspapers your pa owns or how many important people he knows."

Lacey grinned, making her face take on a radiant light that set the aging sheriff's heart to pumping. "Why, Ben Watson, if I didn't know better, I'd say that you liked me."

"I do like you, Miz Spencer, and so do most of the other folks around here, but we ain't the same as you. C. W. owns half this town outright, and he's got mortgages on the other half. That means he owns the people, too. We're not rich like you, and we don't have important men in Washington lookin' out for us. Maybe you are right: Maybe C. W. is too scared of your pa to do you any harm, but that don't mean he can't hurt the rest of us. The truth of the matter is, we may *like* you, but we can't afford to *help* you."

His words sobered Lacey, and she regarded him earnestly. "I don't want anyone hurt because of me, Ben. You know that. But I'm not the problem. C. W. Rawlings and his kind— they're what's hurting this town. Every time he burns out an honest rancher or kills a man like Riley Hanson, he comes one step closer to destroying Willow Springs."

Watson glanced away quickly, and Lacey knew she'd struck home. Riley's death was a dark cloud hanging over all their heads—one no one was likely to forget. Willow Springs had weathered the storm of Will Hanson's arrival in town. The senator had demanded facts but gotten few honest answers. His anger had set off a flurry of activity in Washington and in Cheyenne, the territorial capital, but little had been accomplished. The U.S. marshall, Clinton Rikker, had been fired as a sacrificial lamb, but in the end, all the sound and fury Will created had signified nothing. The vigilance committee had ceased its activities through the month of July, but when things in Cheyenne calmed down, the vigilantes had started up again. They were now more cautious and less deadly in their actions, but they still made their presence and intentions felt through intimidation tactics, including property destruction.

Lacey was sure they had not heard the last from Senator Hanson. She had known him since she was a child, and he wasn't the sort of man to give up his quest for vengeance against those who had murdered his son and daughter-in-law. Yet nothing had been done, and not much had changed since Riley's death.

At times it seemed to Lacey that she was fighting alone. Her newspaper, the only weapon at her disposal, continually attacked the vigilance committee, the WSGA, and C. W. Rawlings. She kept the fight alive, despite C. W.'s attempts to run her out of town, but no matter what she did, she could not rally the citizens of Willow Springs, or this sheriff, around her.

Determined to make Ben see her point, Lacey continued, "Wyoming wants statehood. It *needs* statehood. But we're not going to get it until we prove that we're not a lawless band of renegades."

"But that's just it, don't you see!" Ben cried, thinking she'd painted herself into a corner. "You're the one that's hurting us by printing stories about vigilantes in your paper. And then you send copies to your pa and he prints the stories, too, and all them senators and congressmen sees it and vote us down!"

Lacey swallowed a rapid surge of anger and tried to remember that she was dealing with a man who had little or no education, whose perception of the world ended just a foot or so beyond his nose. If there was one thing she'd learned in the six years she'd lived in Willow Springs, it was never to discuss politics with a man who said "ain't" and drank his coffee from the saucer instead of the cup.

"You're wrong, Ben. The truth never hurt anyone except the guilty. Pretending a problem doesn't exist won't solve anything; it will just make things worse."

Her voice was so soft and sad that Watson realized it was pointless to argue any longer. "You're gonna get yourself killed, Miz Spencer."

"You have my word, Sheriff, that I'll do my best to avoid it." Her grin was contagious, and Watson heaved a long, hard sigh before his craggy face split into a responding smile, showing the wide gap where he'd lost a tooth while breaking up a saloon brawl a few years back. That was the last time Ben Watson had deliberately placed himself in the middle of a fight, and he wasn't about to jump into this one, not even for a pretty thing like Lacey Spencer.

She was right about one thing: He was a mugwump who sat on the fence safe from harm, and he planned to stay there. He had tried to talk her out of this crazy business of going against a man as powerful as C. W. Rawlings; there was nothing else one grizzled old sheriff could do to stop her. And at least now no one could say that he hadn't *tried* to help her. It wasn't his fault if the mule-brained woman wouldn't take his advice.

"Now, I don't suppose you're going to let me see those Wanted circulars, are you?" Lacey asked hopefully, knowing full well that Ben wasn't about to change his mind.

"Sorry, ma'am."

"Oh, well, I should have expected this." She sighed philosophically and stood. Opening the door, Lacey pulled it wide and turned back to Watson as she leaned against the edge. "It's a little thing, to be sure, but C. W. knew it would get my goat so he couldn't resist. He wasn't satisfied with scaring all the merchants into withdrawing their advertising from my news-paper and intimidating the townspeople to the point that they're afraid even to look at a copy of the *Gazette*. No, he had to see if he could keep me from finding any news to print, too."

A thought struck her and her stunning smile widened. "Well, Ben, I guess that means if there's no other news, there'll be that much more space for the long, long editorial I'm writing about the committee's most recent night raid on the ranchers of the co-op. I think C. W. will enjoy that, don't you?"

Her laugh rang out clear as a bell, a throaty, earthy sound that ended in a small sigh as she turned to leave. A shadow fell across the open doorway, though, and Lacey stopped short, then stepped back as a man's broad shoulders filled the entryway. At least Lacey *thought* it was a man. From the condition the newcomer was in, she couldn't be quite sure. He stood on two legs like a man, but for a moment Lacey thought someone had planted a mud statue outside the sheriff's office.

The statue was tall—well over six feet—and the effect of his height didn't diminish much when he took off his wide-brimmed hat the moment he realized he was in the presence of a woman. Where the hat had been, black hair curled damply, but below that an even strip of chalky white dust circled his head, covering the hair that curled around his ears and down to his collar in the back. The dust also concealed the middle of his face, where a pair of sharp golden eyes lent the only hint of color to the pasty coat of grime. The line where his bandanna had covered his nose and mouth revealed the makings of a dark beard, lightly sprinkled with gray.

With all that contrast, he reminded Lacey of an exotic zebra she'd seen in a circus show when she was a little girl. The thought widened her friendly smile, and in return, the stranger grinned back, his eyes twinkling as he realized how he must appear to her. The smile crinkled the corners of his odd eyes, and the outermost layer of caked dust cracked and fell off, revealing still another layer of grime beneath it.

"Ma'am." He nodded in greeting, bowing ever so slightly, but it was enough to set up a stir of dust that made Lacey stifle a cough.

"How do you do," she answered politely, captivated by the

way his eyes held hers. "I take it you've had a long ride."

"No, ma'am," he corrected easily, his voice laced with a hint of a southern drawl. "I've had a long *walk*. My pinto and I had an unfriendly encounter with a rattler three days ago."

"Obviously the rattler won." For some reason, Lacey couldn't stop herself from grinning.

The stranger covered his heart with his dusty hat and lowered his eyes with mock modesty. "A temporary victory only, ma'am. My horse bolted and broke a leg, but the rattler made a mighty tasty evening meal."

Always suspicious of strangers, Sheriff Watson drew himself up a little straighter and cleared his throat to capture the newcomer's attention. "What brings you to Willow Springs, mister?"

"I just followed the river until I came to a road, and the road led here."

"We don't cotton to drifters just lazin' through," Ben warned.

"I'm not looking for trouble, Sheriff, just a bed, a meal, and a shot of whiskey." He looked swiftly at Lacey. "Just to clear the dust, ma'am," he intoned with an apologetic sincerity that was belied by the laughter in his eyes.

"I understand completely," she replied seriously. "For medicinal purposes only, I'm sure."

"Exactly."

Their eyes caught and held again, and Lacey wished desperately that she had even an inkling of what this man looked like. Beneath all that dust and hair could have been a twisted gargoyle, for all she could tell, but something about his eyes intrigued her. They were warm and intelligent, brimming with humor. Physically he appeared to be a fine specimen, with broad shoulders, a lean waist, and powerful thighs, but of course she couldn't be sure of that until she saw him without the mantle of trail dust. After three days on the open road, he could be nothing more than a skeleton layered with forty pounds of dirt.

While Lacey speculated about the stranger, he was doing some evaluating of his own and quickly decided that Willow Springs might be even more appealing than it had looked from the rise where he'd gazed down on the small, widely spread maze of buildings, corrals, and outhouses. After three days of walking, sighting the town had been a relief, but being greeted so pleasantly by this uncomfortably lovely woman with her heart-stopping smile and clock-stopping figure was a blessing from heaven. He wasn't about to question his luck, which was due for a change. Lately it had been all bad.

Her azure eyes, crystal clear and twinkling with laughter, assessed him without judging him—a trait he found most admirable. He detested people who jumped to conclusions, pigeonholing people according to their appearance or the way they spoke. But there was no judgment in this uncommonly pretty face. The lady's high cheekbones and sculpted jawline were pronounced, but they were softened by her rosy complexion. Her nose was a shade too thin, but full, imminently kissable lips made up for that defect; and her hair, pulled loosely away from her face and bound in a chignon at the back of her neck, was a rich, light honey brown that provided a perfect contrast to the vividness of her eyes.

In her slim-heeled high-button shoes, she stood a little above the level of his chin, which made her a bit tall for a woman, but her height was so perfectly proportioned with her figure that he could find no fault whatsoever. She was, quite simply, exquisite.

Lacey was completely aware of his assessing gaze, and though she was surprisingly pleased that he seemed to find her appearance satisfactory, she ignored the rush of pleasure that rose up in the pit of her stomach. "Are you headed anyplace in particular, Mr. . . . " Her voice trailed off as she waited for him to supply a name.

"The name's Morgan."

"Morgan something, or something Morgan?"

"Just Morgan, ma'am."

Lacey nodded thoughtfully. Having been brought up back east, it had taken her quite some time to understand the total lack of concern for names here in the West. Back east a man's name was everything—his heritage and the foundation of his future. But here names were unimportant, particularly to men. A man was judged by what he was and what he stood for, not by the name he called himself. And Lacey also knew that many names were made up, for convenience. Or for protection.

There was an unwritten code in the West that respected a man's privacy, but Lacey's familiarity with that code did not deter her in this instance. She was a reporter, accustomed to sniffing out a good story and getting at the truth. A newcomer in town wasn't much to write about, but to a journalist as desperate for news as she was, anything was better than nothing. And Lacey was intrigued by the stranger. He looked like a dusty trail bum, but his speech betrayed a more than passing acquaintance with education.

Instead of allowing his pronouncement to pass, she fixed him with her most searching gaze. "Morgan. Well, that's simple, to the point, easy to remember . . . and very difficult to trace." Her smile offset the directness of her comment. "Are you a man with something to hide, Morgan?"

His golden eyes instantly lost their humor, but Lacey found it impossible to identify the emotion that replaced it. His smile stayed in place, though. "Don't we all, Miss . . . "

"Spencer. Allyce Smithfield Spencer. And it's Mrs.," she added pleasantly, then wondered why she'd bothered. Having been a widow for three years, that title had little meaning. It wasn't until she saw the obvious disappointment register on Morgan's face that she realized exactly why she'd mentioned it. She'd wanted to know if this unkempt stranger found her attractive enough to regret her apparently married state. How odd! In all the time since David Spencer's death, Lacey had not felt a glimmer of interest in another man. It was startling to realize that she was coming close to flirting with a complete stranger—and one she probably wouldn't recognize if she saw him again without his layer of trail dirt.

"I beg your pardon, Mrs. Spencer."

"That's quite all right."

Their mutually assessing gazes locked, and Lacey knew he was wondering just what sort of person she was. Though her attitude had remained consistently congenial, even friendly, her frank questions were out of character for the proper, well-bred lady she appeared to be. Ladies were shy, demure, and mindful of their place. They did not ask bold, direct questions, as she had.

Watson, unable to fathom the exchange taking place at his office door, cleared his throat uncomfortably. "You got business here, mister, or are you just passin' the time of day?"

With difficulty, Morgan shifted his gaze from the lovely Mrs. Spencer to the much less eye-appealing sheriff. "My first stop once I reached town was at the livery stable, where I stored my gear. A Mr. Applewhite was gracious enough to inform me that I would be required to check my guns with Sheriff Watson. Is that you?"

"That's right. We don't allow no firearms on the street."

Lacey issued an unladylike snort of derision, which Watson ignored. But the sound did not escape Morgan. He looked down at her, only to find himself staring at a lovely but deceptively innocent smile. What on earth was she trying to tell him?

Watson's voice drew him back. "You check your six-shooter and that fancy repeater with me."

"And when do I get them back?"

"When you leave town."

"Or as soon as you find a place to stay," Lacey piped up, taking a perverse delight in contradicting the sheriff. "You *are* staying in Willow Springs for a while, aren't you, Morgan?"

He turned his best smile on her. "For a while. At least long enough to replace my horse. I found out the hard way that walking doesn't agree with me."

"Well, I wish you luck, sir. Though you really shouldn't need it. Lew Dasat should be able to provide you with a mount to your liking at a fair price. His ranch is part of the co-op just north of town. I think you'll find he's an honest horse trader."

"Thank you for the advice."

"Oh, don't thank me." Lacey laughed. "Giving advice is one of the things I do best."

"She just has a mite o' trouble takin' it," the sheriff snapped, eyeing her meaningfully.

Morgan watched the exchange with interest, wondering what advice this fascinating woman had ignored.

Lacey merely smiled benignly at the sheriff. "Good day, Ben." She turned to Morgan as he stepped into the room to allow her access to the exit. "Morgan, it was a pleasure meeting you. I hope you enjoy your stay in Willow Springs."

"Thank you, Mrs. Spencer." He nodded politely as she brushed past him.

At the door a thought struck her and Lacey turned back. "By the way, Sheriff, I should warn you that I'll be receiving a large shipment on the one-fifteen train from Cheyenne this Friday."

"Oh?" Ben's craggy eyebrows shot up in curiosity.

"Yes." Lacey's velvety voice was laced with mild sarcasm. "I'm sure you'll want to find an excuse to be out of town that afternoon. If C. W. decides to meet that train, you won't want to find yourself having to come to my rescue."

The cutting edge in her voice irritated Watson. "Are you askin' for an escort from the station, Miz Spencer?"

She shrugged and held Ben's gaze with a hard look. "There's bound to be trouble. It's merely a matter of whether or not you want to be in on the fun as it transpires . . . or after it's over."

Her voice was deceptively innocent, but her dare was so obvious that even Morgan, who knew nothing of what they were talking about, realized she was taunting the sheriff.

Watson was the first to glance away, obviously uncomfortable with her veiled accusation that he was afraid of trouble. He replied gruffly, "I'll be there, ma'am."

"I'll believe that when I see it," Lacey countered politely.

The sheriff's head shot up, and he pinned Lacey with a sudden flash of anger from which, Morgan noted, Mrs. Spencer did not flinch. "Are you sayin' I'm a coward?"

"No, Ben," she returned softly, a note of sadness lacing her voice. "I'm saying that one of these days someone in this town is going to have to stand up to C. W. Rawlings, and I don't think that someone will be you. Good day, Sheriff. Morgan." She nodded briefly at both men and disappeared. The crisp clack of her heels on the boardwalk punctuated the silence until at last only her accusation echoed in the small office.

Feeling a little sorry for the sheriff, Morgan held his tongue and waited to see how the man would recover from Mrs. Spencer's accusation of cowardice.

Watson seemed to be lost in his own thoughts; it was several seconds before he remembered the stranger standing just inside his doorway. "You gonna hand over them guns or not, mister? I ain't got all day."

Reluctantly Morgan relinquished his Winchester .44-.40,

then unstrapped the holster that housed his .44 Peacemaker. He watched as the sheriff tagged the rifle and placed it in a barred gun case behind the desk.

Watson pocketed the key and turned, accepting the holstered .44. Out of professional curiosity, he slipped the Peacemaker out of the leather holster and tested the balance in his beefy hand. The weight was perfect—the kind of perfection that was expensive. You could tell a lot about a man by the guns he carried, and Watson frowned, not liking what he learned from his brief inspection of the handgun. He eyed Morgan suspiciously. "You a gunslinger, mister?"

"Why would you think that?"

" 'Cause this here fancy Colt's got a pretty fine hair trigger. You could get the drop on a lot more'n rattlers with this thing."

Morgan shrugged indifferently. "There are all kinds of snakes in this world, Sheriff. I'm just a man who knows how to be prepared for any of them."

Watson harrumphed loudly, not liking the answer and liking this stranger even less. Willow Springs had enough problems without another no-account gunslinger stirring up even more trouble. An unpleasant thought struck him, and his frown deepened. "You know C. W. Rawlings?"

Morgan kept his expression unchanged. "Should I?"

Ben stared at him, wishing he could read what was going on behind those weird gold eyes. Morgan's gaze did not waver, and finally it was the sheriff who glanced away. Hell, it wasn't any of his business if old C. W. had gone and brought in another hired gun. He just hoped that if he had, the deal they'd struck didn't have anything to do with Allyce Spencer. The woman had a sharp tongue and a pretty cockeyed notion of a woman's place in this world, but she didn't deserve to be on the wrong side of a cold-blooded killer.

"I guess we'll know soon enough," he grumbled, sitting down to tag the Colt before placing it in a drawer in the cabinet to the right of his desk. He quickly filled out a receipt and tossed it on the desk. "I'll be keepin' an eye on you, Mr. Morgan, or whatever your name is."

"I appreciate that, Sheriff." Morgan grinned. "I'll be back for my hardware as soon as I find a place to stay."

"You gonna be here long?"

Morgan shrugged and went to the door. "As long as it takes, I guess."

The door closed, and Watson watched as Morgan moved past the barred window and disappeared down the street.

In his prime, Ben Watson had been a good lawman; he'd cleaned up towns rougher than Willow Springs had ever dreamed of being. And what had made him good at his job was knowing trouble when he saw it. The prospect of trouble—real trouble—caused the pit of Ben's stomach to churn like cream turning into butter.

Over the years a lot of things had deserted him—a little pride here, a dollop of self-respect there, and as Allyce Spencer had implied, even a goodly amount of courage. One thing he hadn't lost, though, was his instinct for trouble, and right now, Ben's stomach was churning real fast. Mr. One-Name Morgan spelled trouble with a capital T.

Rising slowly, Watson picked up his empty cup and poured it full of mud-black coffee from the pot kept hot on the low-burning wood stove across the room. Thoughtfully he moved back to his desk and from a deep drawer brought out a stack of Wanted circulars. Sipping his coffee, he began sifting through the posters one by one.

For some inexplicable reason he was suddenly reminded of the grim warning Mrs. Spencer had issued four months ago about a storm brewing. Though the sky was clear and the sun shining brightly, Ben could have sworn he heard the rattle of thunder in the distance.

Yes, sirree, Mr. One-Name Morgan was gonna be trouble. Just what kind Ben decided he'd better find out. Quick.

When a storm was coming, a man had to know which way the wind was blowing if he expected to survive.

Chapter Two

Lacey stepped out of the general store, shifting the small bundle of packages in her arms as she closed the door behind her. She'd stopped in to pick up enough dried apples for Berta to make strudel for supper tonight, hoping that her favorite dessert might lighten her spirits. Instinctively, though, Lacey knew it was a futile exercise. Even Berta's luscious confections weren't going to take her mind off the problems her encounter with Ben Watson had painfully illuminated. Their discussion had left a sour taste in her mouth.

Why on earth had she baited Watson like that? Trying to shame him into standing up to C. W. had been a waste of time. Ben was a tired old man with nothing to his name but a job he couldn't afford to lose. Why should he risk that job and maybe even his life over something that wasn't his business?

But damn it, this *is* his business, Lacey thought with a renewed burst of anger. He was the sheriff, for crying out loud! The small ranchers had a right to expect the law to be on their side once in a while. Right now the law was serving no one but C. W. Rawlings, and the injustice of it grated on Lacey. If she had the conversation to do over again, she wouldn't change a word, she decided.

Occupied by her thoughts, Lacey moved onto the boardwalk outside Mr. Underhill's General Merchandise Store without looking, and when she made contact with an extremely solid body, followed immediately by a cloud of dust so thick it set her to coughing, she knew she'd run into Willow Spring's newest guest. Thoughts of Ben Watson and C. W. Rawlings fled, replaced by a flutter of unaccustomed excitement.

"I beg your pardon, Mrs. Spencer." Morgan smiled as he casually brushed off the shoulder of Lacey's velvet jacket where it had collided with his dust-covered buckskin.

"No, it was entirely my fault," Lacey mumbled, her attention riveted on the innocent play of his large hand over her arm. Such strong hands, she noted. Lean fingers, callused palms. Sensual hands. The thought hit her like a bolt from the blue, and she coughed again, this time to cover her embarrassment at the unexpectedly pleasant sensation she was experiencing. Good heavens, the man was a complete stranger!

And yet somehow, when Lacey looked up at him as he stepped back to allow her breathing room, he didn't seem like a stranger at all.

"Sorry about the trail dust," he apologized again, but his eyes were laughing, almost as though he'd guessed the thoughts that had run through her head.

Lacey managed a nonchalant smile. "Don't mention it. That was the first thing I had to grow accustomed to out here in the wilderness. Nothing escapes the wind and the dust."

"Wilderness?" Morgan glanced around, taking in the prodigious number of buildings that lined Willow Springs's wide main street—one of several streets that ran parallel to the Union Pacific railroad line. It wasn't the most cosmopolitan city he'd ever seen, but it wasn't exactly desolation, either. He chuckled. "If you want wilderness, ma'am—real wilderness— I can show you three days' worth starting just outside of town. I got a real good look at it firsthand."

Lacey chuckled. "That won't be necessary. I know this country very well, though I will admit I haven't explored much of it on foot. But you see, when I arrived in Wyoming six years ago, Willow Springs wasn't much more than a wide spot in the road next to the railway. We've grown up considerably since then."

"Or just pushed the wilderness a little farther away." He captured her eyes and held them.

"That's what civilization is all about, isn't it?"

"I suppose so."

They fell silent, staring at each other with an intensity their casual conversation little deserved. A brief wave of tension, as real as a touch, crackled between them, and finally it was Lacey who broke the silence with a little laugh that sounded silly even to her own ears. She turned to head down the street, and Morgan fell in easily beside her.

"You finished your business with the sheriff, I presume?"

"I did," Morgan said, "and I've got a little scrap of paper here to prove it. I hope the sheriff keeps good records. I've already lost my horse—I'd hate to lose my hardware, too."

"Oh, Ben's thorough about things like that. Your weapons are safe with him. So . . . " Her voice was a bright chirp, and she was uncomfortably aware of her uneven breathing and abnormally flushed cheeks. What on earth was the matter with her? A filthy, broad-shouldered, golden-eyed stranger was making her—a grown woman of thirty years—behave like a silly schoolgirl. Quelling the unnatural giddiness, she managed to ask, "Where are you headed now, if I may be so bold as to inquire?"

"I wouldn't have thought boldness was something you worried about, Mrs. Spencer. You didn't seem to have any trouble speaking your mind to me or the sheriff back there in his office."

Lacey cast him a sidelong glance and found it impossible to read the meaning behind his words. Was he making fun of her or chastising her? "You're quite right. If I want to know something, I generally ask."

"And if you have an opinion, you state it."

"Is there something wrong with that?" She came to a dead stop, forcing Morgan to turn to face her.

There was a decided note of defiance in her face and voice, but not a trace of defensiveness, Morgan noted. This woman was obviously accustomed to dealing with men as equals, whether they would grant her that equality or not. No one would ever intimidate or dominate Mrs. Allyce Smithfield Spencer. Morgan wondered mildly just what sort of man her husband was; it would take someone formidable indeed to capture and hold on to such a strong-minded beauty.

Since honesty seemed to be something she waved like a banner, Morgan decided to see just how much she could take herself. He shrugged offhandedly. "There's nothing wrong with saying what you think; it's just not a trait you find too often in women."

"Ah, but that's because men don't care to hear the truth about themselves."

"And you consider it your job to enlighten them?"

He had spoken the words completely without rancor, and Lacey found it impossible to take offense. Keeping her tone as congenial as his, she replied, "As a matter of fact, enlightenment is the most important part of my job."

Surprised by her answer, Morgan started to ask just what sort of work she was employed at, but a wagon rumbled by, stirring up a cloud of dust, and by mutual consent, they resumed their leisurely stroll down the boardwalk. "If you have something to say about my conversation with Sheriff Watson, by all means, say it. That *is* what this is all about, isn't it?"

He nodded thoughtfully. "You were pretty hard on the sheriff. Hacking away at a man's pride is bad enough, but doing it in front of another man is something else altogether."

Lacey looked at him in surprise. "Is that what you think I was doing? Trying to strip him of his self-respect?"

"Sounded like it to me." He had the courtesy to look slightly embarrassed. "Excuse me for saying so, ma'am, but you're a well-brought-up lady with a definite way with words. You're too smart not to know what words like that will do to a man."

"Well, you're right about that," she agreed. "I mean about understanding the power of words. I spoke as I did for a purpose, but not the one you seem to think. You see, you can't very well take something from a man that he's already lost. Ben Watson is a frightened man who's sold his soul to the devil incarnate, and I don't believe in showering someone with pretty words of flattery that aren't true. I only told Ben what he already knows. And maybe, if there's a glimmer of self-respect left inside him, he'll someday reclaim his soul."

"And that means standing up to this C. W. Rawlings I heard you mention? Is he this . . . devil incarnate?"

"That's right."

Morgan chuckled unexpectedly. "I take it you and poor Mr. Rawlings don't quite see eye to eye about something."

That stopped Lacey in her tracks once again. "*Poor* Mr.

Rawlings?" She pounced on his choice of words, deliberately misunderstanding his meaning. Fire danced in her eyes. "I assure you, sir, poor he is not. C. W. owns most of Willow Springs outright, and he controls the rest—in one way or another."

Morgan lowered his voice intimately. "But I have a feeling he doesn't control you, Mrs. Spencer. And I say *poor* man because I wouldn't envy anyone foolish enough to go up against you."

Lacey's face turned bright pink, and her unexpected response to his casual flattery mortified her. Now he had her blushing like a silly little ninny! What on earth was wrong with her today? "Thank you. I think."

A deep chuckle escaped Morgan's throat, and Lacey averted her gaze to stare sightlessly at a frivolous display of feathered hats in the milliner's shiny window. As the window itself came into focus, Lacey saw her own reflection and that of Morgan as well. His gaze had followed hers, but it wasn't hats he was staring at. Even in that hazy reflection of him, she sensed the laughter in his eyes as he studied her, and Lacey decided that beneath that coat of grime there must be a very attractive man. Only strikingly handsome men were as sure of themselves as this one seemed to be.

Simultaneously Lacey and Morgan became aware of the painfully slender pinched-nosed woman who was staring back at them from the milliner's shop, reproof written all over her grim face. Lacey smiled and nodded a greeting, but the woman pointedly ignored the nicety and flounced away from the window.

Morgan's dark brows shot up. "I've always wondered what a 'snit' was, and now I think I know. Don't people around here stop and pass the time of day with one another?"

Lacey smiled mischievously. "Mrs. Carstairs may not be certain that you qualify under the category of *people*. I wasn't quite sure you were human myself when you appeared at the sheriff's door."

Morgan looked down at himself, then sought his reflection in the window. "You mean I'm not a picture of sartorial splendor?"

"I promise you, sir, *that* will not be the rage sweeping the

Continent next season," she quipped, enjoying the sound of her own laughter. It had been so long since she'd had anything genuinely funny to laugh about—or anyone she'd felt comfortable laughing with.

"Well, then, since you profess to be good at giving advice, perhaps you would be kind enough to instruct me on what steps I should take in order to make myself more presentable."

She eyed him speculatively, trying to ignore the warm light in his unusual eyes. "Well, I'd say that you are in need of lodging, a meal, a shave, and a bath."

"Not necessarily in that order. And let's not forget that medicinal whiskey."

"Good heavens, no!" she exclaimed. Mrs. Carstairs returned to the window to glare at them disapprovingly, and Lacey moved off down the walk with Morgan at her side. "Let's see. The whiskey is the easiest of the lot. There are more saloons in Willow Springs than you can shake a stick at. The differences between them are only a matter of quality, atmosphere, and price."

"Begging your pardon, ma'am, but a saloon is a saloon. You can fancy it up, but the objective is still the same."

"In that case I suggest you try the Silver Strike just down there and around the corner on Palmer Street. The decor leaves a lot to be desired, but the whiskey's not too watered down, or so I'm told. As for the rest . . . that all depends on your pocketbook. We have three hotels—the Cattleman's, back there on Center Street; the Palmer House, adjacent to the Silver Strike, and Langhorn's, which is around the corner right . . . there." As they came to the corner, Lacey pointed to the establishment in question just as a wild oath rang out and the swinging doors of the Langhorn Saloon slammed open.

Lacey and Morgan watched as a burly saloon keeper, wearing an apron covered with grime, hauled a drunken, swearing patron through the door and dumped him unceremoniously into the street. The furious bartender muttered a few colorful oaths at the squawking drunk, then slammed back inside.

"I can't say that I'd recommend Langhorn's," Lacey said matter-of-factly, and Morgan laughed as they crossed the street. "The saloon is disreputable, the clientele is rowdy, and the rooms upstairs are shared four to a bed, I understand."

"Definitely to be avoided," Morgan said, still chuckling.

"Quite."

"The Cattleman's, then?" he suggested.

"Ostentatious."

"The Palmer House?"

"Overpriced and grossly overrated."

Morgan frowned. "I do believe you've ruled out all the possibilities. Should I collect my bedroll and head back to the wilderness?"

"Nothing that drastic. Actually, the best place in town is Mrs. Simon's boardinghouse. The rates are reasonable, the beds are clean, meals are included, and Mona Simon is the second-best cook in Willow Springs."

"Who's the best?" Morgan—utterly fascinated by his charming, witty companion—could not resist asking.

"My housekeeper, Berta Kraus."

"Lucky you."

"You have no idea how lucky," Lacey said. Ben Watson had called Berta prune-faced, but the stern German housekeeper was like family to Lacey. Other than Zachary Freeman, her printer at the *Gazette*, Berta was Lacey's only hold on the life she'd left behind with her father in Washington.

Her fondness for the woman showed plainly on her expressive face, and Morgan took note of it. He searched for an appropriate comment, then frowned in confusion when Lacey smiled and spoke a friendly greeting to two elderly matrons passing them on the walk. Morgan tipped his hat respectfully, but the women cut them dead, blatantly ignoring Mrs. Spencer's greeting just as the milliner had. Morgan knew he looked a sight, but that hardly warranted their rudeness to the woman at his side.

Could his assessment of her as a lady of quality have been so wrong? Was she, instead, a woman with a sordid past? Or possibly a prosperous local whore who enhanced her profits by affecting a veneer of ladylike respectability?

Morgan discarded that idea the second it was born. He couldn't speak for the lady's morals, but he did know quality when he saw it, and Allyce Smithfield Spencer was a lady, born and bred. She was decidedly more outspoken than any woman he'd ever met, but that didn't mean she wasn't respect-

able. She was lively, charming, quick-witted, and disquieting-
ly beautiful. He simply couldn't imagine what she might have
done to cause such an overt lack of civility on the part of her
fellow townswomen.

But she seemed to have taken the insult in stride, for she
continued her dissertation as cheerfully as before. "Now, let's
see. Mrs. Simon's boardinghouse takes care of your bed and
meal. We've decided on the Silver Strike for your medicinal
whiskey. That leaves only a shave and your bath."

"My long overdue bath," he corrected.

"You said that, I didn't. A lady always pretends not to notice
such . . . earthy defects."

"And are you?" Morgan stopped abruptly, and Lacey came
to a sudden halt, turning to look at him curiously.

"Am I what?"

"A lady," he replied frankly.

A lesser woman might have been offended, but Lacey met
his direct question with a soft, full-throated laugh that felt to
Morgan like a silken caress. His heart slammed violently into
his rib cage, and he became instantly and acutely aware that it
had been a long time since he'd had a woman. But more to the
point, he couldn't ever recall having had a woman like this. He
felt a sharp stab of disappointment when he remembered that
she'd made a point of letting him know she was married.

"There are differences of opinion on that subject, sir. Ask a
dozen people if Allyce Spencer is a lady, and you'll get a dozen
different answers—many of them exceptionally colorful, I'm
sure. I expect that if you remain in Willow Springs long
enough, you'll be able to make that judgment for yourself."
She turned and resumed her leisurely stroll. "Now, as to your
bath. There again you have an array of choices. What, exactly,
are you in the market for?"

Morgan frowned, wondering what was causing the wicked
little smile that tugged at the corners of her lips. "I usually
bathe with water and soap, ma'am. Did someone come up
with a refinement on the process while I was wandering in
the wilderness?"

"No," Lacey replied with mock seriousness, very much
enjoying this lighthearted repartee. It wasn't often she encountered a man with the education, intellect, and wit Morgan

displayed. His voice was deep and pleasing, with just the faintest hint of a drawl that spoke of a connection to the southern aristocracy. She'd have been willing to bet anything that Morgan had never in his life drunk coffee from a saucer.

"Soap and water are still the usual accoutrements," she assured him. "I was just referring to the . . . accessories that I've been told are available at certain bathhouses. Granville Taylor, just up ahead here, is an excellent barber and has adequate facilities in the back of his shop." She lowered her voice conspiratorially, and Morgan had to lean closer to hear. The delightful, tantalizing scent of roses clung to her hair, and he had to force himself to focus on her words. "However, if you desire the . . . assistance of a nubile maiden in your bath . . . "

Morgan straightened, laughing in surprise and delight. "You are an outrageous woman, Mrs. Spencer. Hasn't your husband ever told you that a gentleman's bathhouse adorned with nubile maidens is another of those earthy topics ladies generally eschew?"

Lacey kept her eyes focused straight ahead. "My husband is dead, Morgan," she replied softly, wondering when she was going to learn to curb her wicked sense of humor. Having grown up around her father's cronies and the dozens of newspapermen who had constantly besieged their home, Lacey had become one of them. She thought nothing of joining their discussions of politics or whatever sensational news item happened to be that day's scandal. The men had grown so accustomed to having her around that their ribald humor frequently slipped out before they remembered that their intelligent, witty companion was a woman.

As a result there was little Lacey had not seen or heard; it was appallingly difficult to offend her. More than once her late husband had been mortified by his wife's lack of propriety. Lacey could be the very soul of sophistication and grace when the situation called for it, but in private she had delighted in teasing David, forcing him to sternly take her to task for some outrageous word or deed, while secretly he did his best to hide the smile she invariably brought to his lips.

The memory of David's strikingly handsome face vainly attempting to suppress laughter assaulted Lacey's memory, and a wave of loneliness washed over her. Her husband was three years dead, and her grief, so intense and painful during that first year after his death, was now little more than a sad friend who accompanied her everywhere she went. She had long ago passed the point of weeping into her pillow at night, having learned to cherish the memories and carry on with her life.

Seldom did she feel the melancholy that assailed her now, but it took no great feat of introspection to see its cause. This stranger, who seemed so little like a stranger, was easy to be with. His warm, smiling eyes coaxed her into a freedom and ease she had not felt in years.

"My apologies, ma'am. I'm truly sorry for your loss." Morgan had sobered with this unexpected news, but though his sympathy was a sincere response to the sudden flash of pain that flickered across his companion's face, he couldn't prevent a surge of relief—or was it expectation?—from coursing through him. Willow Springs might prove to be more entertaining than he'd thought. Surely his employer couldn't begrudge him the diverting company of a lovely woman.

Lacey acknowledged his condolences, then forced herself back into her previous bright mood. In the back of her mind, she was struck by the disconcerting thought that it hadn't taken a great deal to banish David to the recesses of her memory, but she ignored the notion. "So, have you made a decision?"

"Decision?" Morgan frowned, having lost the thread of their conversation.

"As to your choice of bathing services."

"I do believe Mr. Taylor's tonsorial parlor will do just fine."

"In that case"—Lacey stopped a few feet from the barber's door—"we shall have to part company here."

"I am heartbroken, ma'am."

He bent ever so slightly in a token courtly bow, and Lacey laughed. "Yes, but it will be a *clean* break."

Morgan's laugh, deep and rich, was as pleasing as his voice. "Madam, you are truly a wicked woman. I do hope we'll meet again, soon."

"Willow Springs is not large, so I expect it is inevitable that we shall." It astonished Lacey to realize just how much she wished that to be true. Unable to stop herself, she asked, "Do you have business here?"

"Nothing in particular," he said offhandedly. He held her gaze steadily, and Lacey wondered vaguely if he was making a conscious effort to do so. Her instincts as a reporter took over almost without her realizing it.

"Where were you headed before you and your pinto encountered that rattlesnake?" she asked with a disarming smile.

Morgan shook his head and leaned one shoulder against the post that supported the canopy over their heads. "I must confess, ma'am, that I have nowhere in particular to go, nor any particular time to be there."

"And no one awaiting your arrival?"

"Sadly, no."

"But where is your home?"

"Wherever I happen to be. I'm an amazingly adaptable creature," he bragged with a grin.

Despite his charm, there was something guarded in the way he spoke that reminded Lacey of his expression earlier when she'd asked him if he had something to hide. Puzzled, she pressed, "But how do you survive? What work do you do?"

His smile faded a little. "I survive the way almost everyone does—by taking one day at a time."

Frustrated, Lacey eyed him narrowly. "My, but that was uninformative. The only thing I've learned about you is that you don't like to answer questions."

Morgan smiled broadly. "That's more than a lot of people know about me, ma'am."

"Then I'll consider myself fortunate and abandon this interrogation," she said with a resigned sigh. Her curiosity about him would have to go unappeased; after all, who and what he was really had nothing to do with her. That thought, however, was not a pleasant one. "I really should be on my way now."

"You're abandoning me?" Morgan asked, strangely reluctant to allow her to leave. Her questions had raised issues he wasn't ready to discuss with anyone just yet, but for some reason he hated the idea of lying to her. Most of all, he hated the thought of bidding her farewell. Hoping to forestall that moment, he smiled devilishly and asked, "Have you no parting advice for me? Is there anything I should know that will ease my entry into Willow Springs society and keep me out of trouble?"

"Oh, goodness . . . let me see," Lacey said thoughtfully, falling in with his deviltry. "I'll offer you three pieces of advice, and then you're on your own."

"And they are . . . ?"

"First, at all costs you must avoid Dempsey McAdams, the town bully. His father is a prosperous merchant who failed to teach his only son the value of an honest day's work. Dempsey makes the rounds of all the saloons at random, so it is impossible to determine when or where he will strike next. He loves to drink, and when he does, he has a nasty proclivity to pick fights. He's brutal with his fists and is reportedly very quick with a handgun, which is one of the reasons the town council passed the law requiring all guns to be checked with the sheriff."

"I shall avoid Mr. McAdams at all costs," Morgan promised gravely.

"Second, I strongly urge you to eschew any and all contact with C. W. Rawlings."

"Poor C. W.?"

The look Lacey shot him was loaded with daggers, but she ignored the gibe. "Dealing with that man has proven injurious to many—and fatal to some. He knows what he wants, and he has the power of the Wyoming Stock Growers Association behind him."

"He's a cattleman?" Morgan asked casually, but Lacey noted a subtle change in his eyes, a hardening that had not been there before.

"One of the biggest in the territory. Not to mention the most dangerous. And in addition to cattle, Rawlings owns a controlling interest in the local silver mine. In short, he owns this town—lock, stock, and barrel."

Morgan would have liked for her to say more, but she seemed to have finished with her second admonition and he dared not prod her further. "And your third piece of advice on how to avoid trouble in Willow Springs?"

Lacey glanced around dramatically, as though to see if anyone was eavesdropping, but while the street was busy at this late afternoon hour, no one seemed to be paying them any undue attention. "Third, and most important, stay away from the publisher of the Willow Springs *Gazette*, or you might well find yourself in grave danger."

Morgan searched her expressive face for a glint of the humor that had become so familiar to him in such a short time, but though her voice maintained its light, airy humor, there was a bitterness reflected in the sky blue of her eyes. "And why is that?"

"The *Gazette*'s publisher has had the ill fortune to cross C. W. Rawlings once too often, and it is rumored that C. W.'s retaliation may be deadly." She smiled brightly. "And there you have it, Morgan. Everything you need to know in order to have a pleasant stay in Willow Springs. It's been a pleasure talking with you, truly."

She stepped off the boardwalk, prepared to cross the busy street, but Morgan's voice stopped her. "Wait!" he cried in mock panic, stepping to the edge of the walk. It was ridiculous, but he just couldn't let her walk away. "Surely you'll tell me the name of this hapless editor so that I'll know when to run should we meet."

With an enigmatic smile, Lacey retraced the few paces she'd taken and stood before him as she extended her hand formally. "Spencer," she told him significantly as Morgan automatically took her hand. "Allyce Smithfield Spencer. Owner, publisher, and editor-in-chief of the Willow Springs *Gazette*. It's been a pleasure meeting you."

Morgan's eyes widened in surprise as she released his hand and hurried across the street. A newspaper *woman*? Interesting.

Captivated by the graceful sway of her hips, he watched until she disappeared into one of the side streets. What a truly magnificent woman.

Morgan sternly reminded himself that he had a lot to accomplish in Willow Springs, and a woman, magnificent or otherwise, didn't figure into his plans.

Humming a tuneless melody, he stepped into the barbershop and tried to put Allyce Spencer out of his mind, only to discover that the effort was a ridiculous waste of time.

Chapter Three

Lacey slipped the wire-rimmed spectacles off her nose and placed them on the desk before rubbing her strained, aching eyes. She had rewritten her editorial on the vigilance committee three times, trying to get it right, but her anger kept getting in the way of her journalistic training. Since Riley Hanson's death, Lacey had to continually remind herself that it was her responsibility to present her readers with facts and informed commentary, not emotional accusations aimed at C. W. Rawlings—no matter how well founded those accusations might be.

Not that Lacey had any readers to present the facts to. C. W. had seen to that months ago when she had begun her campaign against the WSGA. Now her advertisers were afraid to use the *Gazette*, and her once loyal readers had been terrorized into abandoning her. Only her trust fund and the considerable inheritance left by her late husband allowed Lacey to keep the newspaper in operation, since being seen on the street with a copy of the two-page weekly brought immediate harassment from C. W.'s men, who seemed to be everywhere. Lately it appeared that C. W. had more men patrolling the city streets than he did herding cattle on his ranch west of town.

For the most part the ruffians contented themselves with boosting the profits at the local saloons, but they had an uncanny knack for knowing when Lacey or Zach would leave the *Gazette* office. Invariably, one or more of them would then appear behind her on the street. They seldom spoke to her directly, but they made their intimidating presence known with casual comments and an occasional brush against her shoulder as they passed.

They were always unerringly polite, quick to tip their hats or mumble "Excuse me, ma'am," but the malevolence in their eyes belied their ingratiating words. The Brigade, as Lacey had come to think of them, meant to intimidate her, to remind her that C. W. Rawlings was not happy about her repeated attacks on Willow Springs's wealthiest, most powerful citizen. Were it not for the threatening specter of Lacey's father, three-quarters of a continent away in Washington, Lacey knew she would have been run out of Willow Springs long ago. Having an irate Senator Hanson on the rampage was bad enough; Rawlings and the WSGA had little desire to bring down the wrath of Roland Smithfield's vast publishing empire, too.

Lacey glanced up at the front window of the *Gazette*'s main room and her heart tripped in alarm. As though conjured by magic, one of Rawlings's Brigade stood passively outside the window, staring in at her with a chillingly benevolent smile. How long he had been there, she couldn't guess, but she forced a mockingly polite smile onto her lips and acknowledged the man's presence.

It was Stowe, or maybe Axtell—she couldn't be sure which. All of them looked alike to her—rough, crude men, all cut from the same filthy cloth. The ravages of dissipation and excess were written all over their sinister faces, and Lacey realized it was becoming more and more difficult to ignore them.

Particularly Croft. He was different from the rest. Of all the Brigade, only Croft truly frightened her. The others variously irritated and annoyed her, occasionally startling her as this one at the window had, but Croft was a gunfighter and Lacey despised and feared him, as she did all of his breed. Whipcord lean, with coal black eyes that bored straight through her, Croft watched Lacey with a heated intensity that shook her to the core.

The other men were sheep, grateful to collect a week's wage for the simple task of harassing a harmless widow and anyone foolish enough to be seen with a copy of her newspaper, but Croft was a wolf, vicious and mean. He was like Fogarty, the soulless bounty hunter who had murdered her husband. That was reason enough for Lacey to hate Croft and every other man who made his living with a fast gun.

If C. W. believed he was controlling the animal he'd hired, he was sadly mistaken. Lacey knew that, even if Rawlings did not. Croft might accept his pay and receive his orders, but in the final analysis, he would consider only his own desires, not those of his employer.

That was why he so frightened Lacey, and though she managed valiantly to quell her fear when she encountered the gunfighter, she knew he had sensed it. Every time Croft fixed his eyes on her, looking her over as though she were his own personal property, a chill went down Lacey's spine.

His look seemed to say "Soon," and she lived in terror of that day's arrival. Had she not been so determined and so cussedly stubborn, Lacey would have closed the *Gazette* within a week of Croft's arrival.

But she *was* stubborn, and Willow Springs was her home. The *Gazette* was the dream of her lifetime come true, the only tangible part of David she had left, and she would never give it up. The WSGA stranglehold on Wyoming couldn't last forever, and when the territory achieved statehood, things would change. Lacey was bound and determined to be part of that change. The only way Rawlings could prevent that was to kill her.

Stowe—or Axtell—tipped his hat and nodded politely, then moved on, past the four boarded-up window panes that had been shot out. Lacey had long since given up having the multipaned glass repaired; it was a waste of time and money. The last time she'd replaced the broken panes and had Mr. Donning repaint her sign on the glass—The Willow Springs *Gazette*, A. Smithfield Spencer, Publisher—the central pane had been broken by nightfall, eerily obliterating her name from the sign, like a portent of things to come.

It was becoming a ritual: At least once a week a member of the Brigade would ride past the *Gazette*, whooping and hollering while firing off a damaging shot or two. And of course this ritual was usually performed on nights when a dim light shone through the window, indicating that Lacey was working somewhere inside. Lately she had deemed it prudent to give up her late work habits in order to cut down on breakage.

Now, even though her house was only minutes away from the office, Zach escorted her home every day well before nightfall, watching over her in his quiet, unassuming way. He had even offered to sleep in the *Gazette*'s small back room in the hope of discouraging vandalism, but Lacey had quickly rejected his offer. As important as the newspaper was to her, there was nothing irreplaceable inside the building. Nothing in the world was worth having Zach wounded or killed if he surprised an intruder.

After replacing her spectacles, Lacey reread her editorial with dissatisfaction. In a fit of pique, she crumpled the paper and tossed it into the kindling box next to the wood stove that kept the chill off the room. Trying to concentrate was a waste of time. Maybe she should go home and help Berta with the canning. The last of the vegetables in their summer garden had been harvested, barely escaping the first frost, and though the iron-willed housekeeper had already rejected her offer of assistance, Lacey decided a change of pace might be good for both of them.

"Zach?" Her decision made, Lacey stood as she shuffled the papers on her desk into orderly piles.

"Yes?" Wiping his hands on his printer's apron, Zach stepped through the curtained door.

"We're closing up shop early, Zach. I'm going to help Berta can those beans, whether she wants my assistance or not. I just can't seem to concentrate today."

"As you wish. I've finished setting the columns on the Colorado silver strike, and I'm almost done with the piece on Mr. Cassidy's Wild Bunch. If it's acceptable to you, I'll escort you home, then return and finish."

"That's not necessary, Zach. No one will bother me this early in the day."

"All the same, I will escort you home." He was a rock, completely unmovable, and Lacey knew better than to argue.

"Very well."

"I will be with you in a moment."

Lacey nodded. "I'll secure things out here." Zach turned toward the curtain, but Lacey stopped him. "Oh, and Zach, on those articles, don't forget to credit the newspapers they were taken from."

His shoulders stiffened. "Of course, ma'am." He looked injured that she would even suggest he might forget such an important thing as giving credit to the source newspapers. Except for Lacey's editorials and stories about the atrocities committed by the vigilance committee, the *Gazette* consisted primarily of items reprinted from newspapers across the country. And since C. W. had a way of seeing that her mail was often delayed or managed to disappear completely, whatever news she did finally get to print was sometimes weeks or months old.

"I'll lock up in the back," Zach informed her stiffly, not bothering to conceal his wounded pride.

"Thank you." Lacey smiled fondly as the printer disappeared through the curtain. Ben Watson had been right yesterday when he'd said Zach was getting on in years, but to Lacey he was still the same quiet tower of strength and pride he'd always been. His coarse hair, once thick and jet black, had thinned a little, receding from his wide forehead, and its color was now a dusky gray. The deep-etched lines on his face made him appear distinguished rather than old, and his erect carriage was as straight and proud as it had been the first day she'd seen him more than twenty-five years ago.

A runaway slave who'd worked his way north through the Underground Railroad, Zach had been hired by Roland Smithfield to work in their Washington town house as his valet, but Zach's quick intelligence had soon prompted the newspaper magnate to see that he was properly educated and put to work at the newspaper as a typesetter.

When Lacey and David had set out for Wyoming to begin their married life as joint owners of their first newspaper, Zach had volunteered to join them. Though he claimed it was a need to escape the scramble and clutter of the city that prompted his gesture, Lacey knew otherwise. Zachary Freeman had come along to serve as her overly protective father's eyes and ears in the wild and woolly West.

Together the three of them had established the *Gazette*, and after David's death, when Lacey refused to give up and go home, Zach had remained with her, a pillar of strength, quiet and unassuming, yet always there for her.

And if he secretly made regular reports to Roland Smithfield on the status of his only child, Lacey was more than willing to overlook the spying because she knew it was born of love and concern for her, and that was a great comfort, particularly in times like these.

Moving to the stove, Lacey checked to be certain that it would burn out quickly. She was busy spreading the glowing embers with a poker when the bell over the front door tinkled and she straightened, whirling around in surprise. No one had entered her shop in weeks.

The sun at her visitor's back made her squint to take in the tall, broad-shouldered form, but before she'd even gotten a good look at the face beneath the brushed black hat with its polished silver band, Lacey knew the identity of her caller.

She smiled a warm welcome as she replaced the fire poker in its stand next to the wood box. "Well, well, Morgan, I must say, you did clean up rather nicely," she said and her compliment was no exaggeration. Stepping around her cumbersome printing press, she moved to the long, narrow front counter that separated the office into two sections.

Clean shaven and no longer covered with trail dust, Morgan was more handsome than Lacey had imagined—and last night her imagination had worked overtime on that very topic. It had alternately amused and annoyed her that she seemed unable to push the witty, unkempt stranger from her mind. Seeing him now, as he really was, wouldn't make that effort any easier. His face was bronzed by the sun, a perfect complement to his startling golden eyes, and deep dimples framed the full lips that smiled so easily and often. His nose was long, his cheekbones wide, and when he pulled off his hat respectfully, she noted with pleasure that his jet-black hair, which brushed his collar in the back, still curled in casual disarray.

His long frock coat was crisp black, as were the waistcoat and the form-fitting trousers that hugged his well-muscled thighs. The stark black was relieved only by the dazzling white of his shirt and the sparkling silver of a belt buckle that matched the engraved conchos banding his hat. He was, all in all, the most devastatingly handsome man Lacey had ever seen.

"Thank you for the compliment, Mrs. Spencer. I shall relay it to Barber Taylor. He'll be glad to know his efforts weren't in vain."

Lacey glanced over him appreciatively, immediately warming to the ready laughter in Morgan's eyes. "He had an exceptional specimen to work with."

Morgan chuckled. "Mrs. Spencer, you do have the most disarming way of saying exactly what you're think—" Quite suddenly his voice died and he tensed as his attention shifted over Lacey's shoulder to the back of the office.

Turning to follow his gaze, Lacey found Zach standing quietly in the curtained door to the back room, his Winchester casually cradled in the crook of his arm.

"It's all right, Zach," she assured the printer, who eyed the stranger suspiciously. "This is Morgan. We met yesterday in Sheriff Watson's office." Lacey turned back to her guest to complete the introduction. "Morgan, this is Zachary Freeman, my dear friend and the *Gazette*'s typesetter."

"A pleasure, Mr. Freeman."

"Sir." Zach gave a slight nod to acknowledge the greeting. He looked at Lacey significantly. "If you have need of me, I shall be just inside." He glanced at Morgan to be certain his message was received, then disappeared through the curtain.

"Thank you, Zach," Lacey called after him.

"Nice welcoming committee you have there," Morgan observed, stepping forward until only the long counter separated him from the newspaper's proprietress.

"Zach and I have learned the hard way that it pays to be cautious. We don't get many visitors with friendly intentions." She smiled. "Now, how can I help you?"

"This is purely a social call, ma'am."

"Indeed?" Though she was undeniably pleased, Lacey managed to look reproachful. "I believe you were warned, sir, about the dangers of associating with the notorious publisher of the *Gazette*."

Morgan glanced down modestly. "Well, ma'am, while enjoying a whiskey at the Silver Strike last night, I very judiciously managed to avoid a confrontation with the quarrelsome Dempsey McAdams, and since I haven't seen hide nor hair of *poor* C. W. Rawlings, I figured two out of three left the odds decidedly in my favor. And besides, I must say that you piqued my curiosity yesterday. From what I've learned so far, Willow

Springs is not the peaceful little berg it appears to be on first glance."

Lacey sobered. "Few things are entirely what they appear to be, Morgan."

"Like the publisher of the *Gazette*, for instance?"

"Perhaps."

"Then might I persuade you to enlighten me?"

She looked at him curiously. "About what, Morgan? The publisher or the town?"

He shrugged. "Both. Either."

"Why?"

A trace of a smile tugged at his lips, deepening the dimples in his cheeks. "Have you ever seen a dog settle down to sleep, ma'am? Particularly a stray with no home, who just has to take what he can get?"

Not seeing his point, Lacey shook her head, and Morgan continued. "That old dog, he can't know whom or what to trust, but he's got to sleep sometime, so he'll pick him out someplace that looks quiet and then he'll sniff all around and scratch him out a nest before he finally lies down for the night."

Lacey would have had to be extremely obtuse to miss his point, but she found his analogy fascinating, and his deep voice with its slightly accented drawl was mesmerizing. "And . . . ?" she prompted in order to keep him talking.

"A man's not so different from that dog, Mrs. Spencer. Not a smart man, anyway. A smart man learns to find out which way the wind is blowing before he settles in. And it appears to me, ma'am, that you're caught in the middle of a very dangerous cross draft."

"Not a draft, Morgan," Lacey corrected wryly. "A full-scale tornado. But it has nothing to do with you."

"All the same, I'd really like to know what makes Mrs. Allyce Smithfield Spencer so dangerous to be around."

"Why?" Lacey asked again, with equal parts of suspicion and expectation.

His voice dropped to a thrilling, almost seductive drawl. "If I'm to spend as much time in her company as I'd like, I think it'd be wise to know what to expect."

Morgan was looking at her intently, his expression charming but serious, and Lacey experienced a set of mixed emotions.

Part of her, the utterly feminine part that had been dormant until yesterday, was glowing with delight that this attractive, intriguing man wanted to court her. He was a stranger, about whom she knew virtually nothing, but the idea of coming to know him better made her inexplicably happy.

The other part of her, however, the part trained by her father—the toughest, shrewdest newspaperman on the East Coast—was issuing a warning in banner headlines that there was more to this inquiry than the handsome Morgan was saying.

Always one to examine an issue from all visible sides, Lacey opted to give Morgan the information he wanted, then wait and see if his true motives surfaced. After all, her feud with C. W. wasn't exactly a secret. It was nothing Morgan wouldn't hear around town eventually—or couldn't read about in her own newspaper, for that matter.

"Very well, Morgan. What is it you want to know?"

"You could start with the bully, C. W. Rawlings."

Lacey shook her head. "No, Dempsey McAdams is the bully. C. W. is the devil incarnate."

"Ah, yes. How silly of me to forget." He grinned and leaned lazily against the counter. "So tell me about the devil, preacher."

"If it's a sermon you want, it's a sermon you shall get," she told him good-naturedly. "The congregation may be seated." She moved around the counter and through the swinging gate to the long bench that sat beneath her much abused window. With a caution that was becoming a weary habit, she angled her body on the seat so that she would immediately notice any movement on the street.

Morgan had spent too much time exercising the eyes in the back of his head not to realize what she was doing, and he felt a sudden surge of sympathy mixed with anger. Last night out of curiosity, he'd made it his business to find out all he could about the widow Spencer, and what he learned had made his blood boil. A woman like this should be sheltered and protected, not terrorized to the point that she dared not turn her back on a window.

A wave of protectiveness washed over him, but he quickly pushed it aside, as he had last night. He was truly sorry about the problems that beset her, but he reminded himself sternly that he wasn't in a position to get involved. There was a good possibility that Allyce Spencer could be useful to him, and if that was the case, he'd take whatever advantage was necessary in order to accomplish his goal. One thing he couldn't afford, though, was to let his undeniable attraction to the lovely widow get out of hand.

Carefully maintaining his attentive expression, betraying none of his thoughts or errant emotions, Morgan forced his concentration on the information she was giving him.

"There is very little to tell, really," she began as Morgan sat facing her on the bench. "Wyoming is caught in the grip of the problem that's plagued this country on every step of its westward expansion."

"Cattlemen versus farmers?"

"Or sheepherders or, in this instance, smaller ranchers who cut into the open range. It's a particularly serious problem here because there is so little good range. It takes five or six acres just to graze one head of cattle, and the Wyoming Stock Growers Association believes it has an exclusive right to every acre of land in the territory."

"That must make it hard on the small ranchers who are trying to run cattle on a tiny piece of government land."

"Yes, it does," she agreed. "But the small ranchers are a very determined lot. Last year a group of easterners and a few disillusioned Kansas farmers, seven families all together, formed a co-op. They pooled their resources and purchased several thousand acres of prime land around the Laramie River under the Homestead Act. C. W. Rawlings had been maneuvering to buy that acreage for years, but he couldn't bribe the land agent in Cheyenne. The land was meant for settlers, and the agent was determined that that's what it would be used for."

Morgan raised his eyebrows in disbelief. "An honest land agent! Will wonders never cease?"

"Unfortunately he's now an honest out-of-work land agent. After he sold the river acreage to the co-op, the WSGA put pressure on the territorial governor to fire the poor man."

Lacey saw a tightening in Morgan's face that briefly displayed more than detached interest. Maybe it was just that he abhorred injustice as much as she did, but Lacey once again got the feeling that his curiosity about Willow Springs, and about her, was anything but casual.

Nonetheless, she continued, "Once the co-op moved in, things grew worse than ever. Rustling has always been a problem because the cattle are spread out over hundreds of miles of open range, but Rawlings began complaining that whole herds were being stolen. Of course he offered no proof, just his word that they were gone. By agitating and creating suspicion, he managed to get everyone up in arms. A vigilance committee was formed, complete with secret oaths and a charter, and the vigilantes began terrorizing the small ranchers—not just members of the co-op, but every small operator and farmer in the area. They started with night raids to scatter their cattle and horses, then gradually worked up to wanton property destruction—burning barns and houses, shooting livestock . . . "

Two riders cantered down the street past the *Gazette*. Lacey glanced at them, recognized them as harmless, then returned her attention to her dissertation. "Several ranchers gave up and moved on, figuring it wasn't worth the fight, but most of them have stayed."

"And where do you fit into all this, ma'am?" Morgan asked. "You're not a rancher. This isn't your fight."

"Oh, but it is!" Lacey argued, displaying a flash of defiance that took Morgan by surprise. "This is my home, and I won't stand by and watch good people be destroyed by the greed of one rich, selfish man!"

She caught herself and forced a note of calm back into her voice. "At first I printed occasional editorials denouncing the vigilance committee and did what I could to combat some absurd rumors that the ranchers were organizing to take over the town. Anyone with a lick of sense should have seen that those stories were just lies that Rawlings was spreading to justify his illegal activities with the vigilance committee, but many people believed the rumors, and last June things started getting crazy. A rancher was shot during one of the committee's raids down near Laramie. A week later a ten-year-old boy was trampled to death when the vigilantes stampeded a corral of wild mustangs.

"Suddenly the vigilantes became a pack of wild animals, as

though once they'd tasted blood they had to have more and more and more." Deeply disturbed, Lacey rose and tried to regain her composure.

Morgan sat quietly, fascinated not so much by the story as by the woman herself. Obviously she cared passionately about this crusade. Most of the women he'd known only got this worked up over the injustice of not being able to purchase a new hat or some irrelevant trinket. Mrs. Spencer was a remarkable woman.

After a moment Lacey was finally able to turn to him and continue dispassionately. "The worst of it came in July. The vigilantes hanged Riley Hanson, the leader of the co-op. He was young, but very shrewd."

The effort to remain unemotional was costing Lacey a great deal, and she turned away again so that Morgan would not see the pain she was trying so hard to hide. She didn't turn quickly enough, though, and Morgan saw her effort to hold back tears. "Riley and I had known each other for years. He was the son of a U.S. senator, and we'd more or less grown up together in Washington. They bludgeoned his wife to death and hanged Riley from an oak in his own yard."

In her mind's eye, lightning flashed and Lacey could see her friend's body swaying wildly. She swallowed hard, forcing the image away. She had not cried for Riley and Martha yet; she certainly wasn't going to do it in front of a stranger. "Since their death, I've devoted my newspaper to putting Rawlings and the vigilance committee out of business."

Morgan heard the pain she was suppressing, and his instinct was to go to her and comfort her, but that was obviously not what she wanted. Mrs. Spencer was a very strong lady who had her own way of dealing with grief. Instead, he said gently, "Which makes you pretty unpopular with Rawlings."

"It makes me dangerous to C. W.," she corrected. "He has frightened off my subscribers, threatened merchants into withdrawing advertising, and launched a campaign of terrorism against me—and anyone who associates with me," she concluded, looking at Morgan significantly.

He rose and stepped toward her. "Excuse me, ma'am, I don't mean to insult, but how can the writings of one tiny newspaper possibly warrant such drastic measures?"

"Because I've also taken on the WSGA. They control the territorial government and their lobby in Washington has resulted in the passage of several disastrous laws."

"But I still don't see—"

Lacey chuckled humorlessly and held up a hand to silence him. "You still don't see how one little slip of a woman with a two-page weekly in the wilds of Wyoming could possibly be a threat to anyone. Right?"

"Forgive me, but no. I don't see."

She looked at him archly, a ghost of a smile teasing the corners of her lips. "Have you ever heard of the Washington *Tribune*? The New York *Banner*? The St. Louis *Telegrapher*?" She named only a few of the most prominent newspapers in the country.

"Of course."

"And do you know who publishes those estimable papers?"

Morgan nodded. "Roland Smith . . . " His voice trailed off as he made the connection. He grinned. "Roland Smithfield, venerable father of Mrs. Allyce Smithfield Spencer, I presume."

"Exactly. Father reprints my articles on the WSGA activities and certain select editorials as well. I may be a backwater newspaper publisher, but I am very well connected."

"And dangerous," he finally agreed.

"Yes. But my father is also my ace in the hole, so to speak. If C. W. Rawlings tries to harm me—seriously, I mean, not just through intimidation tactics and petty vandalism—or if he kills me, he knows he's finished. With or without proof, my father would destroy Rawlings, and Wyoming's bid for statehood would be doomed. And the statehood issue is tricky at best. This territory will never have enough citizens to make the population quota, but the WSGA has enough power to solve that problem eventually.

"Roland Smithfield controls public opinion all across the country," Lacey continued. "And he also knows where a hundred dirty little skeletons are buried. He could ruin every senator and representative who dared vote for Wyoming's statehood. Washington knows that, the WSGA knows it, and C. W. Rawlings knows it. He doesn't dare harm me."

"You're playing a dangerous game, ma'am," Morgan

warned softly. "And it sounds to me as though you're sitting at a table where the dealer is desperate. Desperate men don't often see just how much they've got to lose. If you're not careful, you might push Rawlings too far."

"I'm not afraid of him," Lacey replied, summoning all the grit and determination that had kept her going these last months.

"Beggin' your pardon, ma'am," Morgan said, stepping closer, "but you're either a liar or a fool."

Lacey's mouth twitched with the beginnings of a nervous smile. "I'm no fool," she assured him, "but I'm not giving up."

"You're not going to win, either."

Her smile disappeared. "What makes you so sure? Haven't you heard that the pen is mightier than the sword?"

"Check your history books, Mrs. Spencer, and I think you'll find that it's only later generations who look back at the writings of dead patriots and make that claim. The pen becomes mightier only after the sword has struck it down, making the writer a martyr for the cause. I'd hate to see you end up like that."

Morgan lowered his voice intimately and stepped a little closer, making his presence felt in the pit of Lacey's stomach. "It would be a terrible waste of an extraordinary woman."

Lacey tried to ignore the warmth that suffused her. How on earth had this man turned an intellectual political discussion into a conversation that suddenly transformed her into mush? "I won't quit, and I won't be frightened off," she said flatly, surprised at having the power of speech. Her breathing turned shallow as she became aware of Morgan in a completely physical, sensual way. Her eyes wouldn't leave his face no matter how hard she tried to look away, and the clean, masculine scent of bay rum teased her heightened senses, making her heartbeat quicken. Long, dark lashes framed his expressive golden eyes, which seemed to darken intently even as she watched. He wanted to kiss her, and Lacey wanted that kiss very much.

For the first time in her life, Lacey saw retreat as a viable alternative to a situation. One step would have placed her against Morgan's massive body, and from the look on his face, she knew he'd find no discomfort in placing his arms around her and pulling her into a secure embrace. On the other hand, moving past him and behind the counter to put a respectable distance and a solid object between them would be far saner. For the moment, though, Lacey found she could do neither. The magnetic pull of his presence was simply too mesmerizing.

As though reading her indecisive thoughts, Morgan raised one hand and brushed back a lock of wavy hair that had fallen from her neat chignon onto her cheek. It was a gentlemanly move, designed to offer her a choice between the safety of a retreat or the security of an embrace that promised passion—for that was exactly what he was offering, and he was certain Mrs. Spencer knew it.

This was no virginal schoolgirl standing a hairbreadth from his arms, but a vibrant, mature woman who knew quite well that he wanted to kiss her. At that moment, which seemed suspended in time, Morgan's eyes promised a great deal—possibly more than he intended or could deliver—yet he had to leave the decision up to her.

And so he merely touched her hair, allowing his knuckles to brush her cheek. The gentle contact with her soft, smooth skin left him longing to replace the roughness of his hand with his infinitely more sensual lips, but the decision had to be hers. So he waited, astonished that his own breathing had become as labored as that of the very affecting woman in front of him.

He saw himself reflected in her startled eyes, and was disappointed but not surprised when Mrs. Spencer finally stepped hastily around him and retreated through the gate, placing the bulk of the counter between them.

Embarrassed by her retreat, Lacey couldn't bring herself to look at Morgan, but she could almost feel him laughing at her cowardice as she reached for the curl he had been toying with and tucked it back into the chignon. She was amazed to see no laughter in his eyes when she finally summoned the courage to look at him. Instead, she saw patience and understanding, which plainly astonished her. This was no caveman who knew nothing but storming a woman with brute force. This was a gentleman who understood people and who respected women.

In that moment an understanding passed between them, and

Lacey realized it was inevitable that she end up in his arms. Whether it would be for a moment, a night, or a lifetime, she could not predict, but there was something between them that ultimately would not be denied.

Had Lacey been easy to shock, she would have been mortified by the turn of her thoughts, but she was not. As sure as the sun would rise in the morning, Lacey knew that eventually she would surrender to—or share herself with—Morgan. It was an astonishing realization, but it frightened her not in the least.

The moment of sensual awareness between them finally passed, and suddenly the silence became heavy. "Have I given some offense, Mrs. Spencer?" he asked, his mouth twitching to a smile that displayed his dimple.

"Lacey."

"I beg your pardon?"

She smiled, valiantly conquering her breathlessness. "My friends call me Lacey. It's a peculiar little nickname that survived my childhood and chased me into maturity."

"But it is a most fitting one," he said softly. "A truly fine lace is not only beautiful and delicate but strong and durable, too. It is a perfect name for you, indeed."

"Thank you." Lacey felt the flush that crept up her cheeks, but she staunchly ignored it. "And to answer your question, no, you have given me no reason to be offended."

"I'm glad . . . Lacey."

He was looking at her again as though he wanted to kiss her, and Lacey decided she should push the conversation back into neutral territory before she did something truly foolish—like throw herself across the counter into his arms. "So, Morgan, have I satisfactorily answered your questions about Willow Springs?"

Morgan allowed the moment to pass, also, but he was undeniably sorry to see it go. "You've answered some of my questions, but believe me, I find no satisfaction in the trouble you've landed yourself in."

His choice of words plucked at Lacey's pride and she warned him, "Don't condescend to me. I knew exactly what I was getting into when I launched this campaign. I'm not a fluffy little idiot playing newspaper the way some little girls play house.

I'm a journalist. I was born and raised in a man's world, and I know how to fight for what I believe in."

"I can see that."

"Then you'll forgive me if I warn you not to—"

The tinny bell over the door jingled for the second time in one day, but this time Lacey froze at the sight of her newest arrival. As before, Zach appeared with the Winchester, and Morgan swiveled smoothly to look at the newcomer who had turned Lacey to stone.

The man was fifty, perhaps a little older, and of average height. Imposingly built, with broad shoulders and a great barrel chest, he made the tailored suit coat he wore seem out of place. The exaggerated diamond stickpin in his cravat indicated his obvious wealth, and the arrogance on his plain, broad-featured face bespoke a man who had known poverty but had risen to power.

He took the room in contemptuously, staring through Zach as though he were invisible, and spared only a passing glance at Morgan before his condescending gaze alighted on Lacey.

An undercurrent of electricity charged the room and Morgan glanced at Lacey, only to be stunned by what he saw in her magnificent face. Hatred, pure and deadly, had turned her delicate features to cold granite, and her sunlit blue eyes had darkened to stormy midnight. The righteous indignation he'd seen in her earlier had turned to a fiery fury of which Morgan would never have believed this delicate, well-bred lady capable. He needed no introduction to know that their visitor was C. W. Rawlings.

For Morgan this was a most fortuitous turn of events. Here at last was the man he'd ridden six hundred miles to meet.

The game was about to begin.

Chapter Four

"Good afternoon, Mrs. Spencer," Rawlings greeted, his rough voice grating to the ears.

Somehow, Lacey managed a mocking smile. "The sun must be shining today. I see the snakes have started slithering out from under their rocks."

Rawlings's dark eyes narrowed at the insult, but he merely smiled. "As gracious as ever, Mrs. Spencer. It does me good to meet a woman who knows how to make a man feel welcome, don't you agree, Mr. . . . ?" He looked at Morgan, raking him over from head to toe.

"The name's Morgan."

Rawlings glanced at Lacey as though he expected her to complete the introduction, but she stared at him stonily. "Since Mrs. Spencer doesn't seem inclined to do the honors, I'm C. W. Rawlings."

He extended his hand genially, but Morgan ignored it as he leaned negligently against the counter. It wasn't in his nature to insult a stranger, but he wanted to get a gauge on Rawlings, see how he would react to the slight. Morgan's future, maybe even his life, depended on C. W. Rawlings, and he had to learn all he could about the man as quickly as possible.

The insult established the lines of loyalty in the room, but if Rawlings was surprised or displeased to learn that Morgan was Mrs. Spencer's apparent ally, he gave no outward indication of it. That in itself told Morgan a great deal.

Rawlings's hand returned smoothly to his side and he continued, "I own the Double Star Ranch."

"And most of Willow Springs," Lacey added venomously. "Modesty doesn't become you, C. W."

"And sarcasm doesn't become a lady. Or didn't that fine daddy of yours in Washington ever tell you that, missy?" he flared.

"Leave my father out of this."

"Hard to do, ma'am, since you're the one who insists on bringing him into our little difference of opinion."

"I don't call a murder a difference of opinion."

"Murder!" C. W. shook his head sadly and glanced at Morgan as though pleading for assistance. "My, oh, my, where do these women get their ideas? A pretty little thing like this should be putting her mind and talents to work making some man happy, not meddling in business she couldn't possibly understand, don't you agree, Morgan?"

"Do you want something, C. W., or did you just stop by to insult me?" Lacey asked harshly.

Morgan was grateful for her interruption, which spared him having to formulate a reply to Rawlings's question. At this stage of the game, he much preferred to stand back and view the fireworks. Not surprisingly, Lacey seemed more than capable of holding her own with the rancher, and Morgan was learning a lot just by listening and watching.

The business with the handshake had already told him that Rawlings was a man who gave nothing away when dealing with another man. He would be a difficult opponent across a poker table or anywhere else, for that matter. He was tough and shrewd, and whether dealing with a friend or an adversary, Rawlings would never let his feelings show unless it suited his purpose. Morgan had seen his kind before, and he knew them to be quite dangerous. Self-made men always were.

But with Lacey, a woman, Rawlings was less cautious. Evidently Mrs. Spencer was an irritant and a threat, but he didn't consider her a serious opponent.

With what he'd learned about Lacey today, Morgan wondered if that just might be an error in judgment he could somehow use to his own advantage.

"I do admire a body that gets straight to the point," Rawlings pronounced affably, reaching into his vest pocket to extract a paper.

He's playing a game of his own here, Morgan noted, irritated by the insufferably pleased look on Rawlings's beefy face. And this is his hole card. He's tipped his hand already.

"The town council has a little announcement we need printed," C. W. continued as he unfolded the paper and laid it on the counter in front of Lacey.

"You can't be serious," she scoffed, astonished by his gall.

"Well, I've heard rumors that the *Gazette* is in need of business and thought a paying customer would be a welcome change."

"Take your business to the *Clarion*. Douglas Ellerby will be glad to accommodate you. He can use the transaction to pay off some of the gambling debts he owes you."

Rawlings shrugged. "The council's just trying to be fair to all the local tradesmen, spreading the business around to the benefit of all."

"I don't need your business—or that of your flunkies in the town council. I wouldn't walk across the street to spit on you if you were on fire, C. W. I'm certainly not going to do any printing for you." Lacey snatched up the paper and waved it at him. "Now take this and leave."

A muscle twitched in Rawlings's cheek, displaying his displeasure. This was not going at all the way he had intended. "Are you sure you wouldn't like to read it and reconsider?"

Lacey sighed and pulled hard on the reins of her hatred. C. W. was baiting her, trying to provoke her into losing her temper. It was something he did every once in a while just to keep things stirred up. Lacey was bound and determined not to oblige him, but he was also daring her to read the notice he'd brought, and she couldn't back down from that challenge. Obviously it was a public announcement that would be plastered all over town by next week, anyway. She'd know about it sooner or later; she might as well make it sooner so that she could get him out of her office.

Quelling her anger, Lacey turned and marched around the printing press to her desk where her spectacles lay on top of the papers she'd sorted earlier. With a contemptuous glance at C. W., she settled the wire rims across her nose and fixed her attention on the notice as she absently stepped toward the counter.

Though he had no idea what she was reading, Morgan saw the exact moment the import of it hit Lacey. The stiffening of her body as blind fury suffused her was like a bolt of lightning crashing through the room. It was such a palpable, violent thing that Morgan's hand twitched ever so slightly toward his holster before he remembered that his gun was locked in his hotel room. He froze, waiting, as Lacey's head came up slowly, her jaw quivering with barely suppressed rage.

"You bastard," she hissed in a small voice that had the impact of thunder. "You knew I'd never print this trash!" Furious, she ripped the notice in half and let it fall to the floor. "Get out of here. Get out!"

Pleased that he'd finally gotten what he came for, Rawlings couldn't help but give the knife another painful twist. "Does this mean you're rejecting the council's business?"

"*Get out!*"

Rawlings's satisfied leer made Morgan want to smash his face, but he held his peace. This was Lacey's fight, not his. Not yet, anyway. And besides, when he finally did enter the war, it wasn't Lacey's side he'd end up on.

"Now, Mrs. Spencer . . . " C. W. said placatingly. "A truly good businessman—or woman—never lets personal sentiment get in the way of his job. You take Sheriff Watson, for example. Why, do you know that good man had every intention of meeting the one-fifteen from Cheyenne tomorrow. Seems he made a promise to somebody about helping guard a shipment of something or other."

Lacey stiffened, vaguely realizing what he was about to say, yet not able to focus on it. She was still reeling from the pain of seeing the public notice that would soon be plastered all over Willow Springs. Tears were forming deep inside her, but she kept them locked up. Rawlings could make her lose her temper, but he would never have the satisfaction of seeing her cry. Never.

He wasn't quite finished, though. "But you know poor old Watson's getting forgetful in his advancing years. He plumb forgot that tomorrow's the day he's supposed to inspect the brands on my herd up in the north range. I had to remind him of it myself not fifteen minutes ago."

His words finally soaked in, and Lacey squared her shoulders under a weight that suddenly seemed too great to bear. She had known from the start that Ben wouldn't be at the train station when her shipment of newsprint arrived, but somewhere inside she had held out hope that just once the sheriff would stand up to Rawlings and do the right thing. The disappointment she felt in the lawman only added to the rage building inside her—rage that this one despicable man had the power to destroy so many lives.

"I get your message, Rawlings," she spat. "Now get the hell out of here before I do something we'll both regret."

"I do have other business to attend to," he said with a leer. "Got to get to the *Clarion* before Ellerby closes up shop." Rawlings pointed smugly at the torn paper on the floor. "If you'd just be so good as to hand me back my notice . . . "

The look on his face was one more taunting insult than Lacey could stand.

It happened so quickly Morgan wasn't sure he'd actually seen it—or that he truly believed it. One second Lacey was standing in the middle of her office trembling with rage. In the next she whirled to a startled Zach and wrenched the repeater from his arms. She flew to the counter and with swift and frightening efficiency pulled the lever downward and snapped it back up, automatically clicking a cartridge into place.

Before anyone could react, she leveled the muzzle at Rawlings's face, leaving C. W. stunned and speechless. His first instinct was to laugh at her silly bravado, but then he looked past the barrel into her eyes and realized this was no joke.

Very quietly, Lacey murmured, "Get out, C. W. Say one more word and I'll blow your worthless brains from here to Cheyenne."

"Lacey, don't do this. . . . Give me the gun," Morgan commanded, his voice low and hard. She wasn't running a bluff. Morgan recognized her expression all too well; he had seen it a hundred times on other faces. It haunted his sleep. Her eyes held the cold fire of a gunfighter's eyes in those dangerous, telling seconds just before the gun was pulled from the holster. Like a professional gunman, Lacey was suppressing her rage, so that blood was forced to pump furiously as her heart quickened and her breathing became short and controlled.

Knowing they were only moments away from deadly violence, Morgan tried to reason with her again, keeping his voice soft, but commanding. "You don't want to do this, Lacey. Put the gun down, now."

Though Lacey didn't obey him, Morgan was at least relieved to see that Rawlings was finally taking his opponent a little more seriously. Beads of perspiration popped out on his forehead and upper lip. He was a prideful man who didn't take backing down from a woman easily, though, and Morgan could see him mentally weighing the decision whether to retreat or make a grab for the rifle.

"Don't even think about it, Rawlings," Morgan warned. "Just turn around and march out. You came here to start trouble, and you got what you were after. Why don't you just mosey along before that Winchester starts getting too heavy for the lady. You wouldn't want her finger to slip on that trigger."

Rawlings's eyes flickered with one more moment's indecision. He knew a lot about Allyce Spencer—more than he'd ever wanted to know, that was for sure—but he hadn't thought she was capable of this! When she'd begun her campaign against him and the vigilance committee, C. W. had made it his business to find out more about the widow Spencer than just the gossip that was available around town.

Up until a few months ago, she'd been nothing more to him than a silly little widow who was foolish enough to think she could run her late husband's newspaper. Now he knew about her background and that powerful father of hers. He knew about the inheritance her wealthy mother had left her after she died of scarlet fever when Lacey was only three. Rawlings knew how much money she kept in the bank he controlled here in Willow Springs, and he had a pretty good idea of the accounts she kept in Cheyenne, St. Louis, and Washington.

Mrs. Spencer was rich, and she had an even richer father. But she was only a woman. Sure, she was more stubborn and independent than most, but she was just a woman nonetheless. The little twit believed that words were all it took to tame the West, and her hatred for guns was renowned. He'd never believed that anything would tempt her to violence, and he still didn't.

A gun in the hands of a woman was a dangerous thing, but Rawlings decided to take the risk and call her bluff. He'd leave, all right, but he would go with dignity—and certainly not at the point of a gun. Without looking at Morgan, he told him, "It's all right, Mr. Morgan. I don't believe the widow Spencer has it in her to commit cold-blooded murder." He looked at her challengingly. "Do you, ma'am?"

Enough of Lacey's rage had drained away to make her regret the blindly stupid act of pulling a gun on Rawlings, but she wasn't ready to back down, either. Steadying her arms, she lowered the gun, but only far enough to leave the muzzle resting precious inches from Rawlings's massive chest. "Don't tempt me to find out, C. W. Just go. I'd much rather leave cold-blooded murder to cowards like you."

"Coward?" Rawlings's eyes grew hard again. He'd settled this territory when it was nothing but Indians, rattlesnakes, and bushwhackers. No one had ever called him a coward and lived to tell about it.

"Yes, coward!" Lacey shoved the rifle barrel into his chest, forcing him back a step. As he retreated, she rounded the counter, stepping through the gate. Punctuating her words with vicious stabs of the muzzle, she forced him back toward the door. "You are the worst kind of coward imaginable. You ride at the head of a band of vigilantes who terrorize innocent men, women, and children in the dead of night. You hide your faces behind masks. You commit murder, then justify your butchery with secret oaths, pledges, and meetings so righteous that they have to be held behind locked doors! That makes you a coward, Rawlings, and I'm going to prove it one of these days. You're going to make a big mistake soon, and when you do, I'll be right here to tell the world all about it!"

Step by step, Lacey had forced him across the room until his back was against the door and they could retreat no further.

"I'll get no pleasure from watching you hang for murder, C. W.," she ground out viciously, "but believe me, the day I write your obituary will be the happiest day of my life. Now get out of here and don't come back! I've had a real problem with theft lately. I'd hate to shoot you and have to explain to the sheriff how I mistook you for a prowler!"

Her chest was heaving with the force of her wrath, but Lacey stepped back and relaxed her hold on the gun so that it was no longer at his chest.

Rawlings reached behind him for the doorknob that was stabbing at his spine. He opened the door without ever taking his eyes off Lacey. "You're finished in Willow Springs, Mrs. Spencer," he snarled. "I'll drive you out of town if it's the last thing I ever do."

Lacey shook her head and smiled a cold, bloodless smile. "Not in a million years, Rawlings. You can't buy me because I already have money, probably more than you do. And you can't intimidate me because I'm not afraid of you or your gunfighters. That only leaves killing me, and we both know what my father will do to you and the Stock Growers' Association if you harm me. I've heard that down in Texas this is called a Mexican standoff. Right now you're standing on my property, and I don't like it!"

Rawlings nodded, his fury at his own impotence masked behind the oh-so-thin veil of civility and refinement he'd worked hard to cultivate. She was right, and God, how he hated it. And her.

"Good day to you, Mrs. Spencer. You'll be hearing from me again. Soon." With an insolent tip of his hat, he stepped through the door and disappeared.

The room was silent for one long, tense moment as the acrid smell of hatred evaporated. Lacey's relief was a visible thing; Morgan saw it in the slow sagging of her shoulders and the tormented downward tilt of her head. He couldn't decide if what she'd done was very foolish or very brave, or maybe equal parts of both, but he did know he'd never been as moved as he was by this lovely woman's refusal to be broken by a dangerous, powerful enemy.

"It's over, Lacey," he crooned softly, coming up beside her to gingerly pluck the rifle from her hands. Uncocking it carefully, he passed it to Zach, who stepped forward with a grateful look. Clearly, the dignified printer believed that Morgan had taken a stand on Lacey's side, and Morgan had to brush aside a twinge of guilt. Neither Zach nor Lacey knew what was about to transpire in their little piece of the world, but if Morgan was going to feel remorse about the way he might have to use them in the days ahead, he would just have to feel it later.

He turned to Lacey and gently placed his hands on her shoulders, turning her to face him. Tears glistened in her eyes and cut shiny paths down her flawless cheeks. Her tormented look pulled at Morgan's heart. The dangerous woman of a few moments ago now seemed lost and achingly vulnerable.

Behind him he heard Zach returning to the other room, and Morgan lifted one hand to brush away Lacey's tears. "You want to tell me what got you so riled up?" he asked lightly, his voice soothing.

A sob forced its way through Lacey, and she pulled away abruptly, mortified by what she'd said and done to Rawlings and now angry with herself, too, for being so weak that she was reduced to tears. Too overwrought to speak, she whirled from Morgan. With clenched fists, she slammed the counter, then lowered her head and gave vent to her tears.

Torn between wanting to comfort her and wanting to know the cause of her sudden outburst at Rawlings, Morgan slipped behind the counter and retrieved the torn paper from the floor. The pieces fit neatly together and he read the notice: "By order of the Willow Springs Town Council, Territory of Wyoming, be it known to all that on Monday, 13 October, in this year, 1886, the 1,000-acre ranch, formerly the property of the late Orille "Riley" Hanson, cattle rustler, will be confiscated and sold at auction to the highest bidder. Said auction will take place at 8:00 A.M. on the steps of the county courthouse. . . . "

A description of the property followed, but Morgan had read enough. Disgusted, he crumpled the notice and tossed it into the stove before returning to Lacey, who was valiantly trying to conquer her tears and shame.

Gently, Morgan placed his hands on her shoulders and turned her to face him, allowing her to cry in the security of his arms. She clung to him, soft and pliable, letting his strength renew hers. Vainly, Morgan tried to ignore the heat that suffused his loins as she fitted herself against his body.

He held her close until the tears seemed to have run their course. "That was a cruel thing he did, Lacey," Morgan murmured. "He wanted to hurt you, and he succeeded."

Lacey's breath hitched painfully. "God help me, but for a

moment I really did want to kill him. I don't think I ever wanted anything so much in all my life."

"Anyone who's been through what you have would feel the same way. Hanson was your friend. You were the one who found his body and took care of his little boy. . . . You're a strong lady, Lacey, but everybody's got a breaking point." He pushed her away a little so that he could brush at her tears. With one finger, he tilted her head up, capturing her tear-filled eyes with his sympathetic, understanding ones. "This isn't just about that notice, is it? You've been holding in all this anger and pain for a long, long time, haven't you?"

Lacey nodded. Morgan was forcing her to think, and with thinking always came reason. She was grateful to him for comforting her, and just as grateful for allowing her the dignity to recover. "I haven't cried since the night they murdered Riley and Martha," she admitted, clearing her throat to remove the catch in it. It seemed right to talk to Morgan, to let it all out after the long months of keeping everything tightly bound inside. "I was too angry to cry. There were arrangements to be made, and someone had to take care of Timmy, calm him down and help him cope with what had happened. And then the senator came, furious and heartbroken, demanding answers."

She shrugged her shoulders helplessly. "I didn't have any to give him. There was nothing I could prove, nothing I could use against Rawlings to show that he was responsible. All I had at my disposal was the *Gazette*, so I kept turning out stories week after week to make sure that Riley's death was on everyone's conscience. *Everyone*," she said forcefully, capturing Morgan's eyes and praying he would understand. "Not just those who participated, but every one of the docile, sober citizens who allow this butchery to take place right under their complacent little noses! Damn them!"

Fresh tears pooled in her angry eyes. "Damn them all! I love this town, Morgan, but I hate it, too. There are good people here, but they won't fight! They cleared the land and cut out a town. They chased off the Indians and built a nice little nest for themselves, and now they think the fighting is over. They're letting C. W. Rawlings bury them alive, and they don't even realize it!"

Another sob welled up, and Lacey covered her face, vainly

trying to hold it in. Morgan tried to pull her into his comforting embrace once again, but she resisted, moving away with a little shake of her head.

Understanding the pride that kept her from responding to his solace, Morgan reached into his vest pocket and drew out a clean white kerchief. "Here. Dry and blow."

The utterly tactless command reached Lacey in a way sympathy never could have, and she laughed, surprised that she still had the ability to do so. "That's a very indelicate thing to say to a lady, Morgan," she commented dryly, accepting the kerchief and following his directive. "But then, I guess I haven't proven myself to be a very delicate lady today, have I?"

"Delicate doesn't mean weak."

With a resigned sigh, Lacey slipped over to the bench and sank onto it, not realizing until she did so that her legs were still trembling. She fixed Morgan with a gaze that demanded honesty. "What I did was very foolish, wasn't it?"

Morgan joined her. "Let's just say it wasn't exactly prudent."

"That's putting it mildly, I'm sure. Lord, what have I done?" she asked, tilting her face toward the heavens. "Yesterday you accused me of trying to rob Sheriff Watson of his dignity. That must seem tame compared to the stunt I pulled here today—ramming a gun into the face of a man like C. W. Rawlings. God only knows what he'll do in retaliation."

"It could get very ugly, Lacey."

She looked at him sadly. "It already is ugly, Morgan."

She was remembering the horror of a stormy night four months ago—an unspeakable horror that haunted her day and night. As she once again tried to shove away the images that had been burned into her brain that night, something Morgan had said as he held her in his arms, murmuring against her hair, suddenly struck Lacey as odd. "Morgan, how did you know I was the one who found Riley and Martha's bodies? And that I'd taken care of Timmy? I didn't tell you any of that before Rawlings came."

Morgan grinned sheepishly. "I have to admit I came here today under slightly false pretenses. Your row with Rawlings is quite the main topic of conversation about town. Last night at the Silver Strike and later during a friendly poker game at the

Cattleman's Hotel, I made the acquaintance of several gentlemen who were only too happy to fill me in on all the gruesome
details of Hanson's death and the vigilance committee's other
activities."

Lacey stiffened. "If you already knew about that, why did
you come to see me?"

"If you were thinking more clearly, Lacey, you wouldn't
have to ask that question," he replied so softly that Lacey's
heart skipped a beat. "I wanted to see you again—and I wanted
to know why such a beautiful woman had turned into a crusader
against injustice."

"Is that what I am?" she asked quietly, responding to his
tender tone. "A crusader?"

"You are magnificent," he whispered sincerely. "And if I
don't get out of here very soon, I'm going to prove just how
magnificent I think you really are." He grinned and Lacey
found herself wanting to touch him—and be touched by him.
"And I don't think Zach or his Winchester would like that
much. He's very protective of you, I've noticed."

Lacey nodded and rose. He hadn't answered her question.
Not really. He'd merely deflected it and shifted the focus to
her, playing on her vulnerability and her attraction to him in the
hope that she would be too flattered by his attentions to notice
he was being deliberately evasive. But why? What could this
man possibly want from her?

Too emotionally drained to examine his reasons, Lacey
merely said, "Thank you for what you did today."

"I didn't do anything." He stood. "Not one blessed thing."

"Yes, you did. You were here, and no matter why you sought
me out, I'm grateful. Who knows? If you hadn't been here to
reason with me, I might very well have pulled that trigger."

Morgan shook his head. "You'd never have done it, Lacey.
I confess that at the time I thought you might, but you wouldn't
have. You're not capable of murder. Your weapons are courage and words, not guns and violence. Rawlings pushed you to
the brink, but you're the one who refused to cross over it."

"Is that supposed to make me feel better about myself and
what I did?"

"If you let it."

"I'll try."

"Good."

He stepped up to the counter, retrieved his silver-banded hat, then moved to the door, leaving Lacey standing in the golden light streaming through the window. She looked beautiful and somewhat mussed, but heart-rendingly vulnerable, too.

The sanest thing Morgan could have done would have been to say a polite good-bye and leave without a backward glance, but he couldn't seem to do it. His reason for coming to Willow Springs warred with his own demanding need to know this woman better, and though he had never thought of himself as selfish, Morgan gave in to his own needs. It would be better, safer, to do what he had come to do without involving Lacey Spencer. She could be undeniably useful to him, but she could also be brutally hurt. Unfortunately, Morgan couldn't seem to leave her alone. She was too lovely and she had stirred him far too profoundly in ways that went beyond the mere physical.

Despite all his better instincts, he stopped at the door and leaned negligently against the frame. "Tell me, Mrs. Spencer, if I may impose on your font of useful advice just one more time . . . in Willow Springs, how does a man go about courting a woman he finds . . . magnificent?"

Despite all the emotions Lacey was feeling—sadness, remorse, anger, fear—her heart did a little back flip, and a glimmer of happiness bubbled up in her. "This is not so different from most towns, I suppose," she replied with a smile that softened her face and made it glow with inner radiance. "Dinner at a fine restaurant is not unheard of. Church socials are a particular favorite among courting couples, too, I'm told. Or"—her smile turned mischievous—"if you're good with hammer and saw . . . "

"Hammer and saw?" Morgan's dark brows shot up suspiciously. He had the distinct feeling he was about to be roped into more than a simple evening on the town.

"I happen to know, sir, that the publisher of the Willow Springs *Gazette* has made plans to attend a barn raising this Saturday at Lew Dasat's ranch just north of town. It promises to be a fine affair, with a fancy box-lunch picnic and a huge evening meal, followed by a rousing barn dance at sunset. A gentleman seriously interested in courting a lady might escort her there," she suggested lightly.

Morgan's deep gold eyes accepted her challenge. "Saturday?"

"Saturday."

"Eight in the morning?"

Lacey nodded. "My carriage will be leaving my house just about that time, yes."

"And your house is . . . ?"

"Just up the hill at the end of this street. A two-story country house overlooked by twin aspen trees and a windmill. You'll see it if you step outside and look up."

"I know the one already." He grinned. "Quite nice."

"Thank you."

"Then I'll see you Saturday, Mrs. Spencer?"

"I hope so, Morgan," she answered softly.

"Till Saturday." He pushed away from the door frame, then paused. "Oh, and about that box lunch, ma'am. I do have a fondness for fried chicken and apple dumplings."

Lacey chuckled. "I'll bear that in mind."

"Good. And keep this in mind, too," he warned, suddenly serious, capturing her eyes with his startling gold ones that spoke volumes more than words could have expressed. "Saturday I won't be quite so much the gentleman."

"What does that mean?" she demanded, hoping she could be heard over the rapid, expectant thudding of her heart.

"When I start to kiss you Saturday, Lacey, I won't be offering you a choice."

Lacey tilted her head, regarding him sadly. "That's too bad."

Surprised, Morgan asked, "Why?"

"Because you'll never have the satisfaction of knowing which way I'd have chosen." Her chin was lifted proudly, and Morgan detected the residue of tears glittering in her eyes. Dear Lord, but she was beautiful—and dangerously irresistible.

"You're wrong, Lacey. That decision's already been made and we know it. God help us both," he added quietly.

"Amen," she whispered as the door closed behind Morgan, leaving the room quiet save for the echo of his words and the tinkling bell.

Chapter Five

Morgan's view of Center Street from the window of his third-floor room at the Cattleman's Hotel was excellent. Just across the way he could see the sheriff's office with its small barred windows on either side of the stout door, and he had a commanding view of the street itself. No one could come or go down the long, wide dirt avenue without his knowing it. In fact, only an hour ago he had watched with disgust as Sheriff Ben Watson blithely collected his horse from the livery stable and trotted out of town without a backward glance, despite the promise he'd made to Lacey Spencer.

From this high up, Morgan could also see some of the shops on the street that ran parallel to Center Street, and there he fancied he could even catch a glimpse of Mrs. Simon's boardinghouse, where Lacey had advised him to seek a room.

The considerable charms of an out-of-the-way room and the second-best cook in Willow Springs notwithstanding, Morgan had opted to stay at the Cattleman's because it put him in the center of the busy city, which was exactly where he needed— and was expected—to be. The casino, two floors below him, provided ample contact with Willow Springs's most influential citizens, and he could come and go from the hotel as he pleased. The back entrance was very private, making a quick, undetected departure a simple matter. And most important, C. W. Rawlings owned the luxurious hostelry, and it was well known that this was where the cattle baron stayed whenever he was in town. All in all, the Cattleman's suited Morgan's needs perfectly.

The only place of import he couldn't see from his window was the office of the Willow Springs *Gazette*, hidden as it was on one of the back streets at the east end of town. But it was probably just as well that the *Gazette* was out of sight, Morgan had decided earlier this morning. Lacey Spencer was enough of a distraction to him without his being able to see her office and wonder constantly what she was doing—or what Rawlings's men were doing to her.

Morgan pushed aside the filmy curtain and glanced down at the street once again, memorizing each shop, fixing in his mind the faces of those he saw below him, and in general getting his bearings. Long years of caution, of teaching himself to be prepared for any eventuality, made this ritual second nature to him, like breathing or sleeping. His survival instinct was as sharply honed as the blade of the bowie knife concealed in the specially made sheath inside his right boot.

A furtive knock at his door drew Morgan away from the window. His holstered Colt lay on the small round table next to him, and he unsheathed it silently before moving cautiously to stand beside the door.

"Yes?"

"It's Ep."

Morgan lowered the gun and twisted the key. "Door's open." He stood back as Ep Luder swung the door open and glanced one last time into the hall to be certain no one saw him enter. Luder shut the door behind him and nodded toward Morgan's gun.

"Expectin' trouble already, boss?"

"I always expect trouble," Morgan snapped, returning the gun to its holster. "That's why I'm still alive. Where the hell have you been? I expected you early this morning."

Luder shrugged. "Last month you said to meet you at the Cattleman's Hotel on Friday morning, October the third. You didn't say what time. Well, it's mornin', and I'm here."

Morgan resumed his casual vigil at the window, leaning against the wall with the curtain parted only a slit to allow him to see the street. Luder approached the table where the remains of Morgan's breakfast lay mostly untouched.

"You mind?" he asked, pulling the chair up and plopping down unceremoniously.

"It's cold," Morgan warned him.

"It's food," Luder returned. "And believe me, they don't serve nothin' half this fancy where I'm stayin'." Already his mouth was stuffed full, and Morgan had to wonder how a man could put away such prodigious amounts of food and still look as though he were starving to death. Ep's hawkish face, shadowed by an unsightly stubble of beard, was thin to the point of emaciation, just like the rest of his tall, lanky body. But from long experience, Morgan knew that Ep could eat enough at one sitting to feed an army for a week.

"You staying at Langhorn's?" Morgan asked. It was nearly noon, and they had a lot to discuss. He didn't have time to allow his perpetually ravenous guest to eat in peace.

"Yeah." Luder nodded. Between bites, he informed Morgan, "You meet all kinds of interestin' lowlifes there."

"Like who?"

"Like the loudmouthed goons Rawlings has got walkin' the streets. They're a rotten bunch, and they got the townspeople scared half out of their wits. 'Course, nobody's gonna admit that right off, but it don't take long to see how the wind blows." Luder shoveled in another mouthful, then mumbled, "You got in a day early, didn't you?"

When Morgan nodded, he continued, "Yeah, I thought I seed you the other day with that newspaper gal. She's bad news, boss. You better steer clear o' her."

Morgan stiffened at the advice, but Luder was too engrossed in the cold breakfast to notice. "Mrs. Spencer is going to be very useful to us, Ep. Through her I've already become acquainted with C. W. Rawlings."

Ep wiped a glob of egg off his chin with a rumpled cloth napkin and leaned back in the chair, eyeing Morgan speculatively. "Yeah, I heerd about that business yesterday. Stupid. Real stupid, her pullin' a gun on Rawlings like that."

"She had her reasons," he replied tightly.

"And I heered you got in the middle of it, too." Luder frowned and tossed the napkin down with disgust. "Damn it all, boss, what the hell were you thinkin' about? Takin' up for the worst enemy C. W. Rawlings's got ain't exactly the way to get in his good graces, to my way o' thinkin'. Shit, I don't understand none of this nohow! If you want to get yourself on old C. W.'s payroll, why in hell don't you just walk up to him and introduce yourself? I guarantee, you say, 'Howdy, Mr. Rawlings, I'm Justice Morgan,' and that old coot will bust a gut tryin' to hire the fastest gun that ever came out of west Texas. I don't see why we gotta go through all this sneakin' around and playin' games!"

"Nobody's asking you to understand, Ep," Morgan replied softly, his voice hard-edged. "You just do what I tell you when I tell you. I spent two months drifting through Colorado, making sure every miner, gambler, and drifter in the state got to know my face and my reputation. Eventually one of them is going to wander into Willow Springs and recognize me. I even had to duel it out with a fresh-faced kid who wanted to make a name for himself by outgunning the famous Justice Morgan."

Despite the bitterness in his employer's voice and face, Ep pressed, "I still think—"

"Well, don't! Don't think! Don't talk! You're here to keep your eyes and ears open. That's all. Hell, Ep, you think I wouldn't like to do this the easy way? Just waltz up to Rawlings and ask for a job? Well, I can't, because I've got to have that bastard's complete trust. He's got to come after me, got to beg me to work for him, so that there's not a doubt in his mind about my loyalty."

Luder shook his head. "And sidlin' up to that pretty widow is gonna make Rawlings trust you? Hell, that's just about the most cockeyed thing I ever heerd!"

Morgan's smile was patience personified, but his eyes were cold as ice. "As I said, Ep, Mrs. Spencer has her usefulness. First of all, conducting a little romance with the lovely widow gives me a perfectly logical excuse for staying in town instead of just drifting on through. And most important, by standing up for her, I can make sure Rawlings will never suspect what I'm after. But when someone finally does recognize me and Rawlings finds out Mrs. Spencer has a gun on her side, he'll fall all over himself trying to convert me to his side."

"Right," Luder said skeptically. "And when he does, just how are you goin' to justify goin' against your new lady love?"

A veil dropped over Morgan's handsome features, completely obscuring whatever he was thinking or feeling about Ep's
question. He turned back to the window. "I'll take care of that
when the time comes."

The broad back planted firmly against him told Luder that it
was useless to argue further. "Oh, what the hell?" he muttered.
"What do I know? I'm just the eyes and ears of this little party.
You're the brains. I best leave the thinkin' to you."

"I'm glad you finally realize that, Ep. Now . . . " Morgan
turned and took the seat opposite him. "Let's get down to business. I want to know everything you've found out in the month
you've been here. Start with those goons Rawlings has on his
payroll. Who are they? Local talent, or has he brought them
in from out of the territory?"

"Local, mostly," Ep responded, all business. "I got the idea
that a couple of them are wanted up Montana way, but most
of 'em are just drifters Rawlings latched on to in Cheyenne.
The only one you'll really have to look out for is Croft—he's
a real bad 'un. A hired gun from California. Pretty high-tone
muscle from what I can tell."

"Croft, huh?" Morgan searched his memory, but could find
no recollection of anyone by that name. "Any bad paper out
on him?"

Luder laughed derisively. "Now, just how am I supposed
to know that? The local sheriff an' me don't exactly sit down
and discuss Wanted posters over our mornin' coffee!"

Morgan ignored the sarcasm. "What about the sheriff? Is he
on Rawlings's payroll?" Or was he just a coward? he wondered, remembering the way Watson had ridden out of town
despite his promise to Lacey.

"Nobody seems to know fer certain. Some say Rawlings is
payin' him to keep his head turned the other way, and some
say that old Ben's just lost his nerve, that it don't cost Rawlings
nothin' to keep the old geezer out of his hair."

"What have you discovered about the vigilantes?"

"Not a whole hell of a lot, that's fer certain," Ep snorted.
"Secretest damned bunch I ever heerd of. Like most, they got
'em a sworn oath to keep their mouths shut, but hell, you know
how them secrecy oaths usually is. Everybody always knows
who's joined and who ain't. Why, in Kansas I heerd tell they

even published the names of the committee in the local newspaper! But not here, no, sirree. Whoever is on that committee, nobody's talkin'."

Morgan frowned. "How many are there?"

Luder shrugged. "Twenty, maybe twenty-five. Nobody knows fer sure. There may be a coupla locals in the bunch, but my guess is that mostly it's made up of Rawlings's hired men."

For nearly an hour Morgan fired question after question at the lean-faced informant, soaking up the bits and pieces of knowledge passed to him. When they had thoroughly exhausted Luder's observations and his supply of facts, Morgan rose brusquely, checking the gold watch that normally rested in the pocket of his black silk vest.

"All right, Ep, that's enough for now." Luder rose and followed his boss toward the door. "Were you seen coming in the back way?"

"Nope." He grinned, showing a profusion of gold teeth in his lower jaw. "It's as quiet as a church back in that alley. It may busy-up at night when the casino's runnin', but during the day they ain't nobody goes there overmuch."

"Good. Then sneak out the way you came in. I don't want anyone to suspect a connection between us. Is that clear?"

Ep nodded. "But what if I hear somethin' and need to get you quick?"

Morgan thought for a moment before replying, "Tonight at nine I'll be at the faro table in the Silver Strike. If you wander in about nine-thirty and deal yourself into the game, nobody will think anything of us introducing ourselves. After that, if you need to talk to me, we'll just be two acquaintances casually passing the time of day."

"Gotcha." He grinned his gold-toothed smile again and pointed to Morgan's face. "By the way, boss, I like the way you look without the beard. It's a big change."

"I can't get used to shaving every morning," Morgan grumbled. "It's a hell of an inconvenience."

"Yeah, well, don't complain. If you're not careful it might be a vigilante rope that does your shavin' for you."

"I'll keep that in mind. Now you take off. I've got an appointment at the railroad station."

Luder's shoulders drooped in disgust. "Oh, hell! You ain't gonna get yerself in the middle of that, are you?"

"You know about it?" Morgan's dark brows went up in surprise.

"Hell, yes. The whole town knows the widow is expectin' a shipment of paper. Word on the street is Rawlings's got a dozen men waitin' for it. I saw the sheriff ride out early this mornin', so there ain't nothin' gonna stop Croft and his buddies from seein' that Miz Spencer gets shy one load of newspaper."

"Then maybe the odds need to be evened up a little," Morgan suggested smoothly.

"You know, boss, if I didn't know better, I'd say that pretty little widow has got under your skin a mite. You sure you're jest usin' her?"

"Let me worry about Mrs. Spencer, Ep." Morgan's clipped tone brooked no disagreement.

Luder nodded. "Whatever you say, boss." He reached for the doorknob, then stopped abruptly. "Hellfire, I almost forgot. Lookit what I found in the general store the other day." He dug into the back pocket of his worn denim trousers and extracted two dime novels, identical except that the dog-eared pages of one copy told Morgan that Luder had read it. Ep handed over the thin volumes and waited expectantly.

"Damn," Morgan swore softly as he read the title: *Justice for Hire, or the Life of Bounty Hunter Robert "Justice" Morgan.*

Morgan's eyes turned to ice. "Were these the only copies they had? Did you check the other stores?"

"Yep to both questions. That's all they had left."

"Yes, but how many copies of this trash did they sell?"

"Storekeep said he only recollected sellin' one other copy of that particular little gem, but you ain't gonna like who he sold it to."

Morgan tensed. His luck hadn't changed for the better after all. "Rawlings?"

"Nope, but it's almost as bad. Seems old Sheriff Watson reads ever one o' them dime dreadfuls he can get his hands on."

"Damn!" Morgan hurled the books onto his rumpled bed with a violence that startled the smaller man. "That thing was printed two years ago! I would have bet my last dollar that all the copies were out of circulation by now." He looked at Luder, his golden eyes sharp and piercing. "That book could sink us, Ep. You know that, don't you?"

Luder shook his head and corrected softly, "Sink us, hell, boss. That little book could get you killed!"

From the shaded porch of the Willow Springs depot, Minnie Overton glanced nervously down the tracks, worrying that the one-fifteen from Cheyenne might not arrive before trouble broke out. She cast a surreptitious glance at the widow Spencer, who was standing patiently at the far end of the depot. Then Minnie looked at the opposite end, where that despicable gunslinger and two of his cronies were lounging about, looking as though they hadn't a care in the world.

Lordy, Lordy, there was gonna be trouble for sure! Minnie sent up a swift and silent prayer that it wouldn't start until after she had safely boarded the train.

Poor widow Spencer. Minnie didn't hold much truck with women who fancied they could do a job that a man was meant to do, but she liked the widow and admired the way she was standing up under all the pressure C. W. Rawlings was putting on her. Not so many months ago, Miz Lacey had been a frequent guest in the Overton home. But now, with Rawlings threatening to call in her husband's mortgage on the store, Minnie was nervous about even speaking to the woman she'd once called her friend. It wasn't right and it certainly wasn't Christian, but it was completely out of Minnie's hands. If the widow Spencer didn't insist on messin' with politics and rustlers and such, she wouldn't be in this fix, anyway.

Minnie glanced at the widow again, watching as Lacey drew on a heavy pair of workmen's gloves. Dressed in men's trousers and boots, with a bright flannel shirt tucked in at the waist, she looked ready for a hard day's labor or a fight—or maybe both. Her honey-colored hair was bound up in a heavy braid that hung clean to her waist, and from what Minnie could see, her expression was fixed and determined. There couldn't be a doubt in the world that Mrs. Spencer was totally aware of the three men at the other end of the depot, but she was doing a splendid job of staying calm and ignoring them. A body had to admire pluck like that!

"Excuse me, ma'am, but I do believe I hear the train coming."

Minnie nearly jumped out of her skin when the voice spoke right next to her ear, and she whirled toward the speaker, one hand flying to her ample bosom in fright.

Like a menacing bird of prey, Croft stared down at the flustered woman and waved one hand toward his friends. "Harley, why don't you help Mrs. Overton with her baggage?" he suggested, his voice as smooth as oil on water. "I'm sure she'll want to board just as soon as the train comes to a stop."

Though she would rather have touched a snake than allow any one of these vile ruffians near her, Minnie swallowed hard and muttered a terse thank-you. Harley snatched up her overloaded carpetbag and stepped off the porch with it. Croft was watching her, unnerving her with those evil black eyes of his, and Minnie lowered her head, rushing to follow Harley. She twitched impatiently as the train chugged into view and slowed to a halt.

Feeling those eyes still on her, she spared not a backward glance as the porter stepped off the platform of the passenger car and was nearly knocked flat by Minnie in her haste to scramble aboard.

Lacey watched Mrs. Overton's quick ascent with a sad shake of her head. She felt sorry for her, but it was a comfort to know that someone else was scared witless by Croft, too. Even now Lacey could feel his eyes boring into her, making her skin crawl. Every rational impulse in her body cried out for her to abandon her mission and run back to the *Gazette* office as fast as her legs would carry her, but pride held her stiffly in place. Nothing in the world was going to keep her from claiming this shipment of newsprint. She'd never get it back to the office undamaged, but collect it she would, and to hell with C. W. and his Brigade.

"I've brought the wagon up behind the depot, Miz Lacey." Zach had materialized beside her and Lacey had to make a conscious effort not to show how much he'd startled her.

"Fine, Zach," she murmured. "I'll check with the conductor and see which car it's in. If we're lucky, maybe we can get one of the baggagemen to help us load it into the wagon."

Zach shook his head thoughtfully. "I do wish you had let me hire a man or two to assist with the unloading. Any number of men around town are desperate for the price of a drink."

"No, Zach, I refuse to involve anyone else. The last time you paid Whit Sells to help us haul supplies, Rawlings had the poor man beaten within an inch of his life."

"True," he agreed sadly in his deep, melodic voice. "I understand Mr. Sells is now living up in Sheridan."

Lacey cast him a speculative, sidelong glance, but Zachary's implacable face gave away nothing when he continued, "Nice country, Sheridan. Or so I'm given to understand. Very green. Very peaceful."

Even Lacey's best efforts couldn't hide the smile that tugged at her lips. "Is that so?"

"Yes, ma'am. That's what I've heard."

"Zach, are you suggesting that we move the *Gazette* office up north?"

He looked affronted. "I wouldn't presume to suggest anything of the sort, ma'am. But it does appear to me that the air is a bit . . . healthier up there."

"And healthier still in Washington this time of year, no doubt."

"No doubt," he replied briskly, eyes focused straight ahead.

She looked at him suspiciously. "Have you been corresponding with my father again, Zach?"

He leaned forward, glancing around Lacey toward the front of the train. "I do believe I see the conductor now, ma'am."

Lacey grinned, taking his evasion as an answer in the affirmative. "I thought so. We'll discuss your latest report to Father later. For now bring the wagon around to this side of the depot while I find out which car the paper is in."

"Yes, ma'am."

He disappeared as silently as he had come, and Lacey turned. Her fond smile faded as she saw Croft, Harley, and the one she thought was called Kelso standing three in a row like toy soldiers, guarding the entrance to the depot where the conductor had just entered. Taking a deep breath to steady herself, she marched forward, staring at Croft with what she hoped was her most haughty, superior glare.

Raising one imperious eyebrow, she said softly, "Gentlemen, I do hope you'll excuse me, but you seem to be blocking the door. If you'd be so kind . . . "

Croft's smile was as cold as the bottomless depths of his black eyes. "I admire your spirit, Mrs. Spencer, I surely do. We all know you'll never make it to your office with that paper, and yet you insist on carrying out this little charade."

"Ah, yes, Croft. This is quite a little drama, isn't it? So why don't I play my part and you play yours? You growl and look fierce, and then I'll cower and whine."

"I look forward to the day when you do cower in front of me, ma'am."

Somehow Lacey managed a sugary smile. "When hell freezes over, you bastard, and not a day before."

The gunfighter stiffened in anger and Lacey thought she heard Harley snicker, but she dared not take her eyes off Croft. They stared each other down for one long moment, neither giving an inch, until finally Croft stepped gallantly aside and allowed her to pass into the office.

Knowing they were all watching, Lacey refused to give in to her relief. And besides, this was only the first leg of her journey. From experience, she knew that Rawlings had most likely instructed Croft and the others not to make their move until she had the paper loaded and was moving it through town. Setting her wagon ablaze on Center Street where everyone could watch made for a bigger spectacle, and a much more effective object lesson for those C. W. wanted to keep firmly under his thumb. Croft might hassle her here, but things wouldn't become dangerous until later.

Lacey spoke with the conductor and received the information she needed, plus a sympathetic but completely unsupportive nod from the ticket agent. She glided out of the office as regally as any queen, despite her mannish attire. The three men fell in behind her and followed her to the edge of the porch.

"Down here, Zach!" She loped alongside the train, waving the wagon down the line to the car the conductor had indicated. A young baggageman, as agile as a monkey, jumped on the narrow ledge outside the cargo door and unlocked it, sliding it aside to reveal the cavernous, dark interior of the car.

"Do you have four crates for the Willow Springs *Gazette* in there?" Lacey called up.

"You got a bill o' sale?" The worker, with a freckled face and a fresh-off-the-farm look about him, grinned down at her, accepting the sheaf of papers he needed in order to relinquish the cargo. He glanced over them quickly. "Okay, lady, they're all yours."

"My wagon's right here," Lacey said as Zach eased the team next to the freight car. "Can you give us a hand loading them?"

"I don't see why not. I—" His voice died suddenly, and he swallowed hard as he looked beyond Lacey toward the depot. Lacey swiveled and saw that Croft had come off the porch and was standing about fifteen feet away, glaring at the baggageman as he negligently caressed a long, deadly stiletto. He spoke not a word, but his meaning was frighteningly clear.

"Hey, look, lady, I don't want no trouble. The railroad don't pay me to be target practice for no pig sticker."

"Don't worry about it," Lacey reassured him with a sigh. "Just give me a hand up and point out which crates are mine; then you can take off. Mr. Freeman and I will manage it from there."

She held out one hand and braced her right foot on the rusty iron rail below the door. The boy darted a nervous glance at Croft, grabbed Lacey's hand, and pulled, nearly throwing her into the car in his haste.

"They're over there." He stabbed a finger toward the far wall of the freight car, then scrambled out and vanished.

A narrow path sliced the center of the car, and Lacey picked her way to the four crates marked "Willow Springs *Gazette*" and began shoving them into the makeshift aisle. Though they were a little heavier than she had anticipated, she managed to get two of them into the opening. Once they were all accessible, she and Zach could get them on the wagon, but for now she knew that Zach dared not leave the team unattended. Croft would surely spook the horses, and the last thing Lacey needed was a runaway team.

"Looks as though you could use some help."

Startled, Lacey straightened and whirled around. Morgan was lounging against the door as though he hadn't a care in the

world. He wore the wicked cavalier smile that always melted
Lacey's heart, and a genuine flush of delight coursed through
her at the sight of him . . . until she realized that his presence
could ruin everything. If he tried to intervene with Croft, things
could get out of hand and someone might get hurt.

   In a single instant, Lacey saw all her well-made plans crumble to dust, and her welcoming smile vanished.

Chapter Six

"What are you doing here, Morgan?" she demanded, her voice laced with a touch of panic. She was already confused enough by this handsome stranger's sudden appearance in her life; now she was responsible for his safety, too. Why on earth was he doing this? She'd spent the better part of last night trying to figure out what he wanted from her and why he wasn't telling the whole truth about his reason for pursuing her. Though she'd racked her brain, she'd been unable to come up with an ulterior motive. Yet she knew two things for certain: that he did have an ulterior motive, and that she didn't care. For some inexplicable reason, she trusted Morgan completely, and she couldn't bear the thought that he might get hurt or killed because of her.

Morgan read her panic and confusion, but he refused to be put off by her unexpectedly sour greeting. Casually, he replied, "Oh, I just happened to be nearby . . . "

Lacey's delicate brows drew together in a peevish frown. "Do you always hang around train stations?"

"It's one of my favorite pastimes."

"Well, go pass the time somewhere else! This isn't your problem."

The train whistle, impatient and forlorn, drowned out her voice, and though Morgan heard her perfectly, he chose to pretend he had not. Skirting the two boxes in the opening, he grabbed the forward edge of the crate Lacey had been pushing.

"Morgan! I said go away. Stop it! After what happened yesterday, you're in this too deep already."

The whistle blew again. "Lacey, this train is going to pull out of here in about two minutes," he warned amicably. "Unless you want to be on it, I suggest you accept my help."

He was right and she knew it, but that didn't make it any easier to accept his assistance. "Oh, all right! Help me get these loaded; then you disappear!" She waggled a finger at him emphatically, but something told her Morgan wasn't the least bit intimidated.

Morgan tugged as Lacey pushed, and together they quickly slid the remaining crates into the doorway. Zach had positioned the wagon so close to the freight car that they had only to step down in order to be standing in the bed.

Testing the weight, Morgan lifted one box, expecting the crate to be quite heavy, but found instead that it was surprisingly light. He straightened. "How much paper do these hold?"

"Each box holds four bales of paper," she informed him impatiently, glancing over her shoulder as the train whistle prodded them along.

"Lacey, you've been cheated. This box is too light to have four bales of paper inside."

"I said it *holds* four bales! I didn't say there were four in it!" she whispered fiercely. Croft was staring at them, and she could see the conductor coming down the line to hurry them along. "If you're going to help, stop talking and start lifting. And pretend it's heavy, for crying out loud! You're going to spoil everything."

"See if I ever play the Good Samaritan again," Morgan grumbled as he and Lacey lifted opposite sides of the crate. Balancing it low between them, Morgan carefully stepped down to the wagon.

"Let go," he ordered, then grunted dramatically as he lowered the crate to the wagon bed with a loud thump. For good measure he grabbed his back with one hand and wiped imaginary sweat from his brow with the other. "Is that convincing enough?" he whispered conspiratorially.

"Shut up and lift!" Lacey glared at him angrily as she shoved the second box to the edge. Less than a minute later, all four boxes were in the wagon, clumped in the center. Without ceremony, Morgan grabbed Lacey around the waist and loaded her into the wagon, too, despite her surprised shriek of protest.

He resisted the temptation to pull her close and savor the feel of her enticing trouser-clad body sliding along his; such an intimate gesture in front of their unfriendly audience would have been an embarrassment for Lacey. And, too, it might have given their audience ideas Morgan didn't want them to have. Instead, he simply plunked her down in front of him, letting his eyes convey the message he'd wanted to send with his body.

Lacey tried without much success to ignore his heated gaze. She failed, too, in her effort to maintain her irritation. Now all that was left to her was to worry over his safety. Everything had been so carefully planned!

"Thank you, Morgan. Now I want you to—"

"Hold on, please," Zach called from the front, setting the team in motion to get them away from the train, which had begun edging forward noisily. The baggageman appeared from nowhere, jumped onto the freight car to secure the door, then took off toward the caboose as grinding wheels laboriously set the train in motion.

Surprised by the wagon's unexpected movement, Lacey flailed for balance and Morgan grabbed her arm, steadying her, then gently tugging her downward until they were seated side by side on the wooden crates.

"There, that's better." He smiled solicitously. "Are you comfortable? Could I get you a lap robe to ward off the afternoon chill?"

"It's not cold and you are being very foolish," Lacey snapped. "This isn't a hayride, Morgan. I don't want you involved in my fight. Now, get out of here and let me handle this before someone gets hurt!"

"You expecting trouble?" he asked innocently.

"Dammit, you know I am. Why do you think those three men are following us?" Exasperated, she nodded toward Croft and the others, who were leisurely winding their way down the boardwalks, taking the same turns Zach did. "And there will be more of them waiting for us on Center Street."

Morgan shrugged negligently. "Let them wait." He twisted on the crate. "Zach?"

"Yes, sir."

"Did you by any chance happen to bring that Winchester you're so attached to?"

"No, sir."

He frowned. "That's too bad."

"No, it's not!" Lacey gasped. "I don't want any gunplay. No one is going to get hurt because of me. If Rawlings wants to burn this shipment, then let him."

Morgan looked at her, no longer joking. "You know, Lacey, it occurs to me that you're just a little too anxious for those men to get their hands on these boxes. Boxes, I might add, which are lightly loaded and not worth the trouble you—or they—are going to. Would you care to explain that?"

"No, I would not!" She gripped the crate as Zach turned the wagon onto Center Street, where the remainder of Rawlings's Brigade blocked the right-of-way a dozen yards in front of them. Except for them, the street was utterly deserted, though Lacey had no doubt that inside many of the shops, a huge audience had gathered to watch the spectacle from a safe distance.

"There they are, ma'am, just as you expected," Zach murmured softly.

Lacey stood and moved behind Zach. She placed one hand on his shoulder, gathering courage from his solid strength. "We'll play it exactly as planned, Zach. Nothing has changed." She threw a scathing look over her shoulder at Morgan, who still sat placidly on the crate. "You follow my lead, Morgan," she warned softly. "Don't do *anything*."

"Yes, ma'am." He tipped his silver-banded hat graciously and stretched his long legs. "I'm just enjoyin' the ride."

Had she not been so preoccupied, Lacey would have noticed that despite Morgan's languid posture he was as tense as a coiled snake, ready to strike. His eyes sought out the tall, lean, well-dressed man following them—the one who had obviously been in charge at the depot.

This must be Croft, he thought. He recognized the look of a gunfighter about him; it showed in his easy gait and in the level-eyed confidence that fairly oozed from him. Beneath the tails of his coat, Morgan thought he could detect a slightly worn, shaded band where the man normally wore his gun belt, low on the hips. Yes, Morgan decided, that's Croft . . . the dangerous one.

"Whoa! Hold up, there." One of the men, Vance Hoffman,

called for them to stop, leaping forward to snatch the horses' bridles. Zach complied, pulling in the reins.

"You're in our way," Lacey called out, praying her heart would stop its insidious hammering.

"Yes, ma'am, I reckon we are at that," Hoffman agreed.

"Then why don't you move aside and let us pass? We don't want any trouble."

"If you got a problem, lady, why don't you call the sheriff?" one of the men hollered, setting up a whoop of derisive laughter.

"When election time rolls around next month, maybe I'll do just that! Provided, of course, that the people of Willow Springs get fed up with the way C. W. Rawlings rides roughshod over them and vote us a new sheriff!"

"I wouldn't count on that, Mrs. Spencer." Croft eased alongside the wagon, staring up at her. "Sheriff Watson is a real popular man in these parts."

"It surprises me to hear you say that, Croft," Lacey replied lightly. "I thought perhaps *you* might toss your hat into the election arena."

"Oh, no, ma'am," he exclaimed with mock seriousness. Despite Rawlings's low opinion of this woman, Croft truly liked her. He enjoyed her sharp retorts and the courage she displayed with him despite her obvious fear. Bringing the widow Spencer to heel was going to give him the greatest pleasure—in ways that had left Croft sleepless imagining. "I fear I'm not cut out to be a lawman, ma'am. I much prefer the freedom I have to pursue . . . other pleasures."

What those pleasures were showed plainly in his suggestive leer, and Lacey suppressed a shudder. Behind her she heard an almost imperceptible hiss as Morgan drew an angry breath, and she grew terrified that these two men might come to blows over her. She couldn't allow that! Somehow she had to prod Croft into doing what he'd been paid to do before Morgan got himself killed.

Fixing Croft with her steadiest gaze, she ground out, "Pleasures like murder, Croft? Or is arson all you're game for today?"

His eyes narrowed dangerously as he took the bait. "Arson, ma'am? That's a bit strong, ain't it? Why, the boys and I just thought we'd have ourselves a bonfire. Something to warm us up a little. If you and your friends will just step down . . . "

Now. It was time for Lacey to make her move. Her voice strong and clear, she shouted, "Like hell I will! What is Rawlings afraid of, anyway? One woman who dares to tell the truth? Is C. W. Rawlings such a coward that he has to send ten men to do his dirty work? Here, I'll show you what he's afraid of! This is what you've been paid to burn!" She grabbed a pry bar from the wagon bed and spun toward the nearest crate.

Shocked, Morgan stared at her, wondering if she'd suddenly gone mad. She sounded like one of the soapbox suffragettes he'd heard back east, yet her impassioned speech made not one lick of sense. She'd known this moment was coming, so why in hell was she giving way to hysterics?

Or was it hysterics? Morgan wondered as he watched her pry the lid off the crate. No, this wasn't hysterics; it was theatrics. For some reason Mrs. Allyce Smithfield Spencer was putting on one hell of a show.

The other men, likewise stunned by Lacey's sudden outburst, stood and watched as she shoved up the lid of the crate and reached inside with a flourish, ripping at the paper until both hands were full. Then she whirled back to the men, brandishing the sheaves of large, coarse newsprint.

"Blank paper!" she cried. "That's what C. W.'s afraid of! Just pieces of paper! But on that paper I print words that Rawlings is afraid to see, words that tell the world what villains he and his friends in the Stock Growers Association really are! Words! He's afraid of words! And he's afraid of *me*. You're all cowards, just as he is. You take his money to intimidate women and children and decent men who just want to live in peace! Cowards! You're all cowards!"

A sob welled up in her throat and she stopped, giving way to a rush of tears. In apparent frustration, she whirled and swiped at the lid of the open crate, banging it down hard. Another sob escaped and she crumpled the paper in her hands into enormous wads and hurled it angrily onto the wagon bed.

It settled around her, piled high, and finally Morgan understood what she was doing. He couldn't see how it would work to her advantage in the long run, but he had to admire the guts she'd displayed in manipulating everyone so far.

Behind Lacey, Zach was swinging over the seat of the buckboard, apparently concerned about his employer's distraught state, and Morgan decided it was time to join the fun. Rising swiftly, he stepped closer to Lacey and gathered her into his arms.

"There, there, Mrs. Spencer, calm yourself. Nothing you can say will sway these men. You're just going to get hurt if you protest. Come, let me take you out of here."

Surprised by his solicitous tone, Lacey glanced up at him—and the laughter she read in his eyes was nearly her undoing. He knew!

Swallowing back a prematurely triumphant laugh, Lacey nodded mutely, afraid to speak. She allowed Morgan to lead her to the side of the wagon and lift her down gently.

"Mr. Freeman," he called to Zach, "would you be so good as to unhitch the wagon? I'm sure these men don't want to roast a perfectly good team of horses." Meek as a church mouse, Morgan glanced across the wagon at Croft as though seeking his permission for Zach to attend to the animals.

Puzzled, but not sure what it was about this little scene that bothered him, Croft nodded to Zachary, then motioned to Harley and Kelso. "Send it up, boys," he ordered, stepping back as they jumped on the wagon to obey. Just as Lacey had hoped, they bunched the loose sheets of paper around the base of the crates and set a match to them without ever opening the crates. In seconds, a pyre of flame shot up and spread over the wagon bed in deadly, lapping tendrils.

Zach had barely enough time to get the horses out of the way before the entire wagon was ablaze, but the Brigade stood aside and allowed him to pass. He glanced back at Lacey, but it was Morgan who met his questioning gaze and nodded tersely. Morgan's look told the printer that Lacey would be well taken care of, and since that was all that was important, Zach returned to the house.

Stroking Lacey's back comfortingly as he shielded her from the fire, Morgan dipped his head and whispered, "A loud whimper or shriek of hysteria might be effective right about now, don't you think?"

In answer, Lacey punched him sharply in the ribs with one clenched fist and muttered, "Let's not overdo it, shall we? Why don't you just lead the poor, crushed widow woman away and see if we can all get out of this with our hides intact."

"Yes, ma'am," he replied, properly chastised. He started to do as she asked, but Croft stopped them.

"Mrs. Spencer!"

Morgan felt Lacey stiffen in his arms as he turned to face the gunfighter. "What is it, Mr. Croft?" Morgan asked with equal parts weariness and sadness. "That is your name, isn't it? Croft?"

"That's right. And you must be Morgan. Rawlings told me all about you, but I can't say I'm much impressed," he said with a derisive sneer. He truly was disappointed that this stranger hadn't tried to defend Mrs. Spencer and her wagonload of paper. From what C. W. had told him, this newcomer could be a dangerous ally for the widow, but apparently C. W. had been mistaken. Morgan had folded like a house of cards, without so much as a whimper.

If Morgan was insulted by Croft's low opinion of him, he gave no outward indication of it. "As you can see, Mr. Croft, Mrs. Spencer is quite upset, thanks to you and your crew of ruffians. I'd like to escort her home, if you don't mind."

Croft shrugged. "Be my guest."

"Thank you." Morgan turned away again, leading Lacey who, to all appearances, had succumbed to another bout of weeping that shook her shoulders violently. Only when they had turned a corner and escaped Croft's questioning gaze did Lacey pull away, finally giving voice to the laughter that had almost been her undoing.

" 'Crew of ruffians'? That was some performance you gave."

"It was nothing compared to yours, my dear," he said gallantly. "You really should go on the stage."

"Thank you." She was still chuckling as they continued briskly down the boardwalk. "Tell me, when did you figure it out?"

"When you shredded that paper into kindling so that Croft wouldn't have to open the crates and discover they were less than half full. Now, would you care to tell me just what you accomplished with that little charade? When Rawlings hears about how you gave way to hysterics he's going to have a wonderful laugh at your expense."

"Let him," she retorted triumphantly. "Let him laugh all he wants today, because Tuesday when the *Gazette* comes out, the joke is going to be on him."

"You've lost me, my dear."

"Just wait and see. Come on." Quickening her pace, Lacey led Morgan down the side street to her office and unlocked the front door. With Morgan at her heels, she flew through the outer room and shoved aside the curtain to the back. One small window on the rear wall provided the only illumination, but it was enough for Morgan to see, sitting against the back wall, a half dozen crates identical in size to the ones he'd just seen go up in smoke.

Squinting in the dim light, he read "Detrich, Montana, Bibles," on two of the crates, and on the others, "Casper, Wyoming, Schoolbooks."

Though he knew what they really contained, Morgan was so warmed by the glowing triumph on Lacey's lovely face that he wanted to prolong the moment and let her bask in the glory of her victory. "Schoolbooks and Bibles?" he questioned lightly.

Deftly she pried open a crate of "Bibles," revealing the bales of newsprint that should have been in the crates that arrived on the train. "I had the shipment split at Omaha. The ones Croft burned were held over so that they'd be on today's train to give a freight wagon time to get into town with these. The diversion on Center Street gave the freighter the opportunity to unload and make his getaway. By the time Rawlings finds out, it'll be much too late for him to retaliate against the freighter— even if he can find out which one carried this load and where he's bound now."

Suddenly drained, Lacey sank onto one of the unopened crates, her first rush of exhilaration giving way to the intense emotions she'd suffered in the past hour. "I got the bastard this time," she whispered.

Morgan knelt in front of her, his gaze searching and serious. "You got him, Lacey, but that was a dangerous game you played. It won't be so easy next time."

She nodded wearily. "I know that. Next time I'm hiring Pinkertons to deliver the shipment." She managed a wan smile. "Do you realize that this shipment cost me four times what thirty-two bales of newsprint would normally cost? And that doesn't even include the wagon that went up in smoke."

Morgan captured Lacey's face in his hands and whispered tenderly, "It could cost you much more than that, Lace. Please . . . let somebody else pick up the flag and carry on with this fight before you get killed."

Lacey searched his face, enthralled by his eyes, which had turned to molten gold in the dim room. "I can't do that, Morgan. I thank you for your concern and for coming to the depot. It touches me deeply that you wanted to help." Gently she caressed his wrists as she pulled his hands away from her face. Her fingers twined through his, and she gripped fiercely, as though to convey the importance of her message through touch alone.

"I appreciate your kindness, Morgan, but please . . . don't ever ask me to give up. I don't know who you are, because you haven't seen fit to tell me, but I do know this: I didn't ask you to become involved in my fight. In fact, I warned you not to."

"You underestimate yourself, Lacey, if you think you're that easy for a man to walk away from."

His look, so sincere and so very gentle, went straight to Lacey's heart. She needed this so desperately, someone strong and kind to lean on, someone to believe in during this dark period of her life when her friends had all deserted her and anyone could be a dangerous enemy. In a few short days, Morgan had come to mean something to her. Something important.

And yet, what did she really know about him? What was it that made her trust him so completely? Why was it so easy to believe in his tender looks and caring words?

Was it the way he made her heart race? Or perhaps it was the exquisite feelings he had resurrected within her body. Maybe she trusted him simply because she had needed someone to trust, and there he was—kind, concerned, supportive, strong. He looked at her with loving tenderness and made her want nothing more than to melt into his arms.

But that was wrong. All wrong. Suddenly appalled by the depth of what she was feeling, Lacey dropped Morgan's hands as though burned by their touch. She skittered away from him, rising to move across the room for some much needed space.

"Good Lord, but you're glib! Do the right words always come this easily to you?"

"Lacey—"

"What do you want from me, Morgan? Why are you involving yourself in a fight that has absolutely nothing to do with you?"

Morgan stood. "Lacey, I told you—"

"No! You've told me nothing! Every time I ask you a question, you deflect it with sweet words and flowery compliments. Why?" she demanded harshly. "Have you heard that I'm wealthy? Are you looking to seduce a lonely, vulnerable widow lady, or is this just an amusing diversion for you? A pleasant way to pass a few days in a strange town before moving on down the trail to the next town, to the next attractive woman who happens to need a man!"

Morgan moved to her, his face unreadable. "Do you need a man, Lacey?"

"No!" she cried vehemently. "I don't need a man! I need . . . I need . . . " Unexpected tears welled up and Lacey lifted her face to the heavens, fighting the tears and praying for control over her wayward emotions. "I need . . . a friend," she whispered finally. "And I need the strength to go on just one more day, then another and another." She looked at him fiercely. "God, where did this weakness come from? Why didn't I feel it before you walked into my life?"

A faint frown creased Morgan's brow, and he touched Lacey's face, moistening his fingers with her tears. When she did not pull away from him, he gathered her into his arms, comforting and protecting all in the same tender movement. "It's not weakness, Lacey," he crooned. "You said it yourself. It's just *need*, plain and simple. Needing someone else to draw strength from occasionally doesn't make anyone weak. It makes you human, just like the rest of us."

Though she knew it was only the emotion of the moment—how could it be anything else?—Lacey felt safe in Morgan's arms, as though nothing bad could touch her. It was a comforting feeling, but it was also frightening to realize how easy it would be to give herself over to Morgan, a man she knew nothing about. She trusted him, an instinctive, basic trust that told her he would never hurt her. Yet, knowing how vulnerable she was right now, how could she rely on her own suddenly fragile emotions? Did she trust him only because she wanted to? Needed to? For years Lacey had depended only on herself. Why was it that Morgan now made her feel that she couldn't go on another day without his strength to bolster hers?

"Who are you, Morgan?" she asked, raising her face from the hard pillow of his shoulder. "I have to know."

He smiled, and this time Lacey allowed herself the pleasure of touching one of the deep dimples his handsome face displayed.

Her gentle, caressing fingers made Morgan's heart race, tempting him to ignore her question and lower his lips to her enticing upturned face; but he staunchly banked the fires she stirred in him. He had known the moment would come when she would question his reason for appearing so suddenly in her life and in Willow Springs, and he was ready with an answer. It was a lie, of course, and a painful one, considering the fact that he would have given his soul to tell her the truth. But she would accept the lie and believe in him because she needed to believe.

"I'm a gambler, Lacey. I gamble with cards and occasionally with land, gold, cattle . . . whatever will turn the quickest profit."

"Is that what brought you to Willow Springs? The hope of a quick profit?"

He smiled the charming, easy smile that Lacey wanted so much to believe was genuine. "Down in Colorado I heard that the stock growers here in Wyoming were looking for new investors. It sounded tempting, sitting idly in the sumptuous Cheyenne Club, raking in the profits while someone else did all the work."

Morgan felt Lacey stiffen and withdraw from him long before she actually pulled out of his arms and distanced herself several paces away. "So why didn't you go to Cheyenne instead of coming to Willow Springs?"

"I did," he replied, hating the coldness in Lacey's eyes. "I made a few inquiries and found out that there's a small company based here that is actively seeking a new partner."

Lacey knew exactly what he was referring to. About six months ago several Englishmen had formed a company called the Barons and had placed about five thousand head of cattle on the open range. The men were staunch members of the WSGA, and Lacey was fairly certain they also belonged to the vigilante association, but their ranching outfit was small compared to the operation run by C. W. Lacey hadn't heard that they were actively seeking additional investors, but she wasn't exactly in the mainstream of society these days. Anything was possible, she supposed.

"So you're here to become one of *them*," she said disdainfully, referring not just to the Barons but to all stock growers.

"No, Lacey, I'm here to see if they—your hated enemies— can turn me a profit. Frankly, from what I've seen so far, I'd say it doesn't seem to be a wise investment. A feisty news-paperwoman is creating a little too much heat for my comfort."

Somewhat mollified, Lacey also felt a sad sinking in the pit of her stomach. She straightened her shoulders and tried to seem nonchalant. "So you'll be leaving soon? Heading for greener pastures?"

"Not just yet. I thought I might stick around for a while. There are all types of investments, you know—not just money or effort. There's also an investment in people."

"Meaning me."

"Meaning you."

"I see. You've decided to invest some time wooing a wealthy widow to see what rewards it can bring you."

Lacey expected a fervent denial or a shocked, affronted gasp of exasperation followed by more charming flattery. She was surprised when Morgan merely laughed ironically and dropped onto the tall stool beside Zach's print table.

He removed his hat and twirled it between nimble fingers. "Now, that's a trick question if ever I heard one. If I tell you I'm a fortune hunter, you'll send me packing without so much as a fond farewell. And if I deny the accusation vociferously, you'll think I'm lying and send me away. So tell me, how should I answer you?"

"With the truth," she said flatly.

"All right, Lacey." He stood and tossed his hat onto the table. "Here's a truth for you." Crossing the scant distance between them, he gathered Lacey into his arms before she could protest. In one loud, thundering beat of her errant heart, Morgan's lips were on hers, demanding and seeking, advancing and retreating. Soft and pliant one moment, hard and relentless the next. His insistent mouth took her breath away and left her so weak that she swayed toward him, pressing her body against his lean, hard length.

Defenseless, with no sheltering walls to protect her, Lacey responded to his sudden onslaught with all the passion of a woman who had been too long denied the joy of a man's seductive embrace. Her arms twined around his neck, and her soul cried out to his of the long desolate years of loneliness she'd endured. For that moment it didn't matter—if it had ever mattered at all—why Morgan was here or what he wanted from her. She'd known yesterday that this was destined to happen, and now she gave herself over to the moment completely. He was giving her a return to life after a lonely, dreamless sleep, and Lacey embraced that awakening with every fiber of her being.

His arms gentled, holding her not so tightly, and his hands began to rove over the soft flannel of her shirt and down to the stiffer denim that covered the tantalizing swell of her shapely buttocks and thighs. Lacey moaned against his mouth, losing herself in the sweetness of his tongue wooing hers, tasting and exploring. An ageless, almost forgotten heat flooded through her veins and centered itself, throbbing and moist, between her thighs.

When his hand moved back up her body, seeking and finding the fullness of her breast, Lacey moaned again. The bud hardened deliciously, painfully, and the ache between her thighs ignited into a raging fire that demanded quenching. She moved against him, coming alive in his arms, and Morgan groaned, too, as his own body blazed with the ferocious, maddening need to possess. With his hands at her waist, he crushed her against the burgeoning hardness of his loins, and Lacey responded instantly. With sensuous, inflaming movements, she heightened his pleasure—and her need.

He could take her here, now, and she wouldn't protest. Morgan knew it, sensed it, felt it in the straining of her body to reach his. He could lower her to the floor, strip away the clothes that separated them, and thrust into her, putting an end to this scorching heat that engulfed them both . . . but he wouldn't. Couldn't. He couldn't take this precious woman crudely, violently, in a moment of thoughtless passion. Before he had finished what he came to Wyoming to do, he might have to use Lacey in many ways, but he would never take her like a common whore. She was a lady, and she deserved better. She deserved the sun, the moon, and the stars. She deserved the kind of love and security he could never give her.

Though it was unbearably hard, Morgan wrenched his mouth away from Lacey's, determined to put an end to this exquisite moment before it became too late for them to pull back, but Lacey followed his lips, pressing soft, breathless kisses against his mouth. She eagerly took his hand and returned it to her breast, and sanity nearly deserted Morgan. Unable to resist the pleasure, he kneaded the full, luscious mound, and Lacey arched into his hand, wordlessly begging for more. Morgan groaned deep in his throat, knowing he must stop now or there would be no stopping.

"Lacey . . . sweet Lacey." The words were a sigh against her mouth, and when he moved his hand away from her breast, returning it to her waist, intending to pull out of her arms before they made an irreparable mistake, Lacey moaned with longing.

"Please, Morgan, please." She moved against him seductively, and it was one more sensual delight than Morgan could stand.

"Not like this, Lacey," he moaned, somehow finding the willpower to push her gently away from him. "Not like this," he repeated softly, his voice hoarse with need and regret. And guilt.

Stunned, her breasts rising and falling with each fevered, panting breath, Lacey clung to Morgan's forearms, steadying herself as she returned from the passionate void she had been hurtled into so unexpectedly. Her blood was singing, and thought was difficult, but one reality became suddenly clear. Morgan was rejecting her, pushing her away. She had thrown herself at him wantonly, blindly, and he was refusing to take what she had all but forced on him.

The shame and horror of it had barely sunk in, but as Lacey stared into Morgan's molten eyes, all she could see was that she still wanted him desperately. The need was so great that she almost pleaded with him to take her. The words were on the tip of her tongue, where the exciting taste of him still lingered vividly. Her body ached to be possessed, touched, caressed, filled . . . and she was shamelessly ready to beg him for that fulfillment.

The magnitude of her need was so great that, as reason finally began restoring itself, Lacey became horrified, shocked beyond words at her sluttish behavior. In her mind's eye, she saw how she had clung to Morgan, moved against him, encouraged him to touch her intimately. For one dreadful moment, she thought she might die of shame.

Mortified, she whirled away from him and fled from the dimly lit room into the bright sunlight pouring in through the windows of her outer office.

Morgan saw the shame on her face as she fled, and it intensified his growing guilt. He had it in his power to hurt this woman. Not destroy her, perhaps, for she was too strong to be completely devastated by any man, but he could hurt her in ways that would take some of the glorious light out of her azure eyes. Hurting her like that would be a worse crime than taking the use of her body.

Quelling the impulse to rush after her, Morgan allowed them both a moment, one that he desperately needed in order to conquer the throbbing need for her that still engulfed him. He swallowed hard, evening out his labored breathing until the pleasure-pain eased and he could think more clearly. Only then did he collect his hat and push aside the curtain to step into the light of day.

Lacey was seated at her desk, bent forward with her hands covering her face. Her misery made Morgan's heart twist with a pain more fierce than any that had ever come from mere unfulfilled passion.

"Lacey?"

His voice was soft, almost a caress, and Lacey shuddered. She forced herself to look at him, relieved that her eyes were dry. "Well, let's see . . . who was that arrogant woman who claimed she didn't need a man?" Her mirthless smile was filled with self-loathing.

"Lacey, don't. You—"

"Don't what?" she sneered. "Don't apologize? Don't be ashamed of acting like a whore just because it's been three long years since a man . . . since—"

"Stop it!" Morgan came around the desk, but Lacey anticipated him and took flight, escaping when he would have made some gesture of pity.

"*Ladies* aren't supposed to act like that, you know," she continued viciously, placing the bulk of her printing press between them, trying to salvage some pride, but too emotionally confused to know how. "Ladies are supposed to be shocked when a man touches them. They don't pant and moan like a mongrel bitch in heat, do they? Good Lord, how I must disgust you! I disgust myself!"

"Lacey, stop it!" Morgan darted around the press, cutting off her escape. He grabbed her by the shoulders and shook her once, hard. "Don't do this to yourself, Lacey. You don't deserve it." He pulled her into his arms, refusing to release her when she struggled against him, stroking her hair until she calmed. "You don't deserve it," he whispered again, his voice soft and gentle.

Morgan held her until her breathing returned to normal and he could no longer bear touching her without turning his caress into something more than comfort. Only then did he release her. She backed away, studying his face. Her blue eyes sparkled with unshed tears, but other than that it was impossible to read her emotions.

"I think you should go, Morgan."

He nodded almost imperceptibly, then stepped away from her. At the door he stopped and looked back to find Lacey turned away from him.

So vulnerable. So easy to hurt. Self-reproach filled Morgan as fully as passion had only a few minutes ago. He had lied to her, and if he continued to see her, he would only have to build on those lies. And he had also lied to Ep Luder and to himself. He wasn't just using Lacey Spencer. There was nothing he had to accomplish in Willow Springs that couldn't be done without this lovely newspaperwoman. It was selfish of him to pursue her, to involve himself in her life. She was strong and perfectly capable of handling Rawlings without his intervention.

Her weaknesses lay elsewhere, Morgan realized. Just by being with her he could make her need him. He could coax her into leaning on him. He could perhaps even make her love him. She was so vulnerable now that he could hurt her badly. Betrayal was always painful, and ultimately he would be forced to betray her. Better to end it now.

Lacey heard him pause. She knew that he was studying her, but she couldn't force herself to look at him. It was too embarrassing, too humiliating. She had never imagined herself capable of such wanton behavior, and clearly, Morgan hadn't either. It was no surprise when he informed her regretfully, "I think it would be best if I passed on the barn raising tomorrow, Lacey. I'm sorry. For everything."

She nodded, understanding completely. After the way she'd behaved in his arms it was only to be expected. And it was definitely for the best. Her life was in enough turmoil without the complications of falling in love.

Love?

The thought startled her. The bell over the door chimed twice as the door opened and closed softly, leaving her alone.

Love?

No, she didn't love Morgan. Love didn't come so quickly. But she *could* have loved him, perhaps genuinely, deeply, permanently. Or perhaps only briefly, out of awakened passion, loneliness, and need.

But there was no longer a possibility for any of those things now. She had seen to that. And it was all for the best that he had walked out of her life.

All for the best, she told herself sternly.

But if that was true, why were the tears on her cheeks so hot, and why did she feel so desolate? Why was the constriction around her heart so painful?

And why did she still want Morgan more than she had ever wanted anything in her life?

Chapter Seven

Ep Luder sipped the tepid foam off another beer and surveyed the crowded, smoky barroom with far more boredom than he actually felt. His gut was tied in knots, and though he kept his stance at the bar casual, his mind was racing like an out-of-control locomotive barreling down a steep mountain grade.

Across the room, Morgan still sat at the faro table Luder had vacated an hour ago when the stakes climbed too high for his poor pocket. As planned, the two men had greeted each other as strangers, made casual acquaintance, and then gone their separate ways. But as far as Ep was concerned, the man he had pretended not to know really was a stranger tonight. There was a desperation in Morgan that Ep had never seen in his boss.

Oh, outwardly, Morgan was as congenial as ever, but beneath the charming exterior lurked an undercurrent of . . . what? Anger? Frustration? Bitterness?

Ep didn't know what it was, but it bothered him. Having the boss's timing and temperament even a little out of kilter didn't bode well for their survival.

A marginally pretty saloon girl, younger than most of the whores who plied their trade in the Silver Strike, served Morgan another whiskey and leaned just low enough to afford him a glimpse of what she had for sale. Ep had watched her sidling up to the boss like that all night long, and it hadn't surprised him one bit. Morgan was a fine-looking man, and it was the same wherever they went; women flocked to him like flies to honey.

But what was surprising about this girl, in this saloon, was that tonight Morgan was responding to the unsubtle, provocative advances of the whore. Ep was speechless! In all the years he had ridden with this man, not once had Morgan ever encouraged that type. Oh, he was always polite. He teased and joked with them, but he always made it clear that his interest ended with the service of his drink.

Tonight, though, there wasn't a man in the saloon who didn't know that before the night was over the handsome gambler and little Della were going to be spending an hour or two in her bed upstairs.

Ep gave a confused shake of his head and worried his lower lip. What on earth was wrong with the boss? Had that newspaper gal got him so het up he couldn't wait the few days it would take him to sweet-talk his way into her bed? The boss had never been that hard up over any woman.

From the bar, Ep watched as Della straightened, swaying saucily, and Morgan grabbed her with a lusty laugh, pulling her into his lap. He didn't protest when she squealed with mock indignation and managed to bury his face in the deep cleft between her ample breasts. She wiggled her butt enticingly, taking her time about slipping off his lap, and they exchanged a few quiet words, interspersed with laughter.

Amazed, Ep looked on as Morgan carefully dropped a handful of poker chips down the front of her red satin blouse, then tossed his cards to the center of the table, collected the remainder of his chips, and stood. Morgan drained the shot glass and followed the whore, weaving between the tables toward the stairs that led to her room on the second floor.

Muttering a worried curse, Ep drained his own glass dry. His boss paying for a woman? Unbelievable!

Lordy, Lordy, he thought with dismay. What other changes would his friend go through before this whole mess was over?

Morgan stopped just inside the cramped bedroom, pushed the door closed, and leaned against the wall for support. How much have I had to drink tonight? he wondered. More than usual, that was certain. It didn't pay to get so plastered that reason deserted a man completely; stupid mistakes like that could get a body killed. But Morgan was certain he hadn't drunk *that* much. He wasn't staggering drunk; he knew exactly where he was and what he was about to do.

The girl, Della, was already beside the narrow, rumpled bed, swinging her hips from side to side while she blithely unlaced the front of the low-cut blouse that hiked her breasts up to form the deep cleavage she'd been flaunting in his face all night. Her perfume was cheap and cloying, but not intolerably so, and she was pretty in a jaded way that made her seem older than she probably was. She certainly wasn't beautiful, not in the way Lacey Spencer was beautiful . . . and delicate and vulnerable.

Morgan's heart slammed against his rib cage, and he muffled a curse as he tore the string tie from his collar. It was *her* fault, all hers, that he was here tonight, paying a whore to ease the hunger he'd been experiencing ever since he'd first seen Lacey in the sheriff's office, laughing and beautiful. All her fault.

He should have taken her today in her office when she'd practically begged for it. He should have thrown her on the floor and spilled his hunger into her, then buttoned his trousers, walked away, and forgotten all about Allyce Smithfield Spencer.

But he hadn't . . . couldn't. And now he was paying for his noble self-control and compassion. Paying for it literally.

God, how long had it been since he'd bought a woman? Morgan tried to remember, but the liquor had dulled his memory. A long time, he was certain. And even longer since that very first time, when his well-intentioned father had thought he was doing his fifteen-year-old son a favor by taking him to his favorite cathouse to initiate him in the ways of women.

The memories of that time were still bitter to Morgan. It wasn't the cheap, tawdry women who had galled him then, but the sense of betrayal, the disappointment in his father whom he had revered and respected. He'd thought of his mother, beautiful and delicate, waiting lovingly at home for her husband to return, while that same husband was rutting like an animal between the legs of a whore.

At fifteen, even knowing how consuming his own burgeoning urges could be, Morgan had been unforgiving of his father.

He'd kept silent, not voicing his disapproval, but his hero had fallen. Their relationship had never been quite the same after that night.

The whore his father had paid to initiate him had very kindly kept quiet about the fact that no amount of embarrassing coaxing, caressing, or kissing had raised his manhood to the point of making use of her services, and he had left the establishment with his father laughing boisterously about how proud he was of his son. Morgan had only felt sickened.

For years that sick feeling in the pit of his stomach had kept Morgan away from rooms like this. Only desperation or drink ever pushed him this far. Though he hadn't been a virgin when he married Ann Dennison, the girl he'd grown up worshiping, he'd been faithful to her during their marriage. Like the lady she was raised to be, Ann had been shy and reticent in the marriage bed, no matter how careful and caring Morgan was when he came to her. She had tolerated his lovemaking out of a sense of duty, but in all other ways, she had been the perfect wife. She kept their home, gave him a child, and made his life all that it was supposed to be.

He made his second visit to a whorehouse less than a month after he buried Ann and their beautiful two-year-old son. Scarlet fever had claimed them while he was away on business. He'd returned home to find his son in a pitifully tiny grave, and his wife clinging to life only so that she could say good-bye to him.

Crazed with grief, he had found solace in a bottle, and when that was no longer enough to blot out the memories, he stumbled off to the same whorehouse his father had taken him to eight years earlier. Except for the madam, the women were different, yet somehow they were all exactly the same. He had spent three days there, drinking and whoring, trying not to remember.

He had awakened in a room much like this one, his head pounding, his gut twisting, the pain still intact, and with the same sickening disgust he'd felt the first time. In the end, nothing had healed the wounds but time.

Impatient with his memories, Morgan glanced around. Yes, it was a room like this one, only shabbier, maybe, with wallpaper in faded blue flowers instead of gaudy pink rosebuds.

Everything else was the same, though—the narrow bed sagging in the middle, the dressing table with a cracked mirror and dingy, frilled skirt hiding uneven legs. Everything was the same, right down to the anxious-to-please whore in front of him with her overripe breasts, narrow waist, and plump thighs.

No, Morgan thought in disgust. I haven't had too much to drink tonight. I haven't had enough—not nearly enough to make me go through with this. His hands left off unbuttoning his shirt, and he sagged against the wall, suddenly exhausted.

Della swayed toward him with a little sashaying movement meant to entice, and reached out to help with the buttons he had obviously forgotten how to unfasten. "Lost your nerve, mister?" she cooed, pressing against him so that her stomach made contact with his thighs. She moved sensuously and was disappointed to discover that the enormous bulge she'd felt earlier was no longer in evidence. "And that ain't all you lost, is it? Too bad we couldna done it downstairs when you was ready for it, but don't you worry," she promised, sliding her hand between their bodies to cup him intimately. "Della'll get it back up again."

Morgan tensed and pulled her hand away abruptly. "Don't."

Her confidence suddenly shaken, Della eased away, smiling but wary. She liked this one, had liked him from the moment he first came into the Strike two nights ago. He'd virtually ignored her then, treating her with gentlemanly smiles and generous tips, but making it clear he wasn't going to pay for anything more than his drinks.

Tonight he'd been different, though. She'd sensed it the minute he sat down, and her hopes had soared. He was hungry for it tonight, and Della had staked her claim to this handsome gold mine of a man. The thought that he wanted her had pleased her no end. This one was clean and polite, not to mention incredibly handsome. He was a real gentleman, and she didn't get too many of those. With this one she wouldn't have to feign the desire she usually had to work hard to summon in order to please a customer.

But now he was retreating from her, and Della smiled prettily, shrugging her shoulders just enough to make her bare breasts jiggle erotically. "That's okay, mister. We can take our time. Whatever you want." She reached for the flowered robe draped over the end of the bed and shrugged into it. "Would you rather talk about her?"

Morgan's gaze flew to Della's so fiercely that she had to force herself to remain where she was. "Her?" he snapped.

"Yeah, *her*. Whoever it is that's got you thinkin' second thoughts about comin' up here. You got a wife, maybe?"

Morgan relaxed. For a moment, he'd thought the girl was a mind reader. "No, I don't have a wife." Anymore, he added silently, then brushed the thought away. He'd recovered from Ann's death long ago; now was not the time to get maudlin.

"Then it must be Miz Spencer, the newspaper lady," Della guessed, then smiled when she saw her visitor flinch.

"What makes you say that?"

"This is a small town—everybody knows everybody else's business. You been hangin' around her ever since you got into town. Is she an old friend?" she asked with deceptive innocence.

"No. Just someone I met."

"But couldn't get into, huh?"

Her brassy laugh put Morgan off and he began rebuttoning his shirt. He'd come up here to forget about Lacey Spencer. He didn't need the guilt he suddenly felt because he was discussing a lady with a common trollop.

Alarmed that her prize catch was reclothing himself, Della exclaimed, "Hey, I'm sorry. I didn't mean to insult you. The widow Spencer's a real lady—quality, you know? Me and her, we don't travel in the same social circles, if you know what I mean, but I like her. She's got guts."

"Yes, she does," Morgan replied tightly.

He continued rebuttoning his shirt, and Della grabbed desperately at the first thing that came into her head. "And that husband of hers, he was a nice man, too. Kinda stuffy and all Boston proper, but a real gent."

Morgan stopped, suddenly interested. "You knew him?"

"Oh, yeah!" she replied eagerly. If the gambler was talking, at least he wasn't leaving and she still had a chance to get him out of that fancy black suit and into her bed. "I knew him real well."

Morgan's brows drew together in a frown. "Professionally?" Now, why on earth did the thought of Lacey's late husband's infidelities bother him? Morgan wondered angrily.

Because she deserves better, came the immediate answer.

"No, no." Della laughed a little and sat down on the end of the bed, apparently relaxed. She shifted casually so that her wrapper fell open below the waist, exposing her crossed legs to his view. "I wasn't even . . . well, you know, workin' back then. Goodness, that was more'n three years ago, you know. My pa, he had a shop back then, and Mr. Spencer used to come in and take money for puttin' stuff in the paper about the saddles Pa sold. He was real handsome. Citified, but nice to look at."

"Your father?" Morgan teased, knowing very well what she meant.

"No, silly, Mr. Spencer. David, that was his name."

Fascinated, Morgan leaned against the wall and gave up trying to replace his string tie. Talking like this, abandoning her affected sultriness, Della seemed more child than woman. She looked like a painted doll or a little girl playing dress-up in her mother's clothes. The last trace of his desire for her fled, which was only reasonable, since it wasn't desire for *her* that had brought him to this shabby room in the first place.

Curiosity about Lacey and her late husband now replaced his baser thoughts, and though he knew Lacey's name shouldn't even be mentioned in the same room with this waif-whore, Morgan had had just enough to drink to enable him to cast aside whatever guilt he felt. He wanted to know more—anything, everything—about the woman he'd come to . . .

Come to what? Desire? Certainly, that was an obvious fact he couldn't ignore. Care for? Yes, that, too. If he hadn't cared for her he would never have left her today. He'd been raised a gentleman in a gentlemanly society, but he wasn't a saint.

Love?

Morgan thrust that thought aside hurriedly. Now was not the time for introspection. Besides, he certainly couldn't love a woman he'd known all of three days!

Unaware of his thoughts, Della chattered on and Morgan forced his attention to her words. "Yeah, that Mr. Spencer, he was a real nice man. They come to town, oh, maybe six years ago and built that big house on the hill. Why do you know"—Della leaned forward, as excited as a little girl, her eyes dancing—"that house is the only place in Willow Springs what's got runnin' water inside? Even on the second floor!"

Morgan grinned. "You don't say."

"I do so say! And it's true! Water's brought right up from that windmill and held in a big tank back o' the house. Why, the Spencers had runnin' water even before most fancy folks in Cheyenne did! 'Course, now I hear tell they even got 'lectricity in Cheyenne, which Miz Spencer don't have. But she writes things in her newspaper all the time, eggin' on the town council about pipin' in water to make things . . . san-i-tary," she recited carefully. "And stuff about gettin' 'lectricity so's it'd cut down on fires. Her paper says that a little bitty fire in just the right place could burn the whole city of Willow Springs to the ground!"

She grinned impishly. "Can you imagine? Just turnin' a thingamabob an' havin' a room lit up like magic? No matches or coal oil or nothin'?"

Smiling indulgently at her naïveté, Morgan asked curiously, "Do you read the *Gazette*?"

"Nah, I can't read much, but Bart—he's the bartender downstairs—he reads it to us girls ever' week."

"I thought no one dared buy a copy."

Della's eyes twinkled mischievously. "Oh, they don't, but everybody reads it just the same. See, Miz Spencer gives newspapers out free—brings a whole bunch into the saloon, plunks 'em down on the bar, an' walks out. Does that all over town! 'Course, C. W.'s boys are always right behind her, makin' Bart burn 'em or throw 'em away, but Bart, he always manages to hide a copy somewheres. And if he don't get one, somebody else does and we pass it around real quiet like. Nobody'll admit it, but everybody does it."

A horrible thought struck her and Della's eyes flew open wide with alarm. "Oh, shit, you ain't one o' Rawlings's men, are you? I mean, I could get killed fer—"

"No, no, don't worry," Morgan reassured her. "The town's secret is safe with me."

"Whew." Della fell back dramatically, relieved. "You better not be lyin', mister, 'cause I got me a heap o' living to do yet 'fore I cash in. I ain't ready to die until I've took me a train to Cheyenne and got me a fancy room at the big hotel there and took a bath with runnin' water, and seen them fancy 'lectric lights. I'm gonna do it, I swear!"

"I'm sure you will, Della." He chuckled.

"Darlene."

"I beg your pardon?"

"My name's Darlene," she admitted shyly. "But Della sounds so much more . . . well, better. For here."

Morgan nodded and drew a long cheroot from the gold case in his coat pocket. "How old are you, Darlene?" he asked as he crossed to the lamp at the bedside to light his smoke.

She twisted to follow his movements. "Eighteen," she replied proudly, as though daring him to call her bluff.

Morgan accepted the lie, but guessed sadly that she could be no more than sixteen. A hard sixteen on the outside, but with pockets of childlike innocence and wonder inside that would surface less often as the years took their toll. Eventually there would be no softness, no innocence left, just the hardened, painted exterior.

"What happened to your father?" Morgan sat and leaned back in the chair next to the vanity, drawing on his cheroot.

She shrugged indifferently. "He died of the pneumonia two winters ago."

"And you had no other family?"

"Nope. Don't need none."

"So you've been here ever since?"

"Mostly. Pa always said I had bad blood, just like my ma." She shrugged again. "Guess he was right."

Falling easily into her best professional pose, she ran her hand slowly up the rumpled bed until she was stretched along its length with one leg raised to show her bare thigh. "You wanna see just how right he was? I can make you forget just about anythin'."

"No offense, Darlene, but somehow I doubt that," he replied sadly.

With a peevish pout, she lowered her leg and covered it with the tail of her robe. "Well, if you don't wanna fuck, what are you doin' up here?"

"Watch your language, young lady, or I'll wash your mouth out with soap."

"Mister, I ain't any kind of a lady," she informed him honestly, without rancor, though if she had been honest, she would have admitted that this gambler made her feel like a lady, a lady who was good for something besides a few minutes on her back. If they weren't gonna do it—and it was becoming increasingly obvious that they weren't— she should go back downstairs where she had prospective customers waiting. But he was so different . . . so nice, that she couldn't bring herself to throw him out.

Morgan drew thoughtfully on his cheroot, and the question he'd been longing to ask just popped out before he even realized he'd given voice to it. "Darlene, what happened to David Spencer?"

So I was right! Darlene thought triumphantly. This gambler *was* hot for the widow Spencer! Keeping her opinion to herself, she answered, "He was killed in a gunfight."

"A gunfight?" Morgan's dark brows shot up in surprise. Lacey had been married to a gunfighter? That was the last thing he would have expected.

"Yeah, it was real awful. This bounty hunter, name of "— she thought for a moment—"Fogarty. Yeah, that was it. Anyway, this bounty hunter came ridin' in lookin' for some fella with a dead-or-alive paper out on him, and he found him runnin' the livery. Folks hereabouts didn't have no idea old George McKeevey was wanted by the law. He had a wife and two near grown kids and was just as upright a citizen as ever you saw. But that gunfighter, he had proof that George robbed a bunch o' stagecoaches down in the New Mexico Territory some years back, so Fogarty just walked pretty as you please into the livery one day an' shot the old man stone-cold dead. Didn't give him no warnin' or nothin'. Put a bullet in his back, so they said."

Warming to her story, Darlene sat up and leaned forward. Without realizing it, she modestly drew the lapels of her gaudy robe together where it gaped over her breasts. "Well, of course everybody liked George an' felt real sorry for his widow. The whole town got up in arms over it. Fogarty had to wait while Sheriff Watson got his money from Wells Fargo, an' while he was waitin', Mr. Spencer put out this extra edition of the

Gazette and said some awful things about Fogarty and about how wrong it was to kill a man without goin' before a judge.

"He didn't say nothin' that wasn't true, but all the same, that bounty hunter took it real bad. He called Mr. Spencer out and challenged him to a showdown, but Mr. Spencer wouldn't have none of it. Why, he never even carried a gun! Some folks, 'specially Fogarty, called him a coward, but some thought real high of him fer stickin' to what he believed was right."

"So what happened?" Morgan prompted.

"Fogarty, he didn't give up," Della explained. "He kept after him and after him until one day while Mr. Spencer was out o' the office, that gunfighter snuck in and got after Miz Spencer."

Darlene saw the coldness that swept over her guest and had to repress a shiver and the stab of jealousy that pierced her. The gambler sure had it bad for the widow. His fists were clenched as if he'd like to strangle that gunman with his bare hands, and his eyes were as hot as coals and as cold as ice, both at the same time. Sadly, Darlene wondered what it would be like to have a real gentleman like this one care about her just half as much as he obviously cared for the widow Spencer.

Barely managing to control his anger, Morgan ground out softly, "Did he . . . hurt her?"

"No one rightly knows for sure," she replied gently. "Miz Spencer said he just beat her up, but some said he raped her and she just lied to protect her reputation. I don't think that, though, 'cause I heard the sheriff tell Pa that Mr. Freeman, that nigra that works for her, he come in the back way and Fogarty had to hightail it outta there 'fore he had a chance to stick it to her."

Morgan winced at the thought of what Lacey had suffered. He glanced away, but Darlene continued, "So, anyway, when Mr. Spencer found out, he borrowed a six-gun and went lookin' for Fogarty, who was right in this very saloon, downstairs, waitin'. When Mr. Spencer called him out, it was all over but the shoutin', as they say."

Morgan rose restlessly, but had nowhere to go in the small room. His insides were twisted into knots, and he was suddenly stone sober.

"My pa's shop was right across the street, and I saw it all," Darlene went on, wishing that her room were larger so the gambler would have somewhere to pace. "They faced off, outside in the street, and Mr. Spencer drawed first, but Fogarty cut him down with two shots 'fore Mr. Spencer's pistol even cleared the holster. Miz Spencer musta got wind of what was gonna happen, 'cause she ran up just as the shots was fired, and then froze like a stone."

As she got caught up in her memories, Darlene's voice took on a faraway quality. "You know, I ain't never seen nothin' sadder than the look on her face right then. Those big blue eyes was all wide with shock, and tears was runnin' down her cheeks. You just had to feel all the pain she was feelin' . . . but she didn't say a word. Didn't utter not one sound! She just clenched her fists and sorta folded her arms tight across her belly like she was the one that got shot and was havin' to hold her guts inside or they'd fall out. Real slow she walked into the street, and Mr. Freeman and some other man picked up Mr. Spencer and took him up the hill to the house."

"What happened to Fogarty?" Morgan asked flatly.

"Sheriff Watson, he come runnin' up, and everybody said how Mr. Spencer drawed first, so there wasn't nothin' the sheriff could do. But Miz Spencer had other ideas, yes, sir. She walked right up to Fogarty and bold as brass said, 'You bastard.'" Darlene stopped abruptly, glancing at Morgan defensively. "Them's her words, not mine! I heard her say it!"

Despite himself, Morgan grinned. Obviously Darlene had taken seriously his threat to wash her mouth out with soap. "I understand. Go on."

"She said, 'You bastard, I may not see you hang for murder, but you'll spend a long time in prison for salt—'"

"Assault," Morgan corrected absently.

"That's right," Darlene agreed. "'For assault and 'tempted rape,'" she said, proud of her memory. "And she did it, too, 'cause she had the bruises to prove he hurt her. He got sentenced to two years in Leavenworth, but I heard tell he got killed in a fight there and never got out."

She lowered her voice confidentially. "Mr. Spencer's folks was real rich, and some say that they paid money to see that

Fogarty never came out o' prison. They's even those who claim the widow herself paid to have him killed, but I don't rightly believe that. She's too much of a lady to do that, even if she does use words she hadn't oughta."

Morgan smiled again and let the indictment pass. "You have a remarkable memory, Darlene."

She shrugged modestly. "Nah, it just made a real impression on me, I guess. I always envied Miz Spencer, with her nice clothes and big house with runnin' water, and a rich husband that looked at her like he worshiped the ground she walked on. Up till the second she saw her man lying dead in the street, there wasn't nothin' on earth I wanted more'n to be Allyce Spencer."

Tears unexpectedly pooled in Darlene's eyes, tears of sorrow, but not for Lacey Spencer. The tears were for herself, for all the lost dreams of the child who'd wanted to be a lady and had ended up a whore.

Angry at her sudden weakness, she drew herself up stiffly, all business once more. "You got any more nosy questions, mister? 'Cause if you do, they're gonna cost you. They's men downstairs waitin', and I'm losin' money."

Della was back and Darlene was once again buried under the painted face and deliberately seductive pose. Morgan missed the softhearted innocent he'd spent the last half hour with, but there was nothing he could do to bring her back. If she was lucky, eventually some man might see past the sultry Della, find what was left of Darlene, take her out of here, and marry her. He hoped so, for her sake.

"Thank you for your time, ma'am. And for the story."

"If you ever decide you wanna do more'n talk, you know where to find me," she invited coyly.

"Indeed I do." He moved to the door and opened it with one hand while the other fished into his vest pocket. Gold flashed in the lamplight as he tossed a coin into the air toward his hostess.

She caught it easily and nearly fainted. "A twenty dollar gold piece?" she murmured incredulously.

"Della, do me a favor," Morgan said softly. "Buy Darlene a pretty dress with a little lace collar and take her to Cheyenne to see the running water and electric lights."

Della's chin came up proudly and she stiffened against the sudden press of tears behind her eyes. "I just might do that, mister. I just might."

Chapter Eight

Miserable after a long, restless night, Lacey tugged at the sash of her chenille robe and stumbled sleepily toward the kitchen. It was barely dawn, but Berta was already up, a fact borne out by the smell of roasting chicken that permeated the house, making Lacey feel slightly nauseated. It was too early for the scent of a heavy meal, but there was much to be done to get ready for the Dasats' barn raising. Lacey had promised Lew and Sukie she would arrive with a mountain of food, and that meant she was responsible for helping Berta prepare it, or at the very least, tolerate its preparation.

Yesterday morning Lacey had been looking forward to the barn raising because it had promised an entire day with Morgan. She would have come to know him better, learned more about him; perhaps she would even have come to understand why he so attracted her. At the very least, she would have known the joy of a few carefree hours, hours not marred by the ominous threat posed by C. W. Rawlings. Lacey had wanted those hours with all her heart. She had needed them.

And then, like a cheap trollop, she had thrown herself into Morgan's arms. She was ashamed, humiliated. Her logical self argued that it was only natural for her to yearn for the physical love she had lost when she buried her husband, but her pride told her that what she had done was shameless.

And what was worse, she had spent the night inflamed by indecent memories of those few minutes in Morgan's arms. She had tossed and turned until her bedclothes were twisted and damp. She had ached for the feel of a man. She had paced

and fumed, and bathed her temples and wrists in cool water.
She had cried for David, clutching a pillow to her breast, and
then she had cried even harder when she realized that it was
not her late husband she wanted to feel holding her, touching her, filling the void that had opened the moment Morgan
walked into her life.

Sleep had finally claimed her in the wee hours before
dawn. Had it not been for the smells wafting upstairs from
the kitchen, Lacey probably would have slept until noon—
and been grateful for the untortured bliss. Unfortunately, she
did not have that luxury. She had made a commitment to
the few friends she had left in Willow Springs, and she was
not about to break a promise, no matter how melancholy or
fatigued she was.

Wondering how she was ever going to make it through the
day, Lacey stepped into the kitchen and surveyed the spacious
room. Every surface was occupied with some phase of the
meal. Pies lined the sideboard, two roasters of chicken sat
warming on the back of the stove, and another was cooling
on one of the cabinets. On the table, two hampers were already
filled with bowls, platters, and jars of Berta's delicacies—spicy
German potatoes, sweet bread, beet salad, sauerbraten, pickled
pears, Dutch lace cookies. Though some of the food had been
prepared ahead of time, it was obvious that Berta had been
cooking for hours.

Which made Lacey feel terribly guilty. She'd been so
preoccupied last night that she hadn't even realized Berta
was slaving away downstairs while she was wallowing in
self-pity. "Good morning, Berta," she said in the cheeriest
tone she could manage.

Berta Kraus, a tall, rawboned woman with a no-nonsense
mien, glanced up from the stove and frowned. "You lug
teddible."

Out of long practice, Lacey translated Berta's fractured
English to mean "You look terrible," and her smile broadened.
"Thank you, Berta. I feel teddible."

"Sit. I figs you big breakvast."

"No, no, I'll get it," Lacey protested, padding toward the
stove. "I don't think I could handle anything more than tea
and one of those wonderful-smelling biscuits."

Berta's frown—a perpetual fixture—deepened. "You should eat more. It vill be a long day."

"This is plenty," Lacey assured her, pouring a cup of tea while Berta placed the basket of biscuits and a jar of honey on the table. "As soon as I finish eating, I'll help you with the rest of the food. You should have awakened me earlier."

"Acht! I can handle de food. You should go back to bed und sleep." She looked at Lacey sternly. "You ver so quiet last evening. You ate no dinner, and den I hear you pacing de floor all night long. Up und down. Up und down. Vat is wrong vid you?"

Lacey found a small empty corner of the table and sat. "Nothing, Berta. I just had a restless night."

"You are a teddible liar, *Liebling*. Dis has to do vid de handsome man who likes fried chicken und apple dumplings, *ja*? De one who change his mind about coming vid you today?"

Lacey slathered butter and honey on one of the biscuits, refusing to look at the housekeeper. Two days ago she'd told Berta that Morgan would be accompanying them to the Dasats'; last night she'd been forced to tell her that he'd changed his mind. She'd tried to pass the news along casually, as though it was unimportant, but Berta was no fool.

"My restless night had nothing to do with Morgan. I just couldn't sleep, that's all."

Berta made a loud scoffing noise as she removed two more pies from the oven and placed them on the sideboard with the others. "Zachary say Mr. Morgan is a fine-looking man. He also say he vas very brave to help you at de train yesterday."

"It was foolish of him to become involved with my problems," Lacey said nonchalantly, sipping her tea.

"But you were glad he did, *ja*?"

"*Nein*, Berta. I was *not* glad he did, and I am delighted that he changed his mind about accompanying me to the barn raising. The last thing I need at this point in my life is someone else to worry about."

"*Ja*, dis is true. Vat you need is someone to worry about *you*, for a change."

Lacey laughed wearily. "But, Berta, that's what I have you and Zach for. The two of you worry about me so much that anyone else would be redundant."

Berta sighed heavily. "You make jokes when you are sad, *Liebling*."

"I also make jokes when I'm happy, angry, and tired," she pointed out as she nibbled at the biscuit. "What makes you so sure I'm sad now?"

"Because dis Morgan has hurt you. I see it in your eyes."

"Morgan didn't hurt me, Berta. I hurt myself," she said tightly, abandoning the futile attempt to hide her emotions. "Now, could we please drop the subject? I won't be seeing Morgan again, so this conversation is irrelevant."

"Zachary say—"

"Berta, please," Lacey begged, rising, "just tell me what I can do to help you, and forget what Zachary says."

"And you will forget dis Morgan?" the housekeeper asked shrewdly.

"Yes, I will."

Berta grunted and turned to the counter where she had been preparing dough for a chicken pie. "I tink dat not be so easy as you pretend," she muttered.

"You don't even know the man," Lacey said, exasperated. Recognizing the ingredients Berta had gathered around her, Lacey guessed what she was making and began boning chicken for the deep-dish pie. "Why are you making such a big fuss over him?"

Berta shrugged. "Three days ago you come home happy, vith little secret smile a woman wears when her heart is beating faster because she has met a man who pleases her. Then, two days ago, your eyes dance when you tell me of this man, Morgan, and I think, Aha! It is time my *Liebling* embrace love again."

Her hands covered with flour, Berta rolled the pie dough into a ball and slammed it on the bread board repeatedly as she continued. "But last night you come home pretending not to be sad . . . so I pretend not to notice your eyes are red from crying. You hev not cried about anything since we bury Mr. David, so I know dis man, Morgan, he is important to you."

It was everything Lacey could do to bite back a fresh flood of tears, and she hated herself for being so weak. "He was a very nice man, Berta. Intelligent, witty, strong . . ."

"But why did he change his mind about courting you?"

Lacey remembered how vibrantly alive she'd felt in Morgan's arms and cringed with renewed shame. "I'd rather not discuss that."

"But—"

"No, Berta. The subject is closed," she said sternly. "Now, let's finish cooking so that we can leave for the Dasats' on time. Sukie will be worried if we're late."

Berta gave up, and Lacey busied herself getting ready for the barn raising. She pushed Morgan into the far recesses of her mind and prayed that he would stay there until he was nothing but a dim memory.

Somehow Lacey made it through the day with a cheerful, fixed smile that no one but Berta ever questioned, and this she did with nothing more than silent disapproval. Morgan was not mentioned again that day or the next.

On Monday Lacey threw all her energy into finishing the special edition of the *Gazette* that would let C. W. Rawlings know his attempt to put her out of business had failed. By Tuesday afternoon the skimpy one-page edition was ready, with a banner headline that proclaimed "*Gazette* Receives Shipment of Newsprint" and, in smaller type below, "Publication to Continue Despite Rumors to the Contrary."

"Well, Zach, what do you think my chances of distributing the *Gazette* this week are?" Lacey asked as she removed her apron and rolled down the sleeves of her blouse. The papers were stacked on the counter, ready for her weekly ritual of marching through town to give away copies while the Brigade marched right behind, destroying the papers as quickly as she and Zach could distribute them.

"Better than average, I should think," Zach answered. "Since Croft burned the newsprint, the Brigade seems to have relaxed its surveillance of us. If we are circumspect this afternoon, we may be able to blanket most of the town before C. W. realizes what's happening."

"I agree, with one exception. *We* are not going to deliver the papers. When the train for Cheyenne arrives, I want you to go down to the depot and give these to Mr. Gribbs," Lacey said, handing him two packets she'd prepared for the mail. One was to her father in Washington, the other was to her friend, Asa Mercer, who ran the only newspaper in Cheyenne that wasn't controlled by the WSGA. Both packets contained recent copies of the *Gazette*, and both men could be counted on to publish her articles and editorials.

Lacey had learned the hard way that getting her "letters" out of Willow Springs wasn't as simple as taking them to the post office. Though it was a federal offense to tamper with the U.S. mail, Mr. Gribbs, the postmaster, was far more afraid of C. W. than he was of the postmaster general in far-off Washington. Only by handing her mail to Gribbs moments before he put his packet on the train could she be certain it wouldn't get "lost."

Zach didn't care for her plan, though. Not today, at least. "It's not a wise idea for you to deliver the papers alone today of all days," he said, a frown marring his usually placid face.

"Wise or not, that's the way it's going to be. This issue of the *Gazette* is going to embarrass C. W. and Croft, too. I have to be certain that Asa and Father get copies."

"Of course," he agreed. "But if you'll wait until after I've taken this to the mail train—"

Lacey shook her head and cut him off. "That in itself might tip someone off. No, I'll start delivering the papers, and you wait for the train." She glanced at the clock above her desk. "It won't be here for another fifteen minutes. I should be able to last that long before someone figures out what we're up to. By then you'll have delivered this to the train, and I'll have distributed at least a few copies of the *Gazette*. It's the best way, Zach."

"Fine," he finally agreed. "But you should allow me to deliver the papers while you wait for the train. There's far less chance of encountering trouble at the depot."

"That's exactly why I'm going to deliver the papers. Croft and the others won't harm me, but they might not be so hesitant about roughing you up. I want to handle this alone today, Zach." She placed one hand on his arm beseechingly. "Please do as I ask."

Though it went against his better judgment, Zach finally agreed. He loaded a courier pouch with copies of the *Gazette* while Lacey slipped into her jacket and pulled on a pair of dark kid gloves. She placed the pouch strap over one shoulder, then donned her gray woolen cloak. The full, pleated cloak, which brushed the tops of her shoes, effectively hid the pouch.

"Well, that ought to fool them for a while," she said with a grin. Zach did not respond to her attempt at humor, and Lacey impulsively kissed his weathered cheek. "Don't worry, Zach. I'll be fine."

He looked down at her sadly. "You are not indestructible. Please remember that," he said quietly. "If something happens to you, I shall never be able to face your father again."

"That's not going to happen, so stop worrying. I'll be back shortly."

Zach followed her to the door and watched as she left the office. She looked the street over casually and, finding no one from the Brigade lounging about, gave Zach a jaunty wave as she passed the office window.

On Center Street she entered each business establishment and left a dozen copies of the *Gazette* with the proprietors. Without exception, they were all astonished to see her delivering papers as usual. She greeted them enthusiastically. Some spoke to her; others did not. But in every store, the moment Lacey left, the proprietor snatched up a copy of the *Gazette* and quickly read the front-page story of how Allyce Spencer had hoodwinked C. W. Rawlings. Chuckling merrily, they hid a few copies of the paper away, to be shared later with family and friends.

Store patrons read the article, too, and the story began to spread faster than Lacey could deliver the papers. By the time she had methodically blanketed the north side of Center Street and crossed over to the south, she noticed that many of her former friends were no longer averting their eyes when she approached. Wearing secret little smiles, men began tipping their hats to her. Women murmured a pleasant "good day." It was almost like the old days before C. W. had turned her into a pariah, and Lacey was jubilant.

For nearly an hour she was allowed the luxury of basking in her victory . . . until Vance Hoffman and Croft stepped onto the veranda of the Cattleman's Hotel and settled into chairs on opposite sides of the door. Vance surveyed the street while Croft propped his feet on the porch railing and lit a thick cigar.

"Hey, ain't that the widow Spencer comin' up the walk?" Vance said. Croft looked in the direction he pointed just as Lacey disappeared into a shop two blocks down from the hotel.

"Probably doing some shopping." Puffing on his cigar, Croft tipped his chair back and pulled the brim of his hat down over his eyes.

"Yeah, probably. It's for damned sure she ain't delivering papers today," Hoffman said with a crude laugh. "Burning that newsprint put her out of business for a nice long while."

Vance was only parroting C. W. Rawlings, but Croft didn't agree. "I wouldn't count on that if I were you. Burning that shipment was too easy. I expect Mrs. Spencer will be back in business before you know it."

"Whadda ya mean?" Vance said belligerently, coming forward in his chair. "We got the paper that came in on the train, and two weeks ago we dragged every scrap of paper in her shop out into the street and burned it. Just what do you think she's going to print the *Gazette* on? Bed sheets?"

"If she has to," Croft replied amicably. "It would be a big mistake to underestimate the widow."

Vance looked at Croft, frowning. "I don't recollect hearing you express that opinion to Mr. Rawlings."

"That's because C. W. doesn't pay me for opinions."

Hoffman grunted and stood up. His good mood spoiled by the doubts Croft had planted, he moved to the edge of the porch and sat on the rail, looking toward the shop Lacey had disappeared into. Moments later she emerged from the shop next to it and headed straight for the shop next to that, working her way toward the hotel.

"She ain't got no packages," he muttered, then stood. "Hey, Croft. The widow ain't carryin' no packages. You ever knowed a woman to shop and not buy nothin'?"

The front legs of Croft's chair thumped to the floor and he stood smoothly, adjusting his hat as he came out of the chair. He stepped to the edge of the porch and watched as Lacey went from store to store. "Well, I'll be damned," he said with a grin that did nothing to soften his hawkish face.

"Now, what business could the widow have with a tobacconist?"

"Why don't we go see?" As quickly and quietly as a desert rattler, Croft moved off the porch with Hoffman lumbering at his side. They crossed the street that intersected Center while Lacey went from the tobacconist's to the bank. By the time she emerged, they were waiting for her.

" 'Afternoon, ma'am." Croft tipped his hat, admiring the way Lacey swallowed her first startled, instinctive surge of panic when he stepped into her path. Vance joined him and they stood shoulder to shoulder in front of her.

"Croft. Mr. Hoffman. I do believe you're blocking the boardwalk," Lacey said, mustering all the insincere sweetness she could manage. All things considered, she felt lucky to have made it this far undetected, but she would have preferred being discovered by anyone but Croft.

"Out for a stroll, Mrs. Spencer?" Croft asked pleasantly.

"Or maybe you was makin' a deposit at the bank," Vance offered.

Lacey smiled, determined to enjoy her victory as long as possible. "Actually, I was delivering this week's *Gazette*," she said, throwing one side of her cape over her shoulder to reveal the nearly empty pouch. "Would you care for a copy?" She offered one to each of them, but only Croft accepted.

"Don't mind if I do."

Hoffman wasn't nearly as friendly. "Where the hell did you get the paper to print that?"

"Perhaps you should read this and find out," she suggested mildly, then looked embarrassed. "Oh, I'm sorry. You can't read, can you? Surely Mr. Croft will tell you all about it, once he's finished, won't you, Croft?" Lacey asked, a little surprised to discover that Croft was chuckling as he read her headline and the story below.

Croft's chuckle became a laugh, and he hardly took his eyes off the page as he ordered pleasantly, "Hoffman, why don't you step into the bank and fetch the papers Mrs. Spencer left in there?"

But Hoffman made no effort to obey. "What's it say?" he demanded.

Croft smiled into Lacey's eyes, making her shiver with dread. "It says that the lovely Mrs. Spencer made monkeys out of us last Friday. Now, why don't you backtrack and see how many copies you can collect?"

Vance glared at Lacey, then trotted off to do as he was told.

"You'd better hurry," Lacey called after him without taking her eyes off Croft. "I've already canvassed the entire north side of Center Street."

Predictably, Hoffman let go with a string of curses as he disappeared into the bank, but Lacey was a little shocked by Croft's placid reaction. "You don't seem surprised by this, Croft."

"Oh, I'm not surprised at all, ma'am. When you made that hysterical little speech on the street Friday, I knew something was up; I just couldn't figure out what." He waggled the *Gazette* at her. "Very clever, decoying us like that while a freighter delivered the real shipment."

"Thank you." Lacey stepped around him and continued her stroll up the boardwalk. As she expected, Croft stayed at her side, and they had the walk to themselves because everyone who saw them approaching immediately crossed the street to avoid the trouble that was brewing. Lacey wished she could join them, but Croft wasn't going to let her escape so easily. "It was a relief to get the upper hand for a change."

"For a change?" Croft seemed genuinely surprised. Folding the newspaper, he tucked it into the breast pocket of his frock coat. "I'd say you've had the upper hand in this little game from the very beginning, ma'am."

"Oh, hardly," she protested mildly. "With your assistance, C. W. Rawlings has very effectively made my life hell on earth."

"Yet you don't give up."

"And I never will," she promised.

Croft shook his head and chuckled. "I don't know, ma'am. This is the second time in as many weeks that you've embarrassed C. W. You may have just upped the stakes to a more dangerous level."

"Is that a threat, Croft?" she asked, giving him a sidelong glance.

"Nope, just a friendly warning to watch your step from here on out."

Lacey stopped dead and laughed.

Croft looked at her, puzzled. "You find that amusing?" he asked.

"Extremely. Here you are, sweet as pie, warning me to be careful, when we both know very well that if C. W. ordered my execution you'd put a bullet in my head just like that." She snapped her fingers. Her soft kid gloves muted the sound, but the gesture served her purpose. And Croft's, too. Before Lacey could react, he had her hand in his.

"Oh, not *that* quick, ma'am," he said in a soft, husky voice as he stripped the glove off her hand. Lacey tried to pull away, but his grip was unbreakable. Rather than embarrass herself by a useless struggle, she stood frozen as he raised the back of her hand to his lips. "We have some personal business to settle between us before I'd ever carry out an order to kill you," he whispered.

The air was chilly, but Croft's breath on her hand was warm and sickening. His threat was anything but idle, and Lacey wanted to run as far and as fast as her legs would carry her, but pride held her still. "Let go of my hand."

Croft seemed not to have heard her. "You know, ma'am"—he lazily turned her hand over, studying it as he grazed the palm and made shivers run down Lacey's spine—"it might be possible for us to make an adjustment in the arrangements around here."

"Adjustment?" Lacey's voice sounded hoarse even to her ears.

"Uh-huh." He looked at her then, and his black eyes made Lacey's blood run cold. "Haven't you considered the benefits of having someone like me on your side of this little dispute?"

"No, Croft, I haven't. Aside from the fact that I despise men like you more than you could possibly imagine, I don't think you'd have the guts to stand alone against Rawlings and his men, no matter how much money I offered you."

"Oh, you've got something I want a lot more than money, Mrs. Spencer. You've got a big empty bed up in that fine house on the hill. Make it worth my while, and you won't have to worry about C. W. ever again."

He leaned closer, tucking her hand against his chest, and every muscle in Lacey's body tightened as she tried to pull away. She leaned back, but Croft's free hand snaked around her waist, pulling her close. "Let me go!" she demanded, terrified that he was going to take what he wanted right here on Center Street in broad daylight, no less. And the truly horrifying part of it was that no one would try to stop him. He could do anything to her, and the good people of Willow Springs would just cross the street and go about their business as though nothing was happening.

"Aren't you going to give me an answer to my offer?"

"Go to hell!" she spat, going very still because Croft seemed to find her pitiful struggles amusing—and arousing.

"It's quite likely I will, ma'am, but not before I have a little taste of heaven with—"

The unmistakable click of a pistol being cocked brought Croft up short. He looked up and cursed himself for having allowed himself the luxury of being distracted. He hadn't heard the horse, hadn't even seen its approach out of the corner of his eye. But there was a huge horse behind Lacey now, and the rider mounted on the big black devil had a Colt Peacemaker pointed casually at Croft's head.

"I think the lady would like you to go to hell," Morgan drawled lazily. He leaned forward on his horse, negligently resting his arm on the pommel of his saddle without allowing the Colt to waver. "And if you don't let her go right now, I just might be the one to send you there."

At the sound of Morgan's voice, Lacey twisted in Croft's arms and suddenly found herself free. She wanted to cry out in relief and gratitude, but instead, she slowly backed away from Croft, stepping off the boardwalk out of his reach—and out of Morgan's line of fire. "I'm all right, Morgan. Please put your gun away."

With an unconcerned smile, Croft raised his hands, allowing his coat to fall open so that Morgan could see he was unarmed. "Well, well, if it isn't Morgan the Mouse, come to the lady's rescue. I see you do have a little backbone after all."

Laughing, Morgan holstered the Colt and dismounted. His horse shied away, but Morgan's grip on the reins was firm. "Easy, Desperado," he crooned. "This two-legged rattlesnake is nothing to be spooked about." The horse settled down immediately, and Morgan secured his reins to the hitching post.

" 'Afternoon, Miz Spencer," he said, tipping his hat to her. "What brings you out and about?"

"I always deliver the *Gazette* on Tuesdays, and Mr. Croft always takes exception to my deliveries. It's a little game we play," she told him, amazed that she could be so calm now. Morgan's presence made her feel safe, protected. It was ridiculous and improbable, but entirely true. Morgan wasn't going to let anything happen to her—not today, at least.

"Your game's got some interesting rules," he commented mildly, dividing his attention between Lacey and Croft, who was watching him like a hawk while trying to pretend that he wasn't. It was a ploy Morgan understood, because he'd used it many times himself.

"Got some interesting players, too," Croft said. "And more coming all the time, it seems. You dealing yourself in?"

Morgan looked him squarely in the eye. "Could be."

"Could be you'll end up dead," Croft said with a pleasant smile.

Morgan returned the smile. "Don't count on it." As though completely unconcerned by the threat, he turned to Lacey. "Tell me, ma'am, have you got an extra copy of the *Gazette*? I would dearly love to catch up on the news about town."

"Certainly," she said, casting Croft a nervous glance as she dipped into the courier pouch for a paper.

Croft took the glance as a request for permission to give a copy to Morgan, and he quickly assured her, "By all means let him have one. I'm sure he already knows what it says, since he was a principal player in your little charade last Friday."

"Morgan knew nothing about the ruse," Lacey protested, desperate to keep Morgan from becoming more deeply entrenched in her problems. His rescue of her today had already put him in more danger than he could possibly imagine. "He showed up at the train station quite unexpectedly and got caught in the middle. That's all."

Croft gave Morgan a steady warning glance. "The middle of this is a bad place to be, mister. I'd remember that if I were you. Now, if you'll excuse me, I'd best be about my business." He patted the breast pocket of his coat where he'd placed the folded copy of the *Gazette*. "Seems I've got to ride

out to the ranch to pass along some interesting news to
C. W." He turned to walk away, then stopped and looked
back at Morgan. "Oh, one more thing . . . The next time
you point that Peacemaker at me, you'd best be prepared
to use it." He tipped his hat at Lacey and smiled again. "Be
seeing you, Mrs. Spencer. I'm looking forward to finishing
our . . . conversation."

Sighing with relief, Lacey closed her eyes and listened to the
reassuring sound of Croft's footfalls fading into the distance.
When she opened her eyes again, she found Morgan directly
in front of her, holding out the glove Croft had removed from
her hand.

"This is yours, I believe."

"Yes, thank you." She took the glove and concentrated on
slipping it on so that she wouldn't have to look at Morgan.
Now that the immediate danger had passed, she was suddenly
embarrassed, both by the fact that he'd had to rescue her and
by the memory of what had transpired between them in her
office last Friday.

"Are you all right, Lacey?" he asked, his voice caressingly
soft, and Lacey couldn't keep from looking up at him. Remembering the way she'd thrown herself at him, she feared she'd
find disgust in his eyes, but all she found was a gentle concern
that made her heart beat faster.

"I'm fine, truly. Croft was just trying to intimidate me."

"From where I sat, it looked like he was doing a damned
poor job of it. You don't intimidate easily."

"I was terrified," she admitted, then grinned. "But at least
I got a few papers delivered before he realized what I was
up to."

Morgan's gentle smile turned to a frown. "And that's all
that matters, isn't it? Getting your damned papers delivered."

The change in him shocked Lacey. "Yes, it matters. And
you know why."

"What I know is that you could have been hurt today," he
said harshly, unable to stop himself. When he'd ridden into
town and seen Croft pull Lacey to him as though she were a
common trollop, he'd never been so angry. At that moment,
he could have shot the oily gunslinger in cold blood and never
thought twice about it. But now that the tense moment had

passed, his anger was unleashing itself on Lacey. "That man wants you, Lacey. Do you know that?"

"Of course I know it," she snapped back, unable to imagine why he was so furious with her all of a sudden. "He made his intentions abundantly clear."

"Intentions?" Morgan scoffed. "Honey, Croft's only intention is to throw you on the ground and stick himself between your legs. You keep up this newspaper stupidity and C. W. Rawlings is going to sic that rattlesnake on you and sit back laughing while he watches you being raped. Is that what you want?"

Lacey drew back as though Morgan had slapped her. "That was uncalled for. Or maybe it wasn't," she said ruefully. "I haven't given you reason to think much of my morals, have I?"

She turned briskly on her heel and marched away, trying to bite back the tears that had been treacherously close to the surface ever since Morgan walked into her life. She'd known that her behavior in the office had repulsed him, but she hadn't expected him to make his disgust quite so well known. Of course, she hadn't thought she'd ever see him again, so she hadn't really known what to expect. That he considered her the kind of woman who would welcome rape hurt her more than she could have imagined.

Morgan watched her go in stunned silence. What the hell was she talking about? What on God's half-acre did morals have to do with anything? With ground-eating strides, he caught up with her easily. "Slow down, Lacey. I'm not finished with you yet."

"Well, I'm finished with you, so please go away." She was walking very fast, but Morgan stayed right beside her.

"Not until you tell me why you're so angry."

"I could ask you the same question," she shot back.

"I'm angry because you are hell bent on getting yourself killed!"

"That's none of your concern. I never asked you to become involved in my problems."

"Well, I am involved!"

"Then leave Willow Springs and get *un*involved!"

"I can't!"

Lacey stopped and glared at Morgan, who stopped and looked back at her. "Why not?" she demanded. "What's keeping you here?"

Morgan took a deep, angry breath and wondered how the hell he was going to talk his way out of the corner she'd suddenly backed him into. He couldn't tell her the truth. It would be too dangerous, for him and for her, so he told another of the lies he had grown to detest. "I told you before: I'm a gambler, and Lady Luck has been riding my shoulders pretty good since I came here. Only a fool leaves a town where the pickin's are this good."

Lacey was aghast. "You mean winning a few dollars at the poker table means more to you than your life?"

"It's not my life I'm worried about, Lacey. It's yours," he said with a quiet sincerity that robbed Lacey of her anger.

"Morgan . . . don't you understand that by aligning yourself with me, you're digging your own grave?"

An irritated scowl changed the shape of Morgan's features, but did nothing to make him less attractive. "Are you referring to what I did back there with Croft?" he asked. "Hell, what was I supposed to do? Let him rape you right there on the boardwalk?"

Lacey didn't know how to respond. Morgan had come to her rescue, and she was grateful. He was a brave, honorable gentleman, and it was a normal reaction for a man like that to try to protect a woman—any woman—in distress. But Lacey wasn't just any woman. She had dangerous enemies, who were rapidly becoming Morgan's enemies, too.

For a fleeting second, Lacey considered giving up her fight against Rawlings. For months, she'd lived in fear of something happening to Zach or Berta because of her, and now she had Morgan to worry about, too. How could she possibly live with herself if something happened to one of them?

But on the other hand, how could she live with herself if she allowed Riley Hanson's death to go unpunished? How could she face her reflection in the mirror every morning if she abandoned her crusade and the vigilantes were allowed to resume their reign of terror in full force. They were capable of killing without compunction; she had seen bitter proof of that. The articles she wrote were the only thing keeping them from mercilessly slaughtering her friends in the co-op. Could she live with herself if Lew and Sukie Dasat or Rob and Veda Swenson were butchered as Riley and Martha had been?

No, she couldn't. So, either way she turned, someone stood a good chance of dying because of her. It was a heavier burden of responsibility than Lacey's slender shoulders had been meant to bear, but bear it she would.

Keeping her voice soft, she finally told Morgan, "I'm grateful for what you did. Please believe that. But I'm also dead serious when I ask you never to do anything like that again."

"Sorry, Lacey, but I can't promise that. I wouldn't stand by and watch a man abuse any woman. I'm certainly not going to turn my head if *you're* in danger."

What did that mean? Lacey wondered as something that felt like hope blossomed in her breast. Did he mean that she was special to him? He was certainly looking at her as though he wanted to touch her but was fighting that impulse. But if that was the way he felt, why had he changed his mind about courting her? It was best that he had, of course, because she could bring him nothing but trouble. But that didn't keep her from wanting to believe he felt something for her other than disgust.

Nothing about the man made sense to Lacey. And nothing about her feelings made sense, either. "Leave Willow Springs, Morgan," she finally said, her voice strained. "If you can't stay out of my problems, then for your sake and for mine, leave Willow Springs today. I don't want you on my conscience."

Morgan shook his head. "I'm not ready to do that, Lacey. But you can give up your vendetta against Rawlings. Leave it to someone who's better equipped to handle the job."

"And who might that be?" she asked disdainfully. "Ben Watson? He's afraid of his own shadow. The territorial marshal? He was fired, and the legislature hasn't seen fit to appoint a replacement. The governor, whose election campaign was paid for by the Stock Growers Association? Who, Morgan? Who?" she demanded angrily. "Who's going to stand up to Rawlings's vigilantes if I don't?" Without waiting for an answer, she turned and walked away.

Who indeed? Morgan thought as he watched her go. Her shoulders were stiff with pride and determination, but Morgan had seen the fear that lurked just under the surface of everything she said and did. She was justifiably frightened by the magnitude of the job she'd taken on. Yet despite her fear, she would do whatever she had to do, and she would do it all by herself, with no one to share the burden.

More than anything in the world, Morgan wanted to run after her and tell her she wasn't alone. But he couldn't do that; it wasn't part of his carefully worked out plan. All he could do was carry out that plan to the best of his ability, and somehow manage to protect Lacey at the same time.

Morgan suddenly felt the weight of his own burden, and as he turned back toward the hotel, he thought acidly, I'm getting too old for this. He was thirty-five years old; most sane men of his age had long ago settled down with a wife and a steady job. They had children and a place to call home. Morgan had none of that any longer, and until he'd met Allyce Spencer he'd almost forgotten what it was like. Now it seemed to be all he could think of.

The absurdity of the timing made him want to laugh. A man in his line of work, with his current life expectancy, couldn't afford the luxury of falling in love.

He'd been telling himself that for days, but unfortunately it hadn't done a damned bit of good. Lacey had gotten under his skin, deep.

It was a real pity he couldn't let her know it.

Chapter Nine

The bell over the door tinkled as Lacey stepped into the office, and Zach came out of the workroom in the back immediately. "How did you fare?" he asked as Lacey removed her cape and the nearly empty courier pouch.

"Quite well," she answered cheerfully, hoping Zach wouldn't notice that she was still trembling. Whether it was from her encounter with Croft or her confrontation with Morgan she couldn't have said; the only thing she knew for sure was that she was still shaking and she couldn't seem to bring it under control. "I got as far as the National Bank before anyone from the Brigade figured out what I was up to."

Zach frowned. "Who confronted you?"

Lacey moved through the swinging gate and hung her cape on the rack behind the counter. "Croft and Vance Hoffman." She flashed Zach a bright, false smile. "Would you believe, Croft was rather amused? I think he actually enjoys our little game of cat and mouse."

"That is because he has no doubt that he's the cat," Zach muttered darkly. "You have not made the mistake of underestimating him, have you?"

"Of course not."

"What did he say and do?"

"Very little, actually," she lied, moving to her desk to begin the process of sorting through pages of notes she had made for the last edition of the paper. She was uncomfortably aware that Zach was studying her every move. "He read the lead article, laughed a little, then ordered Hoffman to retrace my

129

steps and collect all the issues he could find. I doubt he found very many, though."

"And that was all?" Zach pressed.

"He didn't hurt me, if that's what you're asking," she said, trying not to sound peevish because Zach was pressing her so hard. "Did you have any trouble at the train station?"

"None," he replied pleasantly. "On my way back, though, I took a leisurely stroll down Center Street . . . just as Mr. Morgan pulled his gun on Croft."

She looked up at him, irritated. "If you knew what happened, why did you pretend otherwise, Zach?"

"To see if you would tell me the truth."

"I didn't want you to worry," she said defensively. "Nor did I want you to write Father with another exaggerated story of the danger I'm in."

Zach looked at her with quiet reproach. "My stories to your father have not been exaggerated, and the danger to you is quite real. Croft's actions today proved that."

"C. W. Rawlings isn't going to hurt me, Zach," she insisted impatiently. "The Stock Growers Association is too afraid of what Father could do to them."

"But Mr. Rawlings isn't the Stock Growers Association," Zach reminded her. "He's only one man—mean, vindictive, and powerful. If you push him too far, he will retaliate. But"— he grew distinctly uncomfortable—"that is not the danger to which I referred."

"Oh?"

"Obviously Croft himself has become an extreme threat. Since Mr. Rawlings was convinced he had bested you by burning your shipment of newsprint, I doubt that he had given Croft the authority to physically accost you, yet that is exactly what he did. Rawlings may be bound by the opinions of the WSGA, but in the final analysis, Croft has no such allegiance."

Lacey shuddered as she recalled Morgan's crude appraisal of Croft's intentions toward her. Her own conviction that C. W. couldn't control Croft only added to the fear she was trying to ignore. Obviously Zach held the same opinion.

She wasn't about to give in, though. "I'll handle it, Zach."

"The way you handled it today—with Mr. Morgan's help?"

Lacey went back to shuffling papers. "I've asked Morgan to stay out of it. He doesn't seem to comprehend the risk he's taking by aligning himself with me."

Zach was quiet for a moment. "Perhaps he understands the risk, but takes it anyway because he cares for you."

As much as Lacey wanted to believe that was true, she couldn't allow herself to harbor such delusions. Sighing heavily, she told her friend, "I know you like Morgan, Zach, but please don't waste your time playing matchmaker. Morgan's intervention with Croft was nothing personal. He would have done the same for any woman in trouble."

"No doubt he would. He's a brave and honorable man."

"That's what he appears to be, yes," Lacey hedged.

Zach's graying eyebrows went up in surprise. "You have reason to believe otherwise?"

"No, of course not!"

"Then why do you not accept his help?"

"Because he hasn't offered it, and I don't need it!" she cried defensively. "Zach, please," she pleaded, "stop talking about Morgan, and while you're at it, stop filling Berta's head with the silly notion that Morgan's interest in me is romantic. The two of you are driving me insane with your constant badgering!"

He looked at her sadly. "I do not think that your recent melancholia has anything to do with Berta or me."

"I am not melancholy," she said proudly.

Zach's look told her that he knew better, but he said nothing. After retrieving the courier pouch from the counter, he disappeared into the back.

Feeling very much alone, Lacey tried to straighten her desk, but couldn't concentrate on something as simple as sorting papers and files. She simply wasn't a good liar. Gloom hung over her like a veil of mourning, mingling with her fears and uncertainties, magnifying them, making them seem a hundredfold more threatening than they'd been before Morgan had stepped into her life.

But why should that be? she wondered forlornly, and immediately knew the answer. Morgan's charismatic presence had made her face the loneliness of her existence. He had resurrected emotional and physical needs she had long ago buried with her husband. A week ago she had been strong and self-confident, righteously convinced that the path she had chosen was the right one. Now she was filled with doubts because her needs were no longer totally focused on justice and revenge. The crusading newspaper publisher had been reminded that she was a woman, too. And the man who had reminded her of that fact had waltzed out of her life as easily as he had waltzed into it.

Lacey was so confused she could have wept. But she didn't. Resolutely, she tried to force Morgan out of her thoughts and return her life to its normal pattern.

The effort was pitifully wasted.

His face beet red with anger, C. W. Rawlings crumpled the newspaper and threw it into the fireplace. The heavy newsprint caught fire before it ever hit the blazing logs, and floated, charred and blackened, in the updraft before finally scattering into the grate. C. W. watched it burn without satisfaction.

"God damn that woman! If this gets out, I'll be the laughing-stock of the whole territory!" He whirled on Croft, who had casually helped himself to a brandy and C. W.'s favorite armchair. "How many copies did she distribute before you stopped her?"

Croft shrugged negligently. "I couldn't say. Once we realized what she was up to, Hoffman backtracked and collected twenty-one copies, but I'd be willing to bet she'd passed out three times that many. I'd say by now everybody in Willow Springs knows about her little coup." With a complete absence of concern, Croft glanced around the sumptuously furnished parlor. It was a man's room, with no frills and furbelows, but it reeked of its owner's wealth. Polished mahogany and maroon velvet abounded. Ornate wall sconces lit the room, but it seemed to Croft that no amount of light would chase away the shadows that darkened every nook and cranny of the opulently furnished room. It was a little oppressive for Croft's taste, but he could appreciate anything that bespoke money.

"Dammit, Croft, I'm paying you a fortune to see that things like this don't happen! Why the hell didn't you figure out what she was up to last week? And why didn't you have someone following her today as usual?"

Unaffected by C. W.'s raving, Croft drained his snifter and crossed the room to pour another brandy. "You said yourself that there wasn't any point to following her. You even ordered most of the men back to the ranch because you were certain the widow wasn't going to give us any more trouble for a while." He shrugged and returned to the armchair. "How was I supposed to know her little scene on the street was just a decoy?"

"I pay you to know!" C. W. roared, then made an effort to calm down. He was furious with Lacey and with himself for underestimating her once again, and on top of it all, Croft's casual attitude was galling. Unfortunately, there was little he could do about it. Even he knew that men like Croft were best given a wide berth.

C. W. had been surrounded by rough, rugged men all his life, but this gunslinger didn't fall into that category. He was polished smooth around the edges—slick, cynical, and very smart. And most of all, he was dangerous. C. W. knew better than to push Croft too far; he just might take a walk and never come back. Or worse, he might offer his services to Allyce Spencer, and the last thing C. W. wanted was to be on the opposite side of whatever fence Croft was guarding.

Quelling his irritation, Rawlings returned to the problem at hand. He asked for and got the details of everything that had transpired on the street that afternoon, including the surprise appearance put in by the gambler, Morgan.

"Is he going to be trouble? I thought you said he was harmless!"

Croft shrugged, but his obsidian eyes went cold and flat. "I misjudged him. It's a mistake I won't make twice."

"Well, what the hell was he doing with a gun?" Rawlings demanded. "It's against city ordinance."

"He was on that big black stallion Lew Dasat's been trying to sell, so I'd say that Morgan had just ridden into town from the co-op, where he bought the horse. As far as I know, there's no law against wearing a gun while you're coming into or going out of town." He sipped his brandy thoughtfully. "Could be you need to do away with that gun ordinance altogether, C. W. I told you from the beginning, I don't like being without my sidearm. You make it legal to carry guns on the street, and I promise you Morgan won't ever cause us any worry again."

Rawlings considered the idea and nodded. "I'll take it up with the council at the meeting next week. In the meantime, what the hell are we going to do about Allyce Spencer?" he asked, growing furious all over again. "I'm not putting up with any more of her shenanigans, you hear? I'm going to teach that uppity bitch a lesson if it's the last thing I ever do!"

"Well, I'd suggest you do it pretty quick, C. W., because Kelso told me he saw that man of hers, Freeman, leaving the depot just after the train pulled out. If I had to guess, I'd say that she posted a copy of the *Gazette* to her daddy and maybe one to that Mercer fellow in Cheyenne, too."

Rawlings let go of a string of curses that would have made a God-fearing man blush, and even burned Croft's jaded ears. C. W. could just imagine the scene at the Cheyenne Club, headquarters of the Stock Growers Association, as his fellow members read about how Allyce Spencer had made a fool of him. Most of them understood his problem with the irritating widow, because they were being affected by the negative publicity, too, but they had left it to C. W. to bring Mrs. Spencer under control. His inability to silence her had already damaged his reputation among the wealthy, polished eastern investors and cattlemen C. W. had worked so hard to emulate. Once they found out about this, they would never take him seriously again. If he didn't do something immediately, he'd never be able to show his face at the club again.

As the image of his friends laughing at him slowly burned its way into C. W.'s brain, he made up his mind that it was time to change his tactics. Terrorism hadn't worked on the widow, nor had intimidation, vandalism, or theft of property. Something more drastic was called for.

The logs in the fireplace crackled and popped, sending a shower of sparks onto the stone hearth. Out of habit, C. W. stomped at the red embers, then smiled.

"Croft, we're taking the men back to Willow Springs first thing tomorrow morning," he said, turning slowly. "It's time we arranged for the widow Spencer to have a little . . . accident."

The barroom of the Cattleman's Hotel was too lavish to be called a saloon. Its chandeliers, stained-glass windows, and fine mahogany trimmings were worthy of any big-city establishment that catered to men of wealth and breeding. The prices, too, were a little steep for the likes of a sleepy town like Willow Springs, but there was no one to complain about them, since the only patrons were visitors to town, well-to-do cattlemen, and a few of the men hired by Rawlings to keep the town in line.

Since Rawlings owned the hotel and stayed in his own private room whenever he was in town, Morgan had made it a habit to drop into the Cattleman's luxurious salon every evening in the hope that he might accidentally run into the wealthy cattle baron, but so far no luck. Except for their one brief encounter in Lacey's office, Morgan hadn't seen him, because Rawlings had ridden out to his ranch and stayed there.

Until today.

As Morgan had expected, the news of Lacey's triumph brought him straight into town. For his own sake Morgan was delighted, but instinct told him Rawlings's arrival didn't bode well for Lacey.

Still, he couldn't afford to worry about that now. Lacey had chosen her path; she knew the risks. Getting all mushy and sentimental about her would only make Morgan's job more deadly. Once it was all over, then maybe—

Morgan cut that thought off before it was fully formed. When he'd left Virginia and headed for the wilds of Texas after the death of his wife and son, the first rule he'd learned was that you don't look back and you don't look ahead—not if you expect to survive. His only focus had to be *now*, and right now he was sitting at a green baize-covered table with a full house in his hand, and C. W. Rawlings was sitting across from him. There were two other players in the game, but Rawlings was the only one who counted.

Looking far more at ease than he felt, Morgan pushed a stack of chips to the center of the table, raising the stakes another fifty dollars. On Morgan's left, Ardie Hollis folded, but C. W. only looked amused.

"Oh, come on, Ardie, his luck can't be that good," C. W. said genially. "He's won the last three pots. I think he's bluffing this time."

Morgan shrugged and smiled. "It'll cost you fifty dollars to find out."

"All right." He slid a stack of chips to the center. "I'll see your fifty, and just to make it interesting, I'll raise you another fifty."

"I'm out," Leo Granbury said, throwing his cards down in disgust.

"Too rich for you, Granny?" C. W. asked with a laugh.

"Too rich for nothin' but three treys," Granbury answered. "I'll let you two fight this one out."

"Morgan?" Rawlings was waiting.

Without bothering to answer, Morgan put fifty chips out, then raised another fifty.

Rawlings tried to cover his surprise. "That must be some hand you got there. Call." He met Morgan's raise and waited.

"Full house, aces over queens," Morgan said, spreading the cards.

C. W. tossed his cards onto the table. To his credit, he didn't let his irritation at losing show. "You're a very lucky man, Morgan."

"Some days more than others," he answered, dragging in the pot, which was close to four hundred dollars.

"Like yesterday, maybe?"

Morgan looked at him. "Yesterday?"

C. W. cocked his head in the direction of the bar across the room, where Croft was leaning against the rail watching every move Morgan made. "You went up against Croft and lived to tell about it. I'd say that was lucky."

"I had a gun; he didn't," Morgan said with an easy shrug of his shoulders as he started shuffling the cards for another hand. "I wouldn't exactly call that a fair contest."

"Not fair, maybe, but lucky—that Croft didn't have a gun, I mean. You might not be here to tell the tale otherwise." Rawlings leaned back and pulled a gold watch out of his vest. He'd only been in the saloon an hour, but Morgan had already lost count of the number of times he and Croft had checked their timepieces.

"Or your friend Croft might not be alive to worry about what time it is," Morgan commented mildly, wondering what the men were waiting for.

"You think you're that good?" Rawlings asked with genuine interest.

Morgan stopped shuffling the cards and met C. W.'s gaze squarely. "Let's hope neither one of you ever has to find out."

"Are we going to chew the fat or play poker?" Granbury growled. "Ante up." A prosperous cattleman with the WSGA, Granbury had ridden down from his ranch in Medicine Bow to catch tomorrow's train to Cheyenne. He'd come into the saloon looking for a friendly poker game to pass the time, but he hadn't counted on losing two hundred dollars to this well-dressed stranger. Nor had he counted on getting caught in the cross fire of the tense little game C. W. Rawlings was playing with the gambler.

"Keep your shirt on, Granny," C. W. advised without looking at him. "Morgan and I are just getting to know each other a little better. Right, Morgan?"

"I don't know," he replied lightly as he dealt the cards around the table. "I guess it depends on what you want to know."

"Just the little things, like where you come from and what brought you to Willow Springs."

"And what my interest might be in Mrs. Spencer?"

Rawlings laughed shortly. "Yeah, that, too. You seem to be making a habit of showing up wherever the widow happens to be."

"Pure coincidence."

"She an old friend of yours or something?"

Morgan put aside the deck and studied his cards. "Nope."

"Then why are you risking your life to help her?"

"Is that what I'm doing?" he asked with a smile.

"I'd say so, yes," Rawlings answered, not making too much of an attempt to hide his irritation.

This time it was Morgan who laughed. "Obviously this little run-in you're having with the widow Spencer has blinded you to the fact that she's a very handsome lady, not to mention a mighty rich one."

A slow smile spread over Rawlings's beefy face. "So . . . that's the way the wind blows." Hollis started the bidding, but C. W. ignored him. He leaned toward Morgan intently. "Just how much of a gambler are you, mister? How much are you willing to risk for a pretty face with a big bank account?"

"That all depends on the odds against winning."

"And what do you figure the odds are in this game?"

Morgan sat back comfortably. "Rawlings, I'm not even sure I've figured out the rules and sorted out all the players, but from what I've seen so far, it appears to me that Mrs. Spencer is holding a mighty strong hand."

C. W.'s eyes narrowed dangerously. "Appearances can be deceiving, boy."

"I'll say!" Granbury practically shouted, throwing his cards onto the table in disgust. "It appeared to me that we were play-ing poker, but I guess I was mistaken!" His chair grated against the floor and nearly toppled as he rose and headed for the bar. "Roy! Draw me another draft!"

"Maybe you better deal me out, too," Hollis said quietly, retrieving his chips from the pot.

When he was gone, Morgan said, "Looks like it's just you and me now."

"Looks like," Rawlings agreed, picking up his cards. "It's about time you found out who the players are and who's hold-ing the winning hand."

As though it had been preordained, the persistent, frantic clang-clang of an alarm bell began tolling in the street, and everyone inside the barroom froze—everyone except C. W. Rawlings, who studied his cards far more intently than was necessary. Calmly unconcerned, he began whistling a little dit-ty and dropped twenty dollars into the pot.

The bell continued to toll, and everyone who had frozen was suddenly galvanized into action. There was a stampede for the door just as the desk clerk outside rushed in and yelled, "Fire! Come on, men, there's a fire!"

"Where?" someone shouted in the confusion.

"Where do you think?" the desk clerk shouted back. "The *Gazette* office, where else?"

In a matter of seconds, the room was clear save for Croft, Rawlings, and Morgan, who rose slowly and dropped his cards on the table.

"Like I said, Morgan, it's time you learned who's holding the winning hand." C. W. grinned smugly.

Panic for Lacey's safety settled over Morgan like a stifling cloak, but somehow he managed to maintain a calm, unconcerned facade. "You're a real bastard, Rawlings," he said, looking down on C. W. with a smile.

"I'm a winner, mister. And don't you forget it."

"Somehow I don't think you're going to let me . . . . or Mrs. Spencer," Morgan drawled, then calmly retrieved his hat and coat from the rack by the door and sauntered out.

It wasn't until he was out of Rawlings's sight that he headed toward Lacey's office, running as fast as he could.

Chapter Ten

It was almost more than Lacey could manage, removing the netting and pins from her hair, letting it fall, and brushing the long mane that hung halfway down her back. She had bathed in rose-scented bubble bath and donned her most comfortable brocade dressing gown, but nothing had relaxed her. Tonight she feared nothing would, because something that hadn't happened yet was going to. She was sure of it.

While shopping today, Berta had learned that C. W. had ridden into town early that morning. She had rushed to the office with the news, and Lacey had spent the remainder of the day waiting. She had been primed and ready for a confrontation, prepared for him to march into her office at any moment, but he hadn't come. Not all morning, and not all afternoon. Now it was night, and C. W. still hadn't exacted his retribution for the humiliation he'd suffered at her hands. Unfortunately, the night wasn't over, and Lacey's fear and anxiety were driving her to the breaking point.

She felt as though lighted firecrackers were fizzling inside her, ready for the least little thing to set them off. She jumped at every familiar creak of the house; unfamiliar ones brought her heart pounding into her throat. Logic told her that C. W. wouldn't dare break into her home and try to harm her, but on this dark, anxious night, logic didn't seem to mean much.

Feeling like an idiot for being so jumpy, Lacey finally abandoned the futile effort of brushing her hair; her hands were trembling so hard that she was creating more tangles than she was eradicating. Unable to sit still, she paced her bedroom, then paused at the doors to the balcony that overlooked the front lawn. She pulled aside the velvet curtain, then dropped it when she realized that she was making herself an easy target for anyone who might be watching the house.

Moving through the room, she extinguished the lamps, then returned to the door and tied the dark blue curtain back with a tasseled sash.

Below her, Willow Springs stretched out in odd, familiar patterns of light and shadow. There were no street lamps, but she easily distinguished one avenue from another. Lighted windows in the Cattleman's Hotel, the tallest building in town, made a perfect landmark by which to identify Center Street, and there were lamps burning outside the doors of most of the saloons. Some of them Lacey could see clearly; others only cast ghostly yellow lights that created silhouettes of false-fronted buildings. Tidy squares of light spilled from the windows of homes, and here and there late-working storekeepers had single lanterns still lit as they pored over the day's receipts and recorded their profits and losses in their ledgers.

Lacey had seen this view a thousand times and found it comforting. Tonight, though, comfort wouldn't come.

Staring at the lighted rooms of the Cattleman's Hotel, Lacey wondered which—if any—was Morgan's. Was he in his room now, or in the saloon below, plying his trade as a gambler? Was he alone, or had he found a more suitable companion than she? Was he still in Willow Springs or had he taken her advice and left? How odd that she could find comfort in neither thought.

Lacey lost all track of time as she stared out over the town. Occasionally her eyes would drift in the direction of the *Gazette* office, which was near the end of the street that led up to her house. Only the two-story building Dr. Elias Touchstone had erected across the alley two years ago, with his office downstairs and his living quarters on the upper floor, stood between Lacey's home on the hill and the *Gazette* office.

The faint glow of the lamp Dr. Touchstone always left burning outside his door was all that lit the street, but it was enough to make passersby visible for a brief moment, and to cast a patchwork of light and shadow on Lacey's office next door.

When those shadows began to move, Lacey's heart tripped

in alarm. Two men slipped into the alley between the *Gazette* and Dr. Touchstone's. For a moment Lacey tried to convince herself it was her imagination. When another shadow joined the first two, she tried to tell herself it was only the doctor and two of his friends entering his home via the outside staircase that led up to his apartment. Neither explanation made her heartbeat slow to normal.

And then she saw the yellow-gold glow of fire. Three men in silhouette ran from the alley, and Lacey knew that C. W.'s moment of retribution was at hand.

She had anticipated something like this for a long time, and had even considered herself lucky that Rawlings had not resorted to such drastic measures sooner; but expecting to have her life's work burned to the ground and actually seeing it happen were two different things. Frozen in horror, she watched the glow become brighter. In her imagination, she could see the whole building engulfed in flames—but that hadn't happened yet. The street was still dark. The fire was still young. There might be time. . . .

That thought finally propelled Lacey into action. "*Zach! Berta!*" she shouted, flying through her room, into the hall, and down the stairs. "*Zach!*" As she reached the bottom of the stairs, Zachary met her, and Berta was close behind. "The office is on fire!" she told them breathlessly, not pausing as she ran for the front door.

"Your coat, *Liebling!* Your coat! Zachary, your coat! Is cold out tonight!" Berta reminded them sternly, but they were already out the front door. "*Acht!* Dey vill catch deir death!" she muttered irritably, then hurried through the house to collect wraps for them all.

Zach was right beside Lacey as she ran down the carriage path toward her office. Her bedroom slippers provided little protection against sharp stones that dug at her feet, but she hardly noticed the pain or the stinging cold night air. The street was now aglow with dancing golden shadows, and Lacey could see flames licking the awning over the front door.

She and Zach barreled onto the street just as the fire bell began clanging eerily. With a strangled cry, Lacey headed straight for the office, but Zach grabbed her arm and pulled her to a halt. "There is nothing you can do in there but die," he said sharply. "The alarm has been sounded. The hook-and-ladder truck will be here shortly."

A touch of hysteria edged Lacey's voice as she shouted, "And what do you think they'll do to save my office?"

"There is nothing they can do," Zach replied quietly. Gently, he turned Lacey so that she could take a long, slow, agonizing look at the fire that engulfed the building—inside and out. The front window shattered, and black smoke billowed out, closely followed by licking tendrils of fire.

A dozen vivid images flashed through Lacey's mind. She remembered the day she and David had purchased this small, vacant lot, and had stood in this very spot, imagining how their office would look. She remembered the care her husband had taken with drawing up the simple plans for the building, and the pride that had glowed on his face the day he helped workmen lay the wood planking for the floor.

Tears ran down her face as she recalled the day they had opened for business, and how they had danced around the office like children when the first issue of the Willow Springs *Gazette* came off their squeaky new printing press. Every board and burning timber, every piece of type and every stick of furniture was a reminder of David. It was all she had left of him, and it was going up in flames.

"I can't stand here and do nothing!" Lacey screamed, breaking away from Zach. "This was David's dream! And mine!"

Spectators began arriving in droves, some carrying buckets as though they intended to help, but when they saw for certain that the fire was at the *Gazette* office, they all stopped and drew back, afraid of what might happen to anyone who dared lend assistance to the widow. No one entertained the idea for even a moment that the fire had resulted from an accident.

"Mrs. Spencer?" Granville Taylor approached Lacey cautiously just as she broke away from Zach. "This is a real shame."

His sympathy was genuine, but he was just standing there like the others, doing nothing. Her neighbors' apathy only added to Lacey's anguish. "Save your pity!" she snapped, grabbing the bucket he carried. Not caring that the effort was futile, Lacey ran to the watering trough across the street, and the crowd automatically cleared a path for her as she filled the bucket and raced back to the office. The water sizzled as it splashed uselessly on the outer wall, but Lacey didn't hear it. She was already running for the trough again.

For a moment, Zach watched her through sad, weary eyes, then grabbed the nearest bucket and joined her in the futile effort.

Willow Springs's only hook and ladder truck, operated by a staff of volunteers, finally arrived, its clanging bell clearing the spectators from the center of the street. Ben Watson, in charge of the fire brigade, arrived with the horse-drawn contraption, but even before he stepped down from the wagon he knew the *Gazette* office was a total loss. Nothing could save it now.

Fortunately the building stood alone, with a vacant lot to the east, and a wide alley to the west; otherwise the entire block would already have been ablaze. But the flames were throwing off sparks that might well spread the fire to Dr. Touchstone's office.

Shouting orders at the top of his lungs, Watson ordered his volunteers to begin watering down the side and roof of Touchstone's building. A hose was attached to the huge barrel at the back of the wagon, and four men took opposite sides of the pump lever and began pumping for all they were worth. A trickle of water, then a gush, sprayed up toward the roof.

Without being told what to do, the spectators finally came to life, forming a bucket brigade between the watering trough and the side of the doctor's office, but those without buckets stood back and watched in horrified fascination as Lacey and Zach alone battled the raging fire at the *Gazette* office.

The first thing Morgan saw as he pushed his way through the growing crowd was Lacey running toward the engulfed office. His relief was palpable. As he had rushed down the maze of streets, visions of Lacey trapped in a blazing building had filled him with sickening dread, but thank God those visions had been false.

The second thing Morgan realized once he had gotten past his intense relief was that Lacey and Zach alone were fighting the blaze, while a passive crowd watched. Beyond them, a group was busy trying to save a neighboring building, but it infuriated Morgan that no one was lifting a hand in Lacey's behalf.

Spurred on by anger, Morgan dashed to the water trough just as Zach, exhausted and coughing from smoke inhalation, returned to refill his bucket. Morgan grabbed the bucket from him, and Zach's initial expression of surprise turned to one of gratitude as soon as he realized that someone on their side had finally arrived.

Morgan dipped the bucket, turned . . . and got his first unrestricted view of the fire. He watched as Lacey emptied her bucket onto the porch, then held up one hand to shield her face from the intense heat.

"It's hopeless, sir, but she won't give up," Zach murmured.

Morgan sighed heavily and threw his bucket into the trough. Lacey was running toward him, completely oblivious to his presence, and he hurried toward her.

Grabbing her arm when she would have run past him, he said, "Give it up, Lacey. It's gone."

"Let me go!" she shrieked, not even realizing that it was Morgan who had taken hold of her.

"*It's too late!*" he yelled back, wrenching the bucket from her hand and tossing it aside. He grabbed both her shoulders and forced her to look at him. "It's gone, Lacey," he said more gently this time. "There's nothing you can do about it."

"*I know!*" she cried, struggling against him. And then she stopped struggling and raised her dazed, soot-stained face to his. In the golden, dancing light of the fire, he saw the glistening trail of tears that cut sharp paths down her cheeks.

"Morgan? Oh, Morgan, I lost it," she sobbed. "It's gone." As though Morgan's arrival had released the flood of emotions she'd been holding in check, Lacey's tears became one huge, wrenching sob, and she crumpled to her knees. Morgan caught her, easing her descent, then knelt beside her and pulled her to his chest. Leaning against him for support, she watched the fire as tears of loss and anguish streamed down her cheeks.

The heat was tremendous, but Lacey was shivering from shock and exhaustion. Morgan opened his coat and wrapped his arms around her waist so that they were both enfolded in the same warm garment as they watched the fire blaze out of control.

Lacey's grief was overwhelming, but Morgan held her because it was the only thing he knew to do. Around them, people were pointing and whispering, openly speculating about the intimate way the handsome gambler was holding the widow, but Lacey was oblivious to everything but the fire. Without consciously being aware of it, she drew strength from Morgan's presence. The feeling of safety his arms provided was an illusion, but wrapped in the warm cocoon of his coat, with his strength supporting her, Lacey felt free to let her grief run its course.

Morgan lost track of time as they knelt there, but eventually he saw a woman approach Zach with a coat. They spoke for a moment; then Zach pointed to Lacey, and the woman hurried over. Morgan decided that this must be Berta Kraus, Lacey's housekeeper. She was carrying the cape Lacey had worn yesterday.

"Lacey?" She knelt beside them, but it was several seconds before Lacey was able to focus on the voice and turn her head to Berta.

"He's gone, Berta," she said softly. "David's gone."

The housekeeper's startled gaze flitted to Morgan, then back to Lacey's soot-and tear-stained face. "*Liebling*, Mr. David has been gone tree years."

Lacey looked at the fire again and allowed her head to fall back against Morgan's shoulder. "No, not completely gone. Not until tonight," she whispered.

Morgan and Berta exchanged concerned looks, and Morgan reluctantly reached for the cloak Berta was holding. He placed it over Lacey's shoulders and gently took her by the arms. "Come on, Lacey. Let Mr. Freeman take you home. There's nothing more you can do here tonight."

As though she had lost the will to function on her own, Lacey allowed Morgan to pull her to her feet, but she never took her eyes off the fire. When he tried to urge her away, she held back.

"Lacey, stop torturing yourself," he commanded quietly.

"Yes, come home," Berta said. "I draw you nice hot bath."

"I can't," she said tearfully.

Forcefully Morgan took hold of her shoulders and turned her away from the fire. "Yes, you can. It's just a building! There's nothing here that can't be replaced," Morgan said sternly.

His words were so true that they cut through Lacey's lethargy, allowing anger to surface. Perhaps it was only that she needed a target for her rage, or perhaps it had to do with the guilt she felt because she had betrayed David's memory by caring too much for this man. Whatever the reason, all of Lacey's fury suddenly coalesced and was directed at Morgan.

"What would you know about what I've lost tonight?" she demanded, pulling away from him violently. "When has anything ever meant more to you than a deck of cards or an easy dollar? When have you ever stayed in one place long enough to build something? Or to love someone? When, Morgan?"

A shadow of pain flickered across his face. "A long time ago, Lacey," he said softly. "It's been a very long time."

Lacey saw his pain and was instantly remorseful. "I'm sorry. I shouldn't have said that."

"Why not? I deserved it."

"No. You didn't. You've been nothing but kind to me, and I shouldn't have lashed out like that."

Morgan gave her a wistful smile. "You've had a hard night. You're entitled to vent your anger."

Lacey shook her head a little and turned toward her office just as a portion of the roof caved in. Tiny burning embers flew up and filled the sky like a thousand golden stars. Lacey flinched as another section fell in, but her tears seemed to have run their course for the time being. She watched in numb silence as a dozen men armed with long poles formed a ring around the building and began pushing on the flaming walls so that they would fall inside rather than out. Slowly, one by one, the walls folded like a house of cards, and the flaming rubble was no longer recognizable as the building David Spencer had been so proud of.

Lacey drew her shoulders back and turned to Berta. "Let's go home."

The housekeeper placed one arm around Lacey and glanced at Morgan. "You will come with us, Mr. Morgan, *ja*?"

Protectiveness made Morgan want to accompany Lacey home, but he wasn't sure how she felt about it until Lacey turned to him.

"You're welcome to come, Morgan. Berta will fix us a pot of nice strong coffee. . . . " Her voice trailed off as she became uncertain whether she was doing the right thing or not. Morgan had made it clear he wanted nothing to do with her, and pressing the bounds of his friendship could prove embarrassing for both of them. Yet tonight he had treated her with kindness and concern. He had folded her in his arms and tried to ease the deathly cold that had pervaded her soul. His words didn't match his actions, but Lacey was too emotionally exhausted to try to make sense of his inconsistent behavior. All she knew for sure was that she didn't want to be alone tonight.

Morgan's protective feelings warred with his determination to keep Lacey at arm's length. He wanted to be with her. He wanted to comfort her through what he knew instinctively was going to be one of the longest nights of her life. But he also wanted things from Lacey she couldn't possibly give him, and he couldn't possibly take. Ultimately, the sense of duty he felt to his mission in Willow Springs won out over the intense, tangled emotions he felt for Lacey.

"I think I'll pass, Lacey. You should get some rest tonight," he finally told her. The disappointment she couldn't hide cut at Morgan like a knife.

Lacey stiffened her jaw against a fresh flood of tears. His rejection shouldn't have hurt so much, but it did. "Fine," she said with a little nod. "Thank you for trying to help." Gently, she pulled away from Berta, telling her, "I want to see Sheriff Watson before we go."

"I believe I saw him go into the alley a moment ago," Zach said. "I'll tell him you'd like to talk to him."

"No, Zach. I'll find him." Lacey headed toward the alley, sidestepping the thinning crowd of gawkers. The hook and ladder truck had long since run dry and had returned to the station to be refilled, and the water trough was virtually empty. Still, there had been enough water to douse Dr. Touchstone's office and prevent a second catastrophe.

"Ben? Ben Watson?" Lacey called just as the sheriff emerged from the alley. The smoke was intense and the fire still burned so hotly that Lacey stopped well away from the blaze and waited for Ben to come to her. As she watched him approach, she noticed that he was carrying a kerosene can in either hand.

"I found these in the alley, Miz Spencer," he told her with apparent reluctance. "I'm real sorry."

"Why? You never thought for a moment this was an accident, did you?"

Watson shifted uncomfortably. "No, ma'am, I guess I didn't. But that don't mean—"

Lacey held up one hand to cut him off. "I know. That doesn't mean you can prove who set it. Or who *ordered* it to be set."

"No, ma'am, I can't."

"There were three men," she told him.

"You saw 'em?" he asked, surprised.

Lacey shook her head. "Only in silhouette. I was looking down at the office from one of the windows in my house."

"Keeping watch?"

She shrugged. "I've been expecting—"

"Well, Sheriff, looks like we've had a little accident here!" C. W. Rawlings's booming voice made Lacey shudder. He approached from behind her, and Lacey dug her fingernails into her palms to fight back her instantaneous rage.

"It was no accident, C. W.," Ben said, holding the kerosene cans up to him.

"You don't say!" Rawlings planted himself right beside Lacey and looked down at her with mock pity. "That's a real shame, Miz Spencer. Ben, I expect you to do everything you possibly can to find out who would do something like this."

Watson gritted his teeth. He knew Allyce Spencer would never believe it, but he hated C. W. Rawlings almost as much as she did. "Yes, sir, I will," he replied tersely.

Rawlings nodded thoughtfully. "Probably a couple of kids just trying to have a little fun."

"Oh, stop it, C. W.!" Lacey spat, turning the full force of her anger on him. "Everyone here knows who did this!"

Rawlings's craggy eyebrows went up in surprise. "Why, Mrs. Spencer, that sounds mighty like an accusation. Are you saying I set this fire?"

Lacey glared at him. "If you didn't, you know who did."

C. W. laughed. "Sheriff, I've got a dozen witnesses who'll be happy to tell you I spent the last two hours in the Cattleman's Hotel, playing cards." He looked at Lacey archly. "If you don't believe me, why don't you ask your friend Morgan, over there? He's got about three hundred dollars of my money in his pocket."

Morgan had been about to return to the hotel, but when he saw C. W. arrive, his protective instincts had finally won out and he'd edged a little closer to Lacey, as had Berta and Zach.

"Is that a fact, Morgan?" Watson asked. "Was Rawlings with you at the Cattleman's?"

Though it sickened him that C. W. wanted to use him for an alibi, Morgan couldn't lie. There were too many others who could vouch for him, too. "Yes, Sheriff, we were playing cards right up until the fire alarm sounded," he answered. Then before his better judgment had time to win out, he added, "Rawlings and his man Croft were both there . . . and they were both checking their watches every few minutes. It appeared to me as though they were waiting for something to happen."

C. W. gave him a hard look, but his tone was genial when he said, "I was waiting on your luck to run out, Morgan. And it just may have."

"The sheriff asked for the truth; I told it to him," he replied with a complete lack of concern.

"This is pointless!" Lacey snapped. "I may never be able to prove it, but I know who set this fire."

She looked Rawlings straight in the eye, and he laughed. "Mrs. Spencer, unless you got some proof to back you up, I'd suggest keeping your opinions to yourself. You've done a good job of skirting a lawsuit for libel these last few months. You wouldn't want to risk a slander charge, would you?"

"I'll risk that and a great deal more before this is finished, C. W."

Rawlings lowered his voice dangerously. "I'd say that as of tonight this already *is* finished, ma'am. Why don't you just pack your belongings and trot along home to your pappy in Washington before somebody gets hurt? You got nothing left to keep you in Willow Springs."

Lacey wanted more than anything to tell C. W. that she was never giving up, but arguing was pointless, and anything she said would only give him more reason to watch her every move. It was better, at least for the moment, to let him think he'd won.

Letting her shoulders sag just a little, she looked at the glowing remains of her office. "That's probably the only truth that has ever come out of your mouth, C. W.," she said quietly, then turned away.

Morgan listened to the exchange, but all the time he was watching Croft, who was standing just behind C. W. Until now the gunslinger had feigned a total lack of interest in the conversation, but when Lacey indicated that she just might leave Willow Springs as Rawlings suggested, Croft perked up considerably. He looked at Lacey with something like regret, and then a little self-satisfied smile danced on his lips as though he'd made a decision that pleased him tremendously.

In that instant Morgan knew the danger to Lacey had not fully passed tonight. Croft had plans of his own for her that had absolutely nothing to do with his employer's scheme to run her out of town, and he wasn't about to let her escape before he'd had a chance to take what he wanted from her.

The spectators had shifted their attention from the dying fire to the infinitely more interesting confrontation between the widow and Rawlings. They were clumped in a semicircle a short distance away, and when Lacey turned away from C. W. and saw all the fine upstanding townsfolk who had stood like sheep without lifting a finger to help save her office, her anger surged again.

Fighting the anger, trying to salvage some vestige of pride, she marched past them with Berta and Zach flanking her. Granville Taylor, who'd made the mistake of trying to offer sympathy earlier, erred again. He stepped in front of her, blocking her retreat, and told her very quietly, "We're real sorry, Miz Spencer. Things like this shouldn't happen in a nice town like Willow Springs."

Lacey's hold on her anger slipped, and she retorted, "Things like this will keep happening in Willow Springs as long as all of you kowtow to the likes of C. W. Rawlings!"

"Miz Spencer—"

"You think I'm the only one who's been burned out here tonight?" she asked incredulously, raising her voice so that everyone could hear her. "No, it's you, Mr. Taylor . . . and you, Mr. McAdams! And all the rest of you who won't stand up and fight! For months the Willow Springs *Gazette* has been the only thing standing between you and that monster! And now that the *Gazette* is gone, there's no one left to fight C. W.

Rawlings. He's turned you into complacent cattle, and now he's going to herd you to the slaughterhouse!"

For a moment the only sound was the crackling of the fire that silhouetted Lacey as she stormed away. Morgan hurried to catch up with her, but she stopped when someone at the back of the crowd yelled, "Go home, lady! Go home to Washington."

"Yeah, we don't want you here!" someone else shouted.

Another voice joined that one, and a low rumble swept through the crowd. Like a lioness protecting her cub, Berta Kraus whirled angrily on them, shouting, "Stop that. Stop at once! What she has done, she did for you! For all decent people!"

"You go home, too," the first voice yelled.

"*Scher dich zum Teufel!*" Berta screamed at them, and Lacey grabbed at her arm to pull her away as more voices were raised.

"Stop it, Berta. Let's go home," Lacey commanded, fighting tears. The blatant disapproval was more indignity than she could bear. She loved this town. She cared about the people. That they could turn on her so cruelly was more painful than she could possibly have imagined, but she squared her shoulders and refused to give in to tears. Leading Berta, she hurried past the crowd.

Behind them, Ben Watson tried to calm everyone. "All right, break it up! Go on back to your nice warm houses!" He shouted a few instructions to his volunteer firemen, ordering them to wait for the hook and ladder to return so that they could put the fire out completely before abandoning it for the night.

Morgan stayed behind, looking out over the slowly unraveling knot of people, and Ben moved toward him. "You better go home, too," he advised, keeping one eye on Croft and Rawlings as they sauntered away with the rest of the crowd. "C. W. ain't gonna like it that you made out he was waitin' on this fire to start."

Morgan gave Ben a hard look. "But you know it's true."

Watson glanced around uncomfortably. " 'Course I know. The whole damned town knows it."

"Do you also know that it was one of Rawlings's men who tried to turn the crowd into a mob?"

Ben nodded. "Yeah, it was just Stowe and Axtell stirrin' up trouble. There's not many in town except C. W.'s men who'd speak out bad against Miz Spencer. Everbody feels real sorry for her."

Morgan gritted his teeth. "I don't think it's your pity that she wants, Sheriff," he said tightly, then stalked away. He'd been prepared to warn the sheriff that Croft was going to make a move on Lacey soon—possibly tonight—but Watson couldn't be counted on to protect Lacey from a hangnail, let alone a hired killer.

There was only one person in Willow Springs who might be good enough to go against Croft, and he was already striding up the hill to Lacey's house.

Chapter Eleven

"Out of those wet clothes, immediately! Both of you!" Berta ordered as Zach bolted the front door. The housekeeper hadn't calmed down much since she told her fellow townsfolk to go to blazes, but now she was expending her pent-up energy in doing what she did best—mothering Lacey and Zach.

She shooed the exhausted printer toward his room at the back of the house, but Lacey needed no prodding. She was unbelievably weary, both in body and in spirit. Her clothes were soaked with the water that had sloshed from the bucket on each useless trip she had made from the water trough to her office. Trudging upstairs, she wondered if she would ever be able to wash away the acrid stench of smoke from her skin and hair.

She had just reached the first landing when someone knocked on the front door. She and Berta whirled toward the door and froze, but Zach came hurrying back to the vestibule. He looked up at Lacey, silently asking if he should answer the summons, and she nodded.

What next? she wondered forlornly. How much more could she be expected to endure in one night?

Zach moved across the vestibule and carefully drew aside one of the curtains that draped the long, beveled windows flanking the heavy mahogany door. Somewhat surprised, he turned to Lacey and announced, "It's Mr. Morgan."

Lacey's first reaction was relief, but confusion followed almost immediately. Why on earth had he rejected her invitation, only to change his mind minutes later? What game was he trying to play with her emotions? "Let him in, Zach."

He nodded and unbolted the door. "Mr. Morgan," he greeted noncommittally. Like Lacey, Zach was confused by Morgan's on-again, off-again friendship.

Morgan recognized a cool greeting when he received one. "Mr. Freeman, I'm sorry to intrude, but"—he paused for the merest second, wondering what excuse he was going to give for his change of mind—"I wanted to make certain Mrs. Spencer was all right, and there is something I feel she should know."

"Please come in," Zach invited, stepping aside so that Morgan could enter.

"What is it you think I should know?" Lacey asked, drawing Morgan's attention to her for the first time.

He looked up and saw her clutching the balustrade for support, as though her legs alone weren't sufficient to hold her up. Her dressing gown was a wretched mess, torn, soiled, and wet; her face was smudged and streaked with soot, and her hair was a wild mass of knots and tangles. Morgan had often wondered what her honey-colored tresses would look like if she ever released them from the well-styled buns and upswept curls he had seen her wear. He had wondered what it would feel like to touch it, to wrap it around his hand and bury his face in it. The way her hair looked now hardly fit the fantasy he had built around the sight and feel of it, but unkempt as it was, Morgan found he wanted to touch it no less.

Pulling himself away from that distracting thought, Morgan came to the foot of the stairs. "Actually, there are two things we need to discuss—"

"And dese things can wait until she has changed clothes, *ja*?" Berta interrupted, giving Morgan a look that brooked no disagreement.

"Certainly," he answered.

"Goot. Zachary vill show you to the parlor, and I bring coffee soon."

Berta was trying to shoo her up the stairs, but Lacey resisted, searching Morgan's face for some clue as to what he might want to talk to her about. "Are you certain that waiting isn't inconvenient, Morgan?"

"Positive. You take your time. I'm not going anywhere," he assured her.

"All right." She gestured toward the parlor. "I believe the logs are already laid in the fireplace. Zach, would you take care of that, please? I'll be down in a few minutes."

She went upstairs with Berta, and Zach threw open the doors to a spacious sitting room. From the door, Morgan watched as Zach lit the lamps that sat on delicate tables at either end of a long sofa. As the shadows slowly vanished, Morgan discovered a room that was tastefully elegant without being fussy. A woman's hand was evident in the decor, yet the furniture was substantial enough to make a man feel welcome to sit with ease. There were touches of lace at the bay window overlooking the front lawn, and needlepoint pillows adorned the sofa that faced the fireplace. Comfortable-looking armchairs flanked the fireplace, and there were framed photographs on the spinet and on the writing desk that took up one whole corner.

The room was well suited to its elegant, sophisticated owner, Morgan decided as he stepped to the bay window and found that he could see the commotion that still lingered on the street below. Another lamp was lit, and he turned to find that Zach had finally moved on to the fireplace.

For the first time, Morgan was struck by Zachary's frailty. When he'd met him only a week ago, the printer had seemed almost ageless. Not robust, certainly, but hale and hearty, at least.

Tonight he looked a hundred years old. Morgan wondered how long it had been since Lacey had looked at Zachary intently enough to realize the toll her vendetta was taking on him. "Mr. Freeman, I'd be happy to see to that fire, if you'd like. You must be anxious to get out of those wet clothes and to rest for a bit."

Zach paused, uncertain what to do. "I am, sir, but—"

"But you don't know whether you trust me enough to leave me alone in Mrs. Spencer's parlor?" Morgan guessed.

"It's not a matter of trust, sir."

"Then what?" Morgan asked gently as he removed his coat and placed it across the back of the sofa. "You know, Mr. Freeman, you and I have never exchanged more than a few words, but I am convinced you know that I share your concern for Mrs. Spencer's welfare. Please feel free to say whatever is on your mind."

Zach nodded, then bent to the task of lighting the fire. "I must admit I am confused, sir."

"About?"

"About your contradictory behavior." The kindling in the grate began crackling and Zach stood. "Or rather, the contradiction between your words and your behavior. The *Gazette* office is—*was*"—he corrected—"small. I could not help hearing parts of your conversation with Mrs. Spencer last week, at which time you announced your intention to pay her court. Then, for reasons Lacey will not discuss, you apparently changed your mind."

"Those reasons are a private matter between Lacey and me," Morgan told him uncomfortably, not knowing what else to say.

"To be sure," Zach agreed. "And yet you continue to involve yourself in our lives—the help you tried to give us at the train station, your timely intervention between Lacey and Croft on the street yesterday, and then tonight . . . " He cocked his head to one side curiously. "I have no doubt, sir, that had there been the slightest possibility of saving the office, you would have done everything in your power to do so. And when you saw that there was no hope, you reasoned with Lacey and tried to comfort her. These are not the actions of a man who had no . . . feelings for a woman."

"Zach, I never said I didn't have feelings for Lacey," Morgan explained. "But this is not a good time for either of us to think about courting."

"Obviously your reason has nothing to do with Lacey's current . . . difficulties. If you were intimidated by C. W. Rawlings, you would not be so quick to come to her defense."

"No, Rawlings doesn't intimidate me."

Zach raised one deeply arched brow. "Do you think, perhaps, that he should?"

Morgan laughed. "Are you insinuating that I'm reckless?"

"I insinuate nothing, sir. I am only trying to understand why you say one thing concerning my dear friend and do something quite different. Earlier, when you were invited to be part of our family circle on this very difficult night, you refused. Yet now, here you are. If *I* am perplexed, I can only imagine how confused Lacey must be."

"And you don't want to see her hurt."

"Definitely not, sir."

"Then, Zach, I will have to ask you to trust me when I tell you that our ends are not dissimilar. I don't want to see Lacey hurt, either. That's one of the reasons I'm here tonight."

Zach had been talking about emotional wounds, but he had the feeling Morgan was talking about a more immediate physical danger. Frowning, he said, "If you are referring to a personal matter between yourself and Lacey, I will gladly retire and apologize for having spoken so bluntly on matters that do not concern me. However, if you are suggesting that there may be an additional threat from Mr. Rawlings tonight, I would appreciate knowing about it."

Morgan nodded. "I think you should know, Mr. Freeman." Quickly he outlined the conclusions he'd come to about Croft.

Zach's concern was obvious. "Then you think he might perpetrate some . . . attack on Lacey tonight?"

"It's possible."

"I see." The fire was burning adequately to warm the room, and Zach replaced the fire screen before hurrying toward the door. "In that case, I had best prepare myself for a long night."

"I think you should get some rest," Morgan advised, moving around the sofa to meet him at the door. "If Lacey will permit it, I'm going to spend the night here." He gestured toward the large bay window that overlooked the front lawn. "From that window, I can see anyone who approaches the house. Unfortunately, my guns are back in my hotel room," he murmured as an afterthought. "Is your Winchester the only weapon in the house?"

Zach glanced at the door, and Morgan thought he saw a little guilt in the nervous gesture. "No, sir," he said quietly. "I have a revolver as well, but Lacey is not aware of its existence, and I would like to keep it that way unless there is an emergency."

Morgan frowned. "Why all the secrecy over a handgun?"

"Lacey has not permitted guns of any sort in the house since her husband's death. When the trouble with Mr. Rawlings started, I finally persuaded her to allow me to purchase the Winchester, but when I suggested it would be wise for me to have a revolver as well, she flatly refused."

"But you bought one anyway."

"Yes, sir. On the theory that what she doesn't know may save her life."

"All right," Morgan said with a grin. "You keep the revolver with you tonight, and I'll use the Winchester, if you have no objections."

"None at all." He rose and headed for the hall. "I'll bring it to you immediately, sir."

When Zach disappeared, Morgan returned to the bay window and peered out into the dark night. He pulled the curtain back, making no effort to hide himself. If Croft was outside, he'd think twice before coming in once he knew Morgan was there. The arrogant gunslinger might be confident he could overcome Zach and Berta in order to get to Lacey, but Morgan's presence shifted the odds too much to make it worth the risk. At least, that was the theory Morgan was counting on. He didn't want to fight Croft tonight; he just wanted to quietly warn him off.

When Zach returned with the Winchester, Morgan placed the rifle against the wall, half hidden by the draperies but within easy reach. He suggested that Zach check the house over carefully to make certain all the windows and doors were secure, but once that task was finished, Zach finally took a moment to wash up and change clothes before returning to the parlor with a silver tray bearing a crystal decanter of whiskey and two glasses.

"Would you care for a drink, Mr. Morgan?" he asked formally, placing the tray on a slender table that stood against the wall next to the bay window.

"Only if you'll join me, and agree to drop the 'mister' from my name. It's just Morgan."

"Very well . . . Morgan." He poured two glasses and handed one to the complicated man who continued to confound him. Morgan invited him to share the window seat, and Zach sighed with the simple pleasure of getting off his feet.

Morgan sipped the excellent whiskey. "Mr. Freeman, would I be committing a breach of etiquette if I asked you to tell me about Lacey?"

"You must continue to call me Zachary, or Zach, if you like," he replied. "And as for Lacey, my answers would depend on the nature of your questions. What exactly would you like to know?" he asked, fully expecting Morgan to inquire about Lacey's late husband.

He was surprised, then, when Morgan asked, "What was she like as a child? Have you known her that long?"

"Indeed I have. Lacey was but five when I joined her father's household staff as valet."

"What was she like?"

Zach smiled fondly as he searched for the pleasant memories of Lacey's childhood. "She was like sunshine. Bright and beautiful. She was also mischievous and full of fun. We never quite knew what to expect from her next, but we always knew it would be something to make us laugh or to ease a burden. . . . She was kind and gentle and generous to a fault." He looked at Morgan intently. "Extraordinary qualities, which she still possesses today."

Morgan smiled. "You left out proud, stubborn, and high-principled."

"Only because those qualities seem so obvious." He rose and moved to the fireplace to stir the logs.

"Morgan?" Lacey said softly as she came into the parlor. "I'm sorry I kept you so long."

Automatically, Morgan stood, but it took a moment for him to find his voice. Lacey looked so stunning that she took his breath away. She had bathed and washed her hair, then donned a simple silk garment that flowed around her, concealing more than it revealed with its high collar, long, loose sleeves, and abundance of enveloping silk. Her hair was bound in a turban that matched the subtle print of her gown, but a few damp tendrils escaped down the back and on her forehead. Her costume was utterly feminine and completely modest, yet she still managed to be the most beautiful, arousing woman Morgan had ever seen.

Clearing his throat, he finally found his voice. "You look lovely . . . very exotic, in fact. I don't think I've ever seen a gown quite like that."

Uncomfortable with the compliment, Lacey glanced down at herself. "It's called a caftan. Father sent it to me after he visited the Turkish empire."

"It's lovely."

"Thank you." She tugged self-consciously at her turban.

"Please forgive me for coming down like this, but I thought I might dry my hair by the fire here in the parlor rather than keep you waiting any longer. It's hardly decorous, but the social amenities don't seem to mean much tonight."

Morgan gave her an encouraging smile and gestured toward the fireplace. "By all means, dry your hair by the fire. I would enjoy watching you."

It was such an intimate comment that Lacey did not know how to reply. Instead, she looked at Zach, who was still busying himself with the fire. "Thank you for seeing to our guest, Zach."

"It was no trouble, but if you'll excuse me now, I believe I'll retire."

"Of course." When he moved toward the door, Lacey stepped into his path and put her arms around him. "Thank you for all you did tonight, Zach. I love you," she whispered fiercely, fighting back the tears she'd managed to keep at bay all during her bath.

Gently, Zach kissed her forehead, bade Morgan good night, and left. The room was suddenly filled with a tense silence. To compensate, Lacey took several cushions from the sofa and arranged them before the hearth, then sat and began unwinding her turban. "Won't you join me?" she invited. "It's much warmer here than by the window."

After one last quick glance into the darkness, Morgan crossed to the sofa and eased onto it so that Lacey was between him and the fire. The warm glow silhouetted her, and Morgan wondered how long he could watch her sitting there, soft and vulnerable, before he found it an absolute necessity to touch her.

"Berta is bringing coffee," Lacey told him, vividly aware that Morgan was watching her every move. It both thrilled and frightened her, but tonight she was too drained to deal with either emotion, so she tried to ignore them. "I also asked her to bring some warm cocoa. You may have either"—a thought occurred to her—"unless you'd rather have something stronger, of course. We have some fine scotch left over from my father's last visit."

Morgan gestured toward the slender table. "Zach has already taken care of that, but actually, warm cocoa sounds delicious," he said with a fond smile. "I haven't had any in years. Does Mrs. Kraus serve it with a dollop of sweet whipping cream?"

Lacey nodded. "Topped with shavings of Swiss chocolate."

Morgan closed his eyes in sweet anticipation. "I think I may have died and gone to heaven."

"At least wait until you've tasted it," Lacey said with a grin, then sobered when she remembered that Morgan's visit was not a social call. Glancing away from him, she gathered her damp, tangled hair, pulled it over one shoulder, and began applying a stiff-bristled brush to the ends. "Exactly what was it you wanted to discuss with me, Morgan?"

He hesitated only a moment. "I saw how the crowd's reaction hurt you earlier."

"Yes, it did," she said without looking at him, "though I really have only myself to blame. I shouldn't have called them complacent cattle and expected them to be happy about it."

"You said nothing wrong, Lacey, and considering the circumstances, I don't think anyone holds your speech against you."

She twisted and gave him a skeptical look. "Then why did they turn into a vicious mob and order me out of town?"

"Lacey, that was Rawlings's men, not your neighbors. When it looked as though the crowd had turned ugly, I watched them carefully. Two or three men at the back were doing all the shouting. After you left, I spoke to Sheriff Watson, and he agreed with me."

"Really?" she asked hopefully, feeling a little knot of pain uncurl within her. There was still plenty of pain left to be dealt with, but knowing that her friends hadn't turned against her completely would make what she had suffered tonight easier to accept. "Are you sure?"

"I'm positive of it, Lacey," Morgan assured her, pleased that he could ease some of the torment she was so obviously experiencing. It showed in her eyes, which where flat and lifeless, where once they had danced with wit and vitality. It hurt him to see her so subdued, and he would have given anything, done anything, to return the warmth to her eyes.

"According to Watson," he continued, "a man named Stowe was the one trying to stir up the crowd, but the townspeople weren't going along with him. Frankly, from what I've learned in Willow Springs this last week, I don't think that any right-thinking person in town would speak out against you. These people respect you, Lacey," he told her seriously, remembering the reverence Darlene had shown for her. And there were others he'd talked to, too. "Everyone admires you for going up against Rawlings."

"But they won't fight him," she said sadly. "And they won't stand by me while I do."

"Not in ways you can see, no, but in their own manner they do what they can." He grinned mischievously, and Lacey felt a little tug in the vicinity of her heart that had nothing to do with pain. "Did you know that everyone in town reads the *Gazette*?" he said. "The proprietors of the establishments where you leave copies manage to hide one or two away before Rawlings's men get to them. Those copies are passed around in secret, hoarded like treasure. It's their small way of defying C. W. and supporting you."

The image of her friends squirreling away copies of the paper pleased Lacey. "It's nice to know my journalistic efforts aren't entirely in vain. Thank you, Morgan. I feel a little better knowing that I won't be tarred and feathered. It was kind of you to worry about my feelings, but you really shouldn't."

"I do worry about you, Lacey," he told her seriously, and Lacey shook her head.

"I find that so difficult to understand."

"Zach expressed the same confusion earlier."

Lacey was surprised. "He spoke to you about . . . us?"

"Yes."

She frowned. "He shouldn't have done that. I've tried to explain to him and Berta that you . . . well, that you changed your mind about . . . seeing me. Zach had no right to question your reasons."

"He feels responsible for you, and he loves you very much."

Lacey looked into the fire. "I know."

A small silence fell over them, and Morgan felt the need to change the direction of their conversation. "Zach told me he's been with you since you were a child."

Lacey drew back from the fire, and from the questions she knew she could never bring herself to ask Morgan—questions like why he was so concerned about her and yet so determined to keep her at arm's length. More and more she was coming to believe that his aloofness had nothing to do with the way she had kissed him so wantonly. Even now, as they conversed quietly, Morgan was looking at her as though he wanted nothing in the world so much as to take her into his arms and make love to her. Disgust did not engender the kind of wanting she saw in Morgan's eyes . . . nor did it lead to the kind of regret she also saw reflected there.

But she'd suffered too many wounds tonight to be able to bear the humiliation of questioning Morgan's feelings for her. Better to accept the simple fact that he was here out of concern for her, and take comfort from his presence. And what enormous comfort it was.

"Yes, Zach came to live with us shortly before the outbreak of the war," she told him, turning her back on the fire. Her hair was free of tangles now, and she spread it over her shoulders like a cape, letting the warmth of the fire dry it. "I don't remember a time when Zach wasn't an important part of my life."

"He says you were a beautiful child."

Lacey laughed lightly. "Yes, I was, and believe me, I knew it and milked it for all it was worth. I was incorrigible," she said just as Berta entered with an enormous tea tray. "Oh, Berta, let me help you with that." She jumped up and took the tray.

Morgan turned on the sofa. "Mrs. Kraus, Lacey has been telling me she was an incorrigible child. Is that true?"

"*Ja*, is true," the housekeeper confirmed as she moved a low table to the front of the sofa. "She was spoiled rotten when I come to take over the house."

Lacey placed the tray on the table and gave Morgan an 'I told you so' grin. Berta began rearranging the tray so that she could pour, but Lacey stopped her. "I'll do that, Berta. Why don't you go on to bed?"

Berta started to argue, but when she glanced from Lacey to Morgan, she changed her mind. The last thing these two needed was the intrusion of an old woman. She bade them good night, then left quietly, sliding the parlor doors shut behind her.

Lacey knelt by the table and poured two cups of cocoa from the smaller of the two silver urns on the tray. As she spooned whipping cream and chocolate shavings on top, Morgan told her, "I still don't believe it."

"Believe what?"

"That you were incorrigible. Zach says quite the opposite."

Lacey handed him a cup and saucer. "That's because Zach came to know me when I was younger. When I was five, I was stunningly beautiful and quite precocious. I had only to smile and everyone jumped to do my bidding," she said with a mischievous grin as she took her cup and leaned back against the sofa. "By the time Berta came on the scene, I already had everyone else in the house wrapped around my little finger."

"But Berta didn't wrap too easily?" Morgan guessed, thoroughly enjoying seeing Lacey like this, smiling and at ease.

"Indeed she didn't!" Lacey laughed and tucked her legs beneath her. "You see, I had just turned twelve when Father hired her. Berta hardly spoke any English, and she was quite the most intimidating creature I'd ever encountered. But all my life I'd been charming people effortlessly, and I figured it would only be a matter of time before Berta fell under my spell, too. So I smiled at her a great deal—but she never smiled back. I played innocent pranks on her of the sort that always delighted the rest of the staff, but she was never amused!"

She shook her head ruefully. "I was quite beside myself. And then one day I took a long, hard look in a mirror and realized the source of the problem."

She sipped her cocoa, and Morgan prompted, "Which was . . . ?"

"I was no longer beautiful."

Morgan laughed. "Be serious."

"I am!" she exclaimed. "I was no longer an adorable, stunningly lovely child. I was twelve, remember? And I had shot up like a bean pole. My legs were too long, and my feet were so big that I constantly tripped over them. My hair had turned from the color of corn silk to a dismal shade of ditch water. None of my features fit my face. Overnight, it seemed, I had gone from a beautiful swan to an ugly duckling!"

Morgan chuckled. "That must have been a rude awakening."

"Oh, it was," she said, laughing, too. "I was utterly devastated. My confidence was shattered, and I was convinced that no one ever again would love me."

"A ridiculous conclusion if ever I've heard one."

"Of course it was," Lacey agreed, thoroughly enjoying herself. "But I didn't know it at the time, and I came to detest Berta with a passion, because she was a constant reminder of my fall from grace. I was beastly to her—imperious and argumentative. Open warfare was declared between us, and for months our house was a battlefield. Father was quite beside himself. I demanded that he discharge her, and when he refused I became convinced that he no longer loved me."

"How did the war with Berta end?"

Lacey sipped her cocoa and smiled at her fond memories. It was much the same look Zach had worn when he spoke of the past, and Morgan realized what a warm and loving household Lacey must have grown up in. His own home had been much the same, and suddenly he missed the gracious old plantation where he had spent many nights like this one, curled up by a warm fire, listening to stories of his mother's youth, his uncle's exploits in the foreign service, and his grandfather's tales of growing up in the English countryside.

Desperately Morgan wished that he could share those stories as Lacey was sharing herself with him, but giving her part of his past was something he could never do. The danger was too great, so he simply sat back and listened with pleasure as she continued.

"My war with Berta ended on my thirteenth birthday," she told him. "I had dreaded the day horribly, because it meant I would be another year older, growing uglier by the minute. I took great pains not to breathe a word about my birthday to anyone, praying they would all forget, but knowing all the while that my father would plan a celebration, as he always did."

"And did he?" Morgan asked, unable to bear the distance between them any longer. He slid off the sofa and joined her on the floor. She turned to him as though drawn by a magnet, and they sat facing each other, knees almost but not quite touching, like children sharing secrets.

"No, he didn't!" she exclaimed. "My birthday came, and not one word was said about it. Father went off to work with his usual good-bye kiss on my brow, and all day I waited for someone to bid me many happy returns of the day, but nothing happened. No special cooking was done, no decorations were put up, no secret looks were exchanged between members of the staff to indicate that a surprise was in the offing. My birthday had been completely forgotten, and I was utterly crushed! Here again was proof positive that I was unloved!"

Morgan chuckled merrily as she continued, "All day I clung to the hope that Father would come home and fire the whole staff because they had forgotten to prepare the house for the hundred guests who were coming to celebrate my birthday. I savored all the deliciously cruel things he would say and do to them. I planned how I would gloat over their misery."

"And then?" Morgan said with a laugh.

Lacey rolled her eyes to the heavens. "And then Father came home and I flew to the bottom of the stairs to greet him, waiting for my birthday kiss, but he said not one word! He greeted me absentmindedly and muttered something about having work to do in his study. I stood there, absolutely devastated, and the moment he was out of sight I burst into tears and ran blindly to the kitchen, straight into the arms of Berta Kraus. I sobbed out my sad tale of being thirteen, ugly, and unloved, and Berta comforted me in her broken English, telling me I would one day be beautiful again and that I would always be loved.

"I didn't believe her, of course . . . until she took me upstairs and showed me the surprise that everyone had conspired to keep hidden from me."

"Which was?"

"My first grown-up party gown," she answered, her eyes misting at the memory. "It was the most beautiful gown I had ever seen, rose-colored satin and yards of lace. Berta demanded that I try it on, and then she fixed my hair into an elegant, very grown-up style, and when she was finished she took me downstairs where my father was waiting in his best formal evening suit. He whisked me outside to a waiting carriage and we dined at the Four Horsemen, the most elegant restaurant in Washington. It was the best birthday of my life," she said with a nostalgic sigh.

"And after that, you and Berta became friends?"

Lacey nodded. "Close friends. She saw me through the next few awkward years with her own special brand of love—an uncompromising blend of wisdom and intolerance of my foolish self-pity. I learned a lot from Berta," she said wistfully.

"You're very lucky to have been surrounded by so much love," Morgan said, resisting the urge to touch one of the long strands of hair that curled around Lacey's shoulders like a silken cape. He grinned mischievously, making Lacey's heart turn over. "But I still don't believe you were ever incorrigible—or ugly."

"Then I shall just have to prove it to you," she said. Rising swiftly, she moved to her desk and returned with a cloth-bound album of photographs. "Here, look at this." She leafed through the pages as she sat next to him again. Finally she found an appropriate photograph.

Morgan accepted the book and studied the picture she indicated. The young girl was not the beauty Lacey was today, but she was far from ugly. She was gangly and clearly not at ease with herself, if the sour expression on her face was any indication, but Morgan could see the promise of beauty there.

"Now, contrast that with this one," she instructed, leaning close to him as she turned back the pages to a sepia-toned photograph.

The scent of roses clung to her hair, and Morgan found himself growing intoxicated. With difficulty, he focused on the picture of the most beautiful child he had ever seen, but his thoughts were all of Lacey. This was how her children would look, he thought. Sweet, beautiful, with layers of fair hair and eyes that could brighten a room with a single smile. In that instant Morgan realized that he wanted to see the lovely children Lacey would someday bear—and he wanted those children to be his.

Stunned by the thought, Morgan edged away slightly and began turning the pages of the album as he joked a little breathlessly, "I think you're stacking the deck on me, Lacey. Let me see the rest of these, and I'll make up my mind for myself."

"Be my guest," she invited easily, but she pulled away a little, because she had discovered that being too close to Morgan inhibited her breathing.

Starting at the front, he went through the album page by page, with Lacey narrating. The first picture was of the mother she hardly knew, but Lacey spoke of her with the great affection that had been instilled in her by Roland Smithfield. There were several photographs of Lacey with her father at various stages of their lives together. Everything was arranged sequentially, and Morgan could follow her progress from winsome child to awkward teen to breathtakingly beautiful young woman.

"This was taken at your wedding, wasn't it?" Morgan asked when he finally came to the last picture, which showed a radiantly beautiful Lacey and a tall, handsome gentleman in a cutaway coat with a boutonniere in the lapel.

"Yes," Lacey said, sadness edging her voice. "That's my late husband, David Spencer."

Morgan expected to feel a surge of jealousy for the man who had so obviously occupied all of Lacey's heart, but he found none. All he felt, instead, was a strange kind of pity. Because Lacey had loved him, David Spencer had had more to live for than most men could even imagine.

"How did you meet him?" he asked, needing to know everything there was to know about her.

Lacey reached back and touched the memories with love. Tonight of all nights, it felt right to think about David and remember. "We met thanks to Ulysses S. Grant."

Morgan looked at her in surprise. "Oh, really? I hadn't realized our former President was a matchmaker."

Lacey laughed. "Well, it was quite unintentional on his part, I assure you. David's family moved to Washington when his father, Dolph, was appointed to a post on the President's staff. David and I were both away at college—he in his second year at Harvard, and I in my first year at Oberlin." Morgan wasn't surprised to learn that Lacey had an extensive formal education, but he found himself a little intimidated by the company she had kept. He'd known her father was a powerful man, but he'd never stopped to imagine Lacey socializing with staff members and probably even Presidents.

"Anyway, I returned home from college that year and resumed my role as Father's hostess. The Spencers were among the thirty or so guests who attended our first party of the season, and that's when I met David."

"Did you fall in love with him instantly?" Morgan asked, imagining the scene as she described it.

"Oh, hardly," Lacey scoffed. "David was very attractive, but he was so stuffy and pompous and full of himself that I considered it my duty as a woman to deflate his overblown ego. He had opinions on everything, many of them contrary to my own, and we argued mercilessly all evening. Finally the arguing became so much fun that I began playing devil's advocate, arguing against my own principles just for the sheer pleasure of seeing David's ears turn red as he sputtered with indignation."

Lacey and Morgan both laughed. "You're right. You *were* incorrigible."

In her defense, Lacey exclaimed, "Oh, but it was his own fault." Smiling merrily, she recounted her first stormy meeting with the young, opinionated David Spencer and how their abrasive relationship had finally turned into love after he went to work at her father's newspaper. "I can't really point to the exact moment when things changed between us, but I think that change had mostly to do with David coming to respect my opinions and my right to have them. I was the most outspoken, outrageous woman he'd ever known, and eventually he came to love my stubborn independence."

"And what did you love about him?" Morgan asked softly.

"His goals and his ideals," Lacey answered promptly. "When all his youthful bluster was stripped away, we discovered that our opinions weren't so very different. We both wanted the same things from life—to own our own newspaper somewhere new and exciting. He was my very best friend in the entire world." Her eyes misted over, and she stared into the fire as though she might find David there. When she spoke again, her voice was soft and far away. "And I loved his gentleness, too. I think I miss that most of all," she whispered.

Morgan remembered the grief he'd seen in her eyes as she watched the dream she and David had shared burn to the ground. Unable to stop himself, he stroked her silky, rose-scented hair. "You didn't lose your husband tonight, Lacey," he told her gently. "As long as you have such beautiful memories of him, he'll never be completely lost to you."

Lacey turned to him, her eyes glistening with unshed tears. "You know what happened to him, don't you? Someone has told you how he was killed."

"Yes."

Lacey was relieved that he knew. Tonight of all nights she didn't think she could relive the tragedy. "Why, Morgan? Why do good, loving people have to die while men like C. W. Rawlings flourish and seem to live forever?"

Slowly Morgan pulled Lacey to him, cradling her head against his chest and stroking her hair as he'd longed to do all night. "I don't know, Lacey. I've asked myself that question a thousand times. Death doesn't distinguish between good and evil. It just takes what we love from us and gives nothing in return."

The desolation in his voice was something Lacey understood all too well. Raising her head from his shoulder, she captured his eyes and asked, "Who was she?"

Morgan stiffened. "She?"

"The woman you were in love with. Down on the street earlier you admitted that you knew what it was like to lose someone you loved."

"How do you know I was thinking of a woman?"

Lacey shrugged. "Something in your eyes and in your voice. Am I wrong?"

Morgan looked into the fire, uncomfortable with the direction they were headed. More than anything, he wanted to be as honest and open with Lacey as she had been with him, but he couldn't; the danger was too great. But he couldn't lie to her, either. "No, you're not wrong. There was someone a long, long time ago. She died of scarlet fever."

Lacey heard the hesitancy in his voice. "You don't want to talk about her, do you?"

"No."

"Because you're still in love with her?"

Morgan looked down into Lacey's crystal-blue eyes and felt himself becoming lost. "It's not that, Lacey. I just don't like talking about the past. It serves no purpose."

"You encouraged me to talk about my past," she pointed out, pulling away from him.

"I wanted to know everything about you, so that I could understand why you are the way you are now. Strong and independent—"

"And I want to know about you, Morgan," she interrupted. "I want to know why a man with breeding and education became a gambler. I want to know why someone with your courage and sense of honor has no roots and uses only one name. I want to know what you're hiding, Morgan, or what you're running from."

"Maybe I'm running from myself."

"But why?"

Frowning, Morgan stood and wandered toward the bay window as he considered her question. How strange, he thought. He was keeping so many secrets from her—for her protection as much as his own—and yet this was the one thing he could be completely honest about. "Lacey, a long time ago I lost everything that mattered to me, and ever since then I've been moving from place to place. I guess maybe I've been looking for something without even knowing what I was searching for."

"What will you do when you find it?" she asked gently.

Morgan turned and looked at her for a long, yearning moment. "Stop running and settle down."

Lacey held his gaze steadily, afraid to believe that the tender look in his eyes was meant for her. "After wandering for so long, do you think you'll really be able to do that?"

"Yes."

Lacey wanted to ask if he had found what he was searching for in Willow Springs, but she couldn't. If he said no, it would be another rejection, and Lacey didn't think she was strong enough to bear that right now. Despite all the questions she had about him, she would simply have to accept Morgan as he was—mysterious and unfathomable.

Besides, in her heart she already knew everything she needed to know about him. He was kind, decent, and courageous. He was capable of great loyalty, and he had a strong sense of justice. He was a good man. Learning about his past wouldn't change his character.

Or make her love him any less.

In that moment, as she realized how completely she had lost her heart to Morgan, Lacey also decided she could be patient. Eventually he would either leave Willow Springs or reveal what he wanted from her. If that happened, no matter how much or how little that was, Lacey would give it to him without question. It made no sense to someone who prized a secure, orderly life; but then, the ways of the heart didn't make a lot of sense, either, and Lacey was too tired from fighting the world to fight herself as well.

Chapter Twelve

Morgan found it impossible to guess what was going through Lacey's mind as she sat there, studying him, but he was struck once again by how very vulnerable she seemed. All of his protective instincts surged to the surface, and he turned to the window to search the darkness for some sign of Croft.

That was what he had come for tonight, to protect Lacey from a vicious gunslinger, but Morgan was suddenly stunned by the guilty thought that he was the one Lacey truly needed to be protected from. Yet how could he turn and walk away from her when all he wanted was to take her into his arms and tell her he was falling in love.

Lacey studied Morgan's back, wondering what he found so compelling about the window. Fire crackled on the hearth, punctuating the silence, and finally she said, "When you arrived tonight, Morgan, you said that two things had brought you here. We have touched on only one of them."

"That's right."

"Does your second reason have anything to do with your preoccupation with that window? You have gravitated toward it all night."

Morgan turned his back on the window and faced her. "You're very perceptive."

Lacey ignored the compliment. "What's out there, Morgan?"

As much as he wanted to shield her from the truth, he couldn't. "Croft, I think."

Lacey shuddered. "Why would he be out there tonight? C. W. thinks he's beaten me."

"That's exactly the reason, Lacey. I was watching Croft when you indicated that you might leave Willow Springs because there was nothing left for you here."

"Oh, God," Lacey breathed. She didn't need the situation explained to her further. If she hadn't been so frightened, she would have been angry with herself for not having realized how Croft would react to the knowledge that she might be leaving town for good. "He won't let me go, will he? Not without . . . taking what he wants from me first."

"I don't think so."

"So you came here to warn me."

"I came to *protect* you," he corrected. "That's why I've made myself so visible at this window. If Croft is out there waiting for the right moment to strike, he already knows I'm here. He may believe Berta and Zach are no obstacle to getting to you, but he's not foolish enough to think he can get past all three of us."

Lacey glanced away from Morgan, wondering what she should do next, and for the first time she noticed the butt of Zach's Winchester peeking out from beneath the draperies. "You told Zach about your suspicions?" she asked.

Morgan followed her gaze to the rifle. "Yes. He offered to stand watch, of course, but I couldn't let him. What happened tonight took a terrible toll on him, Lacey. He needs a good night's rest."

She looked at him in surprise. "So you intend to spend the night?"

Morgan nodded toward the cushioned seat in the bay window. "I'll stay right here, with a lamp beside me."

"And make yourself an easy target?" she asked, rising abruptly. "No! I won't hear of it!"

"Lacey . . . " He crossed the room to her. "Croft isn't stupid. Using me for target practice would serve no purpose. The shots would wake up everyone in the house—in the whole damned town, for that matter—and that would hardly leave him free and clear to sneak into the house, dispatch your servants, and have a leisurely tête-à-tête with you."

"No," she agreed angrily, "but it would certainly eliminate you as a potential obstacle tomorrow night and the night after that." She faced him squarely. "Morgan, I will never agree to allow you to spend the night at that window."

Her stubborn streak brought out his own bullheadedness. "You think you can stop me?"

"I can send Zach for the sheriff and have you thrown out of here."

"And leave Zach to fend off Croft by himself? Lacey, Zach's a tired old man who's going to go to an early grave protecting you if you're not careful."

"I'm trying to be careful!" Lacey almost shouted as a sob welled up in her throat. "Don't you think I know someone could get hurt because of me? I don't want it to be Zach or Berta . . . or you, but there's more at stake than just three lives! There's Lew and Sukie Dasat, Rob and Veda Swenson . . ." She named half a dozen members of the co-op. "They all have families, Morgan, and I've seen how good the vigilantes are at making children into orphans."

"Lacey, this isn't about your fight against the vigilantes," he said quietly, hoping his soothing voice would calm her and make her see reason. "What's happening between you and Croft is personal, and my only concern right now is seeing that you make it through the night without that bastard getting his hands on you."

Lacey closed her eyes and shuddered at the thought. "Look," Morgan continued. "If it will make you feel better, I'll sleep on the sofa instead of the window seat."

The fight suddenly drained out of her, and Lacey sank onto the sofa. "All right," she sighed. Confused and miserable, she leaned forward, resting her elbows on her knees and her forehead against her clasped hands. "I don't understand you, Morgan. I don't understand why you've made yourself my champion or why you allow yourself to come close to me and then pull away."

Morgan sat next to her and took her hands in his. "I care for you, Lacey. Surely you must know that."

"At this point in time, Morgan, I don't know what to think about anything."

"Then don't try to think. Just trust me."

"I do," she said honestly. "It doesn't make sense, but I do trust you."

"Good," he whispered, and then because the temptation to kiss her was too great, he stood and returned to the window, being careful not to make himself a target this time. "I'd like to know what you plan to do, Lacey. About C. W., I mean. He thinks he's won, that you'll leave town now."

Once again Lacey was confused. Just when she'd felt convinced that what Morgan wanted most was to kiss her, he had pulled away. Disappointed, she forced her mind to his question. "Do you think Rawlings is correct in his assumption?"

He laughed shortly. "Hardly. I know tonight was devastating for you, but it couldn't have been a complete surprise. Isolated the way your office was, with no abutting buildings, you must have known eventually he'd take the risk of burning you out."

"Yes, I did know," she said, leaning back on the sofa and drawing her legs under her so that she was facing Morgan. "But knowing it was bound to happen didn't prepare me for how much it would hurt. I hadn't realized how much of David was still inside that building."

"So what will you do now?"

"Start over."

"You're not considering rebuilding on that same site?" he asked, concerned.

"No, he'd just burn me out again."

"But no one in town would dare rent you office space," he pointed out.

Lacey gave him a tired smile. "Of course not, but I still have a few cards I haven't played yet. Actually, I'm going to make C. W. very happy tomorrow."

Intrigued, Morgan returned to the sofa. "How?"

"I'm taking the evening train to Cheyenne tomorrow. C. W. will think he's gotten rid of me, but while he's gloating, I'll be completing the contingency plans I've been working on."

Morgan frowned. "Lacey, the headquarters of the Stock Growers Association is in Cheyenne, and that gives Rawlings a very long arm. Until he knows you're safely back in Washington, he's going to be watching your every move."

"Let him watch," she said negligently. "There's nothing he can do about it now."

Morgan wanted to argue that point, but he'd learned that debate was a futile exercise where this woman was concerned.

But there wasn't a doubt in Morgan's mind that if Lacey got on a train tomorrow, Croft would follow her. Unless Lacey had someone to protect her, the gunslinger would choose his own time to take what he wanted.

Knowing that left Morgan with only one possible choice. It wasn't the smartest decision he'd ever made, but he didn't seem to be able to stop himself from saying "All right, I'll go with you."

Lacey knew she shouldn't have been surprised by his offer, but she was. "That's not necessary, Morgan. I'll be fine in Cheyenne."

"Maybe you will and maybe you won't. If I come along, we won't have to find out."

"Morgan—"

"Don't argue with me, Lacey. My mind's made up." He grinned. "It's not such a big sacrifice for me, you know. Cheyenne's a fine city, with lots to see and do. I can think of a lot of chores far worse than squiring a beautiful woman to fancy restaurants and maybe even a night at the theatre."

Lacey knew better than to argue with him. She hadn't won a clear victory in any battle with him yet, and in this instance, she didn't want to. Having Morgan with her in the city, having a reason to wear one of the beautiful gowns she owned, being courted and cosseted and made to feel like a woman again—that was a fantasy Lacey was almost afraid to indulge in. Yet Morgan himself had suggested it. He seemed to relish the idea.

But last week he had relished the idea of kissing her, only to reject her for reasons she still didn't understand. Tonight he had taken her in his arms and then pulled away when she'd tried to learn more about him. The thought of yet another moment of intimacy followed by a stinging rejection was more than Lacey could stand.

Tears pooled in her eyes as she fought back the needs of heart and flesh, which Morgan had reminded her she still possessed. "Oh, God, you confuse me so."

"Lacey, please, just accept my friendship and don't question why it's there," he said quietly, feeling a strange kind of pain in the vicinity of his heart.

"I've spent my whole life questioning things, Morgan. It's not easy to stop when it's something this"—her voice fell to a whisper—"important."

Gently Morgan brushed at the long golden-brown hair that fell over her shoulder, and then, because he couldn't stop himself, he filled his hand with the silken mane. He brought his face close to hers, and Lacey timidly reached up to stroke his cheek. She traced the curve of the deep dimple there, and then of their own accord, her fingertips drifted to his lips.

His breath whispered on her hand, and his golden eyes darkened. "I want you, Lacey," he said, so softly that she almost didn't hear the words. But she didn't need to. Everything Morgan wanted showed plainly in his eyes.

"I want you, too, so desperately that it frightens me. But you always pull away."

Slowly Morgan gathered her into his arms. She was soft, and she smelled so sweet that Morgan thought he might die from the simple pleasure of holding her. "You are so vulnerable, Lacey. For all your strength and courage, your heart is wide open to the kind of hurt that could break it beyond repair." He kissed her hair and murmured reverently, "I don't want to hurt you."

Tears glistening, Lacey raised her face to his and swallowed whatever shred of pride she had left. "You already have, by turning me away."

It was everything Morgan could do to keep from kissing her. His body throbbed with a need that went far beyond the physical; it was a need to hold and protect, to love and be loved, to find his way home after a long, dark journey. In that moment, Morgan made up his mind. There had to be a way to have this incredible woman and do his job, too. Somehow he would find it. But not tonight.

"I want to make love with you, Lacey," he whispered. "More than you could possibly imagine. But not tonight, in this house, in the bed you shared with your husband. I don't think you could live with yourself if you took another man to David's bed on this of all nights."

Lacey closed her eyes and lowered her head to the hard pillow of Morgan's shoulder. He was right. With all she had suffered tonight, it would be too easy to confuse grief and loneliness with love. Perhaps she already had. "Are you trying to save me from myself again?"

Morgan couldn't see her face, but he knew she was smiling. In a soft, caressing voice, he told her, "No, Lacey. I just want to know absolutely that when I fill you, you'll cry out to me, not to David."

The image Morgan created of their bodies joined in fevered passion made Lacey's breath desert her completely. Heat throbbed deep inside her, and the ache she felt was so intense that for a moment she could almost feel Morgan's body covering hers, pressing into hers, filling the sweet void between her thighs. His words should have made her think of David, but only Morgan filled her thoughts and she could feel no guilt for that.

She was in love with him. It was without rhyme or reason, but she loved him, and she knew David would never have begrudged her the possibility of finding happiness in Morgan's arms.

With difficulty, Lacey eased away from him. For a fleeting second, her eyes met his, then fell to his lips, and then she tore her gaze away and rose. "I'll get a blanket for you. And there should be enough logs in the wood box to last the night."

She left quietly and returned almost immediately, but Morgan was at the window again. She faltered for a second, remembering the reason he was spending the night in her parlor.

"It's all right, Lacey. He won't try anything as long as he knows I'm here."

Lacey placed a blanket and down pillow on the sofa. "Zach must have told Berta you were staying. These were on a chair in the vestibule."

"I'll remember to thank her in the morning."

Lacey nodded. "Morgan, please stay away from the window. And be careful."

"I will."

Half the width of the room separated them, but they could have been in each other's arms for all the difference it made to their hammering hearts. "Good night, Morgan."

"Good night, Lacey."

She disappeared into the vestibule. Morgan followed her as far as the parlor door, then watched as she ascended the stairs.

She hesitated for a moment on the landing before she turned the corner and went up to the second floor without looking back.

Standing in the doorway, he listened to the soft creaking sounds as Lacey moved through her room, and when finally all was quiet, he went through the room lowering all the lamps but one, which he placed on the table by the window. He threw another log on the fire, took the blanket off the sofa, poured himself a stiff shot, picked up Zach's Winchester, and finally settled in the bay window with his legs stretched out on the comfortably padded bench and his back resting against the wall.

To his right, the parlor was filled with flickering golden lights and shadows. To his left, the town lay quiet and sleepy below him. But between Morgan and the town, near the spot where Lacey's white picket fence met the carriage road, there glowed a small fire-red disk—the lighted end of a cigar. The dot grew brighter, then mellowed. It moved down a few feet, then up.

Smiling to himself, Morgan lifted his glass in a mock toast and drained it dry. Then he swung the Winchester onto the bench with him, the butt resting against his thigh, the muzzle pointed toward the ceiling, sending a clear message to anyone who cared to look.

Moments later the burning cigar arced through the air, landing a dozen feet away, and the vague shadow of a man disappeared into the blackness.

"Good night, Croft," Morgan whispered.

The next morning while Lacey packed, Morgan went into town to collect a few things of his own. Since he didn't have much more than what he'd come into town with, packing wouldn't take long. He stopped first at the train station to purchase two tickets on the only eastbound train that would pass through Willow Springs that day, and from there he went on to his hotel room. He'd barely had time to remove his carpetbag from beneath the bed and was taking his only change of clothes from the top bureau drawer when someone knocked on his door.

"Who is it?" he called as he quietly removed his Colt from the drawer.

"Ep."

Morgan admitted his associate and returned to his packing. "I'm glad you dropped by, Ep. You saved me the trouble of coming to look for you."

Ep stepped to the foot of the bed and studied Morgan's carpetbag. "I got a message to pass along, but first"—he frowned—"you wanna tell me what's going on?"

"I'm going to Cheyenne for a couple of days."

"You changin' the plan on your own or did you get a change of orders I don't know about?"

"There's been no change in the plan," Morgan answered. "I'm just escorting Mrs. Spencer to the city."

"She's leaving?" he asked with obvious surprise. "After the fire last night I heard some of Rawlings's men say she was gonna hightail it back to her daddy fer sure, but I figured they was just thinkin' wishful. From the way she pulled off that stunt with the paper shipment, I was beginnin' to believe she might actually be good enough to whip C. W."

"Oh, she's good enough, all right. She just doesn't have enough ammunition to use against him," Morgan said with a grim smile. "She's got some plans already made in that regard, but she has to go to Cheyenne to implement them."

"But why do you have to go with her?"

Briefly Morgan outlined the problem with Croft, then changed the subject before Ep had time to comment. "Now what was that message you received?"

Ep let the matter of Allyce Spencer drop, for the time being. "You ain't gonna like it."

Morgan stopped what he was doing and looked at Ep. "What is it?"

"Keenan Stoddard is in Cheyenne."

"Damn!" Morgan threw a starched white shirt on the bed. "What the hell is that paper pusher doing out here?"

Ep shrugged. "I reckon the old man sent him 'cause he's getting tired of waiting. I got a telegram from Stoddard yesterday. Said I was to send my reports directly to him at the Inter Ocean Hotel from now on. 'Course, he didn't say it quite that plain." Ep removed a rumpled telegram from his pocket and Morgan snatched it away. Ep was right. The message was couched in vague terms, but the meaning was clear.

"Dammit, I thought the old man understood that he was to stay out of this and give me time to do the job right."

"I guess he's gettin' itchy about results."

"Well, I don't know why he thinks having that idiot Stoddard in Cheyenne is going to make things happen any faster. I'll be damned if I'm going to report straight to him." Morgan handed the telegram back to Ep.

"You want me to send him a message sayin' that?"

"No, I'll look him up when I get to Cheyenne and see if I can persuade him to leave. I don't like having a wild card in the game unless it's up my own sleeve where I can control it."

"Yeah, that about sums up my feelings, too," Ep said sharply, but he wasn't thinking about Keenan Stoddard.

His face set firm, Morgan gave his friend a hard look. "If you got something stuck in your craw, spit it out."

It was more of a dare than an invitation to speak freely, but Ep took hold of the bed's brass foot rail and leaned forward on it, completely unintimidated. "Boss, if we was back in New Mexico conducting business as usual, it'd never cross my mind to question you about personal stuff, 'cause it'd be none of my business. But we ain't down south, and as long as I'm puttin' my life on the line, I figure I got a right to ask—"

"Yes," Morgan said tersely, cutting him off.

Ep frowned. "Yes, what? I ain't asked nothin' yet."

Morgan stuffed a white shirt into the carpetbag. "You were going to ask if I'm in love with Allyce Spencer, weren't you?"

"Yeah, somethin' like that," Ep said guardedly.

"Well, the answer to your question is yes. I am."

Ep swallowed a smile because Morgan didn't seem any too happy about his pronouncement. "Is this the roll-over-honey-I-gotta-do-this-quick kind of love or the meet-you-at-the-preacher's kind?"

Morgan had to laugh in spite of himself. "Let's just say it's somewhere in between at the moment, and leave it at that."

"And how does the widow feel about it?"

"I'm not exactly sure," Morgan hedged. He'd known Ep for so long that he didn't mind discussing his own feelings, but that freedom of expression didn't extend to discussing Lacey's. And besides, Morgan really wasn't sure how she felt. She cared for him, that much he knew, but he couldn't guess how deep and lasting that feeling was.

Ep frowned. "Have you told her who sent you to Willow Springs, and why?"

Morgan slid his Colt into its holster and placed the gun belt on top of his clothes. "No."

"Are you gonna?" Ep asked, concerned.

"You know I can't do that. The less Lacey knows about this, the safer she'll be."

"This don't make a whole lot of sense, boss," Ep said, shaking his head as he sat on the edge of the bed. "In a few months it'll all be over, and if you survive, you can court the widow free and clear, without keepin' no secrets from her. Can't you steer clear of her till then?"

"No, Ep, I can't, because Lacey is even deeper in this mess with Rawlings than I am, deeper than anybody, including the old man. No matter what else happens, I can't stand by and watch her be destroyed."

"What's she gonna think if you succeed in joinin' the vigilantes?"

Morgan snapped his valise shut. "I'll deal with that when the time comes."

Ep shook his head. "I don't know, boss. It sounds to me like you've put yourself right smack dab between a rock and a hard place."

Morgan picked up the carpetbag and slapped his friend on the shoulder. "Ep, I couldn't have stated it better myself." He grinned. "You need me to bring you anything from Cheyenne?"

"Just yourself in one piece."

"I'll do my best."

"Two tickets to Cheyenne, you say?" C. W. paced the sitting room of his suite at the Cattleman's. The exhilaration of his victory over Allyce Spencer still hadn't worn off, but he was a little puzzled by the latest bit of news Vance Hoffman had brought him. "You sure it was Cheyenne, not Washington?"

"I'm positive, Mr. Rawlings," Hoffman confirmed. "Morgan came down from the widow's house about an hour ago and bought the tickets. Then he came here, packed his bag, and checked out."

"And went straight back to the widow's?"

"No, he stopped at the livery first and paid Applewhite to board that horse he bought from Dasat for another week."

"So that means he's planning to come back to Willow Springs." C. W. turned to Croft, who was lounging on the divan. "What do you make of it?"

"I don't know," he replied, helping himself to a handful of unshelled peanuts from the crystal bowl on the table. "It could mean a lot of things. Morgan has obviously appointed himself Mrs. Spencer's knight in shining armor. Maybe he just wants to make sure she gets safely to Cheyenne. Or maybe he's got plans of his own for her."

Rawlings heard the edge in Croft's voice and wondered what it meant. If he hadn't known better, he would have sworn Croft was showing little signs of jealousy. "You say he spent the night up at her place?"

Croft's jaw was rigid as he concentrated on shelling the nuts. "That's right. He sat in the window downstairs, guarding the place."

C. W. wanted to know just what Croft had been doing up at the widow's after the fire, but he was afraid to ask. He knew Croft had a kind of grudging respect for Mrs. Spencer, and he also knew she was a damned beautiful woman. If Croft wanted to sample some of the widow's many charms, his respect for her wouldn't stop him from doing just that, and neither would a direct order from C. W. To avoid a confrontation, Rawlings let his question go unasked and concentrated on the good news Hoffman had brought.

"I guess I'd better mosey on down to the station this evening and see Mrs. Spencer off."

Croft sighed and dumped a handful of empty shells back into the bowl. "That's a real dumb idea, C. W."

Rawlings rounded on him angrily, then remembered whom he was dealing with. Curbing his irritation, he asked, "Why is that?"

"Two reasons. Allyce Spencer's a very proud, stubborn lady. If you really have succeeded in defeating her, let her leave town gracefully and count yourself lucky. If you go down to the depot and rub her nose in her defeat, she just might change her mind and stay."

As much as it galled C. W. to admit it, Croft's reasoning was sound. "What's the other reason?"

Croft looked at him, making no attempt to hide his amusement. "If you go around blustering and bragging about how you whipped her, you're gonna look mighty foolish if she's not leaving town for good. My advice is that you keep your mouth shut until you know what this little trip to Cheyenne is all about."

Reluctantly, C. W. nodded. "All right. I guess I can afford to let the widow go quietly."

"Good." Croft stood and started for the door.

"Where the hell are you going?"

Without pausing, he answered, "To pack, where else? I got a train to catch."

Of course it was the thing to do—sending someone to keep an eye on Morgan and the widow—but it galled Rawlings that Croft hadn't waited to be told to go to Cheyenne. "Send me a telegram as soon you figure out what's going on," he demanded, but Croft was already gone.

Chapter Thirteen

With every mile that passed between Willow Springs and Cheyenne, Lacey felt the knot of tension inside her unwinding. Morgan had secured tickets for the luxurious Liberty Pullman parlor coach on the San Francisco to Omaha express, and the accommodations were sumptuous to say the least. Hand-carved paneling adorned every wall, specially designed lamps hung precariously from wall sconces, and rich brocade fabrics covered every overstuffed sofa and chair.

Of course, the movement of the train jostled the passengers in the luxury car mercilessly, but the inconvenience was minor considering the surroundings—and the alternative: Passengers traveling second class were squeezed together elbow to elbow on hard benches and suffering a good trouncing to boot.

While Lacey appreciated the opulence of her surroundings, she found far more comfort in Morgan's presence than in the parlor car. With the exception of the hour he'd spent in town, he'd stayed by her side all day, even while she had finished her packing. His presence as bodyguard had been totally unnecessary at that time, but Lacey had found his company irresistible.

Her undergarments and nightclothes had all been packed while he was out of the house, and by the time he returned and sauntered into her boudoir unannounced, she had turned her attention to selecting outer garments. From a chair in the corner, Morgan had randomly passed judgment on her wardrobe. Her green traveling suit was hopelessly out of

187

date, and she couldn't possibly wear it in public, he had decreed with a mischievous twinkle in his golden eyes. Her yellow suit was more stylish, but the color didn't suit her, he'd decided. Finally, a chocolate-covered gabardine with fawn underskirts and trim suited him, and he allowed it to be placed into the trunk.

Laughing with delight, Lacey had paraded most of her wardrobe out for his approval, and she'd had to admit that his taste was impeccable. He chose one day frock because it complemented her complexion, and another he allowed because its severe mannish cut was appropriate for a woman who wished to conduct business and to be taken seriously.

When her room was littered with discarded dresses and her trunk nearly full, Lacey decreed that she was finished, but Morgan had other ideas. Helping himself to her wardrobe closet, he found a ball gown of midnight blue ciselé velvet and demanded that it be included with the others.

"For our night on the town," he had explained. Lacey hadn't even entertained the thought of arguing with him. Carefully she had packed the dress and its matching ermine-trimmed cape.

Morgan was such diverting company that the day passed quickly. At five Berta put out a light supper, and afterward Zach hitched up the carriage. He and Morgan loaded Lacey's trunk, and she had said good-bye to her dear friends.

"You will be careful in the city, *ja*?" Berta said sternly as she helped Lacey into the short dove-gray woolen cape that matched her draped skirt.

"Yes, Berta, I promise."

The housekeeper pinned Morgan with a hard look. "And you will be sure she is careful, *ja*?"

"That's what I'm going along for," he told her with an easy smile. "You and Zach just stay close to home and don't worry about us."

"Don't waste your breath, Morgan," Lacey advised. "Berta was born worrying."

"Your valise, sir." Zach appeared at the parlor door carrying Morgan's carpetbag. "I'll place it in the carriage with the trunk."

He moved toward the door, but Morgan stopped him. "Just a minute, Zach." He took the valise, removed his Colt, then returned the bag. Zach went on to the carriage, and Morgan strapped on the holster with a proficiency that jarred Lacey.

"Is that absolutely necessary?" she asked, frowning.

"I think so, yes."

"I don't like guns, Morgan."

Once the belt was securely buckled, he moved on to the rawhide laces that tied around his thigh. "I know that, Lacey," he said without looking at her. "But this isn't Washington, and until the western territories are as tame as that venerable city, guns will be a necessary evil. There's no telling what we might encounter between here and Cheyenne."

Or who, Lacey thought, remembering the real reason Morgan was accompanying her. As much as she wanted to pretend otherwise, she knew it had nothing to do with the lovely party dress she'd willingly included in her trunk.

Morgan straightened his satin waistcoat and the black wool frock coat that contrasted so dramatically with his white shirt. He was a little rumpled from having spent the night in those clothes, but he still looked impossibly handsome, despite the weapon on his thigh. He shrugged into his calf-length overcoat, and the Colt disappeared, much to Lacey's relief. At least if the revolver didn't show, it wouldn't look as though they were advertising for trouble.

Zach drove them to the station and returned to the house immediately, leaving Lacey and Morgan to wait for the train by themselves. But they hadn't been alone for long. Just as the train arrived, Croft showed up and followed them on board without a word. He, too, had secured a ticket for the parlor car, and once on board, he had given his overcoat to the porter, making a show, Lacey thought, of exposing the ivory-handled revolvers he wore on his hips.

Most of the passengers traveling first class were now in the dining car, leaving the parlor almost empty for the time being. With total lack of regard for Croft, Morgan led Lacey to the front of the parlor car where two chairs flanked a small, ornate round table. They made themselves comfortable, and Morgan kept Lacey so distracted that she was able to put Croft out of her mind completely. And the farther they traveled from Willow Springs, the more relaxed she became, as though she had left the incredible weight of all her responsibilities behind.

After they passed through Laramie, the train stopped at the base of Sherman Hill to take on the additional locomotive they would need to make it up the steep incline. Though the transaction delayed their arrival in Cheyenne, Lacey was grateful for a few minutes of peace and quiet, not to mention a respite from the bone-jarring ride.

Sighing at the blessed stillness, she looked out the window. The moon hung low over the rugged mountain terrain, bathing everything in an eerie, mystical light. "Look, Morgan, isn't it beautiful?"

He glanced at the nearly full moon, but it held his attention for only a moment. "Not nearly as beautiful as you," he couldn't resist telling her. She had removed her cape and was leaning toward the window with her elbow propped on the arm of the chair and her chin resting lightly on the back of her hand. An artist could not have arranged a lovelier pose. A lamp by the window bathed her in a soft golden glow, highlighting her hair and lending her face an ethereal radiance, and the delicate profusion of lace and ruffles at her throat softened the portrait even further. Morgan was awed by her beauty and strangely moved by the flush that crept into her cheeks when she acknowledged his compliment as though it were the first she had ever received.

"Thank you," she said with a sweet, almost shy smile. "Until you came to Willow Springs, I'd forgotten how nice flattery feels. Be careful you don't spoil me."

"You should be told every day how lovely you are, Lacey. But you have so many other admirable qualities that your beauty sometimes gets lost among them. I'll have to remind you of it often."

Lacey's blush deepened and she glanced down, wondering how long he would be around to remind her of such things; but thinking about the end of something that hadn't really even begun threatened to cast a pall over her rejuvenated spirits, and she pushed the thought aside.

Morgan saw the brief cloud that drifted over Lacey's face, and searched for something that would keep her entertained. They were only a few hours away from Willow Springs, but already he could see the signs of strain leaving her. The sparkle was returning to her crystalline eyes, and he intended to make certain that it stayed there. "How about a game of cards?" he suggested, pulling from his inner coat pocket the deck he always kept on hand.

A gambler inviting her to play cards? That was more of a challenge than Lacey could resist. A slow smile spread across her face. "Very well."

"Wonderful." Morgan drew his chair a little closer to the table between them and began shuffling the cards. "What shall we play? Rummy? Euchre? Old sledge? Or how about double canfield?" he suggested. "Just name your game, madam."

Lacey eyed him devilishly. "How about poker?"

Morgan gave her a look filled with mock reproach. "How very unladylike, Mrs. Spencer. Whatever would your father say?"

She shrugged negligently and tossed her head. "What father doesn't know won't hurt him," she said, not bothering to mention that she'd learned the game at her father's knee.

"Very well. What'll it be, ma'am?" he drawled. "Cincinnati? Shotgun? Lame-brain Pete?"

Lacey pursed her lips thoughtfully. "Let's not get too fancy. What's the name of that game where you just hold five cards in your hands and get to exchange the ones you don't like?"

Morgan had a feeling he was being played like a fine violin. "Draw poker."

"That's it!" she said cheerfully. "You deal first."

Chuckling to himself, Morgan glanced around the parlor car, which was more crowded now, and motioned for the porter. The second engine had just been coupled onto the first and they were getting under way again, but the porter crossed the jouncing car effortlessly. "Yes, sir. How may I help you?"

"Where might I procure a set of gambling chips?"

"I'm sorry, sir, but gambling is expressly forbidden in all Union Pacific passenger cars."

"Ah, but the lady and I aren't gambling for money. This is just a friendly game to pass the time."

From the look on his face it was obvious that the porter had his doubts about that, but the five dollar gold piece Morgan surreptitiously passed him immediately cured his skepticism. "I'll see what I can do, sir." He left them and returned only moments later with an ornate wooden box he'd taken from a buffet table near the back of the car. "Here you are, sir," he said formally, then adjourned to his post beside the door.

Morgan opened the box and distributed the chips evenly. Lacey picked up one of the wooden disks and discovered that the Union Pacific crest was boldly emblazoned on one side. "So much for the illegality of gambling on this train," she muttered.

"I would imagine these are holdovers from the grand old days when the railroad catered to the passengers' every whim."

"How did you know the porter would bend the rules so obligingly?"

Morgan grinned. "It's my business to know things like that."

Lacey knew she should be disturbed by Morgan's "profession," but she wasn't; in fact, she found the thought rather tantalizing. She could picture Morgan, steel-eyed and debonair, lounging in elegant gaming rooms, casually submitting to the whims of Lady Luck. The image was titillating, but Lacey knew full well that she was romanticizing what she would otherwise have considered a rather pathetic way of life. And though she knew it was foolish, she chose to ignore reality in favor of a little romance. "Have you fleeced many wealthy sheep in parlor cars such as this?" she asked coquettishly.

His eyes twinkling with mischief, Morgan raised one hand and placed the other over his heart. "I do solemnly swear I have never fleeced anyone who couldn't afford it or didn't deserve it."

"How noble of you," she said with an airy laugh. "Next thing I know you'll be calling yourself Robin Hood."

Morgan sobered a little. "Honestly, Lacey, I never cheat at cards. If I become so desperate that I can't win fairly, I don't play. I've seen gambling become a sickness, and I have no intention of allowing myself to succumb to that fate."

"I never imagined that you were addicted to gambling," she told him honestly. "And while I know that I should thoroughly disapprove of your . . . profession, I find that I cannot."

Morgan reached out and took one of Lacey's hands. "I'm glad. I don't know if I could bear your disapproval."

His hand was rougher than Lacey would have expected of a professional gambler, but she registered that thought only on some deep, subconscious level. It was the sweet sensation of her hand being gently caressed by his larger, stronger one that fully occupied her consciousness. Warmth tingled up her arm, and her breathing became unsteady. His eyes held hers captive, and it was with great difficulty that Lacey finally withdrew her hand and suggested, "Shall we begin?"

"Very well. Ante up." He threw a chip into the center of the table, and Lacey followed suit. Deftly, Morgan dealt the cards, and it soon became apparent that Lacey knew more about the game than she had let on. She bet daringly and bluffed brilliantly—so brilliantly, in fact, that Morgan found himself at a distinct disadvantage. She was not at all averse to batting her eyelashes provocatively and using every woman's wile at her disposal to distract him.

In one game, she pouted as though she had a bad hand, and indeed she did. Morgan won that pot, and the next time her lips pursed into an attractive moue, he bet big—and lost to a straight flush. Her lovely, expressive face was never blank for even a moment, unless it suited her purpose, and Morgan found their match to be the most delightful hour of frustration he'd ever experienced.

"My darling Lacey, you are without a doubt the most delightfully wicked woman I have ever encountered," he commented sweetly as the train whistle announced their imminent arrival in Cheyenne.

"Should I take that as a compliment?"

"By all means," he said softly as he leaned across the table toward her. "You are like an elegantly furnished room with many doors, and I never know what I will find behind the next one I open. I know only that I can hardly wait to open it."

As much as Lacey hated to allow anything to spoil her frivolous mood, she couldn't resist telling him quite seriously, "But you have me at a distinct disadvantage, Morgan. There are no secrets behind my doors, whereas all of yours are locked. I like very much what I have seen thus far, but—"

Morgan reached out and covered her hand. "Then don't question what your eyes tell you, Lacey."

"And what about my heart?" she whispered.

Gently he ran his fingertips across the ridge of her knuckles. "I can't answer that," he told her quietly. "It's your heart,

Lacey, and only you can decide how trustworthy it is or how much of it you dare put at risk."

"Cheyenne station!" the porter called as the train chugged to a halt. "This is only a ten-minute stop, ladies and gentlemen. All through passengers are advised to remain on board."

Lacey held Morgan's intent gaze for a moment longer, then retracted her hand and began gathering her belongings. His words echoed through her mind, but she was afraid it was too late for her to make a decision about putting her heart at risk. It was already fully occupied by the man who helped her into her cape and placed one hand at her waist to guide her through the car.

The other passengers were moving, too. Some headed for the sleeping car where their berths had been made up, while others were bound for the station platform where they hoped to catch a breath of fresh, crisp air. Lacey had her toes stepped on more than once before she reached the door. That was a minor irritation, though, compared to the discomfort she felt when she looked up and found Croft leaning against the wall by the door.

"Mrs. Spencer." He greeted her with a pleasant nod.

"Good evening, Croft," she replied in a tone meant to make the salutation sound more like a good-bye than a hello. She brushed past him quickly and did not see the hate-filled look that passed between Morgan and the gunfighter.

Outside, Morgan preceded her onto the platform and offered his hand to help her descend. "I had managed to forget that he was aboard," she said as she came down the two narrow steps.

"Ignore him, Lacey," Morgan advised. "You should be cautious while we're here, but let me do the worrying about Croft."

She looked at him seriously. "I want you to be cautious, too, Morgan. That man is a professional gunfighter," she said, her voice hard and bleak. "I know from experience how deadly they can be. You must promise me you will not do anything to provoke a confrontation."

"I won't," he said gravely. For Lacey's sake, he hoped he could keep that promise.

Unlike the quiet depot at Willow Springs, the Union Pacific station in Cheyenne was bustling with activity, even at this late hour. Friends and family were on hand to greet the arriving passengers or to see someone off.

Lacey and Morgan fought the crowd as they collected their baggage, and without too much difficulty they found a hack to transport them to the Inter Ocean Hotel. There, two smartly dressed bellboys met the carriage and took charge of the luggage.

The Inter Ocean, a massive three-story structure of brick and stone, was sumptuous by western standards, and over the last few years renovations had been made that were intended to make it the rival of many eastern hotels. In the lobby there were red velvet drapes at the floor-to-ceiling windows, and comfortable chairs upholstered in the same fabric were scattered about in conversational groupings. The floors were covered by Brussels carpets and a huge electric chandelier lit the room.

Behind the front desk, a huge mahogany affair that took up a large part of the back wall, a robust, nattily dressed black gentleman was speaking quietly to the desk clerk. He glanced up, saw Lacey approaching, and smiled broadly. "Mrs. Spencer! How nice to see you again. It's been a while."

Lacey smiled graciously. "Yes, it has, Mr. Ford. It's lovely to see you, too. I'd like to introduce you to my traveling companion, Morgan. Morgan, this is Mr. Barney Ford, owner and manager of the Inter Ocean Hotel."

"A pleasure to meet you, Mr. Morgan."

"The pleasure is mine, sir," Morgan replied, taking note of the warm greeting Lacey had received. Was there any person of importance in the country whom she didn't know? he wondered.

Barney Ford glanced around the lobby. "Zach isn't with you this trip?"

"I'm afraid not. He and Mrs. Kraus are holding down the fort at home."

Ford nodded sympathetically. "I heard you've been having some trouble. It's not true that your newspaper office was burned out last night, is it?" he asked with sincere concern.

"Unfortunately it is true," she told him. "And there's a slim chance that I may encounter some difficulties here in Cheyenne. I'd consider it a great favor, Mr. Ford, if you would let me know if anyone makes inquiries about me or my activities while I'm here."

"Don't you worry about a thing, ma'am. I'll tell the whole staff to be on the lookout for anyone doing any asking or skulking around your rooms or some such."

"Thank you. I assume that means you can supply us with rooms?"

"Mrs. Spencer, for you I'd kick somebody out if I had to, but that won't be necessary tonight."

"Good," Morgan said, giving Ford a congenial smile. "We'd like two adjacent rooms, please, with a connecting door, if possible." He hadn't discussed the arrangements with Lacey, but he hoped she wouldn't protest connecting rooms because of some silly concern for propriety. Ford seemed genuinely concerned about Lacey's safety, but Morgan doubted that the hotel staff could be counted on to protect her. Croft was in town, and Morgan planned to take every precaution necessary. Propriety be damned.

Lacey made no effort to contradict Morgan's instructions. Ford turned to the honeycomb of boxes on the wall behind him and considered the possibilities. "We have a two-room suite with a single next to it. A door in the sitting room opens into the single, connecting all three rooms."

"That will do nicely. Mrs. Spencer will take the suite, and I'll take the single," Morgan said as he signed the register and passed the pen to Lacey. She signed her name with a flourish, and Ford handed two keys to the bellboys.

"Numbers two-oh-five and two-oh-seven. Please see that fires are laid in the stoves immediately," he instructed, and they rushed off to do his bidding.

"Mr. Ford, will you sit down with us while the bellboys prepare our rooms?" Lacey asked.

"Of course." He came around the desk and gestured Lacey and Morgan to a group of chairs on the far side of the room. The lobby was not crowded, but Morgan noted that Ford was leading them to a secluded corner so that there was no possibility of anyone eavesdropping. It didn't take long to figure out why.

"Now, what may I do for you this time, Mrs. Spencer?" Ford asked with a smile as soon as they were seated.

"You know me too well, Mr. Ford," Lacey replied graciously. "I will need some telegrams sent first thing tomorrow morning."

"Consider it done."

When Morgan looked at Lacey curiously, she explained, "I've made a number of arrangements these last few months, Morgan, and I've kept them secret by using second parties and fictitious names. Experience has taught me that if I send a telegram myself, even here in Cheyenne, C. W. or one of his friends learns the contents almost immediately. And if there is a reply, they usually know what it is long before I do."

"So Mr. Ford sends your telegrams?" Morgan guessed.

"Among other things," Lacey answered.

"It's only one of the many services we perform at the Inter Ocean," Ford told him. "Our clerks frequently take messages to the telegraph office and have the replies delivered here. We even keep telegraph forms at the desk for the convenience of our guests." He looked at Lacey again. "What name will we be using this time?"

"William Crawford."

"Ah, yes, the photographer."

Morgan looked from Lacey to Ford, completely lost. Obviously, he was the only one who hadn't a clue as to what was going on. Lacey promised that after breakfast the next morning she would give Ford the messages she needed sent, and the hotel owner promised to keep the replies safe if she was not at the hotel when they arrived.

With that business taken care of, Lacey inquired about Ford's family, and they chatted like long-lost friends. While they were visiting, Croft checked in at the front desk. He saw Lacey and Morgan on the far side of the lobby, and Lacey pointed him out to Ford as someone to be wary of. As soon as he had mounted the stairs to the second floor, she and Morgan started upstairs, too. Ford bade them good night and insisted they call on him if they needed anything at all.

"Do you have devoted followers everywhere you go?" Morgan asked as they started upstairs. "Obviously Mr. Ford was serious when he said he would have evicted someone in order to give you a room."

"He has become a dear and trusted friend. We met through Zach, who saved Mr. Ford's life twenty-six years ago when they were both fleeing a posse of slave hunters. After they escaped to the North, they lost contact with each other until Zach came west. Their accidental reunion was a very moving sight, believe me." She went on to explain how Barney and Zach had maintained their friendship the past few years with frequent visits between Willow Springs and Cheyenne.

Morgan shook his head. "For someone so quiet and reserved, Zachary Freeman has led a rather eventful life."

"And it's getting more eventful all the time," Lacey said quietly, thinking of the occurrences of the past few days. "Oh, Morgan, I wish I could persuade Zach and Berta to go back to Washington. When I think of what could happen to them I get so frightened."

"They'd never leave without you, Lacey. You know that."

She sighed. "I know. But how will I ever live with myself if one of them gets hurt because of me?"

"You can always go back to Washington, Lacey—not permanently, but just for a little while," he added quickly before she could protest. They had reached the second floor, and Morgan stopped in front of room 205. "Give up whatever plans you've got in the works and take a vacation back east until all this ugliness is over."

He pushed the door open, and Lacey stepped into the room, looking up at Morgan with a puzzled expression. "You talk as though this is going to end soon. Why would you make an assumption like that?"

Morgan cursed himself. How could he have forgotten how perceptive Lacey was? "Sooner or later conflicts like this always end, Lacey. It's inevitable. One of these days Rawlings will go too far, and someone will put a stop to his vigilante activities."

Lacey frowned, suddenly growing angry at his offhand attitude. "He already has gone too far, Morgan, and I'm the only one who's been trying to bring him to justice!"

With an irritable sigh, Morgan gestured for Lacey to enter the room, where the bellboys had just completed the task of lighting Franklin stoves in all three rooms. They had unbolted the door between Morgan's room and Lacey's suite, and as far as Morgan could see, everything was in perfect order.

He dismissed the bellboys with generous tips, and once they were gone, he turned to Lacey, who was warming herself by the stove. "I don't want to argue about C. W. anymore. Why don't we drop the subject?" he said crisply.

"All right," she agreed briskly, unfastening her cape. "We've covered this territory before, haven't we?"

"All too often," he muttered, wondering why their good mood had suddenly turned sour. It seemed that the moment they'd set foot in the sitting room, tension had sprung up between them for no apparent reason. Its source confused Morgan, and since he hated being confused, he chose to ignore it for the moment.

Moving purposefully around the lavishly appointed parlor, he studied the layout and inspected the view of Hill Street below. Ignoring Lacey, he stepped into her bedroom and noted with satisfaction that the only way in or out was through the little parlor. The only other door in the bedroom led to a bathing room that was barely large enough to accommodate a huge claw-footed porcelain tub and pedestal lavatory. The other facilities were down the hall, he presumed.

Lacey watched him inspect her apartment, and something about his efficiency bothered her. It was almost as though he had performed this little ritual before, as though attending to matters of security was second nature to him. It was just one more thing that didn't fit his image of a carefree gambler. The inconsistency only added to the inexplicable agitation she'd begun to feel the moment they'd come into this room.

Once Morgan finished checking Lacey's quarters he moved on to his own bedroom, on the opposite side of the sitting room from hers. Everything was in order there, too, and after securely bolting the door to the hall, he started back to the sitting room and found Lacey standing at his door, watching him.

"You're very proficient at this," she commented as he neared.

"I'm just being cautious."

"Then caution must be a habit with you."

She was looking at him with so much suspicion that it irritated Morgan. "It is," he said, brushing past her into the sitting room.

She leaned against the door frame, studying him. "Why?"

Morgan ignored the question. "We'll sleep with both these doors open," he told her, gesturing to her bedroom door and his. "And you are not to leave here without me, not even to go downstairs to the lobby. Understood?"

Though she had no idea why, Lacey was already upset, and Morgan's evasiveness and authoritative tone didn't improve her disposition. "Please don't order me around," she said sharply. "I know you're doing this for my protection, and I am grateful, but I don't like being told what to do, nor do I appreciate your dictatorial attitude."

In a voice that was clearly not apologetic he said, "Sorry. I'll try not to become too much of a despot."

Lacey studied him a moment, examining her agitated emotions. It simply didn't make sense that she should be so upset with him for no reason. "Why are we on the verge of an argument, Morgan? Until a few minutes ago, we were the most congenial companions imaginable."

Morgan found it difficult to look at her. "I suppose it's because we differ over the approach you should take to dealing with C. W. Rawlings. Perhaps we should consider that subject off limits for the remainder of our stay in Cheyenne," he said, but his explanation was only subterfuge. The real reason for his discomfort was that he was finally alone with Lacey in a setting that could be made very romantic with just a little effort, but he didn't know how to proceed. He felt like a clumsy, overanxious schoolboy, and he didn't care for the sensation one bit.

Lacey studied Morgan, completely unconvinced by the reason he'd given for their argumentative attitudes. They'd quarreled about C. W. before, and probably would again. No, the uneasiness she felt now was far different from any she'd experienced during their previous disagreements.

Finally she made a concerted effort to suppress her irrational irritation and said, "Very well. For the duration of our stay in Cheyenne, we shall pretend that C. W. Rawlings doesn't exist." A thought struck her, and she grew pensive. "But if we take away that topic of conversation, I wonder if we'll discover that we have absolutely nothing else in common."

The thought seemed to disturb her so much that Morgan felt much of his discomfort vanish. "I doubt that, Lacey," he told her gently. "I don't imagine we'll have any trouble keeping each other occupied."

His tone mesmerized Lacey, and she found she couldn't look away from him. "No?"

"No. I haven't been able to think of anything but you since we met ten days ago. That's not going to change now, whether we find anything to talk about or not."

Lacey's heart leapt into her throat, and she suddenly recognized the source of her previous agitation. It had nothing to do with their argument and everything to do with the fact that she would be sharing these three small rooms with Morgan. She felt silly for not having realized it before.

A little overwhelmed, Lacey cleared her throat nervously. "I, uh, think I'll unpack my things and turn in," she said, heading for her room. "It's been a very long day."

Morgan was disappointed but not surprised by her retreat. "All right, Lacey. I'll see you in the morning."

She stopped at the bedroom door and turned to him. "Thank you, Morgan. For everything."

"You don't have to thank me, Lacey. I'm exactly where I want to be."

His golden eyes held hers for a moment, and Lacey felt her heartbeat accelerate. "Good night," she said finally.

"Good night." They watched each other for another long, intense moment; then Lacey turned and disappeared into her bedroom. Morgan turned out the lights in the sitting room, but did not leave. Choosing a comfortable chair, he settled in, put his feet up, and for nearly an hour listened to the soft, feminine rustle of Lacey moving around her room unpacking, undressing, bathing, slipping into bed.

Only when her room was dark and still did he prepare for bed. As he had instructed, the doors between their rooms remained open.

It was a small intimacy that made for a very long night.

Chapter Fourteen

The next morning they rose early so that Lacey could get a good start on the mysterious business she had come to conduct. They breakfasted in the Inter Ocean's dining room and afterward returned to their suite so that Lacey could draft her telegrams. As promised, Barney Ford appeared about an hour later to see that they were properly dispatched, and Lacey and Morgan left the hotel to handle some "other arrangements."

Lacey's first stop was at her attorney's office, and while she was closeted with him for nearly an hour, Morgan lounged outside, surveying the street for any sign of trouble. He was a bit surprised that Croft had not picked up their trail yet, but there was no sign of the gunfighter or any of Rawlings's other men. If anyone was paying attention to Lacey's comings and goings, Morgan couldn't spot him.

Though it was the end of October, the day was relatively warm as compared to the chill of the previous days, and the streets of Cheyenne were quite busy. Once Lacey left her lawyer's, she informed Morgan that there was nothing else to be done until she began receiving replies to her telegrams.

Free of any time constraints, they spent the rest of the morning wandering casually down the avenues. They shopped, and Lacey introduced Morgan to several trusted acquaintances who ran businesses in the city. Around ten-thirty, Morgan noted that Croft had joined their promenade. He followed at a discreet distance, making no effort to hide himself, but neither did he force a confrontation.

Lacey was so thoroughly enjoying herself that she didn't

notice their unwelcome shadow, and Morgan was grateful. She was blossoming before his very eyes. The day they had met, Morgan had thought Lacey was vivacious and charming, but today she was even more so. Gradually the haunted air of tragedy ebbed away as she forgot all her troubles, and Morgan was completely captivated. She smiled freely and often, making his heartbeat quicken, and when she laughed, he knew that if he died with that joyous, seductive sound in his ears, he would die a happy man.

She solicited his advice on all her purchases, which Morgan thought were modest, considering her wealth. He helped her choose a saucy little hat and pick out presents for Berta and Zach. As it neared time for lunch, they dropped off Lacey's packages at the hotel, then strolled down the block to Grosvenor's, one of the city's leading restaurants, where Lacey had arranged for her friend, Asa Mercer, to join them.

Though she assured him that he would like Asa, Morgan had his doubts. She spoke of Mercer with such respect and affection that by the time they arrived at Grosvenor's, Morgan had grown more than a little jealous. According to Lacey, Mercer had established his newspaper, the *Northwest Live Stock Journal*, three years ago, just a few months before David Spencer's death. When Mercer learned of the brutal murder of unarmed, unsuspecting George McKeevey at the hands of a bounty hunter, he was appalled. He made a special trip to Willow Springs to get the facts, and it was then that Lacey met him for the first time. When Mercer learned a few days later that David, too, had fallen victim to the gunslinger, he used the *Journal* to speak out against a judicial system that made it legal for men like Fogarty to kill with impunity.

Though he barely knew her, Mercer was a great comfort to Lacey throughout her period of mourning, and they became good friends. What else they had become was anyone's guess, Morgan thought glumly, and the more Lacey praised Mercer, the more he became convinced that their relationship had long since progressed beyond mere friendship.

By the time Mercer arrived at Grosvenor's, where Lacey and Morgan were already seated and waiting, Morgan was prepared to hate Mercer on sight. Jealousy was such an unaccustomed emotion, that he barely knew how to handle himself.

But Morgan's jealousy eased considerably the moment Asa arrived. At forty-seven years of age, he was a tall, thin man with spectacles and a receding hairline. He treated Lacey in a thoroughly respectful manner, and it was soon clear that the basis of their friendship was nothing more than the common bond created by their profession and by the principles they both held. For the sake of Mr. Mercer's continued good health, Morgan was delighted, because he discovered that he very much enjoyed the company of the educated, well-traveled man.

"A proper gentleman probably wouldn't ask this, Allyce," Asa said when they'd finished their meal, "but I am burning with curiosity to know what these mysterious plans of yours are. Would you feel comfortable telling me how you propose to survive the blow Mr. Rawlings has dealt you?" Asa knew a great deal of what had gone on in Willow Springs from the copies of the *Gazette* Lacey sent him every week, and she'd spent most of lunch catching him up on the more recent events.

Morgan looked at the two of them, finally settling his gaze on Lacey. "Yes, I'm curious to know that myself. I've had enough of your secrets this morning to last a lifetime, and I have absolutely no idea what you're up to."

Lacey smiled at both of them. "I don't mind telling you," she answered, glancing around to make certain no one was within earshot. They had dawdled so long over their meal that most of the dining room had cleared out, and Lacey felt free to talk. Keeping her voice quiet, she said, "Last month I purchased a building on Center Street in Willow Springs, adjacent to the Cattleman's Hotel."

"What?" both men said simultaneously, but Morgan got the next word in first. "How on earth did you manage that? Doesn't C. W. own that entire block?"

"Yes," Lacey said with a justifiably satisfied smile. "But as far as he knows, that building was purchased from him by a Mr. William Crawford for the purpose of operating a photographic studio."

Morgan remembered the name as the one Lacey had told Mr. Ford would be used on all the telegrams she planned to send. "And does this William Crawford really exist?" he asked.

"Of course. The whole venture is quite legitimate, I assure

you. William Crawford was a college chum of David's. He was the best man at our wedding, as a matter of fact."

"And he purchased the building for you?" Asa inquired.

"More or less. You see, a number of years ago, David, William, and I formed a partnership to create a company called Crawford Photographic Studios. Since I am still part owner of the business, I was able to buy the property from C. W. using the company name."

Though Morgan greatly admired her ingenuity, her plan worried him. "Lacey, when Rawlings finds out—"

"It will be too late to do anything about it," she said sternly, cutting him off because she didn't want to listen to a list of everything that could go wrong with her plan. "He can't possibly burn me out this time, because the building abuts the Cattleman's Hotel, which is C. W.'s pride and joy. His own living quarters are there."

But yours aren't, Morgan wanted to say. If C. W. couldn't destroy her place of business, he might decide that burning down her house was the next best thing. But clearly, Lacey didn't want to hear reasonable arguments. Having her office destroyed was such a crushing defeat that she needed to bask in victory, if only for a little while.

Knowing he couldn't talk any sense into her, Morgan sat back and listened as she went on to explain the other arrangements she'd made. A printing press would be sent out of her father's newspaper office in St. Louis, and in Chicago supplies were being purchased and prepared for shipping. Thanks to William Crawford, the building in Willow Springs had already been renovated and furnished to her specifications.

Morgan and Asa exchanged worried looks. "Allyce dear, C. W. is not going to take this well," Asa said when it didn't appear that Morgan was going to speak up.

"That is something of an understatement," she replied wryly. "But what else can I do, short of giving up completely?"

Because he wished she'd do just that, a wave of frustration washed over Morgan. But it was useless to argue with her, so he sighed heavily and gave Asa a crooked smile. "Mr. Mercer, I am going to leave it to you to talk some sense into our lovely companion. I have a few errands to run, and I'm sure you and Lacey would appreciate some time to yourselves." He grinned at Lacey. "Can I trust you to remain here with Mr. Mercer until I return?"

Lacey was dying to know what business Morgan could possibly have in Cheyenne, but she was too much of a lady to ask. "Of course you can trust me. Croft has been following us all morning, and I have no desire to run into him while I am unaccompanied."

Morgan was surprised. "You knew Croft was watching us?"

"Of course. He made no effort to hide himself."

"Who is Croft?" Asa asked, looking from Morgan to Lacey.

"One of Rawlings's men," Lacey explained.

"I'm afraid he's here to do Lacey some harm," Morgan added. "That's why I don't want him to find her alone. May I count on you to stay close to her until I return?"

"Of course."

Morgan stood. "I shouldn't be more than an hour," he told them. Again, he cautioned Lacey not to leave the restaurant, and then departed.

Lacey watched him go, admiring the broad cut of his shoulders and the masculine grace of his walk. He paid for their meal, then left.

"Your gentleman friend is quite devoted to you," Asa commented mildly, studying the expression of longing on Lacey's face. "And if you'll forgive me for being so bold, I would say that you are equally devoted to him."

She sighed deeply and turned her attention back to Asa. "I'm afraid my relationship with Morgan is"—she struggled to find the right word—"undefined. We've known each other only a short time, but he's been so kind and helpful that I don't know how I would have survived this last week without him." She glanced toward the long row of velvet-draped windows that overlooked Ferguson Street and watched as Morgan passed by on the busy boardwalk outside. "He is truly a remarkable—"

"What is it?" Asa asked when she stopped in midsentence. He turned in his chair and looked out the windows, following the line of her gaze. The street was busy and Asa recognized several people he knew, but he couldn't tell what had so distracted Lacey.

"That man, there, in the bowler hat. Do you know him?" she asked, pointing, but before Asa could get a good look he had passed the last window, headed in the direction Morgan had gone.

"I'm sorry, Allyce. I didn't see him clearly. Why? Do you know him?"

"Yes, I do. At least, I think I do." She frowned. "But I can't imagine why he would be in Wyoming."

"Who is he?"

Lacey looked completely befuddled. "If it's who I think it is, his name is Keenan Stoddard. He's an aide-de-camp to Senator William Hanson."

Asa glanced at the window again, though the man was long gone. "Could he be making inquiries into Riley's death on behalf of the senator?"

"That's the only logical explanation I can think of. But why would he come to Cheyenne instead of Willow Springs? And why hasn't he contacted me?"

"Perhaps he's only just arrived and has stopped over in Cheyenne en route to Willow Springs," Asa suggested.

Lacey frowned. "We could speculate for hours and still draw no accurate conclusions. The only sensible course is to ask him," she said, rising as she gathered up her gloves and reticule.

"But you promised Morgan you'd remain here," Asa reminded her as he stood as well.

"That was before I knew Keenan Stoddard was in town," she replied, hurrying through the dining room.

Asa had to move quickly to keep up with her. "But what about Croft?"

That brought Lacey to a dead stop. "Damnation," she muttered, then turned to her friend. "Will you walk with me, Asa? I don't think he'll accost me in broad daylight if he sees that I have a companion."

Asa smiled at her. "Since I promised Morgan I'd keep an eye on you, I don't see how I can refuse."

"Good." Lacey hurried outside and scanned the busy street. The first thing she saw was Croft, who was lounging in the door of a tobacco shop just across the wide boulevard. With a subtle gesture, she pointed him out to Asa, then blocked his presence out of her mind and searched the crowded boardwalk in the direction Stoddard had disappeared. Morgan, two blocks ahead of her, was easy to spot because he stood so much taller than practically anyone else on the street, but it took a little longer to find the diminutive Keenan Stoddard. Finally she saw his bowler hat bobbing not far behind Morgan, and she moved off in pursuit so quickly that she was almost running.

"Won't Croft think this is somewhat peculiar?" Asa asked, dodging passersby as he struggled to keep up with Lacey. He glanced across the street and saw that the gunfighter was moving parallel to them, keeping pace without expending any effort whatsoever.

"I don't care what he thinks," Lacey replied, keeping her quarry firmly in sight. "I'm positive that man is Keenan Stoddard, and I have to know what he's doing here."

"Your determination is admirable, but you've told me more than once that Senator Hanson will never abandon his quest to bring his son's murderers to justice. What if he has some covert plan in the works that involves Stoddard? Surely you wouldn't want to do anything that might call undue attention to him."

Lacey slowed down a little, considering the logic of Mercer's suggestion. She saw Morgan turn a corner and disappear, but Stoddard was still in view, and that was all that concerned her. "You may be right, Asa. It would be foolish of me to force a confrontation here on the street. Why don't we just follow at a discreet distance? If I can discover where he's staying, perhaps I can confront him in his room this evening."

Asa nodded. "That's a much wiser course, Allyce." They stopped at the end of the street, waiting for a chance to cross the busy intersection, and Stoddard turned down Fifth Street, just as Morgan had.

With Stoddard out of sight, it was difficult for Lacey to move at a sedate pace, but she managed it. Finally she rounded the corner at Fifth and scanned both sides of the street, praying Stoddard would still be in view. Again, she spotted Morgan first. He had crossed the street, and Lacey paid little heed to him as he entered a shop on the corner of Fifth and Hill.

It came as something of a surprise, then, when she saw Stoddard enter the same shop.

Frowning thoughtfully, she continued down the block until she was directly across from the store, which turned out to be a tailor shop that also advertised ready-made menswear. She and Morgan had passed there earlier, and Lacey had commented that the silver brocade waistcoat on display in the window would look wonderful on him. The logical assumption was that he had gone there to purchase the vest to please Lacey. But that didn't account for Stoddard's presence. There were a dozen stores in Cheyenne that carried men's clothing. Why had Stoddard chosen this one?

Lacey thought back over the last few minutes that she had been following Stoddard, and realized that his behavior had been remarkably similar to hers. He hadn't been out strolling. He'd bobbed and weaved his way past the other pedestrians as though he was following someone: And that someone was obviously Morgan.

"Do you believe this is a coincidence, Asa?" she asked pensively.

Mercer, too, had seen both men enter the same shop. "Are you suggesting that your friend Morgan is acquainted with Stoddard?"

"That is exactly what I'm suggesting. Look through the window. See?"

Asa did as she asked and saw Morgan towering over Stoddard, exchanging words that didn't seem friendly. Their conversation was brief, and when they were finished, Stoddard abruptly left the shop. Lacey stepped behind Asa so that she wouldn't be spotted when Stoddard glanced around nervously before disappearing down Hill Street.

"Don't you intend to follow?" Asa asked.

Lacey's head was spinning, and she made no move to pursue Stoddard. Was Morgan somehow involved with Will Hanson's efforts to bring C. W. Rawlings to justice? It seemed incredible, but if it was true it would explain many things. And it also made one thing painfully obvious.

I am somehow part of the plan, Lacey thought with sickening certainty. She had fallen in love with a man who was, in all probability, only using her.

Numb with confusion and unable to shake a horrible sense of betrayal, she murmured, "I think I'll go back to the hotel now, Asa."

He looked at her, concerned. "Allyce, what's wrong? If your

suspicions are correct, I should think you'd feel like dancing in the streets. Help has arrived, my dear."

"Yes," she agreed quietly, "but the help has lied to me, deceived me, and used me." She looked at him with tears glimmering in her eyes. "Please. Will you accompany me back to the hotel? I need time to think."

"Of course." He offered his arm and escorted her back to the Inter Ocean.

Though his errands had taken much longer than expected, Morgan returned to Grosvenor's feeling inordinately proud of himself. The brocade waistcoat had already been delivered to the hotel, as had the lovely sapphire broach Lacey had admired in a jeweler's window. Morgan was proudest, though, of the two tickets he'd acquired to this evening's performance of *Hamlet, Prince of Denmark*. The renowned Shakespearean actor, Hamilton Schuyler, was appearing for three nights at the Cheyenne Opera House, and tickets for opening night were scarce. It had taken a small fortune and the assistance of Barney Ford, but finally Morgan had found someone willing to part with two of the best seats in the house.

Whatever it took, Morgan was determined to make this evening one of the most special nights of Lacey's life. After the theatre, they would dine at the Tivoli, and when they returned to the hotel, a bottle of champagne would be awaiting them.

It was the search for theatre tickets that had made him late in returning to collect Lacey at Grosvenor's. That, and his unexpected encounter with Keenan Stoddard. Morgan still didn't know how the obnoxious little man had spotted him or how he'd managed to follow him without being detected, but when he approached Morgan in the tailor's shop, in full view of anyone who might have been looking, Morgan had been furious.

"We must talk," Stoddard had said without preamble. "I want to know what the devil you're doing in Cheyenne cavorting with some little tart while you should be in Willow Springs!"

"Keep your voice down," Morgan ordered harshly, grateful that the tailor's shop was empty except for a clerk who was preoccupied at the back with the only other customer. "That little *tart*, as you call her, is Allyce Smithfield Spencer, a friend of Senator Hanson's, and I don't appreciate the fact that the old man didn't tell me there was a woman involved in this mess."

Stoddard went pale at the mention of Lacey's name. "Damn, I didn't know she was here, too. I saw you go into that restaurant earlier, but I didn't get a good look at the woman," he explained, then regained some of his composure. "But that doesn't change anything. I still want to know what's happening with Rawlings."

"And I want you to get out of Wyoming before you get us all killed," Morgan growled.

"But Senator Hanson—"

"I don't give a damn about Senator Hanson. He'll get his reports through the channels we agreed upon or I'll take my men and walk off this job. Now you deliver that message to the old man personally and make a believer out of him. If he wants his son's murderers caught, he's going to have to trust me."

"But—"

"No more buts," Morgan whispered angrily, stepping so close to Stoddard that he towered over him in the most intimidating fashion imaginable. "You haul your ass out of Cheyenne today or so help me God, I'll kick it all the way back to Washington!"

Based on the man's scared-rabbit look, Morgan had felt confident he would obey. He had turned away abruptly, and Stoddard had left without another word.

Concentrating on his plans for the evening, Morgan managed to put the incident out of his mind. He was whistling merrily as he approached Grosvenor's, but his jovial mood died when he noticed that Croft was no longer lounging in the door of the tobacco shop, across the street. If Lacey was still inside, why would Croft have left?

Stepping up his pace, he hurried into the restaurant. The place was almost completely deserted, and Morgan's heart tripped in alarm.

"Where is she?" he demanded, grabbing a young waiter.

"What?" The startled waiter tried to pull away, but Morgan wouldn't allow it.

He jerked his head toward the table where he'd left Lacey.

"Where is she? The woman who was sitting with me earlier. Where did she go?"

"You mean the lady who left with Mr. Mercer?"

"That's right. When did she leave?"

"Just a couple of minutes after you did," the waiter replied, and Morgan released him so abruptly that he stumbled.

"Did either of them say where they were headed?"

"No, sir. They didn't speak to anyone, just rushed out like the building was on fire."

Morgan frowned. Why on earth had Lacey left so suddenly? Puzzled, he muttered a hasty thank-you to the waiter and rushed out. Cheyenne was a good-sized town, and Lacey could have been almost anywhere. The logical place to start a search, though, was the hotel. Perhaps she'd become so anxious to know if there were any replies to her telegrams that she'd gone back there. Morgan prayed it was something that simple. He also prayed that Asa Mercer had kept his promise to watch over her.

By the time he reached the Inter Ocean his heart was pounding with fear. Images of Lacey desperately fighting Croft filled his head to the exclusion of all else, and the closer he came to her room, the worse the images became. He dashed through the lobby and took the stairs two at a time up to the second floor. The door to Lacey's suite was locked, and Morgan resisted the urge to batter it down. Instead he unlocked his own room and drew his Colt as he rushed into the parlor through the adjoining door.

"Lacey? Lacey, are you here? Lacey, answer me!"

He was halfway across the room when Lacey appeared at her bedroom door. "Yes, Morgan. I'm here."

"Thank God." Relief flooded through him, and he holstered his gun, then quickly gathered her into his arms, holding her close because he needed to prove to himself that she was really safe. "When I returned to the restaurant and you weren't there, I was scared half to death."

"I'm sorry I worried you," Lacey said in a toneless voice. She didn't struggle to get away from him, but she didn't return his hearty embrace, either. She was still confused by her discovery.

Morgan immediately sensed that something was wrong.

Without releasing her, he drew back and studied her ashen face. "What happened, Lacey? Did Croft—"

"No," she reassured him quickly, pulling out of his arms. His concern seemed so genuine, but at that moment, Lacey didn't know what to believe about the man she had fallen in love with. "Asa escorted me back to the hotel. Croft followed, but made no effort to intercept us."

"Then what's wrong?" Morgan asked, watching Lacey closely as she moved stiffly to the sofa and sat, arranging her skirts meticulously around her. She had never seemed so inaccessible, and to Morgan, that was almost as frightening as her disappearance.

"After you left Grosvenor's, I saw a man I recognized pass by the restaurant windows. I followed him." She looked Morgan squarely in the eye. "What were you and Keenan Stoddard arguing about at the tailor's?"

Morgan still clutched his room key tightly in his left hand, and he hurled it angrily onto a chair. If Keenan Stoddard had been present, Morgan would have strangled him—and Will Hanson, too. This was all their fault! "Damnation! I didn't want you involved in this, Lacey!"

Clearly he was furious, but Lacey didn't think his anger was directed at her. "Involved in what, Morgan? How do you know Keenan Stoddard?"

Trying to control his anger, Morgan wiped one hand across his face. What should he tell her? The truth had to come out, obviously. But did he dare tell her all of it? Unbidden, he thought of his friend, Ep Luder, who was putting his life on the line in Willow Springs. No, he couldn't tell Lacey everything. There were too many lives at stake, including hers. "Lacey, I met Keenan Stoddard through Senator William Hanson. But you've already figured out that much, haven't you?"

Lacey nodded and looked away from him. "Yes. If I had to piece this together on my own, I'd guess that the senator has involved you in a plot to bring C. W. Rawlings to justice."

"That's right."

"So you didn't come to Willow Springs to invest money with the Barons."

"No."

"What have you and Will Hanson planned?"

Regretfully he answered, "I can't tell you that, Lacey. The less you know, the safer you'll be."

She laughed shortly. "Oh, that's rich. Were you thinking of my safety the day you came to my office to ask questions about C. W.? The same day you expressed your admiration for my courage and asked permission to come courting? Was it for my own good that you kissed me, then cast me aside, allowing me to believe you were disgusted by me?" She stood abruptly and faced him, her voice loaded with sarcasm. "Tell me, Morgan, please, which of your many contradictory, incomprehensible actions were meant for my *safety*?"

"Lacey, please . . . " He moved to her with his arms outstretched as though he meant to touch her, but she darted away quickly. Morgan lowered his arms and watched her. "You're angry—with good reason—but you're not thinking clearly."

"Well, you're half right, Morgan. I'm not thinking clearly, and I haven't since the day we met. But you're wrong about my being angry. I'm not. I'm hurt. You've been lying to me, using me. Considering the way I've been deceived, the very least I deserve is to know how I fit into the senator's plan."

God, what a mess, Morgan thought with a heavy sigh. The last thing in the world he'd wanted to do was hurt this incredible woman; yet he'd done exactly that because he hadn't had the strength to stay away from her. "Lacey, I know I haven't given you much reason to trust me, but you must believe me when I tell you that you were in no way part of the scheme that brought me to Wyoming. When I was approached about taking on this job, the situation was explained to me in what I thought was complete detail, but as God is my witness, I was not told about you. I guess Hanson didn't want you involved."

Lacey wanted to believe him, but there were too many unanswered questions and too many inconsistencies. "If that's the case, why did you seek me out? I can accept that our first meeting in the sheriff's office was a coincidence, but that doesn't explain why you came to my office the next day."

This was the hard part. Of all the things Morgan had done since he'd met Lacey, this was the one he regretted most. All he could do was tell her the truth and pray she would understand and forgive him. "As you said, our meeting in Watson's office was a coincidence, Lacey. And if you had been less intriguing, not quite as charming, and not nearly so damned beautiful, I probably never would have seen you again. You were all of those things, though, and I was captivated by your wit, intelligence, and grace. But," he reluctantly confessed, "after I learned who you were and how you were single-handedly fighting Rawlings, I convinced myself that you might be useful. I cultivated your friendship for a very specific purpose."

Lacey felt as though a monstrous fist were squeezing her heart. She barely had the breath to ask, "Which was?"

"It's vital to the success of my plan that Rawlings never suspect I came to Willow Springs because of him. He must believe I just happened to wander in and decided to stay for a while."

"And how did cultivating my friendship accomplish that?"

"Courting you would have given me a logical reason to remain in Willow Springs, and aligning myself with C. W.'s worst enemy seemed like an excellent way of drawing his attention to me without arousing suspicion that I was actually cultivating him."

Lacey regarded Morgan coldly. "Has it worked?"

He nodded, hating himself and what he was telling Lacey because it was the truth. "Yes. The other day he questioned my interest in you, and I convinced him that I'm a fortune hunter trying to seduce a lonely widow."

Lacey frowned, suddenly more confused than ever. "No, wait. That doesn't make sense. If courting me was part of the plan, why did you change your mind about accompanying me to the Dasats' barn raising? Why did you make no attempt to see me after"—her voice faltered as she remembered the way Morgan had kissed her and the way she had kissed him back— "after what happened in my office?"

Crossing the room slowly, Morgan approached Lacey. She didn't flee him this time, but stood stiffly as he placed his hands on her arms. "Because I realized I'd been lying to myself. I could accomplish my goals in Willow Springs without involving you. The real reason I was pursuing you was that I wanted you more than any woman I've ever met, and the only way I could justify being close to you was by convincing myself that you were useful."

He brushed the back of one hand against Lacey's pale cheek.

"But that day when I kissed you, and you responded with such sweet passion, I had to stop lying to myself, because I realized that I had it within my power to hurt you very deeply."

Lacey wanted to believe him. "So you decided not to use me because you felt sorry for me. You pitied the poor lonely widow."

"Pity has nothing to do with what I feel for you," he protested. "If you can't believe any of what I'm telling you, at least believe what you know in your heart—that you and I feel something unique and wonderful for each other. That's why you've been so confused. Hell, it's why *I've* been confused. I'm falling in love with you, and it's been tearing me in a dozen different directions. My heart keeps pulling me toward you, and my head keeps telling me to push you away so that you won't be hurt by the job I have to do."

Lacey heard the words "falling in love," and her heart melted. His explanation made sense. It was, in fact, the only thing that could completely account for Morgan's irrational behavior. But there was one more thing she had to know. "Tell me honestly, Morgan. Did you use my troubles with Croft as an excuse to come to Cheyenne so you could meet with Keenan Stoddard?"

"No," he told her firmly. "I had already purchased our train tickets when I learned that Stoddard was in Cheyenne. I did plan to see him while I was here to tell him to get out of Wyoming, but I had no idea I was going to run into him today. My reasons for coming here with you have nothing to do with our plans for Rawlings." He lowered his voice to a husky drawl, and he cupped her cheek in one hand, brushing his thumb over her lips. "Your safety has come to mean more to me than anything. I don't want anyone to hurt you. Especially me."

The words, his gentle touch, and the look of absolute honesty in his golden eyes swept away the last of Lacey's doubts. "I want to believe that so desperately."

"Believe it, Lacey," he said, lowering his face to hers until his lips were only a whisper away. "Believe that I'm in love with you."

Lacey's heart thundered in her breast, and she gave up the battle with her own emotions. "I believe," she murmured as his mouth closed over hers. She opened her lips to him hungrily, and Morgan's tongue pressed deep into her, mating his desire with hers.

They kissed with a passion born of suppressed longing and a desperate need for reassurance. Lacey's hands feverishly traveled up Morgan's arms and across his shoulders, until her fingers were entwined in the soft black hair that curled at his neck. Morgan's hands could not be still, either. He pulled Lacey to him, fitting their bodies together like two pieces in a puzzle. He caressed her back. He cupped her face in his broad hands while his mouth drank the headiest wine he'd ever tasted.

"Make love with me, Lacey. Now," he murmured fervently.

Lacey barely heard the words, but she knew exactly what Morgan wanted, because she wanted the same thing. Right or wrong, this was inevitable, and she had no more strength to resist him now than she'd had that afternoon in her office.

"Say yes, Lacey," he whispered as his mouth blazed a trail of fire down her throat.

"Yes, Morgan," she breathed softly, clutching at his shoulder with one hand while the other guided his mouth back to hers.

"Oh, Lace . . . " he moaned as he started to kiss her again, but Lacey captured his face between her hands and forced him to look at her. "*Yes*," she said again, stronger this time. "Yes, Morgan. Now."

Her sky-blue eyes had darkened to the color of midnight, and her lips, parted and breathless, looked as though they had been kissed by an early morning dew. Her hair was an elegant mass of upswept curls, and as Morgan held her intense gaze he slowly began removing the pins that held it. One by one they fell to the floor until her hair was free and fell in a silken mantle around her shoulders.

"Now," he whispered. Sweeping Lacey into his arms as though she weighed nothing, he carried her into her bedroom and gently lowered her onto the bed.

Chapter Fifteen

"It's the middle of the afternoon," Lacey purred as Morgan's lips meandered down the back of her neck. She was nestled snugly against his hard-muscled chest with his arm around her waist, holding her close, and one of his legs draped intimately over her thigh. A light flannel sheet was their only protection against the slight chill of the room, but for the last hour they had created their own heat—a fiery passion that had scorched them equally and exquisitely.

"What does the time of day have to do with anything?" Morgan mumbled, completely fascinated by the graceful arch of Lacey's neck. His lips moved forward, and he discovered that the delicate lobe of her ear was fascinating, too.

Lacey sighed with pleasure and managed to explain, "Only terribly wicked women take lovers in the middle of the afternoon."

Morgan chuckled and urged Lacey onto her back. "What do you know of wicked women and their lovers?"

"More than I did an hour ago," she told him wryly, glancing down at his hand, which curled intimately around the lush underside of one of her breasts. The sight of his large, sun-bronzed hand against her pale skin gave her almost as much pleasure as the feel of it did. Morgan glanced down, too, and grinned. He lowered his head to her breast and took the hard crest into his mouth. With lips and teeth and tongue, he teased the rosy nub until Lacey arched her back and moaned with pleasure. She dug her hands into his hair and guided him to her other breast so that he could give it equal treatment.

She gasped as his hand moved lower on her body, down over her stomach, until his fingers were buried in the soft tangle of hair between her thighs. He explored her intimately, taking liberties Lacey had never imagined, and she bit hard on her lower lip, trying not to cry out, because if she did, she knew her words would be a plea for more. She moved against him, feeling his growing hardness against her thigh, and finally the pleasure he gave her was too great to be denied. She heard her own voice, hoarse and breathless, begging Morgan to take her completely, and he was only too willing to comply.

Bearing his weight on his forearms, Morgan moved over Lacey and kissed her deeply. His tongue slid into her mouth in imitation of a bolder act, and Lacey arched against him. She was on fire everywhere, but most of all, she needed to feel Morgan's hardness inside her so that she could be certain this exquisite pleasure was not a dream.

With breathless words, she begged him to come to her as she wrapped her legs around his waist and arched upward just as Morgan plunged into her.

Morgan was drunk with the taste and feel of Lacey, intoxicated by the perfect way her body closed around him, squeezing him like a silken glove, but when she cried out sharply as he filled her, he stopped all movement. He captured her face in his hands, and saw that her eyes were filled with tears.

"Oh, love, have I hurt you?" he whispered urgently. He started to withdraw from her, but Lacey wrapped her legs more tightly around him, taking him into her even deeper.

"No, oh, no," she murmured. "This is more wonderful than I ever could have imagined. Oh, Morgan, please . . . please . . . " She rocked against him, and this time it was Morgan who cried out.

"Lacey . . . Lace . . . Oh, God." They moved together as one—one body, one heart, one soul dancing in perfect harmony, until they cried out in one voice as their passion exploded into the heat of a million suns.

Gasping for breath, they came back to earth together, holding each other tightly. Morgan slid to one side, taking his weight off Lacey, then pulling her with him as he moved. Too overwhelmed to speak, Lacey rested her head on Morgan's shoulder and let her hand curl into the dark, downy mat of hair on his chest. He was perfect in every way. This day was perfect. This very moment was the most perfect of all, because she knew that she had touched Morgan as deeply as he had touched her.

His arms were a protective shield that kept the world at bay, but Lacey was afraid to pray that it would always be so. She took the moment, reveled in it, and tried not to question what tomorrow would bring.

"I love you, Morgan," she said, her breath as soft as a sigh. She raised her head to look into his eyes and discovered that he had drifted into a deep slumber. Smiling, Lacey caressed his cheek, then brought two fingertips to her mouth and transferred a kiss from her lips to Morgan's. "Sleep well, my love."

Lacey studied her reflection in the vanity mirror, wondering if she'd applied a little too much kohl to her eyelids. Her cheeks were rouged with a delicate rose pink, and her hair was perfectly in place, but her eyes were a little overdone, she finally decided. With a soft cloth, she dabbed at the lines until they were little more than a suggestion. It had been so long since she'd had to dress for a formal occasion that she was woefully out of practice in the delicate art of enhancing her features.

Donning her complicated gown without Berta's assistance had been no easy chore, either, but the effort had been worth it. Or it would be if Morgan was pleased by the way she looked in the midnight blue velvet dress he had picked out for her.

"And if he doesn't like it," she told her reflection, "that's just too bad, because this is as good as it gets." With one last, unnecessary gesture, she checked the pearl-encrusted combs that held her hair in place, and then lightly touched the sapphire brooch at her throat. Morgan's gift had been unexpected and touching. The mysterious errands he had run this afternoon had all been for her benefit. Theatre tickets, the brooch, everything . . . all were considerate, romantic gestures.

The meeting with Keenan Stoddard had been an accident— the one blight on an otherwise perfect day—but Lacey wasn't sorry she had discovered Morgan's connection to Senator Hanson. Even after an afternoon of intense lovemaking, Morgan still refused to tell her more about the plan that had brought him to Wyoming, but at least Lacey was less confused than she'd been before. Her instincts about Morgan had been right. He had asked for her trust, and Lacey knew she was right to give it to him, just as she'd been right to give him her heart. He was a good man. He believed as strongly in justice as she did, otherwise he would never have become involved in this dangerous situation. He wasn't a footloose gambler, he was a man of conscience and principle.

And he was also her lover.

As she'd lain in Morgan's arms, Lacey had tried to find some shame in that, but none had arisen. How could it be wrong to love and be loved? How could it be wrong to give and receive a pleasure that went beyond the physical and touched the soul? How could being happy for the first time in years be shameful?

If Lacey had found any guilt at all during her soul-searching, it was in the strange sense that she had somehow betrayed David, not by loving Morgan, but by loving him so very much. David had been her dearest friend, but his touch had never set her on fire the way Morgan's did. The physical side of her marriage had been sweet and satisfying, but with Morgan, there was something more. Lacey hadn't figured out what it was yet, but it was intense and so powerful that it almost frightened her.

Or it would have if she had let it. Instead, she focused on Morgan and turned all her thoughts and energy to the pleasing task of making him as happy as he had made her.

That was why she was so obsessed with her appearance tonight. Everything had to be perfect for Morgan, so she checked her kohl-darkened eyelids one last time and rose from the vanity, carefully adjusting the panels of her overskirt and the folds of the long train.

Unable to resist, she glanced in the mirror, which now showed her from shoulder to thigh, and studied her dress. Even modesty could not keep her from admitting that it was as fashionable as any in the current issues of *Harper's Bazar*: narrow waist, a perfect V-shaped bodice, and a modest but pronounced protrusion of a bustle, which would have looked comical had not her gown draped it so perfectly.

Laughing at herself, Lacey told the mirror, "You are becoming vain, Allyce."

"Are you going to talk to yourself all night, or may I expect to be allowed into the conversation eventually?" Morgan asked, rapping on the door between Lacey's room and the parlor, which was closed for the first time since their arrival last night.

"I shall be only too happy to speak with you, my love," Lacey called out. Moving quickly, she plucked her cape and ermine muff off the bed. "What would you like to talk about?"

Morgan stepped back as she opened the door, and his witty retort died in his throat. "My God, you're beautiful," he breathed. And she was. Swathed in velvet, with ecru Chantilly lace at her throat and wrists, and butterfly bows of the same color on her draped skirt, she was the most elegant vision Morgan had ever seen. The velvet basque of her gown formed a deep V at the neckline and buttoned with a row of tiny pearls, and in that V, sheer black lace covered what would have otherwise been a scandalous décolletage. Even so, Morgan could make out the luscious swell of her breasts.

Utterly enraptured, he stepped closer to her and lowered his voice intimately. "I have seen every inch of you, Lacey. I have even tasted every inch of you. Our lovemaking this afternoon should have sated me for a lifetime, but seeing you in that gown makes me want you all over again."

Lacey's breath grew short and a blush darkened the rouge on her cheeks, but she did not look away from his mesmerizing gaze. With one hand, she reached out to touch the silver brocade vest he'd bought just to please her. His white shirt had tiny ruffles down the front, and just those little changes in his wardrobe had transformed him into an elegant courtier. It also pleased her that for the first time since their arrival in Cheyenne, Morgan wasn't wearing his revolver. "You look handsome, too, but I think I prefer the way you looked this afternoon as you slept"—her blush deepened—"and just before you slept."

A vivid image of the moment she described flashed into his mind, and with it came all the sensations and emotions that had accompanied their lovemaking. He felt a tightening in his loins and regretfully took a step back. "If you remind me too much of that moment, we'll never make it to the performance."

Lacey smiled, delighted that with nothing more than words she'd been able to move Morgan as profoundly as he had moved her. "You're the one who wanted to talk, remember?" she teased. "But since you went to so much trouble to obtain theatre tickets, I suppose we should table any further . . . discussion until later."

Morgan grinned. "How much later?"

"You promised me an evening of theatre and dinner at the Tivoli," she reminded him. "It may be quite late before it is safe to continue this conversation."

"Then by all means, let us be off. The sooner we begin, the sooner we can return."

It was only a short walk down Hill Street to the opera house, where carriages were lined up for blocks in every direction. Fighting the crowd, they entered the elegant foyer, and Lacey gave herself over to the pleasure of being one of the gala crowd. Amid the noise and hubbub, Morgan took her cape, and while he checked it at the cloakroom, Lacey surveyed the room. The opera house seated one thousand people, and it seemed to Lacey that they were all crowded elbow to elbow in the enormous lobby, yet more were arriving all the time from the steady stream of coaches outside.

"Quite a spectacle, isn't it?" Morgan asked as he rejoined her. He offered his hand, and Lacey placed hers on top of it so that he could lead her on a sociable stroll through the room.

"Indeed it is," she replied, leaning her head slightly toward his as she spoke. "Do you realize that nearly every person of importance, every cattle baron, and every politician in the territory will be gathered under one roof tonight? One well-placed stick of dynamite could rid Wyoming of a number of vexatious problems."

"Allyce Spencer! What a shocking thing to say," Morgan told her with a laugh. "Your suggestion would destroy Wyoming's economy in one fell swoop."

"Oh, I know that. I was only joking," she assured him, then sighed wistfully. "And besides, it would be worth the effort only if C. W. were here, and I haven't seen him. Fortunately."

Morgan laughed again, ceaselessly pleased by Lacey's wit. Despite what Rawlings had put her through, she could still joke about him. "Since we won't be blowing up C. W. and his cronies, would you care to point out some of the local luminaries to me?"

"Of course." As they passed through the milling crowd, Lacey named off an impressive list of distinguished gentlemen and ladies. She conversed casually with several couples, and though their responses were sometimes cool, Morgan was relieved to see that she wasn't being snubbed in Cheyenne to the disheartening degree that she was in Willow Springs.

"Oh, my," she murmured as she and Morgan moved on through the lobby. "Be on your best behavior, darling. The governor and his wife are headed this way."

"Hmmm . . . As I recall, you said some rather unkind things about the estimable Governor Paull in the last issue of the *Gazette*."

Wide-eyed and innocent, Lacey stopped and turned casually to Morgan. "Why, darling, are you suggesting that the governor might have objected to being called an arrogant, self-serving demigod?"

"It's entirely possible," Morgan muttered under his breath just as the governor hailed them.

"Mrs. Spencer, what a lovely surprise to find you here."

"Indeed it is," his wife added.

If Lacey hadn't been every inch the well-trained socialite, she would have choked on the couple's sugary greeting. "And what a pleasure it is to see you, Governor, Mrs. Paull." She introduced Morgan to the most powerful twosome in the territory, and though the ensuing conversation was unerringly polite, the level of veiled animosity between Lacey and the governor was startling. By the time they parted company, Morgan knew without a doubt that neither the governor nor his wife approved of Lacey or anything about her.

"Well, that was certainly interesting," he commented as they entered the elaborate auditorium and searched for their seats.

"Did you think I was going to comment on Mrs. Paull's opinion of my 'little newspaper hobby'?" Lacey asked with a laugh.

Morgan chuckled. "Comment? No, but I was worried that

you might tear her hair out. Tell me, Lacey, doesn't it bother you to be so unpopular with someone as important as the governor?"

"Being actively disliked is never pleasant, Morgan, but I think what you're actually asking is why I am not intimidated by powerful men."

"I suppose you're right. That is what I want to know."

"It's because power is an elusive thing," she said seriously as she settled into her seat on the center aisle. "All my life I've seen men rise to prominence only to fall into obscurity with a crashing thud. The only thing that lasts is integrity. A man who possesses it doesn't always achieve greatness in the eyes of the world, but in the hearts of his friends he is always treasured."

"A noble sentiment."

"I believe in nobility."

Morgan took her hand and raised it to his lips. "You are the most remarkable woman I have ever known, Allyce Smithfield Spencer, and I adore you," he whispered.

Lacey's heart turned over in her breast. "Because of my integrity?"

Morgan gave her a wolfish grin. "Among other things."

The immense chandelier began to dim, and the single-jet lights on the walls were suddenly extinguished. The red velvet stage curtain rose slowly in scalloped, draping folds, and the play began with the entrance of sentinels, Bernardo and Francisco. Five acts and three hours later, the audience rose as one to cheer the excellent ensemble of performers as they took their final bows.

It took some time for the audience to file out of the theater, and by the time Morgan collected Lacey's cape it was nearly eleven-thirty. "You must be famished," he commented as they moved into the crush of people awaiting their carriages in front of the opera house. "It's quite a walk to the Tivoli. Shall I try to find a hack?"

"In this mob? It could take days," she said with a laugh. "Frankly, I'd rather walk." She leaned close and whispered, "If you'd ever sat for three hours in a bustle and corset, you'd know why."

Morgan laughed. "Then by all means let's walk. It's a fine

night for it." He guided her through the crowd until they finally reached the point of being able to walk freely.

"What did you think of the play?" Lacey asked.

"It was an excellent production," Morgan replied. "The sword play between Hamlet and Laertes was the best I've ever seen."

"Have you seen the play often?"

Morgan nodded. "Several times. In fact, I played Laertes once while I was at William and Mary."

"Really?" Lacey asked, delighted. She had known by his speech and manner that he was well educated, but this was the first solid piece of information about his past he had ever given her.

"Don't be too impressed," he advised her. "The production was strictly amateur, and I was atrocious. I did love the duel, though. In my younger years, I fancied myself quite the blade."

"The sword is an elegant weapon. Much more civilized than a six-gun."

"I've always thought so, too," he agreed. They strolled on, discussing fencing, the theatre, and a myriad of other mutual interests, but eventually Morgan made the mistake of steering the conversation to politics and received a stinging lecture on the woman suffrage movement. He made the comment that equality for women would ultimately evolve naturally in their society, but Lacey didn't agree.

"No, Morgan. It may be inevitable, but it won't happen by itself. We are only now coming to an age where women are considered human."

Morgan frowned. "That statement is a bit extreme, isn't it?"

"No! Think about it. The war between the states freed the Negroes from slavery, but where is emancipation for women? Our battle for equality will surely be less bloody, but it will take much longer than four years, have no doubt. Why do you think David and I chose to settle in Wyoming?"

Morgan had to think a moment, but once the answer came to him it seemed ridiculously obvious. "Because this territory gives women the right to vote?"

"Exactly. In Wyoming women are afforded the same rights as men. We can vote, sit on juries, own property outright, and even hold elected office!"

"Oh, God," Morgan groaned comically. "Don't tell me you're going to enter politics!"

"Well, why not?" she asked saucily. "I think I'd make a damned fine governor, don't you?"

"Of course you would," he agreed heartily. "But what about me? Can you see me as the governor's consort, sitting around the mansion serving tea to the ladies of the Wednesday Afternoon Garden Society?"

The ridiculous image made Lacey laugh, but when she realized the significance of what he had said her laughter died. His suggestion implied that someday she and Morgan would marry. The thought was thrilling, but Lacey dared not take his jest seriously. He had only been making a joke in keeping with their lighthearted conversation; surely he didn't realize what he'd said.

"Lacey, what's wrong?" Morgan asked, concerned over her sudden silence.

"Nothing. Nothing at all," she said brightly trying to recapture their playful mood. "Frankly, I think you could charm the skirts off the Wednesday Afternoon Garden Society."

But Morgan refused to be fooled by her false cheerfulness. "Oh, no, you don't. Tell me what I said that upset you."

"Nothing!" she swore again.

"Lacey . . ."

"Really, Morgan, you're making a fuss about nothing," she said with an exasperated sigh.

"And I'll continue to do so until you tell me what took that glorious smile off your face," he warned. "Now, confess."

"It's silly," she said hesitantly. "I know you were only teasing, but you said it so casually that, well . . . it made me stop and think."

"Said what?" Morgan asked, trying to remember his exact words.

Lacey waved her muff. "Just that silly business about you being the governor's consort. You just seemed to take for granted that we might marry someday. See? I told you it was nothing."

"You didn't think I was serious?" he asked gravely.

"Well, of course not," Lacey said blithely.

"But I was serious, Lacey," he told her. They had turned

a corner and were walking against a stiff, cold breeze, but Morgan took care of the chill by pulling Lacey into the recessed doorway of a shop. He pinned her lightly into the corner and searched out her face in the shadows. "I love you. How could I not be serious about wanting to marry you?"

Lacey could barely breathe. "Morgan, please. Don't tease me. I haven't asked for anything from you, and I don't intend to, but please don't joke about something as serious as this."

Lovingly, Morgan brought his lips to hers and pressed the gentlest of kisses there. "I'm not joking, love. I told you once that when I found what I've been searching for, I'd happily settle down. Surely you must have known that I meant you."

"I didn't know, Morgan," she whispered, enraptured by his voice and his loving words and the way the shadows danced on his handsome face. "I wanted to believe that, but I didn't dare."

"Then believe it now, Lacey. I've been searching for you without even knowing it, and now that I've found you I don't intend to let you slip away." He kissed her again, deeply this time, pouring so much of his love into her that Lacey was trembling by the time he released her.

"Tell me, Lacey." His warm breath fanned her cheeks.

"Anything," she said breathlessly.

"Tell me you love me."

She drew her head back and sought his eyes. "I thought surely you knew, Morgan. I love you with all my heart."

"And when I'm free to ask you to marry me, you'll say yes?"

She nodded, enthralled by the contrast between the intensity of his voice and the tenderness on his face. "Take me back to the hotel, Morgan."

A slow smile spread over his features. "I thought you were famished."

She nodded again and wound one arm around his neck, drawing his lips down to hers. "I am."

They kissed deeply, until they were both so warm that the night cold meant nothing, and then turned back in the direction they had come.

Chapter Sixteen

Lacey spent most of Saturday pacing the floor of her sitting room, waiting for telegrams to arrive. Morgan watched her pace, and though he could think of a number of ways to divert her attention, every time he initiated one another telegram would be delivered. Lacey would dash off a reply and then resume her pacing. Finally Morgan gave up trying to divert her. He found a novel Lacey had brought with her and read while she concentrated on her business.

It was apparently time well spent; by the end of the day all her preparations were finished. Her new printing press, furniture, and supplies would all arrive on the train that passed through Cheyenne early Monday morning, she announced happily.

"Wonderful. Does that mean I have your undivided attention until then?" Morgan asked, not bothering to look up from his book.

"My attention and anything else I have are all yours," she promised coquettishly. "But since my business is finished, we could leave for Willow Springs at any time."

"Not on your life." He tossed the book away and pulled Lacey into his lap. "We'll take the train on Monday, and until then you are all mine."

Lacey slid her arms around his neck and fitted her torso to his. "Do with me as you will, sir. I am entirely at your mercy."

Morgan laughed as he moved to the edge of the sofa and stood with Lacey in his arms. "I suppose there's a first time for everything."

He headed for the bedroom, and Lacey's heart began pounding with expectation. "Are you insinuating that I'm too strong-willed for my own good?"

"Of course not! You're perfect."

"No, I'm not."

Morgan drank in her wicked smile and lost another piece of his heart. "No, you're not," he agreed. "But I love you anyway."

"Prove it," she challenged boldly.

"It might take a while," he warned.

With one gentle fingertip, Lacey traced the outline of Morgan's lower lip. "We have thirty-six hours until our train leaves. Is that enough time?"

"Well, it's a start," he said with a lecherous smirk, then dropped her unceremoniously onto the bed.

The next day and a half were the most romantic of Lacey's life. As promised, Morgan proved he loved her in a dozen different ways. Saturday night they had a candlelight supper at the Tivoli, and later they returned to the hotel and sat on the bed, laughing like naughty children while they sipped champagne and told outrageous stories. They made love with raucous delight until they collapsed into each other's arms, exhausted and giddy while outside, Mother Nature blanketed Cheyenne with a pristine white snow.

They breakfasted in the dining room the next morning and later played chess in an intimate corner of the Inter Ocean's magnificently appointed billiard room. After lunch Morgan insisted that Lacey dress in her warmest clothes, then spirited her outside where a sleigh was waiting to take them for a long drive through Lions Park several miles north of the city.

In town, the roads were rutted and muddy, but the rugged landscape outside of town was a fantasyland of pure white ridges and rills. Trees that had been leafless and desolate yesterday were trimmed with delicate webs of snow, and the silent splendor was broken only by the slow clip-clop of the dappled mare pulling the sleigh. In Lions Park, the lake was not yet frozen over, but in sheltered coves a thin glaze of ice glistened as patches of sunlight tried to break through the gunmetal gray clouds.

"Are you cold?" Morgan asked solicitously as the sleigh left the beautifully landscaped driving park and headed back toward town.

"How could I possibly be cold?" Lacey asked with a laugh. "You have me smothered under a whole herd of buffalo robes. If I get any warmer, I'll have to take a dip in the lake to cool off."

Morgan chuckled. "That I'd like to see."

"You and about half of the population of Wyoming," she commented dryly, twisting in Morgan's arms so that she was facing him. "But seriously, thank you for this. I can't remember the last time I had a sleigh ride or felt so completely carefree. In the midst of all this beauty and serenity I could almost convince myself that I haven't a care in the world."

"Enjoy it as long as you can, love," he murmured, pressing his lips to her forehead.

"I intend to, but . . . " She grew pensive and lowered her head to his shoulder. "What's going to happen to us when we return to Willow Springs, Morgan?"

He sighed, and his warm breath formed a crystal fog around Lacey's face. "I'm not sure. I suppose you'll set your new publishing empire into place, and I'll try to find some way to protect you and do my job at the same time."

"I've put you in an untenable position, haven't I?" she asked, raising her head to look at him. It had started snowing again, and she discovered that a few hardy flakes had attached themselves to his hair. Lovingly she brushed them away, and Morgan captured her gloved hand in his own.

"I'll manage."

Lacey glanced at the coachman driving the sleigh and lowered her voice so that there was no chance he might overhear. "Morgan, please promise me that when we get back to Willow Springs, you'll stop worrying about me and concentrate totally on whatever you have planned to stop C. W. and his vigilantes. With Zach's help, I can take care of myself. You must do your job, whatever it is, and end this thing quickly, for all our sakes. Will you promise me that?"

Morgan knew that Lacey's troubles with Croft and with Rawlings, too, were far from over, but that only made it more imperative that he get on with his plan. He was surprised that no one had recognized him yet and made Rawlings aware of his identity; maybe it was time to take the laws of chance into his own hands. For Lacey's sake, the sooner he infiltrated the vigilantes the better. He could probably protect her better from the inside, anyway.

Finally he nodded and, mindful of the driver, kept his voice low as well. "All right, Lacey. I'm going to send a telegram of my own tonight and see if I can't speed things up a little. But you must promise me two things."

"What?"

"First, don't be foolish or do anything impetuous—like pointing a gun at C. W. or walking the streets of Willow Springs without Zach at your side. Agreed?"

Lacey nodded. "Of course I'll be cautious. I'm stubborn, but I'm not foolhardy, Morgan."

He grinned at her. "Let's save that argument for another time, shall we? Right now I want a second promise from you."

"Anything."

His grin faded, and his look grew intense. "You must trust me, Lacey. Once we're back in Willow Springs, I may not be able to see you, talk to you. And I certainly won't be able to explain what's going on."

"I understand that," she told him, her countenance as serious as his.

"Good. But no matter what happens, no matter what I'm forced to do or say, no matter what you hear about me, you must believe that it's all part of the plan. Can you do that for me? For us? Do you love me enough to trust me, no matter what?"

Lacey felt tears forming beneath her long, snow-tipped eyelashes. "Morgan, I love you enough to put my heart and soul in your hands," she told him, her voice filled with emotion. "My trust is only a small part of what I long to give you."

"Lacey, you have already given me more than I could ever have imagined or possibly hoped for." He touched his lips to her forehead and pulled her tightly into his arms. "And it's far more than I deserve," he whispered.

Lacey pressed against him, and they rode back to town in silence, letting the falling snow form a shield around them that kept the rest of the world at bay for a little while longer.

When they returned to the Inter Ocean, the boardwalk, which had earlier been swept clean, was turning white again, and Morgan was very careful in handing Lacey out of the sleigh onto the walk.

"Here you are, Mr. O'Rourke," he said, handing several bills up to the driver. "You have a very surefooted horse and a well-oiled sleigh. The lady and I thank you for the lovely tour of Lions Park."

"My pleasure, sir," Cleary O'Rourke answered, pocketing the fare plus the generous gratuity that had been included. "We'll be havin' a nice fresh snow again afore mornin', so if you an' the lady'd be likin' another ride, you just send for old Cleary, ya hear?"

"We'll keep that in mind, won't we, Morgan?" Lacey said graciously. "My thanks to you, Mr. O'Rourke."

"A genuine pleasure." The beefy coachman tipped his high hat and watched as the gentleman escorted the lady into the hotel. When the doors closed behind them, his ingratiating smile faded, and his look grew thoughtful. "Morgan, is it?" he muttered to himself as he signaled his horse to move on. "Now, ain't that interestin'."

Though the streets were slushy, O'Rourke made good time back to the stable and pulled in bellowing at the top of his lungs, "Johnnie! Johnnie, lad, come unhitch the mare, and be quick, now!"

A boy of thirteen with hair as black as coal stuck his head out of the hayloft and looked down at his father. "Trouble, Pa?"

"Not trouble, lad. Money. There's cold hard cash on the barrelhead to be earned if we're quick. Now get down here and take care of old Bess!"

Johnnie O'Rourke scrambled down the ladder. "What's happened?"

Cleary removed his gloves and held his hands next to the potbellied stove in the corner. "Do ya remember that man, Hastings, who was in here yesterday askin' questions about a man by the name o' Justice Morgan?"

Johnnie nodded as he began unhitching old Bess. "Sure. He was offerin' fifty dollars to anyone who could tell him where he might find the devil who'd murdered his son down in Colorado. Said he was a big man with black hair and strange golden eyes."

"That's right. And I've just seen that very man, and the lady with him called him by the very name, Morgan."

Johnnie let out a wild whoop. "Fifty whole dollars, Pa! We'll be rich."

Cleary gave his son a lopsided grin and cuffed him on the shoulders. "At least till the end o' the year, lad. That fifty dollars is goin' to look mighty good to your ma. I only hope the man with the money ain't left town yet." He shoved his hands back into his gloves and started for the door.

"Pa?"

Cleary stopped and looked back at the boy, who was wearing a strange, puzzled look. "What?"

"What do you reckon Mr. Hastings'll do when he finds this Justice Morgan?"

Cleary shrugged. "Kill 'im, I suspect. It's what I'd do if anyone laid a hand on my boyo. Now get that mare unhitched and rub 'er down good!"

They had completed their breakfast quite some time ago, but Lacey was still sipping coffee as she stood pensively at the sitting room window, studying the nearly deserted street while Morgan finished dressing. Last night's snowfall had added several more inches, and because it was so early, the streets of Cheyenne were still blanketed in white. There were a few wagon tracks, and one or two industrious shopkeepers had shoveled the snow from the front of their businesses, but overall, the city was as sleepy-quiet as it had been more than an hour ago when Lacey and Morgan had risen to get ready for the trip back to Willow Springs.

"You're very restless this morning, love," Morgan commented as he stepped into the parlor, buttoning his vest. "Are you worried about the train being on time?"

Lacey turned to him and smiled. "Not really. When the bellboy came for our luggage a few minutes ago, he assured me that at last report everything was running on schedule."

"Then why are you so jittery?" He moved toward her, and Lacey set her cup on the windowsill so that when Morgan took her in his arms, she could wrap her arms around his waist.

"I'm experiencing a definite conflict of emotions," she told him as she rested her head on his shoulder and soaked in the luxury of being safe and loved. "I'm anxious to get home to Berta and Zach, yet it saddens me to think of leaving this hotel suite." She looked up at him. "These last three days have been the most wonderful of my life, thanks to you, and I don't want our time together to end."

"Then don't think of it as an ending, Lacey. Think of it as the beginning of an intermission. I promised you last night that I'd finish this business with Rawlings as quickly as possible, and when it's done, we can be together for good."

He made it sound so simple, but Lacey knew better. Morgan was involved in a dangerous game, and there were bound to be a hundred little things that could go wrong. The real cause of her anxiety this morning was that she had a frightening premonition that everything between them was about to change—drastically. No matter how hard she tried to tell herself that she was being silly, the fear of impending disaster wouldn't go away.

But Morgan didn't need to know that she was terrified of losing him; that would only make his job harder. Lacey wished she knew exactly what that job was, but Morgan couldn't tell her, and she'd given up asking. She'd promised him her trust; now she had to honor that promise and allow him to do the job he'd come to Wyoming to do. The best way she could help him was by reassuring him that she would be fine until his work was completed.

Rising on tiptoe, she pressed a light kiss to his lips. "I'll hold you to that promise, love. And now we should be going." She started to pull out of his arms, but Morgan tightened his hold on her, fitting her body perfectly to his.

"Oh, no, you don't. It may be a while before I have another opportunity to kiss you properly. I don't intend to let this chance pass me by." He lowered his face to hers, and Lacey yielded to him completely. Automatically her lips parted to receive him, but Morgan took his time, painting her mouth with his tongue, nipping lightly at her lower lip, and teasing her with his warm breath until Lacey moaned softly and began mimicking his attempt at slow torture. And then it was Morgan who moaned with pleasure. Their kiss deepened as passion ignited between them, and by the time Morgan finally raised his head, they were both breathless.

"Maybe that wasn't such a good idea after all," he said huskily. Lacey was snuggled tightly against his loins, and even through her several layers of skirts and petticoats, she could feel his arousal.

"It's a real shame that train isn't going to be late," she told him, her voice just as hoarse as his.

"Yes, it is," he said dryly, then resolutely placed his hands on Lacey's shoulders and set her away from him. "And if we don't go now, it won't matter whether it's on time or not, because neither of us will be at the station when it arrives."

Lacey laughed lightly and moved to the sofa where she'd laid the gray velvet redingote that matched her traveling suit. Morgan helped her into the floor-length beaver-trimmed mantle, and while she worked at the fastenings, he disappeared into the bedroom. He was gone several minutes, and when he returned he was wearing his frock coat. Over that, his calf-length overcoat hung loose, and somewhere underneath was his Colt. It still disturbed Lacey every time he wore it, but she was trying hard to adjust.

"I told Mr. Ford to send our baggage on to the station and asked that he have a hackney waiting for us," Lacey told him.

"Good. I'll settle our account with him and—" Morgan stopped in midsentence, looking at Lacey questioningly. "When did you see Mr. Ford this morning?"

Lacey sighed. This was something else she'd been dreading, because she knew Morgan was going to protest. "When the waiter brought our breakfast tray, I asked him to send Mr. Ford up to see me. He came while you were bathing, and . . . " She hesitated slightly.

"And what?"

Lacey moved toward Morgan, one hand held out placatingly. "Please don't be upset with me, and please don't argue the issue. You see, I've already settled our account."

Morgan frowned. "Lacey—"

"Darling, please don't be insulted. I knew if I waited until we went down to the front desk you'd never allow me to pay for my room, so I took matters into my own hands. You've spent a great deal of money this weekend, and my conscience wouldn't rest if I allowed you to pay for our lodgings as well."

"Lacey, I'm not a pauper. I can afford—"

"I'm sure you can," she said, cutting him off quickly. "But this trip was my idea. It was solely for my benefit, and I can't allow you to bear the cost of my business expenses." Her look begged for his understanding. "Are you angry with me?"

Morgan laughed shortly and pulled her into his arms. "How can I be angry when you pout so prettily?"

"I do not pout!" she said indignantly. "Only simpering young girls pout, and in case you haven't noticed, I am a full-grown woman."

"Oh, I noticed that, all right," he told her, his golden eyes twinkling merrily. "Every time I hold you in my arms, I say to myself, This is a lady who's full-grown—in all the right places!"

Lacey blushed. "You are a cad, sir. And I love you for it."

"I love you, too. Pout and all." Playfully Lacey pushed against him, and Morgan released her with a laugh. "All right, let's be off."

He collected their room keys and escorted Lacey downstairs. Barney Ford was just emerging from his office as they descended to the quiet lobby, and he greeted them with his usual good cheer.

"I'm so sorry to see you leave. Next time you come, you must bring Zach with you."

"I will, I promise," Lacey said, extending her hand, which he shook warmly. "I can't thank you enough for all you've done. I could not have conducted my business so smoothly without you—not to mention all the other kindnesses you've shown us."

"For you, dear lady, I would move heaven and earth."

"And you have once or twice this week," Morgan said, offering his hand as well.

"It has been my pleasure. Here, let me take those for you," he said, referring to the room keys Morgan was holding. "Mr. O'Rourke is already outside waiting to drive you to the station."

"In his sleigh?" Lacey asked.

Ford nodded. "Yes. Some of the low-riding hacks are finding the streets difficult this morning. Oh, and speaking of difficulties, I've heard an unconfirmed report that the train might not be on time, after all. Something about a troublesome snowdrift in Eagle Pass. You should probably go on to the station, just in case the report is false, though."

"We will," Morgan said.

And Lacey added, "Just as soon as I've seen the desk clerk to retrieve my valuables from the vault. Will you excuse me a moment?" She hurried off to the front desk, where she had turned over the magnificent sapphire brooch Morgan had given her.

Barney Ford watched her go, then turned back to Morgan, his smile no longer in evidence. "I'm grateful for a moment to speak with you alone, sir," he said seriously. "This may mean nothing, but I didn't want to alarm Mrs. Spencer."

Morgan frowned. "What is it?"

"Someone has been asking about you."

"Who? Croft or another of Rawlings's men?"

Barney shook his head. "No, I don't believe so, sir. He was looking for you, not Mrs. Spencer. At least that was the desk clerk's understanding. Last evening, about an hour after you and Mrs. Spencer returned from Lions Park, a tall, rough-looking man came in asking for the room number of a man named"—Ford grew distinctly uncomfortable, as though he hated to even say the name—"Justice Morgan. According to the desk clerk, the description he gave fit you perfectly."

Morgan's whole body tensed. This was what he had been waiting for, but he hadn't expected it to happen this way, and he had absolutely no idea who might be inquiring about him. That in itself was troublesome. "Did the man give his name?"

"No." Ford searched Morgan's face, looking for some evidence that this considerate, well-bred gentleman was a ruthless, cold-blooded killer. It didn't seem possible, but he had to know. "Is it true, sir? Are you . . . Justice Morgan?"

Morgan liked Barney Ford a great deal, and over the last few days he had come to believe that the respect was mutual. Now that respect was about to crumble. "Yes," he answered finally.

Ford stiffened and his manner became distant. "I see. Well, I can certainly understand why you choose to use only one name."

"I'm sorry you feel that way, Mr. Ford."

Barney sighed deeply. "How else could any upstanding,

law-abiding citizen feel, Mr. Morgan? Though I must admit that having met you, I find it hard to reconcile my casual knowledge of you with your deplorable reputation."

Morgan almost smiled. "I suppose I should thank you for that."

"It's not necessary," Ford said coolly, and Morgan nodded in understanding.

"Tell me, did your desk clerk give my room number to the man who was looking for me?"

Ford shook his head. "No. I had made it clear to the staff that Mrs. Spencer was not to be discussed with anyone, and the desk clerk assumed that directive applied to you as well. He told the man that no one fitting your description was registered here, though he said it was clear the gentleman didn't believe him."

"Remember to thank the clerk for me," Morgan said. "And my thanks again to you." He bade Ford a good morning, then moved across the lobby to Lacey, who was still at the desk.

Ford watched him go, wondering if Allyce Spencer knew that her companion was a ruthless bounty hunter. Considering her past, it seemed impossible that she would willingly associate with such a person, but her private affairs were none of Barney's business, and he quickly returned to his office before he could give in to the urge to enlighten her.

"What's wrong? Did the clerk forget the combination to the safe?" Morgan asked as he joined Lacey.

"I was beginning to wonder the same thing myself," she answered. "What were you and Mr. Ford discussing so intently?"

"Nothing. Just small talk."

"Really? It looked like something more serious than—" Her voice faltered as she glanced past Morgan and saw Croft emerging from the hotel dining room. "Oh, damn. I'd almost forgotten about him."

Morgan turned and saw that Croft was headed toward them. "Don't let him disturb you, Lacey."

"Easier said than done. When we didn't see him at all yesterday, I almost dared to hope that he'd returned to Willow Springs."

Morgan gave her an effortless smile. "I was hoping he'd left the territory."

The clerk returned with Lacey's valuables, and she signed for them just as Croft arrived. " 'Morning, Miz Spencer, Morgan. Going for another sleigh ride?"

"As a matter of fact, we are," Lacey answered coldly, wondering how he'd known their whereabouts yesterday. "Only this trip is to the depot."

Croft feigned a puzzled frown. "Aren't you a little confused? This morning's train is westbound, and you should be headed east."

"Whatever for? My home is in Willow Springs."

A slow smile spread over Croft's hawkish face. "So you're not licked yet, eh? I had a feeling you were up to something." He stabbed a glance at Lacey's companion. "Spunky lady, isn't she?"

Morgan held his gaze steadily. "Yes, she is."

"And who would know better than you, right?" Croft said with a little sneer.

Morgan's hand clenched into a fist, but he resisted the urge to wipe the smug look off Croft's face. "Keep your assumptions to yourself. Come on, Lacey. Mr. O'Rourke is waiting." With one hand at her waist, he led her away, but Croft's laughter followed them.

"I'll let C. W. know you're on your way home, Miz Spencer! He may want to arrange a welcome party!"

Morgan felt the shudder that rippled down Lacey's spine as they reached the door. "Don't think about it, love. It'll all be over soon."

"I pray to God you're right, Morgan," she muttered softly, stepping through the door he held for her. Unable to help herself, she glanced over her shoulder and discovered that Croft was casually sauntering toward the door. Apparently he was going to see them off.

"Good morning, Mr. O'Rourke. Sorry to have kept you waiting," Morgan said to the friendly coachman, but the Irishman didn't seem quite so chipper this morning. In fact, he blanched when he saw Morgan and Lacey.

"Top o' the mornin' to you, sir," he replied, but the greeting seemed forced. He glanced around nervously.

Morgan handed Lacey into the coach and waited while she arranged her skirts and mantle. "Something wrong, Mr.

O'Rourke? You seem vexed this morning."

"Oh, 'tis nothin', sir, nothin' at all. I just had a wee bit too much to drink last night. Celebratin', don't you know."

"A happy occasion, I hope," Lacey said.

O'Rourke ducked his head. "Well, yes and no," he said with some reluctance. "I come into a spot of money. Sort of an inheritance."

Lacey gave him a sympathetic look as Morgan tucked a buffalo robe around her legs. "I'm so sorry. Has someone died?"

Cleary gritted his teeth. "Not yet," he muttered under his breath, cursing his luck. When the boy from the Inter Ocean had come to the stable saying there was a fare to be earned, he hadn't suspected it might be this couple. If he had, he wouldn't have come within a dozen blocks of the Inter Ocean.

Fighting the snow that clung to his boots and slowed him down, Morgan moved around the back of the sleigh to the other side. "Well, we'll make this trip worth your while, Mr. O'Rourke," he promised. A stiff breeze billowed his open coat, and he wrapped it around him as he placed one foot on the runner of the sleigh, preparing to hoist himself in.

"That's far enough, Mr. Morgan. I finally found you, and you ain't goin' anywhere!"

Halfway into the sleigh, Morgan froze for a fraction of a second, then slowly lowered himself back to the ground. Lacey whirled toward the man who had called to Morgan from across the street, and her heart began pounding with fear. The man was fifty years old, at least, but even from this distance Lacey could see that his eyes were twice that age, as though he'd seen far too much in his lifetime. He was tall and brawny. He hadn't shaved in a week, and there were dark circles under his eyes from lack of sleep or too much drink, possibly both.

What frightened Lacey, though, was that in his gloved hand was a cocked revolver—pointing directly at Morgan.

Making no sudden moves, Morgan turned slowly. "Do I know you, mister?"

"No, but I know you," Owen Hastings said, his voice filled with hate. "I know all about you, Mr. Justice Morgan. I been trailin' you for six weeks now, prayin' that nobody else would get to you first, 'cause I'm gonna be the one that has the pleasure of shootin' you dead."

"Any particular reason, or are you just lookin' to make a name for yourself?" Morgan asked, though he had a sinking feeling he knew what was coming. Six weeks ago he'd been working his way through Colorado, and there had been a boy . . . a stupid, trigger-happy boy who'd wanted to make a name for himself. The boy's father had been out of town, but Morgan had been warned that the old man might come looking for him.

It appeared that the day of reckoning was at hand.

Morgan's insides were coiled like the spring of a tightly wound watch, but outside he gave no indication of the tension.

"You murdered my son," the man seethed. "Ain't that reason enough to want to see you dead?"

Lacey listened to the exchange in horror. *Justice* Morgan? There was some mistake, some terrible mistake. She knew that name—everyone knew it. Justice Morgan was a cold-blooded bounty hunter who paid no heed to the words "dead or alive" on a wanted poster; he always brought his quarry in dead because it was easier that way. The last story about him Lacey had read claimed that Robert "Justice" Morgan had brought thirty-five dead men to justice; most of them had been unarmed when he'd taken them.

"Morgan, what is he saying? Tell him he's got the wrong man!" Lacey begged. She slid across the seat and grabbed his shoulder, but Morgan shook off her hand.

"Shut up, Lacey," he growled, never taking his eyes off the gun pointed at his heart. Slowly he stepped away from the sleigh, moving into the center of the street so that Lacey would be out of the line of fire in the event that he couldn't talk his way out of this mess. "Your name wouldn't happen to be Hastings, would it?"

"That's right. Owen Hastings. And the boy you shot dead was Joshua," he said. Following Morgan's every move with the pistol, he, too, stepped into the street.

"Mr. Hastings, your boy Joshua called me out because he wanted to make a name for himself by killing Justice Morgan. When I refused to draw on him, he tried to back-shoot me as I was leaving town. There were at least a dozen witnesses who swore I shot him in self-defense."

"What else was they gonna say?" Hastings roared. "They was all afraid you'd come after 'em if they told the truth!"

"You're wrong," Morgan said with a calm he didn't feel. "I didn't want to kill your son."

"But you did! You humiliated him in front of the whole town by refusin' to fight him, an' then you shot him when he wasn't lookin'." With a trembling hand, Hastings holstered his gun. "Well, I'm lookin' at you, Justice Morgan, and you're not going to refuse to fight me. Now, I know you got a gun under that coat somewheres, so you just pull it back and free up your gun hand so we can get this over with."

Morgan shook his head. "You're making up the facts to suit yourself, Hastings. And I'm not going to draw on you."

"If you don't, I'll shoot you where you stand! Take your pick!"

Knowing he had no choice, Morgan slowly unbuttoned his frock coat and with his left hand reached behind his back and pulled the right side of both coats back, freeing his Colt.

"Stop it! Stop it!" Lacey screamed, scrambling out of the sleigh. Slipping in the snow, she ran toward Hastings, who was so surprised by her sudden movement that he went for his gun as he whirled toward her.

"Hastings, no!" Morgan yelled, his heart slamming against his rib cage with fear for Lacey's life. His gun was in his hand long before Owen Hastings's weapon had cleared leather, and his shout tore the man's gaze from Lacey back to Morgan. "Don't do it!" he ordered. "Lacey, get back!"

Lacey stopped, staring with disbelieving, pain-filled eyes as Morgan moved toward Hastings. She had never seen anyone as lightning quick on the draw as Morgan.

Hastings froze when he saw that Morgan had the drop on him. His gun was still in his hand, halfway out of the holster, and for a brief second, he seemed to toy with the idea of continuing the motion. Morgan read his intention and quietly demanded, "Don't even think about it, man. Drop the gun back in."

Morgan had cut the distance between them by half, and when Hastings did as he was told, Morgan moved the rest of the way to him.

"You killed my son," Hastings whimpered in a broken voice.

"I didn't want to. Believe that. He just didn't give me an alternative. Now go home, Mr. Hastings, please," Morgan begged. Gently he laid one hand on the man's shoulder, but Hastings jerked away from his touch. Cowed like a whipped puppy, he turned and trudged away.

Morgan watched him for only a second, then turned to Lacey, who had slowly backed away from them. Her face was ashen, and tears were streaming down her cheeks. "Lacey, it's all right. It's over."

"You *are* Justice Morgan, aren't you?" she asked, her voice hardly more than a whisper.

He paused for a fraction of a second. "Yes," he said, extending one hand to her, but Lacey whirled away and ran toward the hotel. "Lacey, come back. Let me explain," he ordered, following her.

"Explain what?" she demanded, whirling on him as she reached the boardwalk. "That you're a cold-blooded bounty hunter, just like the one who killed my husband?"

"No!" Morgan grabbed for her and managed to get hold of her shoulders.

"Oh? You're not really Justice Morgan?" she asked viciously.

"Yes, I am, but—"

"Then let me go!" she cried, struggling to get away even as she clung to his forearms for support because tears were coming stronger now, and the pain in her heart was suffusing her whole body. "Why didn't you tell me? You should have told me!" she sobbed, and the tears finally won. Her struggles ceased, and she looked up at him with agony in her eyes. "Oh, God, Morgan, why did you let me love you?"

Morgan had never seen so much pain in any woman's eyes. The secret he'd needed someone from Willow Springs to discover was finally out. Not only did Lacey know it, but Croft knew it as well. He'd been standing just outside the hotel door, watching everything, and now he would tell Rawlings, and Rawlings would try to hire Morgan over to his side. He would infiltrate the vigilantes and ultimately put an end to Rawlings's reign of terror.

Knowing that should have made Morgan happy, but it didn't, because he was looking into Lacey's eyes and seeing brutal pain, confusion, and a growing hatred that stabbed like a knife straight into his heart. The "truth" had cost him the woman he loved. "Lacey, I'm sorry. I didn't mean for you to find out like this."

"You're sorry? Sorry!" She pushed away from him so abruptly that he stumbled back, and when he reached for her again, she demanded, "Don't touch me! Don't ever touch me again."

His hand had caught a fold of her coat, and as she twisted free, Lacey found herself facing the street. Behind Morgan no more than a dozen feet, Owen Hastings was drawing his gun.

"Morgan, behind you!" she screamed, but the look on her face had been an even earlier warning. Before the words were spoken, Morgan had pushed Lacey against the wall as he pivoted and drew his revolver. He dropped to one knee just as Hastings's bullet whizzed past the spot where he'd been standing. The deafening report of Morgan's Colt came only a fraction of a second later, and Owen Hastings fell dead, his blood staining the snow a bright red.

Sagging against the wall, Lacey stared at Hastings, but she wasn't seeing the grief-stricken older man. She was seeing David Spencer and reliving the horror of losing her husband and dearest friend. She felt the pain of his death as acutely as she'd felt it three years ago, only this time it was worse—much worse—because she'd betrayed David's memory by giving herself heart and soul to Morgan, a gunslinger, a bounty hunter, the same kind of man who had murdered her husband.

"Lacey . . . are you all right?" Morgan asked. He reached out to her, but she cut him dead with one cold, hate-filled look.

"You killed him."

"He didn't give me any choice, Lacey. You know that."

Lacey straightened and shook her head. "There are always choices, Morgan," she said in a flat, lifeless voice that was more frightening to Morgan than anything she could have said. "You made your choice years ago when you picked up a gun and set out to earn a reputation as the fastest man alive. And now you're killing grief-crazed men and foolish boys. Congratulations."

"What's goin' on here!" Deputy Ira Wells elbowed his way through the crowd that had been summoned onto the nearly deserted street by the two gunshots. He checked the lifeless body and turned toward Morgan. "This your doin', mister?"

"He was about to shoot me in the back," Morgan replied.

"Is that a fact?"

The hardest thing Lacey had ever done in her life was to step toward the officer and tell him, "Yes, Deputy, that's a fact. His name is Owen Hastings. A few minutes ago he tried to force Mr. Morgan into a gunfight, and when he failed, he sneaked up on him from behind. Technically it was self-defense."

"Anybody else see it that way?" Wells asked the crowd.

Morgan gestured toward the door of the hotel, where Barney Ford and his bellboys were now clustered. "There was a man named Croft standing in the doorway the whole time. I don't know where he disappeared to, but he can tell you what happened. And the coachman, Mr. O'Rourke, saw it all, too."

"That right, Cleary?" Wells asked.

Reluctantly O'Rourke nodded. "Aye, I saw it all," he answered with a resigned sigh. He hadn't moved a muscle through any of what had transpired. At first he hadn't wanted to move the sleigh for fear of provoking the Hastings man into doing something stupid, and later he'd been too fascinated by the quarrel taking place in front of the hotel. If he'd known Hastings was going to come back, though, he'd have whipped up old Bess and gotten her out of there quick.

"Well, all of you are going to have to come over to the office so we can take your statements." Wells gave Morgan a hard look. "And until we get this sorted out, I'll have to take your Colt, mister." Morgan handed over the weapon, butt first, and the deputy tucked it into the waistband of his trousers. Another deputy had arrived on the scene, and Wells issued a string of orders that cleared the crowd and put someone onto the task of notifying the undertaker. "O'Rourke, help this lady onto your sled and take her over to the office. And you"—he jabbed a finger at Morgan—"come with me."

Barney Ford stepped forward quickly and helped Lacey into the sleigh as the deputy said, "By the way, mister, you got a name?"

"Morgan," he replied. "Just Morgan."

Lacey froze as the painful memory of the day she'd met Morgan flowed over her. She'd stood in the door of the sheriff's office, intrigued by the well-spoken stranger, and asked, "Are you headed anyplace in particular, Mr. . . . ?" Her voice had trailed off as she waited for him to supply a name.

"The name's Morgan."

"Morgan something or something Morgan?"

"Just Morgan, ma'am," he had answered.

Just Morgan—short for Justice Morgan. He had told her who he really was, she just hadn't realized it. Somehow his clever little play on words made his deception even worse.

Sick and numb, Lacey settled into the sleigh, and as Cleary O'Rourke drove her to the sheriff's office, she wondered how she was ever going to cope with the hideous pain that was squeezing the life out of her heart.

Chapter Seventeen

After Lacey gave her statement at the sheriff's office, she left immediately. Morgan tried to speak with her, but she could hardly bear to look at him, and so she hurried on to the train station. Fortunately, the rumor about a snowdrift in Eagle Pass turned out to be true, and the train had been delayed for nearly two hours. It pulled in to the depot only minutes after she arrived, and she barely had time to send a telegram to Zach requesting that he pick her up at the station in Willow Springs. Her head reeling and her heart numb, she returned home.

Three days later, the numbness still hadn't worn off. She wandered around her house, wrapped in a cocoon of sorrow and shame from which she simply could not escape. Her printing equipment, labeled as photographic supplies, had been delivered to her new office, but she couldn't bring herself to go down the hill into town. She gave herself lectures on commitment to her profession, but the will to continue her journalistic fight seemed to have deserted her. She reminded herself of Riley and Martha and the need to avenge their brutal murders; but that only made her think of Senator Will Hanson's mysterious plan for revenge—and Justice Morgan's part in that plan.

Thinking of Morgan drove a knife into Lacey's heart, and nothing she did could drive away the pain. She had loved him—still loved him—and yet he was a brutal murderer. Bounty hunting was legal, but he was a murderer nonetheless. The knowledge that she had given herself so totally to someone like Justice Morgan made Lacey physically ill, but the sweet memories of loving him wouldn't go away.

And that was the worst thing of all. How could someone so kind and loving be a ruthless killer? It didn't make sense. In her mind, Lacey relived every minute she had spent with him, searching for some clue she had missed, some sign she had been too blind to see, but she could find nothing. The man she had fallen in love with was wonderful; the man she had discovered him to be was not.

She tried to convince herself that she hated him, but the effort was to no avail. The love in her heart simply wouldn't go away. Only time could cure that. Until then she would have to live with the guilt and the pain.

It surprised her that Morgan had made no attempt to contact her, but she was relieved that he had stayed away. In Cheyenne, she had said all that needed to be said, and nothing Morgan could tell her would change the way she felt. He had come to Willow Springs for the noble purpose of bringing C. W. Rawlings to justice, but that didn't alter the fact that he was a cold-blooded bounty hunter.

While Lacey tried to find a balm for her aching heart, Zach and Berta treated her with extraordinary care. Giving few details, she had told them what she had discovered about Morgan. They had filled in the rest for themselves when she asked that they never mention his name again. Once or twice they tried to encourage Lacey to discuss the emotions that were obviously tearing her apart, but she refused, and finally they gave up. They supported her with tender silence and prayed that their friend would overcome her terrible grief.

By Thursday morning Lacey had shown no sign of doing so, and they were both relieved when Asa Mercer arrived unexpectedly from Cheyenne. While Berta hurried upstairs to inform Lacey she had a visitor, Zach escorted Asa to the parlor.

"I'm very glad you're here, sir," Zach told him. "Lacey has not been herself since she returned from the city."

Asa sat on the edge of a chair by the hearth. "So you know what happened?"

"Some of it. She described the unfortunate shooting that led to her discovery of Mr. Morgan's identity."

Asa looked distinctly uncomfortable. "I know that must have been a terrible shock to Allyce. It certainly was to me, but . . . " He paused for a moment. "Has she explained why she decided not to return to Cheyenne?"

Zach's brows went up in surprise. "Return? Why should she?"

Asa's frown deepened. "Don't you know? Haven't you read the papers? Didn't Allyce tell you what was in the telegram?"

It was Zach's turn to frown. "We received no telegram, Mr. Mercer, and we have not left the house since Lacey returned."

"Then she doesn't know?" Mercer asked, coming to his feet.

"Know what, Asa?" Lacey asked as she stepped into the parlor.

He turned and was shocked by her appearance. She was as pale as death, and there was no animation in her eyes. She moved stiffly, her torso erect, and the pain etched on her face tore at Asa's heart. This was how she had looked after David's death, when only pride and courage had sustained her. "Allyce dear, are you all right?" he asked, hurrying across the room.

"I will be, Asa," she promised, taking his hand. Zach slipped quietly out of the room, and Lacey escorted her friend to the sofa, where they sat together. "It's just taking time for me to sort through . . . everything. I assume you've heard what happened Monday morning."

"Everyone knows what happened, Allyce," he told her gravely.

"I expected no less. It isn't often the territory is visited by someone as famous as Justice Morgan," she said bitterly. "Now, what was it you thought I should know?"

Asa regarded her with concern. "Allyce, you were sent a telegram yesterday, but Zach said it never arrived."

Lacey shrugged. "There's nothing unusual about that. The telegraph agent never delivers my messages until C. W. has seen them. He's probably out at the ranch—"

"No," Asa interrupted her. "He's in Cheyenne. And you have no idea what transpired there after you left Monday morning?" She shook her head, and Asa's shoulders sagged a little. "I am somewhat relieved, though I do dread being the one to give you the news. I assumed you'd heard, or had read the story in one of the newspapers."

"Asa, I have no idea what you're talking about. What happened after I left?"

"Allyce . . . Mr. Morgan is in jail. He has been charged with the murder of Owen Hastings."

Lacey leaned forward on the sofa. "That's impossible! The shooting was self-defense. I told the sheriff that, and as I was leaving his office I heard Cleary O'Rourke swear to the same thing."

"I know. Cleary gave his statement and left, but he returned an hour later with the gunfighter, Croft, and they both told quite a different story. According to them, Owen Hastings confronted Morgan with words only. Morgan shot him with absolutely no provocation and then removed the poor man's gun from his holster so that it would look like self-defense."

"That's absurd!" Lacey said, rising in agitation. "What reason did O'Rourke give for changing his story?"

"He claims that Morgan threatened his life."

"Oh, and I suppose he decided to tell the truth after Croft promised to protect him," she said sarcastically. "Damn that man! Croft is the one threatening O'Rourke!"

Asa shook his head. "I doubt that, Allyce. Cleary O'Rourke isn't a bad man, but it's well known that he'll do anything for a dollar. I imagine Croft waved a few bills under his nose."

"Then you believe my version of the story? That Morgan is innocent?"

"Of course. I know you'd never lie about a thing like that, Allyce. Obviously Morgan is being framed."

"But why?"

Asa shrugged. "I have no idea. Based on what you told me about Croft, he could be acting on his own in order to get rid of someone he perceives as a rival, or this could be Rawlings's doing. Personally I'd put my money on Rawlings. He arrived in Cheyenne Tuesday morning, and it has taken a considerable amount of influence to make things happen so quickly."

"How do you mean?" she asked, returning to sit on the sofa.

"The coroner's inquest was held Wednesday. At that inquest Morgan was charged with murder, and the trial has been set for Friday."

Lacey sprang to her feet again. "So soon? How is that possible?"

"Judge Commestock has canceled everything else on his docket."

"That's unheard of!"

"I know, but he claims this is such a heinous crime that justice should be meted out quickly."

Lacey raised one hand to her face, fighting a wave of dizziness. This couldn't be happening. Morgan was going on trial for a murder he didn't commit. No matter how she felt about him and the terrible things he had done in the past, she couldn't allow an innocent man to hang. "You're right," she said faintly. "C. W. must be behind this. Only he and his friends have the power to control Judge Commestock."

"And only you have the power to save Mr. Morgan," Asa said gently. "You must come to Cheyenne and tell the jury what really happened. Morgan's lawyer and I have done everything we can to locate another witness, anyone who might have seen what happened and would be willing to come forward and tell the truth."

"Your efforts were a waste of time, weren't they?"

Asa nodded. "Of course. We feel confident that at least two shopkeepers saw the shooting, but both of them refuse to admit it. They've either been paid off or intimidated in order to keep them silent."

"Then I'll have to go to Cheyenne," Lacey said, more to herself than to Asa. Then she looked at him as a thought occurred to her. "Asa, did Morgan send you to get me?"

"No," he said gravely. "In fact, he asked that you not be involved."

Lacey frowned. "Why?"

Asa looked uncomfortable again. "He feels that he has hurt you enough already. He doesn't want you to suffer more because of him."

Lacey closed her eyes and fought back a rush of tears. His was a foolish, impractical sentiment, but it was so like the man she had fallen in love with. Still, she no longer dared to trust her impressions of Morgan's character.

"Asa, how is it possible for one man to be two different men? The Morgan I knew was considerate and loving, the kind of man who would try to shield me from hurt, even if it meant harm to him. But Justice Morgan . . . " She looked at him in bewilderment. "Justice Morgan is a ruthless killer. Men like that aren't capable of self-sacrifice."

Asa shook his head, clearly as confused as she was. "Allyce, no one is totally good or evil. Every personality has shades of gray. Yet I must confess that your friend Morgan is more complex than anyone I have ever met. I've heard all the stories about Justice Morgan, and I can't reconcile the man I know with the legend that surrounds him."

"Neither can I."

He heard the pain in her voice. "Learning his identity must have been devastating."

"That is something of an understatement, Asa," she said with a sad smile.

"Cleary O'Rourke has been telling everyone who'd listen how you denounced Morgan after the shooting. Most people are convinced that's the reason you haven't returned to Cheyenne to refute Croft's story."

Lacey shook her head. "Asa, no matter how I feel about Morgan, I wouldn't allow him to be convicted of a crime he didn't commit."

"That's why I felt I should come and see you. I knew you couldn't be aware of the situation. Charles Green, Morgan's lawyer, asked me to come. He would have made the trip himself, but he's busy mounting a defense."

"Naturally." She reached out her hand to him and he stood. "I'm glad it was you who came, Asa."

He squeezed her hand. "So am I. But now we should really start thinking about how to get to Cheyenne. There isn't another train out of Willow Springs until late tomorrow morning, and by then it will be too late."

Lacey thought for a moment, fighting back her dread. She didn't want to go back to the city—the idea of seeing Morgan was unbearable—and yet she had no choice; the thought of Morgan hanging from a rope was unbearable, too.

Glancing at the clock on the mantelpiece, she finally told Asa, "The short line between Laramie and Cheyenne runs at three o'clock. If we hurry, we should be able to catch it."

Morgan sat in a little chamber adjacent to the courtroom, staring at the handcuffs on his wrists. His lawyer was taking care of some last-minute details, and there was a guard at his door. He'd spent the last four nights in jail, and in a few minutes he would be paraded in front of a jury and the farce would begin.

He'd known this job would be dangerous, but being hanged for murder wasn't one of the hazards he'd anticipated.

There was a way to escape the gallows, of course. Ep Luder had already taken care of the details, but Morgan didn't want to play his trump card yet. If he did, his entire scheme to bring down C. W. Rawlings would collapse, and since Morgan was convinced Rawlings was behind the attempt to frame him, he wanted to see what the unscrupulous cattle baron was up to.

Morgan was mystified. He had no idea what C. W. thought he could gain from the charade, but it was certain he had a motive of some sort. In order to find out what that was, Morgan was going to allow himself to be put on trial for murder. Not a pleasant prospect.

The guard came in and motioned for Morgan to accompany him. They entered the courtroom through a side door, and the crowd immediately fell silent. There wasn't a vacant seat in the gallery, and spectators were lining the walls two and three deep; the trial of the infamous Robert Justice Morgan was the best show in town. Morgan scanned the back of the room and spotted Ep Luder, who gave him a subtle nod to indicate that his plans were all in place should his intervention be needed. Morgan acknowledged him with a barely perceptible nod, then glanced over the rest of the crowd. C. W. was there—on the prosecution's side of the room, of course—and Croft was right beside him.

Seated at the defense table, Charles Green looked up from the papers he was studying and gave his client an encouraging half-smile, but Morgan looked past the attorney and was shocked to see Lacey. She was frighteningly pale, and she stared straight ahead, her posture so stiff that it was almost painful to look at her.

For Morgan, it would have been painful to look at her, even if she hadn't been so rigid. He still couldn't forget the last words she'd said to him and the look of loathing in her eyes. She hated him. There was nothing he could do about that, but God, how it hurt.

"What's Mrs. Spencer doing here?" he demanded quietly as he rounded the table.

Green glanced over his shoulder at Lacey. "She arrived in town late yesterday afternoon."

The guard removed the handcuffs from Morgan's wrists. "That doesn't answer my question," he said as he sat.

"She's here to testify," the attorney said reluctantly, knowing his client wasn't going to like the news.

"The hell she is!" Morgan growled. "I don't want you to put her on the stand. I told you that two days ago."

"She's the only one willing to tell the truth," Green argued.

"Her testimony won't make any difference. It will be her word against that of Croft and O'Rourke."

Green nodded. "That's right. But Mr. Croft is a transient gunfighter, and everyone in town knows that O'Rourke is a mercenary. Mrs. Spencer, on the other hand, is a lady of quality and substantial influence. That will mean a great deal to a jury."

"That won't mean a damned thing to a jury," Morgan said, scowling. "This trial has already been bought and paid for by C. W. Rawlings."

"You don't know that for sure."

"Yes, I do," he said hotly. "I don't want Lacey to testify. She's been through too much already because of me."

"So you said, but she's the only chance I've got to keep you off the gallows, and I'm going to put her on the stand!" Green took a deep, calming breath. He'd had some strange clients in his time, but Justice Morgan had to be the strangest. It almost seemed as though he *wanted* to be convicted of murder. "Look, Mr. Morgan, unless Mrs. Spencer testifies, this is going to be a very short trial. You're being railroaded, and she's my only hope of obtaining an acquittal."

Morgan shook his head to clear it of images of Lacey on the stand being grilled about the nature of her relationship with him. If their affair was made public, her reputation would be ruined. "Don't you understand? If the prosecutor has any brains at all, he'll crucify her."

"I don't see how that's possible."

"Then you're an idiot," Morgan snapped. Was he going to have to spell it out for his attorney? "Look, this is my trial. It's my life on the line, and I'm telling you Allyce Spencer is not going to testify. After the prosecutor presents his case,

I want you to ask for a recess. Get the trial postponed until Monday if you can."

Green frowned. "Why?"

"Because C. W. Rawlings has something up his sleeve, and I want him to have plenty of time to play his cards."

Green knew that Morgan believed Rawlings was somehow going to use this predicament to blackmail him into working for him, but Green had his doubts about that. "And if he doesn't?"

"Then you'll put me on the stand. Once I'm finished testifying, there won't be any need for Mrs. Spencer to do so."

The attorney was mystified. "Mr. Morgan, you behave as though you're the one with cards up your sleeve. Is there something you're not telling me?"

Morgan thought about his connection to Senator Will Hanson and, more important, his association with the Department of Justice in Washington. "Yes," he said succinctly, "but I have no intention of involving you in this unless it becomes absolutely necessary."

"Involving me in what?"

"You don't need to know that right now."

Green ground his teeth in frustration and would have given his client an earful had not Judge Commestock entered the courtroom just then. Everyone rose on command, and once the judge was seated, the proceedings got under way. The jury was brought in and both attorneys presented their opening arguments.

With her hands clenched in her lap, Lacey tried to listen to the lawyers, but it was difficult. Seeing Morgan had shaken her to the core. His eyes had met hers and her heart had melted. She loved him. And what was worse, he loved her. She could see that he'd been arguing with his lawyer, and Lacey knew she was the cause of that argument. He didn't want her to testify. He was trying to spare her the ordeal.

And that just didn't make sense. Morgan was in desperate trouble; yet he was more worried about her than about himself. Asa had told her that, and so had Charles Green when she'd talked to him last night. And Morgan's behavior this morning bore out the truth of their claim. How was it possible for a vicious gunfighter to behave so nobly?

Asa Mercer, sitting to Lacey's right, reached over and gently patted her hands, offering what little comfort he could. Lacey gave him a weak smile, grateful for his support. And on the other side of her sat Barney Ford. His presence was a comfort, too, and yet Lacey was a little puzzled because he had been subpoenaed to testify for the prosecution. He had been inside the hotel at the time of the shooting, and Lacey couldn't imagine what the prosecutor was going to question him about.

Croft was the first witness, and his testimony was devastating. With absolute conviction, he told the preposterous story of how Owen Hastings had meekly confronted Morgan, accusing him of having murdered his son. He said Hastings made a halfhearted threat, and Morgan shot him dead, then removed his gun from the holster to make the shooting look like an act of self-defense.

Charles Green did his best to shake the story, but Croft held firm. The best Morgan's attorney was able to do was to get Croft to admit that he was a gunfighter who'd been hired by C. W. Rawlings in Willow Springs.

The coroner was called next, and though his testimony was entirely factual, it was very damaging. He described in chilling detail how a single bullet had pierced Owen Hastings's heart.

"It took someone with incredible skill to place that shot so precisely, didn't it?" Felix Asher, the prosecutor, asked.

"That's right," the coroner replied.

Asher paced thoughtfully in front of the witness. "And it would also take a man with ice water in his veins to shoot an unarmed man, wouldn't it?"

Charles Green was on his feet instantly. "Objection, Your Honor."

"Sustained," Commestock said gravely. "Mr. Asher, please confine your questions to those the coroner is qualified to answer."

"Of course, Your Honor." Asher returned to his chair. "I have no further questions."

Green stood. "Dr. Lipscomb, when you arrived on the scene did you find a gun on the person of Mr. Hastings?"

"Yes, sir."

Green frowned and moved toward the witness. "You found a gun *on* the body? Mr. Hastings's gun was in his holster?"

"Well . . . no," Lipscomb admitted. "The gun was on the

ground just a few inches from Hastings's hand."

Green turned and gave the prosecutor a hard look. "So he wasn't 'an unarmed man.' "

"No."

"No further questions," he said, satisfied that he'd made his point.

"Mr. Asher, call your next witness," the judge intoned as the coroner left the stand.

"I call Barney Ford, Your Honor."

Giving Lacey a reassuring pat on the arm, Ford stood and took the stand. Once he was sworn in, Asher approached him with a stern mien. "Mr. Ford, would you state your occupation?"

"I'm the owner of the Inter Ocean Hotel."

"Did Justice Morgan take a room at your establishment a week ago last Thursday?"

"Yes."

"Was he alone?"

"No, sir."

"Who was with him?"

Barney squirmed a little in his chair. "Mrs. Allyce Spencer."

A murmur rippled through the courtroom, and Asher allowed it to die down before he continued. "What room did they occupy?"

Realizing where the prosecutor was leading, Barney said firmly, "They took *two* rooms, sir. Numbers two-oh-five and two-oh-seven."

"Mr. Ford, is there a door connecting those two rooms?"

Reluctantly Barney admitted, "Yes, there is. But there's a sitting room between the two bedrooms," he added quickly.

"Isn't it true that Mr. Morgan specifically requested connecting rooms and the only way you could accommodate him was with this three-room suite?"

Barney looked down at his hands. "Yes."

"Did Mr. Morgan make any other requests of you while he was at the Inter Ocean?"

"Like what?"

"Didn't you procure theatre tickets for him? And didn't you serve them a champagne supper in their room the following night?" Barney had to answer yes to both questions. "So Mr. Morgan and Mrs. Spencer had a romantic weekend, didn't they?"

"Objection!" Green was on his feet again, surprised by this line of questioning. Already the prosecutor was setting himself up for cross-examination of Allyce Spencer so that he could discredit her testimony; clearly he was insinuating that Morgan and Mrs. Spencer were lovers. So this is what Morgan had wanted to avoid! Green cursed himself for not having foreseen what was coming. He cursed himself, too, for not having asked Morgan if the implication was well founded. "That question calls for a conclusion."

"I withdraw the question, Your Honor," Asher said quickly with a sly wink at the jury. "I'm sure we can all draw our own conclusions. I have no more questions for this witness."

Lacey felt physically ill. If she'd been thinking more clearly, she might have anticipated what the prosecutor would do to refute her testimony, but she hadn't even considered it. She was here to tell the truth, nothing more. But it was also the truth that she and Morgan had had an affair, and if that became common knowledge, Asher could easily convince everyone she was lying to protect her lover.

Green took his turn and tried to undo some of the damage that had been done to Lacey's credibility by asking Ford to explain some of the other things he had done for Lacey and Morgan during their stay. Barney told the jury about the telegrams he'd sent on Lacey's behalf.

"So Mrs. Spencer was in Cheyenne conducting business," Green concluded.

"That's right. Her newspaper office in Willow Springs had been burned to the ground, and she was trying to replace what she had lost."

"And was Mr. Morgan's presence ever explained to you?" Green asked.

"It was." Barney pointed to Croft. "That gunfighter, Croft, meant to do Mrs. Spencer some harm, and Morgan was here to protect her."

"Objection," Asher said, standing. "That's hearsay, Your Honor. Just because Mr. Ford was *told* that doesn't mean it's the truth."

"Objection sustained," the judge intoned. "Just stick to what you know for a fact, Mr. Ford."

"I know for a fact that Croft followed Mrs. Spencer everywhere she went. That's proof enough for me," Barney said hotly.

The judge cleared his throat and warned him against any further outbursts. Morgan's attorney asked a few more questions, clarifying Lacey's business dealings, then ended his cross-examination.

"Call your next witness, Mr. Asher," Commestock instructed.

Asher stood. "Your Honor, I'd like to call Mrs. Allyce Smithfield Spencer to the stand as a hostile witness."

"You can't do that!" Morgan shouted, jumping to his feet. He whirled toward Lacey and saw that all the color had drained from her face. One trembling hand was at her throat, and Asa Mercer had placed his arm around her protectively.

"Mr. Morgan, sit down!" the judge ordered, but Morgan refused to comply.

"He can't do that! I don't want her to testify."

"Well, that's too bad," Commestock said irritably. "Mrs. Spencer gave her deposition to both attorneys last night when she arrived in Cheyenne, and that entitles Mr. Asher to call her as a witness. Now sit down, Mr. Morgan, or I'll have you restrained."

Morgan sat and leaned toward Green, speaking urgently. "Call for a recess. You've got to do something to stop this. Now."

Green asked for a moment to confer with his client, and the judge waited impatiently while they spoke in hushed tones.

"Look, there's nothing we can do about this," Green argued. "Asher will question her sooner or later, anyway."

"No, he won't, dammit," Morgan said, gritting his teeth. "I told you, I won't let it come to that. If I have to, I can put a stop to this farce with my testimony. And there's another witness on the way from Washington who can clear me. We don't need Lacey. I won't let Asher drag her reputation through the mud."

Green gave him a hard look. "Are you and Mrs. Spencer lovers?"

Morgan sighed deeply, regretfully. "Yes," he whispered.

"Dammit, why didn't you tell me?"

"Because you didn't ask, and I didn't think it was any of your business. I told you I didn't want Lacey to testify. Why didn't you listen to me?"

Green wiped one hand over his face. "Well, there's nothing we can do about it now. The prosecutor has called her, and she has to testify."

"Then ask for a recess. *I'll* testify."

"You can't," Green snapped. "I can't put you on the stand until the prosecution has rested its case. A recess wouldn't help."

"We can talk to the judge privately, get him to drop the charges."

Green looked at Morgan in amazement. "Just what the hell is this information you think is going to save you?"

"Ask for a recess and get us out of here; then I'll tell you."

"All right." Green rose. "Your Honor, I need some time to confer with my client about some new evidence that has just come to light. I'd like to request a recess—"

"Request denied, Mr. Green," Commestock said, cutting him off. "I won't allow you to employ delay tactics. Mr. Asher, continue with your next witness. Will Mrs. Allyce Spencer please take the stand?"

Green protested again, but the judge overruled his objection, and Lacey stood. A hundred pairs of eyes bored into her like knives. Morgan's eyes were the cruelest cut of all, though. She saw them when she took the stand and turned to face him. He was in agony. With his eyes, he told her he would have done anything in the world to save her from what was about to happen, but he was powerless to do so. Love, regret, and remorse were written on his face, and Lacey had to fight back tears.

She was sworn in, and she sat, carefully arranging her skirts around her. "Mrs. Spencer," Asher began, "were you in front of the Inter Ocean Hotel on the morning Owen Hastings was shot?"

"I was."

"After the incident, did you give a report to Deputy Sheriff Ira Wells?" Lacey answered in the affirmative, and Asher requested, "Would you please repeat the substance of that sworn statement?"

Summoning all her strength, Lacey kept her voice firm and clear as she related what had really happened that morning.

"So it is your contention that Mr. Hastings drew his revolver before Mr. Morgan did."

"That's right. I saw that Hastings was about to shoot Morgan in the back. I called out a warning, and Morgan shoved me aside, turned, and fired."

Asher paced back and forth in front of Lacey. "Mrs. Spencer, why did you give that statement to Deputy Wells?"

"Because it's the truth."

"Is it?"

"Yes," she said firmly. "If it wasn't the truth, why did Cleary O'Rourke tell exactly the same story to the deputy?"

"I'll ask the questions, Mrs. Spencer. What Cleary O'Rourke did or didn't tell the deputy isn't at issue here. We're talking about you at the moment."

"And I'm telling the truth."

Asher nodded. "So you said." Clasping his hands behind his back, he turned away from Lacey and moved toward the jury. "Mrs. Spencer, did you share a suite with Justice Morgan at the Inter Ocean Hotel?"

Lacey's hands were folded together so tightly that her knuckles had turned white. "Yes."

"Did you attend the theatre together last Friday?"

"Yes."

"Did Mr. Morgan give you an expensive sapphire brooch?"

Lacey's heart skipped a beat. How on earth had Asher found out about that? "Yes, he did."

"What was the occasion?"

"Occasion?"

Asher turned toward her. "Was it your birthday? An anniversary of some sort? An early Christmas present?"

"No."

"Then why did Mr. Morgan give you such a lavish gift?"

"I don't know. He just gave it to me."

The prosecutor returned to the witness box and leaned against the rail, studying Lacey closely. "Mrs. Spencer, you are a widow, are you not?"

"That's right," she replied softly.

"Your husband, David Spencer, was killed in a gunfight with a bounty hunter approximately three years ago?"

Pain knifed through Lacey, and her voice was barely audible as she answered, "Yes."

Asher paused again, letting that information soak in. He let the anticipation build until there was absolute silence in the courtroom, and then he asked, "Mrs. Spencer . . . are you and the bounty hunter, Justice Morgan, lovers?"

The bold question sent a ripple of shock through the room, and Charles Green's protest was barely audible. "Your Honor, I object. Mrs. Spencer's private life is irrelevant to this case."

"On the contrary," Asher argued. "If this woman is involved in a sordid love affair with Justice Morgan, her private life is entirely relevant! A woman in love will do many things to save the life of her paramour. She will even lie!"

"Objection, Your Honor! The prosecutor isn't asking questions, he's making speeches!"

Judge Commestock banged his gavel and looked at both men sternly. "Quiet down, both of you. I'll allow this line of questioning and direct the witness to answer the question. Mrs. Spencer, are you and Justice Morgan lovers?"

Charles Green was still on his feet, and all the spectators held their breath, waiting.

Lacey tried to shut them out of her mind and answered the question the only way she could. With the truth. "Yes," she whispered.

"I'm afraid you'll have to speak up," Asher directed maliciously.

Lacey glared at him and took a deep breath. "Yes. Justice Morgan and I have been lovers."

The shock rippled through the room again, and Lacey closed her eyes to fight back the tears that welled there.

Morgan had never felt so helpless in his life. His hands were clenched into white-knuckled fists, and he wanted to vault the table and strangle Asher. Yet he could do nothing but sit and listen as the prosecutor systematically destroyed the reputation of the woman he loved.

"Tell me, when did your illicit love affair with this bounty hunter begin?" Asher asked.

Sickened, Lacey dug her fingernails into her palms. Asher was making something wonderful sound depraved and disgusting. On Monday morning before she'd discovered Morgan's identity, she had felt no shame for having loved him, but that was no longer true. All week long, shame had consumed her, and now everyone was going to know exactly how Allyce Spencer had betrayed the memory of her husband with a vicious bounty hunter.

With difficulty, she confessed, "It began last week after we arrived in Cheyenne."

"And how many times did you have sexual relations with the defendant?"

"Your Honor, I protest!" Green shouted. He rose, keeping one hand on Morgan's shoulder to hold his client down. "Mrs. Spencer has admitted the nature of her relationship with Mr. Morgan. It's hardly necessary to degrade her with this line of questioning!"

Asher turned to the judge. "Your Honor, I am merely trying to determine the depth of Mrs. Spencer's commitment to this man."

"Then do so," Commestock said, "but keep your questions within the bounds of propriety."

"Yes, sir." Asher returned to Lacey. "Mrs. Spencer, did Justice Morgan force himself on you?"

"No."

"So you were a willing participant in this affair."

Lacey felt that she was dying a little inside with each question the prosecutor asked. "Yes."

He stepped away from the witness box and moved to the jury again, not looking at Lacey as he asked, "Are you in love with Justice Morgan?"

Lacey looked at the man who had shattered her heart and wished that she could lie. Or better yet, she wished that she could tell Asher she didn't love Morgan and know that such a statement was the truth. Neither was the case, though. "Yes, I am in love with him," she answered quietly.

"Are you aware that if he is convicted of murder he will be hanged by the neck until dead?"

"Yes," she said, a little stronger this time.

Asher returned to her. "Mrs. Spencer, is there anything you

wouldn't do to save the life of the man you love?"

Lacey drew her shoulders up proudly. "Mr. Asher, I wouldn't lie in a court of law to save anyone's life. And in this case, I don't have to lie, because I've told nothing but the truth."

"So you say."

"Dammit, if I'm a liar, why did I admit to having an affair with him? Why didn't I lie about that, too?"

Asher looked calmly at the judge, who rapped his gavel and ordered Lacey to control herself. The prosecutor asked a few more questions, but the damage was done and Charles Green's gentle questioning did little to help the situation. Under his guidance, Lacey described the situation that had existed between her and Croft. Finally, blessedly, she was allowed to stand down.

Lacey wanted to run as far and as fast as her legs would carry her, but she held herself erect and returned to her seat. She kept her face averted from Morgan and in so doing, looked directly at C. W., who was grinning malevolently.

He's won, she realized with nauseating certainty. This is his revenge. He framed Morgan so that he could destroy me.

"Come, Allyce, let me get you out of here," Asa whispered solicitously as he rose and took Lacey's arm, but she shook her head and sat.

"No. I'm not going to run away. That's what C. W. wants, and I won't give him the satisfaction."

She sat like a statue, beautiful and cold, while the trial proceeded. Asher questioned Cleary O'Rourke, who told the same version of the story that Croft had told. In cross-examination, Green read Cleary's original statement into the record, but the Irishman claimed he'd only told that version because Morgan had threatened his life. Nothing Green said to him made him change his story.

Lacey listened to the testimony with growing fear. Morgan was going to hang. The jury hadn't believed her, and Green hadn't been able to discredit O'Rourke. There was no one left to save Morgan from the gallows—no one but C. W. Rawlings. And only one thing would persuade him to do so: Lacey's complete and total surrender.

When O'Rourke left the stand Asher rested his case, and the

judge declared a two-hour recess for lunch. "We will reconvene at one-thirty so that the defense may present its case," he told the jury and adjourned the session.

As soon as the judge and jury had left, the courtroom erupted into chaos. People pushed and shoved toward the exits, everyone talking at the same time, but Lacey sat silently between her two friends, waiting for the room to clear. Morgan had turned toward her, but she refused to look at him as a deputy cuffed his hands and escorted him out of the courtroom. Several reporters rushed forward, calling to Lacey, but Barney Ford blocked their path and kept them at bay.

"Allyce, I'm so sorry," Asa said, placing a comforting hand on hers.

"It's not your fault, Asa. I did this to myself."

"But if I hadn't come to Willow Springs—"

"If you hadn't come, someone else would have," she said, cutting him off. "This was what C. W. wanted all along. He's finally succeeded in bringing me under control."

Asa frowned. "I don't understand."

"You will soon enough." She rose stiffly and glanced around the room, but Rawlings was gone.

"Mrs. Spencer, come on back to the hotel with me," Barney Ford urged. He'd finally convinced the reporters they weren't going to get near Lacey, and they had left. "You come, too, Mr. Mercer. I'll have lunch served in Mrs. Spencer's room where you won't be disturbed."

"Thank you, but no," Lacey said, giving him the best smile she could manage. "I have something else to do. You go on, Asa. I'll join you when I've finished."

"Are you going to see Morgan?" Asa asked.

Lacey gave a quick shake of her head, shuddering at the thought. "No. I couldn't bear that."

"Then what . . . ?"

She turned to him. "I have some business with C. W. Unless I'm mistaken, he's waiting for me at the Cheyenne Club."

Asa looked shocked. "But, Allyce, that's the headquarters of the Stock Growers Association. Women aren't allowed to set foot in there."

"Oh, they'll be only too happy to admit me," she said with

a ghost of a smile. "In fact, they'll probably toast my health before I leave."

Barney regarded her gravely. "What are you going to do?"

Her expression bleak, Lacey stared at the empty chair Morgan had vacated. "Whatever I have to do to save his life."

Asa sighed regretfully as he finally realized the immense sacrifice she was about to make. Justice Morgan had cost her so much already, and now he was about to take away the only thing she had left. "Do you love him that much?" he asked gently.

"It's not a question of love, Asa," she said tearfully. "He's innocent, and I'm the only one with the power to save him. I couldn't live with myself if I didn't."

"And afterward? Will you go to him?"

Lacey felt twin tears escape her control and cut down her pale cheeks. "How can I? I hate everything he stands for."

"But you love him," Asa pointed out gently.

She brushed at her tears. "I'll just have to learn how to stop," she murmured, hurrying out of the empty courtroom.

Chapter Eighteen

By the time Lacey reached the elegant Cheyenne Club her grief had turned to anger. She marched up the steps, crossed the wide veranda, and knocked boldly on the door. An impeccably dressed British butler answered the summons, and Lacey swept past him into the foyer before he could protest.

"Please inform C. W. Rawlings that I'm here," she said imperiously, drawing off her gloves.

"I'm sorry, madam, but ladies are not allowed in the Cheyenne Club. If you'd like to leave a message—"

"I would not." She fixed the butler with a stare that brooked no disobedience. "You will tell Mr. Rawlings that I am here to see him or I will search the club myself until I find him."

The butler drew himself up huffily. "Madam, I can have you removed—"

"But you won't. Because if you try to remove me by force, I will raise a ruckus the likes of which this club has never seen. It will be much simpler and much less disturbing to your members if you just do as I ask." She moved to a brocade-covered settee and made herself comfortable. "I shall wait here."

The butler paused indecisively for a moment, then finally moved off toward the dining room where most of the members were having their lunch.

Alone in the foyer, Lacey glanced around, taking in her surroundings. The room was decorated in the style of an English hunt club. From where she sat, she could see part of the lounge and also a slice of the sumptuously furnished billiard room.

At any other time, she would have been delighted for the

opportunity to survey the private men's club, but now she was only trying to hold on to her anger. C. W. had engineered the destruction of her reputation and had delighted in watching her brought low in the courtroom. She wouldn't give him the pleasure of watching her suffer more. Lacey had lost their hard-fought battle of wills, but she would face her defeat with her head held high.

"Mrs. Spencer, what a pleasant surprise." C. W. came into the foyer with Croft right behind him.

Lacey stood. "It may be pleasant for you, C. W., but I doubt that it's a surprise. You knew I would come looking for you."

Rawlings grinned. "Well, let's just say I suspected you might. Shall we find someplace quiet to talk?" He gestured toward the billiard room, and Lacey preceded him. "Please have a seat. Make yourself comfortable," he invited.

"No, thank you. This won't take long."

Croft followed them into the room and closed the doors, but C. W. generously asked, "Would you rather we do this alone?"

"No, he can stay. This concerns him, too."

A little surprised, Croft moved to the billiard table and sat on the mahogany rail, studying Lacey who was on the other side of the table. "I'm honored, Miz Spencer."

"Don't be," she snapped without looking at him. All her attention was focused on C. W. at the head of the table. "Now, C. W., shall we get down to it?"

"Down to what, Mrs. Spencer?" he asked innocently.

"You know very well what. You've won. I'm here to negotiate the terms of my surrender."

Rawlings grinned and glanced at Croft. " 'Surrender.' The word has a nice ring to it, doesn't it, Croft?"

"It certainly does," the gunman said, studying Lacey like a ravenous wolf.

"Now, what exactly do you want to negotiate, Mrs. Spencer?" C. W. asked.

"The release of Justice Morgan," Lacey said, steeling herself for what she was about to do. "You are to make Croft and O'Rourke tell the court what really happened and get the charges dropped."

"And what will you do in exchange?"

Lacey took a deep breath. "My newspaper will never mention your name again. I will never write another article about the vigilantes or make an attack on the WSGA."

C. W. burst out laughing and moved to a chair near the door. "Now, that's funny, Mrs. Spencer. As I recall, you don't have a newspaper to write articles in."

"You know better than that, C. W.," she said harshly. "You heard Barney Ford's testimony about the arrangements I made, but I imagine you knew something about my plans before you got to court today. Otherwise you'd never have set up this elaborate scheme to frame Morgan. Croft was following me last week. He knew I was up to something."

Rawlings fanned the air with one hand as though waving away an offensive odor. "I know you've ordered some equipment and supplies, but that doesn't mean you have a place to set up shop."

"Oh, but I do," she said, delighted that she would at least have one last laugh on the smug bastard. "You see, I've already purchased a building in Willow Springs."

"Impossible."

"Really? Do you recall selling a piece of property to a photographer by the name of William Crawford?"

Rawlings's scowl was answer enough. He came to his feet in indignation. "You set me up! That's fraud!"

"No, it's not," she replied calmly. "It was all perfectly legal. I'm half owner of Crawford Photographic Studios, and Willie never actually told you the building would be used for a picture parlor. You made that assumption on your own."

"You bitch," he growled. "I'll get you for this."

Lacey laughed humorlessly. "Oh, but you've already got me, C. W. Thanks to you, I'll never be able to hold my head up in Willow Springs again. And you'll never be punished for the murder of Riley and Martha Hanson."

That calmed Rawlings considerably. "You're really giving up?" he said with some surprise. He'd been sure about her before, only to be proved wrong.

Lacey nodded. "On two conditions. You've already heard one: I want Morgan cleared of the charges you trumped up."

C. W. scowled. "What's the other one?"

She looked at Croft. "Keep him away from me. I haven't

decided yet whether I'll stay in Willow Springs or return to Washington, but if I do stay, I don't want any trouble with Croft. I don't want to see him; I don't want to hear any veiled threats or innuendo from him. I don't want to have to worry that he's going to break into my house and assault me. Keep your mad dog under control or the whole deal's off. If he comes near me, I'll resume my attacks on you and the vigilance committee as vigorously as ever." She paused and looked at C. W. imperiously. "Those are my terms. Do you accept them?"

"I can't believe you'd even consider remaining in Wyoming after what happened today. Not a decent person in this territory will associate with someone of your low moral character."

Lacey clenched her hands and stiffened her jaw. "News of this trial won't be confined to Wyoming, C. W. My reputation will be just as black in Washington as it is here. I may be better off in Willow Springs where I won't be an embarrassment to my father." Lacey swallowed hard, fighting back a sudden rush of tears. Until the words were out, she hadn't really considered how deeply this was going to hurt her father. Roland Smithfield would be crushed by the news that his daughter had had a scandalous love affair.

Rawlings smiled at her, enjoying the expression of pain that flashed across her face. "If that's the case, Mrs. Spencer, I'd pack up and move someplace new if I were you."

Lacey drew herself up again. "Well, you're not me, C. W., and I won't be bullied into making a decision yet. Will you agree to my terms?"

Absently he toyed with one of the balls on the billiard table, relishing the opportunity to make the high-and-mighty Allyce Spencer squirm. "Why should I? When all is said and done, I don't think you'll be able to take the pressure of living in Willow Springs. You'll end up back in Washington where you can't do me any harm."

Lacey's facade of calm vanished, and her fury erupted with such quiet intensity that C. W. was riveted by its force. With slow deliberation, she stepped toward him until only the corner of the table separated them. "Let me make something crystal clear to you, C. W." Her quiet voice lashed him like a whip. "If Justice Morgan hangs, you'll never see the last of me. I can do just as much damage to you in Washington as I can in Willow Springs—maybe even more. Unless you agree to my terms, I will launch a full-scale attack on the Stock Growers Association. With my father's help, I will strip Governor Paull of power. I will lobby for legislation that will destroy the economy of Wyoming and postpone statehood for decades."

She placed her hands on the rail of the billiard table and leaned toward him menacingly. "Even if it costs me every penny I have, I will destroy you. I will take you and your petty little empire apart piece by piece, and you'll never know what hit you. Now, do we have a deal?"

He believed her: With her wealth and her father's connections, she could make good on every one of her threats. Right now the other members of the Stock Growers Association were on his side, but if he didn't neutralize the threat Allyce Spencer posed, his friends would turn on him.

C. W. decided he'd better accept her offer before she changed her mind. "All right. It's a deal."

He offered his hand, but Lacey ignored it. "You agree to *all* the terms? Including the part about Croft?"

He nodded. "Croft won't give you any trouble."

Lacey heard a rustling behind her as Croft moved, but she didn't look at him. "Court reconvenes at one-thirty. You'd better get busy, C. W." She swept past him, threw open the door, and disappeared into the foyer. The clack of her heels on the parquet floor echoed eerily in the room.

Croft moved to Rawlings, who had turned to watch Lacey's departure. "You had no right to involve me in your deal, C. W.," he told him.

"You work for me; you'll do as I say," Rawlings replied, turning to him. "And I say you leave Mrs. Spencer alone."

"What if I don't?"

"Then you become one more annoyance that will have to be eliminated."

Croft laughed and sat on the rail of the billiard table. "Now, just who do you know that's good enough to deal with me, C. W.?"

Rawlings looked Croft squarely in the eye. "I've heard that Justice Morgan will kill anybody for the right price."

All traces of amusement left Croft's face. "He would never work for you."

"Really? After the way you helped set him up for murder, I imagine he'd take great pleasure in killing you." C. W. smiled jovially and clapped Croft on the shoulder. "She's not worth the trouble, son. No woman is. That was a fine idea of yours, framing Morgan for murder so that Mrs. Spencer would lay off us. Let's not spoil things now, okay? There's work to be done in Willow Springs, and I'm going to need every gun hand I can get. What do you say we forget all about Mrs. Spencer?"

It took a moment, but Croft finally nodded. "All right. For the time being."

Croft meant just until Morgan had left town, C. W. realized, controlling a sudden flash of anger. He'd worked hard to get rid of Allyce Spencer, and he wasn't about to let a two-bit gunslinger undo everything he'd accomplished. He would have to disempower Croft before he did something stupid.

But first he had some business to conduct with Judge Victor Commestock.

"Come on," he said, clapping Croft on the shoulder again. "Let's go find Mr. O'Rourke and pay a visit to the judge."

Lacey hurried outside, praying for the strength to make it back to the hotel. Fortunately the answer to her prayers was standing in front of the Cheyenne Club. Asa Mercer and a hired coach were waiting for her, and Lacey nearly stumbled into his arms in relief.

"Oh, Asa, get me out of here, please."

"Of course, my dear." He helped her into the closed carriage and instructed the driver to take them to the back entrance of the Inter Ocean Hotel.

"Thank you," she said as he climbed into the carriage and sat beside her. "I'm not sure I could have made it on my own."

Asa smiled gently and patted her hand. "A number of reporters are waiting for you at the hotel, and I thought this might be the best way to outwit them. Mr. Ford is keeping the back entrance clear for us. Now tell me, what happened with C. W.?"

She stared straight ahead. "The murder charge against Morgan will be dropped as soon as court reconvenes."

"But at what cost to you, my dear?" he asked sadly.

"I promised to abandon my newspaper campaign against C. W. and his cohorts." She looked at him. "What else could I do?"

"Nothing. You really had no choice, but it does sicken me to think that Rawlings will never be brought to account for the crimes of the vigilantes." A thought suddenly occurred to him. "Unless, of course, your supposition that Morgan is working for Senator Hanson turns out to be true. Were you right about that, Allyce? Did you ever confront Morgan with the fact that you saw him talking to Keenan Stoddard?"

If Lacey hadn't trusted Asa implicitly she never would have admitted the truth, but she did trust him. "Yes, I confronted him after you left the hotel that day, and he did admit that he is involved in some sort of scheme to bring down C. W. He refused to give me any details, but I do know there is a plan at work."

Asa smiled encouragingly. "Then perhaps all is not lost. And who knows? This may have worked out for the best. I know that what happened in court today has been devastating, but at least now Morgan will be free to carry out the senator's plan, and you won't have to worry about C. W.'s retribution."

Her voice trembled slightly as she replied, "You may be right, Asa, but at the moment it's difficult for me to see any good that might come from this ordeal."

"You're strong, Allyce," he told her firmly. "In time you will be able to put your life back together."

Lacey choked back a tearful sob. "How, Asa? How can I ever live down what I've done? How will I ever be able to face my father and my friends again?"

Asa placed a comforting arm around her, wishing he could take away her desperate pain. "Those who love you will understand, my dear, and no one else matters."

They completed the ride to the hotel in silence, with Lacey trying to bring her tumultuous emotions under control. By the time they arrived, she had succeeded in resurrecting the wall of pride that had protected her thus far. They slipped through the rear entrance and hurried up the back stairs to her room. As Barney Ford had promised, a simple meal had been laid out for them on the table in the sitting room.

"We have one hour before court reconvenes," Asa said as he helped Lacey out of her cloak. "Please come and have something to eat."

She took the cloak from him, shaking her head. "Not just yet. I'd like to freshen up first."

"Very well." Asa stepped toward the table as Lacey headed for the bedroom. "Allyce, there are some messages for you here. Apparently Mr. Ford sent them up from the front desk."

Lacey stopped in her tracks and turned toward him, her heart racing. He was at the table holding a stack of notes. Some were in envelopes, others were just folded pieces of paper, and one was a small package wrapped in brown paper. "They're probably requests for interviews," she said faintly, wondering if one of them might be a message from Morgan. The thought filled her with anticipation and dread in equal measure. "Would you look through them for me, Asa? If they're all from reporters, just toss them into the fire."

"Certainly, dear, but what about this one?" He separated the small package from the others and held it out to her.

Lacey accepted the package and tore off the wrapping. It was a book, and on top was a note: "My dear Mrs. Spencer, as you are a journalist yourself, I feel confident that you will be only too happy to grant me an interview so that the public may become acquainted with the full details of this unfortunate episode. I hope, too, that you will be willing to comment on the contents of the enclosed biography of your paramour, Justice Morgan. Most sincerely yours, Quentin Tesserman, Denver *Daily News*.

Lacey crumpled the note and looked at the cover of the book. A wave of nausea rolled over her as she read the title, *Justice for Hire, or the Life of Bounty Hunter Robert "Justice" Morgan*. "Oh, God, get this out of my sight," she moaned, handing the trashy dime novel to Asa as though it burned her hands. "Destroy it, please." Fighting back tears, she hurried into the bedroom and closed the door behind her.

Asa looked at the thin volume and shook his head in revulsion. The cover depicted a man—presumably Justice Morgan—holding a smoking gun as he stood over the body of a rough-looking outlaw. The drawing was atrocious, for the man on the cover looked nothing like Morgan. That was hardly surprising, though, since dime dreadfuls like this one seldom made an effort to stick to the facts.

In Asa's opinion, it was a shame that writers were allowed to glamorize the exploits of men like Justice Morgan. And it was an even worse shame that some callous reporter had not realized how cruel it was to send this book to Allyce Spencer. Yet despite his aversion to such trashy journalism, Asa had a perverse desire to read the book, perhaps because he knew Morgan and had become caught up in the web of his very complicated life. Whatever the reason, Asa felt compelled to see what the author had to say.

But Lacey had asked that the book be destroyed, and Asa was disgusted by his compulsion to read it. Irritated with himself, he tossed the book onto the table and quickly perused the other notes. All were requests for interviews, and he took them to the stove and tossed them in. He stirred the waning fire until it was blazing properly and started to throw the book in after the notes.

His hand was inches from the fire when his morbid curiosity finally overcame him. After a furtive glance at Allyce's closed door, he opened to the first page, intending to read only a paragraph or two. Ten minutes later, when Lacey emerged from her room, he was seated at the table, still reading.

He was so absorbed in the book that it took him a moment to realize that Lacey had returned. "Allyce dear, you must read this," he said, rising. She joined him at the table, and he held out a chair for her.

"Please, Asa. I don't think I can bear to be reminded of Morgan's grisly past, no matter how romanticized it may be."

"No, that's not it, my dear," he said, returning to his chair and leaning forward intently. "It's . . . well, there's something you should read. It may mean nothing, but it does have me puzzled."

Knowing her friend would never subject her to such an ordeal needlessly, Lacey sighed with resignation. "All right. What is it?"

Asa quickly flipped back several pages and handed her the book, pointing out the paragraph he wanted her to look at: "With eyes as black as coal, the bounty hunter stared down the vicious outlaw. 'I'm not taking you back alive, Bart,' Justice

Morgan said. 'So draw, or I'll shoot you where you stand.' "

" 'Eyes as black as coal'?" she murmured, glancing up at Asa.

"That's right," he said, nodding eagerly. "The author, Timothy Braxton Prentiss, repeatedly describes Morgan's eye color as 'cold and dark.' " He took the book from her and found another page. "And listen to this: 'His cold eyes were the most prominent feature in a face that never smiled. As black as midnight, and filled with the promise of certain death, they had the power to bore through his victim.' What do you make of that?"

Lacey was baffled. That certainly didn't sound like the smiling, good-humored Morgan she knew. Of course, he hadn't been smiling when he confronted Owen Hastings. Lacey's mind was still filled with the image of the cold, hard look on Morgan's face as he'd faced the grieving father. Perhaps that was what Timothy Braxton Prentiss had seen when he interviewed Justice Morgan and followed him around collecting material for the book.

But that still didn't account for such a flagrant mistake in the color of Morgan's eyes. The Justice Morgan Lacey knew had hazel eyes that often looked gold, and yet Prentiss repeatedly described them as black.

Overcome with curiosity, Lacey took the book from Asa and began reading from the beginning, skimming the material quickly, ignoring the sensationalized gunfights and melodramatic dialogue. A few minutes later, she looked at her friend, more puzzled than ever before. What she was thinking seemed impossible. "What does this mean, Asa? Granted, Timothy Braxton Prentiss is an atrocious, melodramatic writer, but why would he print such obvious mistakes? Look at this." She handed the book to Asa. "It says there that Morgan was the son of an itinerant handyman and had almost no formal education. But Morgan once told me that he attended the College of William and Mary."

Asa nodded. "I found the mistake in eye color strange as well," he told her. "That's why I thought you should look at the book."

"But what does it mean?" Lacey asked, wishing that she could think more clearly. It had been such a devastating day that she wasn't capable of absorbing anything, and now this book had her thinking wild, improbable thoughts. "Is it just poor reporting or was Braxton taking literary license?"

Asa grew thoughtful, hardly daring to give voice to his suspicions. "Allyce, you've asked me a number of times how Morgan can seem to be two different men. If he really is involved in a plot concocted by Senator Hanson to bring Rawlings to justice, is it possible that . . . " He paused for a moment before putting what they were both thinking into words. "Is it possible that the man we know as Justice Morgan is an impostor?"

Lacey was immensely grateful that Asa had expressed the thought for her. It was so farfetched that she hadn't wanted to voice it for fear that her friend would think her mad. "I don't know, Asa," she said, rising in agitation. "In a way, it makes a great deal of sense, but I don't trust my own judgment anymore. I would give anything in the world to be able to believe that the man I fell in love with isn't really a bounty hunter. But just because I *want* to believe it doesn't make it so."

"Yet it does seem possible," he replied.

"It seems . . . preposterous," she said firmly. "But it also makes sense. The man I know has principles, compassion, and courage, none of which could possibly be possessed by a man like Justice Morgan, who takes pride in shooting unarmed outlaws."

"Allyce, if you go to Morgan and ask him—"

Lacey shook her head and cut Asa off. "No. If he is an impostor, he'll only lie to protect me."

"Are you sure?"

Lacey ran one hand over her troubled brow. "I'm not sure of anything, Asa. But I know how I can rectify that," she said as a plan suddenly began to take shape. Swiftly she went to her bedroom. Asa followed her to the door.

"What are you going to do?" he asked as she hurriedly stuffed her only change of clothing into the carpetbag Berta had packed for her yesterday.

"As soon as the charges against Morgan are dropped, I'm going to Washington. When does the next eastbound train depart?"

Asa smiled at her. Her fighting spirit had returned, and color was coming back into her cheeks. "At two o'clock, I believe."

"Then I should be able to make it," she said resolutely. "I'll send father a telegram from Omaha and have him launch an investigation immediately."

"Quietly, of course."

Lacey stopped what she was doing and gave Asa her first genuine smile in days. "Of course. But I'm going to find out what the devil is going on here, even if I have to tear Will Hanson apart to do it!"

Sick at heart, Morgan entered the packed courtroom, searching for Lacey and praying he wouldn't find her. He didn't want her subjected to the judgmental stares of the curiosity-seeking crowd. She had suffered too much already. Later, after he'd given his testimony, he would find her and tell her the truth. He would beg her forgiveness for the way his deception had ruined her reputation. He would tell her he loved her and make good his promise to propose marriage.

Once he finished testifying, his plan to infiltrate Rawlings's vigilance committee would be public knowledge. His failure to complete his mission would be a black mark on his record, but his career would still be salvageable. If Lacey would only forgive him, he would happily spend the rest of his life trying to make up for the pain he had caused her. Right now that was all that mattered. In a strange way, he was almost relieved that the masquerade would soon be over.

And as for C. W. Rawlings . . . well, eventually he would face a day of reckoning. Morgan had to believe that.

As he moved around the defense table, he raked his gaze once more across the crowd and found Lacey standing at the back of the room. As before, Asa Mercer was at her side, but this time Lacey met Morgan's gaze. She stared at him steadily as though she was searching for something, but Morgan couldn't imagine what it might be. She did seem different, though. This morning, pride and courage had been the only things holding her together. Now there seemed to be something else—a determination and a sense of purpose that hadn't been there before.

Reluctantly Morgan turned away from her and allowed the

deputy to remove his handcuffs before he sat. Charles Green was already at the table, but he didn't look happy. Morgan had spent most of the recess explaining the complicated series of events that had brought him to Wyoming, and the lawyer was now confident that his client would be acquitted; he just wasn't too pleased about having been kept in the dark.

Green did not speak as Morgan joined him. He was too busy poring over his notes, so Morgan sat quietly, waiting. It would all be over soon, he reminded himself. The judge arrived, the jury returned, and Commestock gravely made an announcement that shocked Morgan to the vary marrow of his bones.

"Ladies and gentlemen of the jury, during our luncheon recess some new information was brought to my attention, and it is with my sincerest apologies to you that I must declare this case a mistrial."

Shocked murmurs rippled through the room, and Morgan sat back in his chair, stunned.

"Apparently," the judge continued, "two of the prosecution's witnesses committed perjury this morning. In a laudable act of conscience, Mr. Croft and Mr. O'Rourke have both come forward to admit that their testimony was totally false and that Mr. Morgan shot Owen Hastings in self-defense. Perjury is a serious crime, and in the days ahead I will consider whether or not charges are to be brought against these men. But in the meantime Mr. Justice Morgan is cleared of the murder charge against him and may go free with the court's apology." Commestock stood and banged his gavel. "The jury is dismissed, and this court is now adjourned."

Absolute chaos broke out in the courtroom as the judge hurried toward his chambers, ignoring the questions that were shouted at him by stunned reporters and spectators.

"What the hell was that all about?" Green asked, turning to Morgan with absolute surprise on his face. "Croft and O'Rourke recanted? Why?"

"I don't know," Morgan muttered, his head reeling.

"Rawlings must have changed his mind about wanting you framed," Green speculated.

"Yes, but why? He wouldn't have done this unless he'd gotten what he wanted, and I know better than that because he hasn't contacted me."

Green shrugged. "Have you considered the possibility that *you* weren't the one he wanted something from?"

Morgan scowled, and his heart began hammering in double time. "You mean Lacey? He did this to set up Lacey? My God! Why didn't I realize that? Damn!" He came to his feet instantly, searching the crowd for her, but there was so much confusion that he couldn't spot her. Several reporters surged forward, but Morgan ignored them as he began pushing toward the spot where he'd last seen Lacey.

"You'll never make it through that crowd," Green said, grabbing his arm.

"I have to find Lacey," he growled, pulling away. "I have to know what Rawlings did to her—or what he made her do."

"Then go out the side door," Green urged. "I'll try to keep the reporters busy for a minute. And let me know what you learn!" he said, but Morgan was already hurrying toward the exit. "This is the damnedest mess I ever saw," Green muttered to himself, then turned to the reporters who were scrambling over the rail in pursuit of Morgan. "Gentlemen, please. May I have your attention? My client will return to speak with you in a moment. In the meantime I have a statement to make."

The reporters paused indecisively, and Green launched into a verbose, absolutely meaningless speech about the integrity of the judicial system. By the time the reporters realized they were being hoodwinked, Morgan was long gone.

The streets outside the courthouse were a tangled mass of carriages and pedestrians. Morgan was recognized instantly and had to fight his way through the crowd. Lacey was nowhere to be seen, but that made sense. She'd apparently been standing at the back of the courtroom because she'd known what was about to happen and wanted to be able to make a speedy escape.

What have you done, Lacey? he wondered. What did you have to promise C. W. in order to secure my release? What else has loving me cost you? He asked the questions over and over in his mind, but the only person who could answer them was nowhere to be found. He reached the Inter Ocean across town as quickly as he could, but the desk clerk refused to give out any information about Lacey. Morgan demanded to see Barney Ford, but was told that he was not available.

Asa Mercer would certainly know where Lacey was, but Morgan wasn't sure he'd get any answers from him, either. Still, Asa was his only hope. On the street in front of the hotel, he obtained directions to Mercer's newspaper office, but when he got there, he found that the doors were locked. Frustrated, he returned to the hotel just as Barney Ford walked into the lobby.

"I want to know what room Lacey is in," Morgan said sternly, not bothering with the amenities.

"Mrs. Spencer doesn't want to see you, Mr. Morgan," Barney replied. "She made that very clear."

"Well, *I* want to see *her*, and I'll tear this hotel apart if I have to! Now, where is she?"

Barney sighed impatiently, wondering how long he could stall this determined madman, but the faint sound of a train whistle relieved him of the problem. "Mrs. Spencer is not at this hotel," he said finally.

"Then where is she? I saw her in the courtroom not thirty minutes ago. She can't have left Cheyenne yet."

"Oh, but she has. I just returned from escorting her to the depot, where she caught the two o'clock train for Omaha."

Morgan felt as though he'd been kicked in the stomach. "Omaha?"

"That's right. Her final destination is Washington. She felt compelled to see her father. After the ordeal she has suffered because of you, she needs the strength and support of a loving family."

"Is she coming back?" he asked quietly.

Despite the trouble Morgan had caused Lacey, Barney Ford felt sorry for him. He didn't know the details of everything that had transpired during the last few hours, but he realized that Morgan was an innocent pawn in the deadly game Lacey had been playing with C. W. And one other thing was clear: No matter what his reputation, no matter what he had done in the past, right now Justice Morgan loved Allyce Spencer desperately. "I don't know if she's ever coming back," Barney said, gentling his tone to express the sympathy he felt. "But I am sure that she is doing what she thinks best. Please respect her decision."

Decision? What decision was that? Morgan wondered as he

thanked Ford and left the hotel. She had apparently decided to cut him out of her life forever. And he could hardly blame her. She believed that he was Justice Morgan, a despicable bounty hunter, and her reputation was in shreds because of her association with him.

And perhaps worst of all, she had abandoned her campaign against C. W. Rawlings because she'd thought that was the only way to save Morgan's life. Nothing less would have made Rawlings get the charges against him dismissed. And nothing less would have made Lacey leave Wyoming. As long as she was fighting to avenge the death of her friends Riley and Martha, nothing could have forced her to return to Washington.

Now, though, she had no reason to remain. On his own, C. W. Rawlings hadn't been able to break the indomitable spirit of Allyce Spencer. It had taken Morgan's inadvertent help to do that.

But at least now she was out of danger, Morgan thought, trying to find some good that could come from what Lacey had suffered. *I can do the job I came to do without worrying that Lacey might be hurt,* he told himself. *I can bring C. W. Rawlings to justice . . . and I'll be doing it for her. All for her.*

Even if it cost him his life, he was going to finish the job she'd started.

Chapter Nineteen

With a half-empty glass of whiskey in one hand, Morgan stood at the window of his second-story room at the Dyer Hotel. It was night, but the street seemed busier than usual, probably because of the number of people who had flooded the city to see the hanging of Justice Morgan.

There wasn't going to be a hanging, but Morgan suspected he was the only one who was happy about that; an execution always livened things up in any town, and from the looks of the street below, Cheyenne was itching for a good party.

Irritated by his gloomy thoughts, Morgan drained his glass and poured another one from the bottle he'd brought to the room. He wasn't drunk, but he wished he could be. Maybe it would keep him from thinking about Lacey. But considering the circumstances, losing all his sensibilities in a bottle wasn't a bright idea.

A knock on the door brought Morgan away from the window immediately. He drew his Colt and quietly stepped close to the wall beside the door. "Who is it?"

"C. W. Rawlings."

Morgan wasn't surprised. He'd half expected the cattleman to seek him out, but nothing had gone the way it should have since Morgan arrived in Wyoming, and he'd become skeptical about his instincts. Still, Rawlings was here now, and Morgan had a pretty good idea why he'd come.

Maybe the game was about to take a turn in his direction after all.

Gun still drawn, he threw open the door and stepped back. "What the hell do you want?"

"A little friendly conversation," C. W. replied, sauntering into the room without an invitation.

"After the way you set me up for murder, do you really think we're going to be pals, C. W.?" Morgan asked incredulously.

Rawlings didn't bother to deny the accusation. "Pals, no. But I do have an offer you might be interested in."

"I'm not interested in anything you have to say. Now get out." Morgan waved his gun toward the open door, and in reply, Rawlings closed it.

"Now, don't be hasty, son. Don't you want to know what your lady friend, Allyce Spencer, did to save your hide today?"

Morgan's jaw turned to granite. "I already have a pretty good idea. She promised to leave you and the vigilantes alone."

"That's right." C. W. moved across the room and made himself comfortable on the bed. "You know, Morgan, you and I could have become friends a lot sooner if you'd made your identity known as soon as you came to Willow Springs. I need good guns and men who aren't averse to using them for a price."

"I wasn't looking for employment opportunities in Willow Springs," he answered negligently.

"But you're a long way away from home, aren't you? Just what brought you north?"

Morgan shrugged. "Things were getting boring in Texas."

C. W. laughed. "You mean you finally ended up on the wrong side of the law down there."

"There aren't any warrants out for my arrest," he replied with a touch of defensiveness.

"But you're not anxious to go back."

"It's a big country."

"And Wyoming's a big territory. I could find plenty for you to do around here."

Morgan snorted with derisive laughter. "You gotta be kidding. I'd just as soon kill you as look at you."

"Oh, I don't think you'd go quite that far. You've been through a pretty rough time these last few days, and I'd like to make it up to you."

"And just how do you think you could do that?"

"By offering you a job."

This is it, Morgan thought. The months of planning were about to pay off. Now he simply had to play hard to get. "You're crazy. Why on earth would I work for a snake like you?"

"Because from what I've heard, you'll do just about anything for the right price," he answered. "And I'm prepared to offer that."

"Why?" Morgan asked, feigning suspicion.

"You're one of the best guns in the country, and I need good guns."

"What for? You've already got Croft."

Rawlings scrunched up his face in an exaggerated frown. "Croft is . . . unpredictable. In fact, he may soon become something of a liability."

"Then why don't you fire him?"

"I've thought about it, but that could get tricky." He looked at Morgan closely. "I guess you already know that Mrs. Spencer supposedly left for Washington this afternoon."

Morgan kept his expression neutral. "Supposedly?"

C. W. stood and meandered around the room. "Morgan, one thing these last few months have taught me is that Allyce Spencer is a very resourceful but mighty unpredictable woman. She may be gone for good. Then again, she may show up in Willow Springs tomorrow. I've finally learned not to underestimate her."

"You think she won't honor her promise?"

"Oh, no," he said quickly. "She'll keep her word as long as I keep mine."

"And you've already done your part," Morgan pointed out.

"Only half of it," C. W. replied. "You see, Mrs. Spencer drives a mighty hard bargain. In exchange for ceasing her newspaper campaign against me, I had to promise not only to release you but also to see that Croft doesn't cause her any trouble."

"Smart lady," Morgan said, not bothering to hide the admiration he felt for Lacey. Considering how much she'd sacrificed, she deserved to get something in return. But of course, there was a big difference between what Rawlings could promise and what he could deliver when it came to Croft. "Did your pet gunslinger agree to keep that promise?"

C. W. nodded. "For the time being, but I'm a little worried about him." C. W. sighed with mock regret. "If Mrs. Spencer does come back to Willow Springs and Croft defies my order to leave her alone, she will resume her publishing activities. That disturbs me, Mr. Morgan. I've gone to a great deal of trouble and expense to persuade that woman to stop harassing me, and I now have a vested interest in seeing that she remains healthy."

"So you can't fire Croft because then he'd go after her for sure."

"That's right. And since I can't fire him, what I need now is someone who can manage him if he gets out of hand."

Morgan holstered his gun finally and dropped into a chair. "Are you admitting that you can't manage him?"

"Let's just say I'm not qualified to try. But you are. So what do you say? After what Allyce Spencer did for you today, I think that's the least you owe her."

Morgan laughed. "Now, that's rich, C. W. You want to hire me to protect her? After all you've done to her?"

"It seems like a good idea to me."

Morgan regarded C. W. narrowly. "What if she doesn't come back to Willow Springs?"

C. W. shrugged. "Then I'm sure I can find something else to keep you busy."

"Such as?"

"Oh . . . I have some plans in the offing."

"For your 'friends' in the co-op?"

"That's right."

"But you're not going to tell me what they are."

C. W. shook his head. "Not just yet. You see, I'm pretty well convinced that your relationship with Mrs. Spencer is finished. Cleary O'Rourke says that when she found out you're a bounty hunter she said she never wanted to see you again. She tried to save your neck and destroyed herself in the process, but she did that because she's an honorable woman, not because she's planning on having a future with you."

"So what?" Morgan asked, carefully hiding the pain that truthful assessment brought him.

"So I think it would be safe to say that for the right price I could guarantee your loyalty to me, but I'm not quite sure yet. If Mrs. Spencer doesn't come back from Washington, I may let you in on my plans."

"Why should I trust you, C. W.?"

Rawlings shrugged expansively. "Because I've got nothing against you. That murder business wasn't personal; you just happened to get caught in the middle of my tug-of-war with Mrs. Spencer."

"And that's supposed to make it all right?"

He laughed and clapped Morgan on the shoulder. "Son, we're both practical men. I was just doin' what had to be done. You can understand that. Now I'm trying to make it up to you, and if you're smart, you'll accept my offer."

Morgan looked at the hand still resting on his shoulder. "I haven't heard an offer yet, C. W. Just how worth my while are you prepared to make this little setup?"

Rawlings laughed again. "That's more like it." He named a figure that was far from insulting. "And if it means anything to you, that's more than I've been paying Croft."

"It had better be," Morgan warned.

"Then we have a deal?" C. W. asked, delighted.

Morgan thought for a moment, then stood. "Yeah. We've got a deal. I'll make sure Croft doesn't give Lacey any reason to renege on her promise."

"Wonderful!" C. W. extended his hand to seal their agreement, and though it nearly choked Morgan, he shook it firmly. "There's a train leaving for Willow Springs at eight tomorrow morning. Can I expect to see you on it?"

"I'll be there."

Smiling C. W. headed for the door. "Morgan, I think this arrangement is going to work out very nicely for everyone concerned."

Morgan thought of the months of planning that had gone into setting up this very moment. He thought of the innocent people Rawlings had ruthlessly murdered. He thought, too, of the devastation Lacey had suffered because she'd been caught in the middle of it. "I think you're right, C. W.," he said finally as he saw Rawlings to the door. "This arrangement is going to work out perfectly. You have my word on it."

* * *

The train slowed as it chugged toward the station. In the Pullman parlor car, Lacey stared out the window, twisting her kid gloves nervously. She was nearly home. In the telegram she'd sent her father from Omaha, she had made no mention of the debacle in Cheyenne, but she held out not a single hope that she might be the one to tell Roland Smithfield that his daughter had disgraced him. That news had already been reported in several Chicago newspapers, and if Chicago papers were carrying the story, newspapers in the East were, too.

Knowing that she was causing her father great pain was almost more than Lacey could bear, and she dreaded facing the disappointment she knew she would see in his eyes. But on the other hand, she desperately needed to see him. She needed his strength and his love now more than ever, and she knew that no matter what she had done, her father would not deny her either.

The train finally pulled into the cavernous station and slowed to a stop. With a trembling hand, Lacey picked up her valise and left the car. Since Roland knew the time of her arrival, he would certainly have sent someone to pick her up—probably a member of his household staff—and Lacey searched the crowd for a familiar face. The one she found surprised her and sent a sharp pain stabbing through her heart.

Roland Smithfield had come himself. He was standing a little apart from the crowd, watching her, waiting for her to notice him. Except for the lines of sadness around his eyes, he looked unchanged from the last time Lacey had seen him earlier in the year when he'd come to Willow Springs to celebrate her birthday. He was still tall and broad-shouldered. His full head of graying hair was as unruly as ever. His mustache was neatly trimmed and waxed, and his clothing was impeccably tailored.

He was the most wonderful sight Lacey had ever seen.

Fighting back tears, she worked her way toward him, and when he was close enough to touch, he wrapped her in arms that were as strong as iron bands. Those arms had sheltered, comforted, and protected her when she was a child, and when Lacey rested her tear stained face against his shoulder she felt as she had back then—as though nothing in the world could possibly harm her.

"Welcome home, honey," Roland said. His voice sounded a little gruff because he was fighting back a mist of tears.

Lacey pulled away from him, wiping at the moisture on her face. "Oh, Papa, it's so good to see you."

Roland searched his daughter's face, looking for some sign of the scarlet woman he'd been hearing about for the past two days. All he saw, though, was the beautiful, sad, exhausted daughter he loved more than his own life. "You look terrible," he said with a fond smile.

"Try spending three nights sleeping in your clothing in a Pullman berth and see how you look," she said wryly. "I think we should join forces and do an exposé of Mr. Pullman's false advertising campaign. His coaches look fabulous, but where comfort is concerned, they leave much to be desired on long trips."

"I'll make that your first assignment as soon as you return to the *Tribune*," he said, relieving her of the valise.

Lacey frowned. "Papa, that's not why—"

"Now, where are Mrs. Kraus and Zachary?" he asked, cutting her off because he didn't want to hear that she wasn't home to stay. "I have a coach waiting out front."

"Berta and Zach didn't come, Papa. I was in Cheyenne when I decided to make this trip. Asa Mercer volunteered to get a message to them asking that they remain in Willow Springs until they hear from me."

"Then you must send for them immediately," he said, giving her his sternest look.

"Not just yet," she replied, moving aside to avoid being knocked down by a porter who was overloaded with baggage. The area was becoming more congested by the moment as passengers poured out of the train.

"Now, look, Allyce . . . " He'd been preparing for this fight since the moment he received her telegram, but the exhaustion and vulnerability on his daughter's face brought him to a grinding halt. She had her jaw set, ready for the argument, but Roland couldn't bring himself to initiate it. "Oh, never mind," he said irritably. "We'll postpone this discussion until you've had a chance to freshen up."

"Thank you, Papa."

He ushered her out of the station, and they made the fifteen-minute journey to Roland's town house without saying anything important. Lacey commented on the changes in the city since her last visit, and Roland pointed out some of the newer businesses that had sprung up in the growing metropolis, but their conversation was stilted at best. It was the first time Lacey could ever recall having been ill at ease with her father, and the feeling was quite distressing.

When they arrived at the town house, Lacey immediately went upstairs to her old room. Mrs. Brinley, the housekeeper, drew her a bath, while Lacey searched her closet for something to wear. All of the clothing she'd left in Washington was hopelessly out of date, but style was the least of her concerns. She laid out a loose-fitting cambric dressing sacque to be pressed while she was in her bath and, nearly an hour later, returned downstairs.

Roland was waiting for her in his study, and Lacey slipped in quietly, observing her father unnoticed as he stared out the window into the little courtyard that served as an oasis of greenery between this house and the one next door. His shoulders were slumped, as though they carried too much weight, and Lacey fought back tears because she knew she was the one who had placed that weight on him.

"Papa?"

Straightening in surprise, Roland turned and regarded his daughter. Her damp hair had been pulled away from her face by a single bow and was flowing freely down her back. The white ruffled dressing gown made her look young, and her fresh-scrubbed face reminded him of days gone by, when Lacey had visited his study every evening at bedtime to kiss him good night. "I haven't seen that gown in years, princess. It makes you look like a little girl again."

Lacey sighed deeply. "But I'm not a little girl, Papa."

"No, you're not," he replied, unable to keep an edge of sadness out of his voice. "You're a grown woman. Stubborn, strong-minded, and independent."

"Qualities I inherited from you," she pointed out quickly.

"And which I am proud to have passed on."

Lacey fought a sudden rush of tears. "Oh, Papa, I have made such a mess of my life."

Roland sat on the sofa and patted the space beside him.

"Come and tell me about it, Lacey. I know there must be a great deal more to the story than what I've heard and read."

Lacey moved farther into the room but did not sit beside him. She needed a little distance in order to be able to talk. If she sat beside her father, she would only throw herself into his arms and cry like a wounded child—not the action of a grown woman who was fully prepared to face the consequences of her folly. "What have you heard?"

Roland looked down at the floor. "I've heard about the trial, and most of my rival newspapers have delighted in reporting your testimony. I've been hoping you'd arrive and tell me it's all a lie, but I know you would not have sworn to something so . . . devastating unless it was the truth."

"It is true, Papa," she said, burying her fingernails in her palms. Admitting her indiscretion to a roomful of strangers had been mortifying, but that was nothing compared to the pain of admitting it to her father.

He looked up, pinning her with a hard stare. "Did you at least love this man?"

Lacey felt her barely contained tears spill onto her cheeks. "Of course I loved him! How could you even ask such a thing?"

"How can I ask?" Roland exclaimed, coming to his feet. "What a ridiculous question! You have subjected yourself to the vilest sort of malicious gossip—and all of it true! Your reputation has been tattered to shreds, and all for what? For a few hours of illicit pleasure in the arms of—"

"That's enough!" she protested, indignation overcoming her shame. "I loved Morgan. We were planning to be married!"

"Then you should have waited until after the wedding to consummate your union!"

"Oh? The way you and Mrs. Simpson have been waiting for the past fifteen years?" Lacey asked hotly. "Why is it perfectly acceptable for you to keep a mistress, while I am vilified for something far less sordid?"

Roland went pale at the mention of his longtime companion. "Mrs. Simpson and I are friends!"

"Oh, Father, everyone knows you've been paying Gladia Simpson's bills for years. Her late husband's fortune wasn't nearly enough to keep her in the style to which she had become accustomed, so you've been picking up the slack. And you have been compensated quite handsomely for your generosity!"

"Now, see here, young lady," Roland said, advancing on his daughter. "You will show a little more respect for your father. Gladia Simpson is a gracious lady—"

"Who is still accepted in polite society despite her liaison with you," Lacey countered, cutting him off. "The only difference between Gladia and me is that I was forced to make my affair public."

"That is not the only difference!" Roland thundered. "You are my daughter!"

Lacey calmed her voice. "But I'm not a saint, Papa," she said quietly. "I fell in love with a man who was intelligent, kind, and very gentle. He gave me his arm to lean on when I desperately needed to feel that I was not alone. He brought back to life a part of me that I thought had died with David, and he made me feel like a woman again." Lacey's tears returned, and she made no attempt to stop them. "I loved him, Papa. I still love him, in spite of what I have learned about him and everything that has happened. Can you understand that?"

Roland Smithfield melted like a pat of butter on a hot summer day. "Of course I understand, sweetheart," he said, drawing her into his arms. "It just hurts me so to see you suffer, and I've known for days now that you must be suffering terribly. Your conflict with Rawlings, then the fire, and now this. I've been worried sick about you."

"I know. And I'm sorry," she said, raising her face from his shoulder. "I've hurt you, and I regret that more than I can ever express. But I need you now, Papa. In so many ways."

"Tell me what I can do."

"Just hold me," she choked out. "Just hold me a little longer so that I can pretend everything is going to be all right."

"Oh, it will, darling, it will," he said, stroking her hair, rocking her gently to and fro while she cried against his shoulder as she had when she was a child, as she had when she'd buried her husband. Then she had sobbed in his arms as though her heart would never mend, and Roland had comforted her as best he could, ignoring the feeling of helplessness that pervaded him. His child was the most precious thing in his life; she had her mother's wit and beauty, but more than that, she was strong and independent. She had the capacity to care about things deeply and the courage to act on her convictions. Roland Smithfield had built an empire that stretched across the country, but his greatest achievement in life was the girl he held protectively in his arms.

Lacey's tears finally began to subside, and she felt cleansed. She was still exhausted and confused, but at least as far as the discussion with her father was concerned, the worst was over. He might never again be able to look at her in quite the same way, but she had not lost his love, nor had she for a moment feared that she might.

"Are you ready to talk now, or should we yell at each other some more?" Roland asked with a grin as he handed her the kerchief from his breast pocket.

Lacey smiled at that. "It has been a while since we've had a good donnybrook, hasn't it?"

"I've missed them," he admitted. "You always could give as good as you got."

"That's something else you taught me. How to stand up for myself." Lacey wove her arm through his, and they moved to the sofa.

"I may have taught you too well," he said wryly. "I suppose it was naive of me, but I had no idea you were aware of the nature of my relationship with Gladia Simpson."

Lacey looked sheepish. "Sorry. That was a low blow, wasn't it?"

"But not undeserved. Now tell me what's happened, Lacey. I know you were in Cheyenne last week, carrying out your plan to relocate the *Gazette*. Start there, and tell me all about the trial and this mysterious Justice Morgan."

Lacey noted something odd in her father's voice—something strange in the emphasis he gave to the word "mysterious"—but she did as he asked, leaving nothing out save the most intimate details.

"Lacey, I can hardly bear to think about the danger you've been in. C. W. Rawlings is a madman," her father said, rising in agitation.

"No, he's just a very rich, powerful man who believes he's above the law."

"Then we shall have to teach him that he's wrong."

"Not yet, Papa. I gave him my word that I'd leave him alone, and I intend to honor that bargain, for the time being, at least. And anyway, Will Hanson may be taking care of C. W. himself. Have you been able to discover anything about his plan and how Justice Morgan fits into it?"

"A little," he admitted, moving to his desk and extracting an envelope from the top drawer, "though not without great difficulty, let me assure you. I didn't want to go directly to Will until I had something specific to ask him, so I've been calling on some of my private sources around the Senate and in the Department of Justice."

"What have you learned?" Lacey asked anxiously, sliding to the edge of the sofa.

"Several things. And in light of what you've just told me, they make a great deal more sense now than they did a few minutes ago."

"What do you mean?"

Roland sat beside her. "I learned yesterday that about two months ago a new U.S. marshal was assigned to the Wyoming Territory to replace the one Will Hanson had fired."

"I haven't heard anything about that," Lacey told him.

"That's because the man apparently hasn't reported to Cheyenne yet. It's all being kept very hush-hush."

"Why? Because he's part of Hanson's plan?"

"I believe so."

"Do you know his name?"

Roland nodded. "Travis Blackburn."

"What else do you know about him?" Lacey asked anxiously.

"I'll get to that in a minute," he said, eliciting a deep sigh from his daughter. There was nothing in the world Roland Smithfield enjoyed more than dragging out a tale as long as he possibly could. The journalist in him loved to milk a story for every last drop of suspense. Knowing this, and knowing that it was pointless to demand that he lay out the facts succinctly, Lacey sat back, prayed for patience, and played her father's game. It was the very least she owed him.

"I think we ought to discuss this first." He reached into the envelope and extracted a copy of *Justice for Hire*. "You mentioned that a copy of this had fallen into your hands, correct?"

"Yes. The inconsistencies I found in that book prompted me to come to Washington."

Roland leaned forward intently. "What exactly were those inconsistencies?"

"A lot of little things about Morgan," she replied, remembering the myriad of small inaccuracies she'd found when she read the entire book on the train. "The color of his eyes and the description of his background were the primary contradictions, though. The Morgan I know has golden eyes and claims to have attended college. The Morgan in that book has dark eyes and almost no formal education."

"Did he ever say, by any chance, what college he attended?"

"William and Mary."

"That's it! I knew it!" Almost bouncing with delight, Roland came to his feet and began pacing furiously. "Now it makes perfect sense."

"What does, Father? Tell me!" Lacey demanded, coming to her feet as well.

He took her by the shoulders. "Lacey, it's obvious you suspect that the man who calls himself Justice Morgan is an impostor."

Lacey looked into her father's eyes and felt the tightly wound coil of pain inside her begin to unwind. "Are you saying that I'm right to think so? Papa, I want to believe that's true, but—"

"The other important piece of information I uncovered is a rumor that the real Justice Morgan is dead. According to my source, he was killed several months ago while attempting to rob a bank in the New Mexico Territory."

"But if he's really dead, who is the man who's impersonating him? The new marshal?"

Roland nodded. "That would be my guess. Here, look at this." He reached into the envelope and handed Lacey several sheets of paper. The handwriting was atrocious, which meant that the author had either failed penmanship or had been in a terrible hurry when he'd written it. "This is a hastily made copy of Travis Blackburn's file. I bribed a clerk in the federal marshal's office to give me access to his records."

"Shame on you, Father," she murmured without a bit of censure in her voice. She scanned the page for some clue that the

man she loved might actually be a U.S. marshal, and Roland
stood beside her to point something out.

"Look there, under his educational background."

Lacey's relief and joy were palpable. "Travis Blackburn
attended William and Mary."

"That's right. He's the son of Collier Blackburn, a wealthy
Virginia plantation owner. Tobacco, I believe."

"Really?" Lacey's head was spinning with a hundred questions about Morgan. No, not Morgan, she reminded herself.
Travis. Travis Blackburn. A U.S. marshal, not a bounty hunter. A kind, honorable man of the law, not a ruthless, money-
hungry killer. A man who was risking his life in a deadly game
to bring a dangerous man to justice. A man who . . .

A painful memory assaulted Lacey, and her legs suddenly
felt so weak that she had to sit down.

"What is it, dear?" Roland asked, moving to her solicitously.
"I thought this news would please you."

Lacey raised her face to his, her eyes brimming with tears.
"Oh, Papa, he begged me to trust him. On the day before the
gunfight, he made me promise that I would believe in him, no
matter what happened, no matter what he was forced to do or
say. I didn't do that, Papa," she cried. "Oh, God, why didn't
keep that promise?"

Roland gathered her into his arms. "How could you possibly
have kept it, Lacey? You had no way of knowing he wasn't
really a bounty hunter."

"But I did," she said fiercely, pulling away and drying her
ears. "I knew the man I was in love with wasn't capable of the
horrible deeds Justice Morgan had committed. I should have
known immediately that he was an impostor, and later, when
began to suspect it, I should have trusted my instincts."

"My darling daughter, you are not clairvoyant, and as you
just pointed out to me, neither are you a saint. You're a woman
in love who's been under terrible stress."

"But he asked me to trust him," she said plaintively.

"And what you gave him instead was worth just as much.
Believing what you did about him, you still did everything in
your power to save his life. You sacrificed your reputation
and humbled yourself before your worst enemy. What greater
act of love could any man ask for?" He gently brushed at the

tears on her cheeks. "Mr. Morgan—or Blackburn or whatever the hell his name is—is a very lucky man."

It meant so much to her that her father could believe that. "Thank you, Papa."

"You're welcome, my dear." He kissed her brow. "So, what will you do now? Wait until Marshal Blackburn has completed his job and then go to him, or wait until he comes for you? You know, with my connections, I could very easily get him a job here in Washington. There's no reason for him to remain permanently in that godforsaken Wyoming."

"Whoa, Papa, slow down," Lacey said with a laugh. "Morg—Travis and I have a great deal to settle between us before we can even consider marriage."

"Of course you'll consider marriage!" Roland said indignantly. "You'll consider it all the way to the altar, even if I have to take you there at gunpoint! No man is going to compromise my daughter and then walk away scot-free!"

Lacey found his fatherly indignation amusing. "Papa, what I meant was that we don't even know for a fact that Justice Morgan is dead or that the man impersonating him really is Travis Blackburn. Nor do I know what he has planned for C. W. Rawlings. He's still in grave danger."

"But that's his job, and you must allow him to do it," Roland argued sternly.

"Of course I will. But I'm not going to let this thing rest until I know all the facts. Will Hanson owes me a few answers and I'm going to get them."

"I'm afraid that will be a little difficult, my dear, because Senator Hanson left yesterday for New Orleans."

"What? Are you sure? Could he be headed for Wyoming because his plan is coming to a head?"

Roland shook his head firmly. "No. The trip to New Orleans is legitimate government business. There have been a number of complaints from foreign shipping interests about corruption within the Port Authority, and the President sent three members of the Senate down to initiate a formal investigation. Will tried to get out of the trip, but the President was adamant."

"When is he expected back?" Lacey asked, frowning.

"Next Monday, if all goes well."